THE MANUAL

THE MANUAL

SHERRYLE KISER JACKSON

www.urbanchristianonline.net

Urban Books, LLC
1199 Straight Path
West Babylon, NY 11704

The Manual copyright © 2009 Sherryle Kiser Jackson

ISBN- 13: 978-1-60162-935-7
ISBN- 10: 1-60162-935-4

First Printing October 2009
Printed in the United States of America

10 9 8 7 6 5 4 3 2 1

This is a work of fiction. Any references or similarities to actual events, real people, living, or dead, or to real locales are intended to give the novel a sense of reality. Any similarity in other names, characters, places, and incidents is entirely coincidental.

Distributed by Kensington Corp.
Submit Wholesale Orders to:
Kensington Publishing Corp.
C/O Penguin Group (USA) Inc.
Attention: Order Processing
405 Murray Hill Parkway
East Rutherford, NJ 07073-2316
Phone: 1-800-526-0275
Fax: 1-800-227-9604

Dedication

To Janette Ashford, my aunt and angel,
I'm eternally grateful to your gracious support.

Acknowledgements

To God, in whom I live and breathe and have my being. Like the Verizon Wireless company, I am aware that book marketing and promotions are only as good as the network that I am on. I would like to thank God for linking me up with the following: Lewis, Delores and Monique Kiser, Arvell, Nylah and Arvell Jr., my Soulfood crew, my Writer's Workshop crew—forever dedicated. To Pastor Anthony G. Maclin and the entire Sanctuary at Kingdom Square family—thanks for spiritually feeding my family and edifying our souls. My fellow Urban Christian authors, my fellow Mochas of Mocha Moms Inc., especially the Waldorf Chapter, Delta Sigma Theta Sorority Inc., particularly my home chapter of FWAC, Ella D. Curry of EDC Creations, Sankofa Literary Society and Black Author's Network—is there no end to your innovation, United Black Writers, Urban Literary Review & 3 Chicks On Lit, I've learned so much just being a listener to your blog talk shows. To the very talented authors who have joined Everywhere Gospel, it is refreshing to have an opportunity to share and promote our craft. As a book club's best friend, I'd like to thank The Sweet Soul Sisters Book Club, Black Women's Book Group, Sistahs with Books, Sisters of Soul Book Club, B~More Readers with W.I.S.D.O.M., FWAC Book Club, Virtuous Woman Book Club, Mochalicious Literary Divas, and the Divas of Color Book Club, RAW Sistaz and KC Girlfriends Book Club for reminding me why I write.

. . . a threefold cord is not quickly broken.

Ecclesiastics 4:12

Prologue

October 1984

Andre Hicks angled the tip of the aerosol can with his finger and guided the stream of black colored paint into an arc above the letters he had just painted on the utility door of his high school. The design spelled out his tagname, HICKORY, in disjointed branch-like letters, which he smeared with a rag to create his signature effect. He stepped back to glance at his burner like a painter would his canvas.

"Yo, Hick, let's get out of here, man," said Theo Kelley a.k.a. Theory, who had just painted the cove of the delivery area with their crew's name.

"Hold up. I'm gonna sneak into the gym for a minute."

"That's not a good idea to leave your tag and hang around until people start to leave the joint, man."

"I want to check out this shorty."

"Yo, is this man talking about that church girl again. She got my man buggin' out," said Keith Jackson, a.k.a. Gemini One.

"She looks better than all the other girls put together; especially your girl." Andre said.

"She's probably in there all dressed up and grinding with Suit Coat," Theo said, dancing and dipping an invisible partner in front of Andre. "You know what Cindy Wilson said when she came to our class peddling those tickets."

"This will be a respectable dance where everybody dresses up and dances with their dates, so all you wannabe New York break dancers can just stay home," Keith said in his best impersonation.

"Wannabe? Watch how I mark that skeezer," Theo said, forming the first letter of Cindy's name using a neon green jumbo marker.

"What you doing, man? You gonna mess it up." Andre bumped Theo's elbow, causing his pen to create a line across the letter he had just written. "Just wait for me, all right?"

Andre capped his spray cans and turned his gloves, stained with fresh paint, inside out. He tossed the items into his duffel bag and tried the doors around the back of the school until he found one propped open.

Perfectly stenciled signs pointed the way to the Homecoming dance for those few unfortunate enough to have to use the back parking lot, but Andre went into the opposite direction than the signs indicated. He was sure the DJ brought his equipment through a different entrance than the students entered. Once again he tried the doors and was pleasantly surprised when one yielded across from the student locker rooms. He eased in the door to find a middle-aged man leaning over a crate full of records. Andre had to tiptoe around the man who was tethered to the sound system by a set of headphones that he wore around the neck.

Andre managed to navigate the narrow space between the wall and the DJ booth without alerting the DJ or upsetting the record he was playing. His heart thumped

from the bass of the speakers that blared a song by Rick
James. The room was dark except for the fluorescent lights
that highlighted the throne for the soon to be crowned king
and queen. They used the lights that spilled in from the
hallway to provide illumination on the refreshment table
on the opposite wall.

Guys in tapered suits with slender ties danced a con-
siderate distance from girls in neon party dresses with
fishnet stockings. Andre's eyes scanned the gym until he
saw her. Deidre Collins stood with her friends in the back
drinking party punch. She wore a pink dress that had a
bodice connected to spaghetti straps and a ballooned
mini skirt.

Andre, dressed in a hooded sweatshirt and baggy
army fatigues with tennis shoes, remained in the shadows of the DJ booth. He started to turn and leave the way
he had come when he made eye contact with the DJ.

"My man, can you liven this place up with Eighth
Wonder or Apache by the Sugarhill Gang or anything by
Kurtis Blow?" Andre asked.

"I was told to play Top 40, brother. Apparently your
Homecoming Committee does not want anyone to work
up a sweat and really dance in here," the DJ said, taking
one side of the headset away from his ear to respond
over the Michael Jackson cut he was mixing onto the end
of the fading song.

"Can you play me something fresh; I'm planning on
putting on a show."

"I hear you. Give me a few seconds to see what I can
do."

Andre took that opportunity to move toward his target. He had been mesmerized by this freshman girl
named Deidre whose locker was outside his shop class.
His woodworking class was buried in the vocational
wing or the wasteland, as the area where the automotive,

plumbing and woodworking classes was called. Only a few members of the huge freshman class had the misfortune of having to trek down to the vocational wing to their lockers. Boys who weren't on the college track usually chose a trade in the wasteland. Girls, on the other hand, who were in the family way or otherwise weren't academically inclined were encouraged to take business courses like typing and office practice that were housed down there also.

Most of the freshman girls whose lockers were in the wasteland would run in and out of their lockers as if they had to travel through an alley and feared being abducted, but not Deidre. Andre had noticed how unhurried and unconcerned she was to be mixed with the troublemakers of the school. She was one of those girls destined to be Ms. Popularity or Most Likely to Succeed by senior year, yet she didn't give off the air. She was generous with her smile and made Andre feel as if he were the direct recipient of it. To the disgust of her friends, she even took the time to sway to the beats he and his classmates would bang out on the walls, lockers, and window seals between classes. She had become his obsession.

Andre thought she was the best looking girl at the dance. She was a tall curvaceous young lady with thick shoulder length auburn hair, who in Andre's opinion could easily take home the crown and sash from any of the Homecoming Princesses there tonight.

Andre stared at Deidre who was standing on the edge of the dance floor swaying and waiting as if she wanted someone to ask her to dance. *Just talk to her before her girlfriends come back,* he thought. He put on a confident swagger, ignoring the looks from his classmates at his choice of attire.

"Hi," Andre said.

"Hey," Deidre replied.

"You think your boyfriend will mind if I ask you to dance?"

"I don't know, I'll ask him," Deidre said. She looked around as if she were searching for someone. "Sike." They both smiled, then looked off in opposite directions, temporarily lost for words. One of her girlfriends came back, and she and Deidre huddled and laughed as if hearing something hilarious.

"Excuse me, but we were about to dance," Andre said, growing impatient.

"Do you even go to this school?" Deidre's friend, Sheila, said, rotating her finger in his face.

"I've seen him around." Deidre stepped in between them.

"I haven't."

"That's 'cause I wasn't looking to be seen by you." Andre said, this time rotating his index finger in her face. "Come on." He began swaying back and forth to the beat. He backed up while extending his hand for Deidre.

Deidre moved toward him. She didn't know why, but she was drawn to him. Andre heard the familiar bass and down beat of one of his favorite cuts, Neucleus's "Jam on It." He cupped his mouth as if letting out a battle cry and screamed out, "Ho." A few people responded in kind.

Andre started a backward glide that curved until he completely encircled Deidre. She tried to back up while he approached her like a puppet on a string, dangling his arms from side to side. Then he stopped directly in front of her and began pop locking, moving the parts of his body as if they were controlled by a machine. He grabbed her hand in his and placed it close to his chest, then pulsed it back and forth as if his heart were beating outside of his chest.

Kevin and Theo burst through the crowd that had formed a circle around Andre's one man show. He glided back to allow himself some room and began shaking as if he had stuck a finger in a light socket. Summoning the energy from the crowd that was now chanting, "Go, go, go," he threw a wave to Theo who appeared to catch it across the floor. Theo allowed the energy to go through one arm, down his right leg which he collapsed to the ground and back up again before returning up his other leg and out through his left arm. Keith picked up the pulse that set his feet into a frenzy. In one fluid motion he was on the floor spinning on his back until he stopped into a pose a few seconds after the last beat of the song.

Andre wiped his face from perspiration and tried to find Deidre who was hidden amidst the crowd of people jamming to another Hip Hop record. Their performance and the reaction from the crowd had given the DJ permission to jam. Andre found Deidre on the side among three other girls. This time her friend smiled as he approached, obviously impressed.

"Where did you learn to dance like that?" Deidre's friend asked.

"Like anything, shorty, God-given talent and a whole lot of practice." He knew his time was limited, and he didn't want to get into the years he lived in New York, his home state and the home of break dancing. He looked at Deidre. "Can I talk to you?"

Deidre's friends pushed her forward. He beckoned for her to follow him and she did until they got just outside the doorway.

"Come on, I want to show you something," he said, proceeding to the exit until he felt her stop.

"I'm sorry; I don't know you that well to just walk off with you." She looked apprehensive. In the light they could see one another better. His hairline where his deep chocolate skin met his small afro that was faded close on the sides was moist with perspiration and he wiped it with the length of his forearm. He saw her grimace and decided to extend the other hand for her to grab. He could tell that she wanted to go with him, but once again apprehension took hold.

"Yo, Dre, that was fresh in there, but Cindy and her crew are going ballistic because we messed up her event. So you need to put your play on pause so we can get out of here," Kevin said as he and Theo jogged by them.

"I'll be right out. Yo, don't leave me. I ain't playing," he called after them.

He looked at her as if his pending departure would change her mind. "I'm hurt you are treating me like a stranger off the street or some kind of murderer."

"Well," Deidre said, backing up to just inside the shade of the cafeteria. She noticed his dejected expression and gently touched his arm and smiled. "No, I know exactly who you are. You're the one that almost got me in trouble the other day standing outside my house."

Andre thought back a few weeks ago when he was visiting a buddy and saw Deidre staring outside an upstairs window of her house. It was as if he had stumbled upon a buried treasure discovering where she lived. The dark shudders around the panes of glass and her melancholic expression made it seem as if she were in prison. He remembered beckoning for her to come outside and how she shooed him away with such ardent fervor that it had taken him this long to approach her again.

"Yeah, and you dissed me."

"I'm sorry, but my mother doesn't play that. She won't allow boys to come visit me, you know, unannounced," she added.

"Oh, you got one of those overprotective moms. What she holding on so tight for? You're in high school."

"I'm her baby. Don't you have someone holding on to you?"

Andre didn't. He had an uncle who tolerated him because his brother, Andre's father, couldn't handle life let alone a kid since his wife died. He didn't want to tell her that.

"That's why I'm trying to talk to you, so I'll have someone to hold on to." Andre held a smile as Deidre blushed and looked away.

"You just got to know my mom. She's so worried I'll get in trouble and not graduate like so many of my cousins who got caught up with the wrong . . . influences."

"I guess I would be one of those influences," he said.

She didn't reply, and Andre wondered what she was thinking. He followed her glance inside the cafeteria where the house lights were brought up and they could hear someone speaking on the microphone followed by cheers from the crowd.

"They are introducing the homecoming court," she surmised.

Andre noticed Deidre glancing over her shoulder several more times as if it were killing her to miss out on the festivities. He didn't want to try her patience. He knew she wanted to get back into the dance. That was her element, and he needed to catch up with his buddies outside.

"I definitely think we should get together sometime. Maybe you can . . . uh, rightly influence me." He smiled. "Let me get your number."

"Wait. You mean to tell me that you came in here, cheated me out of a real dance so you can dance with your boys and then leave?" She dismissed him with a wave. She was sassy, but he could tell that she was considering whether she should part with her number—considering her and him.

"So come on, give up the digits."

She gave another thoughtful look before letting out an exasperated sigh. From her purse, she pulled a small memo pad like the ones sold in the school store. She tore a piece of paper and wrote the digits of her phone number neatly on the line under her name. Andre smiled. He had worn her down and vowed to have the same effect on her mother.

"Bust it, when you're riding home tonight. Drive around back where the big trash dumpsters are. Check the writing on the wall. I left a message for you." He leaned in close.

"Stop playing," she said, backing away from a kiss he was trying to give her.

"I gotta go. I'll see you around."

Deidre went back into the dance. She refused every guy who asked her to dance for the rest of the evening, preferring to listen to the music and trying to feel the energy left in the room by Andre and his boys. After the formalities, and despite arguments with Cindy, the DJ maintained the excitement of the crowd by playing one dance cut after another.

After piling into the car with three of her friends and filling them in on the conversation Deidre had had with Andre, they drove from the front lot to the back of the school.

On the loading doc wall, lit by the street lamps, Deidre could see a city scene with yellow letters outlined in black: MO' IN STO' 4 U THE OUT 2 GET U CREW.

Chapter 1

Deidre Collins was enjoying the click of her freshly manicured nails across the keyboard of her personal computer. She did not know what she enjoyed more about her day off, the invigorating wash, blow dry, and curl at Prim Rose Beauty Salon, the luxury of having someone else do her nails or the leisure time she had to delete old emails and drift through cyberspace. By the third page of email scams and spam, Deidre was saving time by clicking the button to select all the mail on that page and purging them unless something in the message line prompted her to open it. The top line of page four read, FINDING NYMPHO. She wondered how the webmaster of this site could get away with exploiting a wholesome Disney title to sell filth. That would be all her fourteen-year-old son, DeAndre, would need to see before his curiosity would have him viewing a lot of things she has tried as a God-fearing parent to keep him from. Lord knows he was on the computer more than she cared to be. *The devil is everywhere*, she thought to herself as she checked the parental control options.

Just as Deidre was about to delete page four, an email caught her attention with a message bar that read, TARDY NOTICE FROM PEMBERTON MIDDLE SCHOOL. She had remembered thinking how progressive the school systems had gotten when they asked for email and cell phone information on the parent contact form at the beginning of the year. She read the note informing her that DeAndre was tardy for school on March 19th. That was over a month ago. Deidre wondered why they hadn't called. Then she remembered that DeAndre typically came in two hours before her. Naturally he had erased the message with no intentions on telling her. She knew her son; he wasn't a saint. Lately his behavior wasn't even close.

Deidre examined her emails more closely. She found two more tardy notices: March 28th and April 15th. Despite feeling angry, she couldn't help but feeling a little guilty about not checking her messages more regularly. And when was the last time she had been to his school to check on him? She had only been to Pemberton Middle School twice since he started there last year as a seventh grader.

Deidre couldn't understand what was stopping DeAndre from getting to school on time. After winning the battle of getting him out of bed each morning, all he had to do was walk a few yards to the bus stop and get on. She purposely worked the swing shift, from 11A.M. to 7P.M., at least three times a week to make sure he was prepared for the day. Most of the time she left nothing to his imagination in regards to what she expected from him when he came in by himself in the afternoon. Head nods and barely audible grunts let Deidre know he had at least heard her to-do lists. Only God knew how many other notices she had deleted in her haste to empty her email box.

Deidre was up before DeAndre this morning to make her nine A.M. hair appointment and was sitting in the nail shop by 12:30. Her best girlfriend's wedding was the next day for which she was an attendant. The latter didn't thrill her in the way she would have been in her twenties or if she were married herself by her present age of thirty-eight.

The single phone line she used for both the telephone and the computer rang the moment she logged off of the Internet. It was probably Sheila asking her to pick up yet another thing she or her overpriced wedding coordinator forgot.

"Hello, I'm trying to reach Mrs. Hicks. This is Jeff Riley, the principal at Pemberton Middle School where her son, DeAndre, attends."

"This is Ms. *Collins*. I am DeAndre's mother." Deidre's upper body tensed the way a person would in preparation for receiving a shot.

"Ms. Collins, DeAndre has gotten himself into trouble, and I was wondering if it were possible for you to come down to the school and pick him up."

"I don't understand. Are you saying he's been kicked out of school?"

"Yes ma'am, he will be suspended."

"Excuse me." Deidre yielded to a short coughing spell from the lump rising in her throat. "What did he do?"

"This is why we want you to come in. When a child has been suspended, we have what is known as an exit conference where the school explains the circumstances surrounding the suspension."

"That is what I am asking you. Why was he suspended?"

"It allows you to meet with a team that includes De-Andre's teachers and counselor, so that there are many perspectives on how DeAndre can be more effective when he returns to school." He continued speaking as if he didn't hear her question.

"And when will he be able to return, Mr. Riley?"

"The day DeAndre will be permitted back to school will also be explained at the conference. Rather than upset you further on the phone, it would be best if we sit down and discuss his conduct in detail."

"Are you telling me you're kicking my child out of school, but cannot tell me why over the phone?"

"Calm down, Mrs. Hicks. Is transportation a problem?"

"It's Ms. Collins. DeAndre's father and I aren't married. To answer your question, transportation is not a problem. Mr. Riley, I am a supportive parent, and I am also a Christian. You can be assured that before I leave for the school I will be praying for an outcome that aligns with my faith. Just like you have prepared your team to be a united front when I arrive, I would like to be equally prepared.

"He's being suspended for sexual harassment."

"I'll be right there."

Chapter 2

Pemberton Farms was one of the last areas of pure grazing and farm land left in Prince Georges County Maryland until it became home to fast growing estates two years previous. City developers built high priced homes and equally high priced townhomes around the development of new neighborhood schools, one elementary, one middle, and one high school that would be completed sometime in the near future. All named after the newly developed city of Pemberton. These state of the art facilities were the jewels of a county that was still struggling with desegregation of schools in the name of diversifying their population.

Pemberton Middle School was a stone's throw from Deidre's home in the well established neighborhood of Kettering. DeAndre and other children in his neighborhood rode a school bus; not because the walk would kill them, but rather crossing the six lane thoroughfare may. Deidre mindlessly raced through her block cutting through the neighborhood of Lake Arbor. This took her past Pemberton Nursery that still gave the community a sense of its rural beginnings. She sat in the car a few minutes after pulling into a parking spot on the side of the school. *Another prayer won't hurt,* she thought.

Buses began pulling in for dismissal so she hurried to make sure DeAndre would not get on his bus. Something about the principal's office made her feel like she was going into central booking down at the police station to bail out a loved one. Deidre walked into the administrative suite and sat next to a teenage girl who looked as if she were ailing. Neither secretary who sat at chunky wooden desks looked up until a friendly looking postman arrived.

The mail guy waited with the package extended in his hand for some indication as to where to put it. Deidre also waited for someone to acknowledge her presence.

"Can you tell Mr. Riley that Ms. Collins, DeAndre Hicks's mom, is here for an exit conference," Deidre said.

The secretary dialed an extension, whispered into the phone and shielded the receiver as if either of them could hear Mr. Riley's reply. "Mr. Riley will be out in a moment."

Mr. Riley was shorter than Deidre imagined a principal of a middle school would be. She wondered if he were any taller than DeAndre. She soon realized that what he lacked in height, he more than made up for in confidence. Mr. Riley signed for the release of the package and took it from the awaiting postman. He questioned the girl next to Deidre about why she was in the office before turning to Deidre.

"Ms. Collins, glad to meet you," Mr. Riley said. They shook hands. "I sent DeAndre to his last period class. What class does he have at the end of the day?"

"Um, I don't know," Deidre said, shifting in her chair.

"That's quite all right. Mrs. Tate, can you pull up De-Andre Hicks's schedule and call him down to the office? Also, can you call Mr. Talbert to join Ms. Collins in my conference room?" He looked at his watch. "The team will be joining you momentarily after the dismissal of students."

Mr. Riley walked over to another student who had just come in with a green hall pass and indicated to him to go back from where he came. He sighed of satisfaction much like a family physician would who had success-fully cleared his lobby of patients.

Deidre took a notepad and pen from her purse. On the first clean page, she wrote: *get a copy of DeAndre's sched-ule*. A bell toned followed by the voice of Mr. Riley that signaled the end of the school day. A man who looked not much older than the neighborhood high school kids came in and walked up to Deidre.

"Ms. Collins, I'm Mr. Talbert, DeAndre's counselor. We can go in Mr. Riley's conference room and wait for the team in there."

Deidre followed Mr. Talbert down the hall into a small room almost entirely consumed by a gray Formica table. Deidre sat close to Mr. Talbert in hopes of finding out more about her son's behavior in school.

"So, do you work directly with my son?"

"I am the eighth grade Guidance Counselor," Mr. Tal-bert said, twiddling his ink pen.

"I see."

"I see DeAndre quite often in the hallway. One day, he came past my office with a friend of his who had an ap-pointment. I'm not quite sure why he was there. Nice boy. I saw a drawing on his folder, and we started talking about Art Education."

"Oh?"

"I told him if he were serious about his drawing, that maybe he should consider going to one of the Creative Arts Magnets for high school. Told him to come by and talk to me about it, but he hasn't made it by yet."

Now that Deidre was thinking about it, she had seen DeAndre drawing in a sketchbook. She just thought the sight of him scribbling in a notebook with his headphones on was his way of tuning out the world. She let him get away with it except at dinnertime or when she was talking directly to him. Deidre never bothered to take a look at any of his school papers anymore, let alone his drawings. She decided not to ask Mr. Talbert any more questions for a while before it became apparent that she didn't know anything about who her son was becoming.

DeAndre came in the room before his team of teachers. Deidre was horrified at his appearance. He wore a white tank top with a standard blue and yellow issued gym shirt around his neck like a towel and grey shorts so long they almost met with the top of his slouch socks. His hair was braided back into cornrows except for a section on the end that was sticking straight out from the scalp.

"What happened to you?" Deidre asked.

"I got in trouble."

"To say the least, but why do you look like that?"

DeAndre shrugged the way he did when he knew no explanation would be good enough for her. He sat across from his mother and Mr. Talbert so that his back was toward the door. He leaned back in the executive style chair and stretched out his legs.

Silently, Deidre thanked God for the width of the table because the Lord knew that she could have just choked the boy. "Don't shrug at me. And sit up. Is that what you had on this morning?"

"I was at gym before they sent me to the office. Then Mr. Riley sent me to my last class, so I had to go like this."

"Put your gym shirt on then. I sure hope you don't walk around in a tank top all day."

DeAndre grudgingly slipped his gym shirt over his tank before slouching back into the chair. He avoided her eyes by looking up at the ceiling. *Don't say nothing else, Deidre,* she told herself

Mr. Riley escorted DeAndre's team of teachers into the conference room. There were six in all. He introduced each one, and Deidre rose to shake their hands before they took their seats. She got a warm vibe from his English teacher and his History teacher, both African American, both female, probably with kids of their own. The other teachers looked disgusted and overall disinterested. She wondered if it were the result of a hard day or an expression caused by what they had in mind to tell her about her son.

"Ms. Collins, it's unfortunate that we all have to meet under these circumstances. DeAndre was sent to my office from gym class when Mr. Richards caught him with his hands in a female classmate's shorts."

Deidre clutched the cross around her neck. She felt as if all eyes were on her except, of course, DeAndre's. He had detached himself from the proceedings with a stoic expression.

"Is Mr. Richards here?" Deidre asked.

"No, he had to leave early. By procedure he wrote his side of the incident down on a PS-74, which is a legal incident report." Mr. Riley cleared his throat. "He wrote the following. *The class was told to line up in squads for a dribbling exercise. DeAndre lined up behind one of his classmates at the end of squad four. As I was giving instructions, I looked up to see DeAndre crouched behind a female classmate with his right hand up her shorts.*"

Deidre was angry. She was angry at Mr. Cleveland, DeAndre's math teacher, for fidgeting in his chair, angry at Mrs. Graves, his science teacher, for grading papers as if she were unconcerned. She was mad at Mr. Riley for airing this incident in front of her son's other teachers so they could form a lasting impression of DeAndre as a pervert. But most of all, she was mad at DeAndre's stupidity.

"I don't understand why all his other teachers are here and not the teacher whose class the incident happened in," Deidre said.

"Ms. Collins, DeAndre was caught doing something inappropriate," Mr. Riley said. "DeAndre, do you want to tell your mother what you were doing? Be honest, because I'm sure a couple of your classmates saw the whole thing."

"DeAndre doesn't have to lie," Deidre said, wishing he would tell them this was all a big joke. "You know as well as I know about teenagers and hormones. They get curious. I'm not condoning his actions, but if this girl is going to let my son put his hands down her pants, then I am not the only parent you should be contacting."

"Ms. Collins," Mr. Riley said, exasperated, "you can understand the position I'm in as a principal. This young girl is going to go home and tell her parents what has happened to her during gym class. Let me tell you, I've talked to the girl in question, and I can tell you that she's pretty humiliated. When her parents call this school I want them to feel satisfied that we did a little more than slap your son on the wrist for putting his hand down her shorts."

"I didn't put my hands down her shorts. I put it up her shorts, but I wasn't trying to touch her or anything."

"Boy, shut up," Deidre wanted to say. Why can't he

just let his poor old mother hold on to the thought that he was a lot smarter than his actions presented? Let her believe that some loose girl let him put his hands down her pants.

"Rajah had been playing with me in gym, trying to embarrass me by pulling my shorts down in front of everyone and what not," DeAndre said, this time looking down. "So when Mr. Riley told us to get into our squads, I was behind Lorraine Dupree. We always tell jokes about her because she's all skinny. So I got Rajah's attention and showed him how I could put my hands up her shorts without her knowing because her pants were so baggy."

Deidre surrendered. She rested her head in her hand and didn't say another word.

"DeAndre will be suspended for ten days," Mr. Riley said.

"Ten days?" Deidre and DeAndre said in unison.

"Ms. Collins, the county wants to send a strong message against sexual harassment to our students and parents alike. What seems like innocent antics to you and your son will likely be viewed differently in the little girl's household. Violating a person's private area will not be tolerated."

"Am I supposed to take off work for ten days?" Deidre looked at the faces around the table.

"Ms. Collins, the more DeAndre understands what an inconvenience this is to you, the more it will deter him from this kind of behavior in the future. Perhaps his father can help you out during his time off. Maybe he can accompany either of you to work."

Deidre thought this was really a punishment for her. She would have to think of something, but she was quite sure it would not include DeAndre's dad.

Mr. Riley excused himself and turned the meeting over to Mr. Talbert and DeAndre's teachers. Deidre sat nearly in tears as each teacher shared how, just like in the gym incident, DeAndre regularly followed the lead of his peers. They also spoke of disrespect, poor test grades, and his overall disinterest in school.

Deidre could not read DeAndre's blank stare. She only hoped he felt as embarrassed as she felt.

"Ms. Collins, the team has compiled a list of assignments DeAndre can work on while at home. When he comes back to school in ten days, I'd like to meet with him and discuss some goals and maybe put him on a weekly progress report," Mr. Talbert said.

"Thank you, I'd appreciate it, really," Deidre said, allowing her back to rest on the back of the chair for the first time since the meeting started.

"Maybe we can talk about art and where talented boys like he can go in this county to receive training," Mr. Talbert said pointedly, trying to get DeAndre out of his trance.

"I'd just like to say, I'm sorry on behalf of my son. While he is home, he will be writing his own apologies. This has been a wake up call." Deidre paused. "It's been hard raising DeAndre by myself. Don't get me wrong, he knows his father, but he has had to rely on me for the past seven years. I mean, DeAndre is a good boy. He knows right from wrong. I brought him up in church, although you probably can't tell by the way he has been acting lately."

"Like I said before, the couple times I've seen DeAndre in the halls he has always been respectful. He's just like any number of our kids who are willing to follow the pack. We just need to direct them in the right path," Mr. Talbert said.

"That is my prayer also. DeAndre is going to have to

make some decisions on his own, wear out his own knees and start praying for himself. With the grades I've seen today, he might not make it to high school next year, let alone a Magnet Art school. He's got some thinking to do, and ten days will give him plenty of time to do it."

Chapter 3

Deidre rose in the hotel bed that she shared with her best friend, Sheila, the bride-to-be. They had talked and laughed well into the night about the antics of high school and fell into a labored sleep around three A.M. They had been friends for over twenty years. Deidre awoke with thoughts of her son's trouble and suspension from school. She hoped it would not put a damper on the day ahead.

Deciding to pray, Deidre eased her body to the floor so as not to awaken Sheila and whispered what was on her heart. Weddings were much like a fairy tale. She prayed that God would help her play her role in her friend's fairy tale without the feelings of jealousy and envy.

Deidre felt the movement of the bed as she got up from the floor.

"Today's my wedding day," Sheila shouted as if announcing it to the entire area.

"Girl, hush. It is nine A.M. and some people in this hotel don't care what day it is. I have a surprise for you that should be arriving shortly before you get in that gorgeous dress," Deidre said with as much enthusiasm as she could muster.

Sheila jumped up on the bed like a kid on a trampoline and hopped to the floor. "I better take a shower."

"Slow down before you hurt yourself," Deidre warned. "I can't imagine having to explain to Keith why his bride is coming down the aisle in a wheelchair."

Sheila laughed hysterically from the bathroom. *She was way too giddy*, Deidre thought. *But wasn't that the way it should be*? Today she would be receiving what she always wanted.

"Oh did I tell you . . ." was all Deidre could make out after Sheila turned on the shower.

"Girl, I can't hear you. Wait until you get out."

Deidre thought about DeAndre who was at her sister's house. Her thoughts were interrupted when the doorbell rang. Two ladies she met at the hair salon stood at the door. They were giving fifteen-minute chair massages for customer appreciation day. Deidre had not purchased a bridal shower gift, thinking surely her friend didn't expect her only attendant to bear the cost of throwing her a shower and purchasing a gift. When Sheila told her some friends from her job were giving her a shower, she knew she at least owed her a sensational gift.

Karla and Beth were both petite women, but from what Deidre remembered, Beth could maintain firm pressure with her hand and forearm. Deidre paid in advance for Sheila's full body massage and couldn't pass up a chance to have a full body massage herself. The ladies set up their tables between the bed and the television in the spacious hotel suite.

"Sheila, your surprise is here," Deidre said, signaling to Karla and Beth to be quiet.

Sheila peeked out from the bathroom door and squealed with delight when she saw the massage tables. Karla congratulated Sheila and beckoned for her to lie face down on her table so she could begin her thirty-minute massage. They had almost every waking hour scheduled, so Deidre figured she'd better hurry up before the primping and pictures began. Beth plugged in her CD player nearby. A rhapsody of rolling rapids filled the air. Deidre grabbed her travel cosmetics bag and retreated to the bathroom.

Deidre smiled at the look of utter peace on her friend's face when she emerged from the bathroom in a towel. She positioned herself on Beth's table. Beth concentrated on her shoulders and back, kneading at a bundle of nerves with the force of her thumbs and forefingers. Deidre, whose mind had again shifted to her son, began relaxing as each nerve was unwound from the knot in her shoulder.

Sheila's massage had progressed to her back. She lifted her face from the recessed headrest and cradled her head on her hands. "Thank you so much for this. I'm so glad you agreed to be in my wedding." Sheila's eyes began to tear up. She reached a hand across the divide for Deidre to grab and squeeze in return.

"Stop it this instant; if I start crying, I won't stop."

They grew silent for a long while, allowing the serene music to take their minds to different destinations. As hard as she tried, Deidre couldn't get her mind off her present woes. She had temporarily lost control, but vowed she would reel in her wayward son after this weekend.

Sheila extended her arms forward in a luxurious stretch as Karla worked on her calf muscles. "I'm glad I kept the wedding simple. At thirty-eight, I didn't need twenty bridesmaids. Plus, you have been there since the beginning; you and Andre."

"Yeah, and you and Kevin have outlasted every one of my so-called relationships."

"Dee, he RSVP'd."

"Who?"

"Andre," Sheila said, sounding concerned. "That is what I was trying to tell you from the bathroom."

Deidre felt the knot return to her shoulder, her nerve endings were the string being wound up into a yo-yo after a trick. She rubbed her shoulder herself as if she could repeat the technique Beth had used to work out her kinks.

"Good," Deidre said, feigning indifference. "Now I can tell him about his son's latest antics."

"What's happening with DeAndre?"

"Your godson put his hands in a little girl's gym shorts and got himself suspended for ten days. I could have killed him."

"I thought he liked that little girl from church that can sing real good."

"Me too. And her mother, Marilynn, is in our Sunday School class. It's embarrassing all the way around. I told him he's going to break that little girl's heart. He's taking a page straight from his father's book. I declare . . . all men must read from the same manual. Like Momma used to say, the pages are long and the book is thick, 'cause a man has got a lot of tricks."

"When did all this happen?"

"Yesterday. But hey, I don't want you to worry about all this," Deidre said, waving it off. "You're getting married in a couple of hours."

"I haven't seen my godson in a while now," Sheila said. "It's a shame I'm going to have to pull him up at the wedding for showing off."

"Oh you've seen him. He's the one in the mall being

obnoxious and talking all loud. He's one of the guys on the corner with the rim of his boxer shorts showing and a hairdo that looks like Buckwheat from *The Little Rascals*."

"You make it seem like he's suddenly become a stranger."

"No, he's not a stranger. He's so much like Dre, with his nonchalant attitude, it isn't even funny."

Sheila once again reached across to grab Deidre's hand across the gap between their two tables. "Well, I definitely think it's a good idea that you and Dre have a talk. It's long overdue if you ask me. I just wanted to warn you that he would be there so you would be cool."

"I'm cool just as long as he is," Deidre said, partially rising up to her elbow. She didn't expect him to be anything but cordial. Blame it on a lack of temperance, but it was usually she that dredged up some catalyst of an argument.

"He's coming alone."

"Trust me. I'm not thinking about Andre Hicks like that anymore. I'm so over that relationship." Deidre laid her head back down on the massage table.

Sheila pushed down from the table, her half an hour massage time elapsing. She admired the glow of her skin in the mirror before sitting on the bed opposite Deidre. "Yeah right. Face it. You were in love with Dre and will always love him."

The room fell silent. Deidre felt like everyone awaited her admission, including Beth and Karla whom she realized had been privy to details about her son and his father. She sat up and pulled her foot from Beth's grasp. She wrapped the towel around herself and signaled to Beth that she was ending their session prematurely.

"Don't go there." Deidre stepped down from the table gingerly holding the towel closed with one hand.

"Come on, Dee, he was your first love and is the father of your child."

"Yeah, well, first loves may linger in your thoughts, but the flame is gone in my heart."

Deidre turned away from her friend so that she could not see how upset she was getting. Karla and Beth, who had been signaling to one another with their eyes, began packing up their things, sensing from the conversation that it was time to leave. Deidre removed her purse from the top drawer of the hotel's night table and took out two ten dollar bills as tips for the ladies. Deidre walked them to the door. Sheila waved, not wanting to lose her point in the conversation.

"It's okay to still love him. You were together since you were teenagers. I just think that if you were entirely over him, you wouldn't be this bitter." Sheila held up a hand to silence Deidre's comeback. "You're emotionally tied to him. He was your first true love. Think about it. Your first love can be a powerful thing."

"C'mon, can we talk about something else?" Deidre said, studying her friend. She knew Sheila and sensed she meant well by her comments. "I admit I wish things could have been different between Dre and me. It ended so abruptly. I mean, sometimes I still wonder what happened."

"We've all had relationships to end like that." Sheila brushed a wisp of hair from Deidre's crestfallen face. "It felt like he was snatched from you. Remember that time when DeAndre was small, and we let him crawl around the basement carpet at my mother's house? We were so busy watching television. I'll never forget we turned our back and Man-Man had picked up a box cutter left on the floor and was playing with it. Remember what you did?"

"I took it from him," Deidre said assuredly, although she vaguely remembered the incident.

"You saw the danger and immediately snatched it from

him with such force that Lil' Man was left dumbfounded in the middle of the floor."

"I remember he started hollering so loud I thought about retracting the blade and giving it back to him."

"Think about it, that's what God does for us. All you know is that you're having fun playing, and then Daddy snatches our play thing from us. Remember Ronnie Jeffries? Yuck. What was I thinking? Anyway, if I hadn't met Keith, I would still be waiting for a return call from him. He dropped me, and then stopped speaking to me as if I did something to him."

Ronnie Jefferies was a far cry from Andre Hicks as Deidre recalled. Deidre and Andre had been on the threshold of matrimony, at least that's what she'd thought. They had just gotten their cart in front of their horse.

"Why didn't I wait?" Deidre said. "Who knows? If Dre and I had waited to have DeAndre, to have sex period, we might have been married by now. I feel like I'm ruining DeAndre's life sometimes, raising him alone."

"A lot of us have done the crime. The question is have you been forgiven?" Sheila said, starting to pull out her undergarments, hosiery, and crenlin slip from her suitcase and garment bag.

Deidre decided to do the same. "You know I've repented."

"Then stop condemning yourself."

Deidre smiled at Sheila as she received what she had to say. It was exactly what she needed to hear. "I'm supposed to be helping you today, and look, you're supporting me again. I go to church and sit beside you every Sunday, but it seems like I can't hold on to half of the Word we hear in the services."

"Hide the Word in your heart." Sheila poked Deidre in

her chest right above the monogrammed hotel emblem on the robe she now wore. "There is something else I think you need to hear. You have to forgive Dre and let him see his son when he wants to."

"Dre can see his son anytime he wants to see him now that DeAndre is a teenager. I just didn't want him sashaying in and out of his life like the time he skipped town."

"Yeah, but now he has to report to you about every little thing like you are his parole officer or something."

"Sheila, you don't know what you are talking about."

"All I'm saying is DeAndre obviously needs his dad in his life right now. You should see what kind of impact Keith is having in the life of his nephew. I'm talking a 360-degree change. You say you don't like the direction DeAndre is headed. I mean it's worth a shot to let him spend more time with his dad."

There was a knock on the door before Deidre could respond. She figured Keith must have told Sheila to say those things on Andre's behalf. That was the annoying thing about best friends dating good friends. Sheila's words soured Deidre's mood as she gathered her things and plopped on the bed. There were a lot of things she had to get straight in her personal life. She just wished she didn't have to think about it all now.

A smile returned to both Deidre and Sheila's faces when they saw Ms. Betsy, Sheila's mother. Ms. Betsy was an original diva. The way that Ms. Betsy called Deidre *darling* always made her feel as if she were the prize pupil in her charm school. Deidre got dressed and then assisted when needed while Ms. Betsy orchestrated, and Enrique, the hairdresser, worked his magic. In the end, Sheila was gorgeous. Once again, Deidre felt the oozing of envy. She caught a glimpse of herself in the mirror behind Sheila and planted on a smile she hoped would carry her through the ceremony, sessions with the photographer, and the reception, where she already planned to make an early departure.

Chapter 4

One kiss, two "I do's" and 200 pictures later, the bridal party entered the halls of the elaborately decorated banquet hall. Deidre was able to relax and enjoy herself a little as the day wore on except for fleeting thoughts about DeAndre or running into his father. They spoke briefly when he called to speak to DeAndre, but it had been about six months since she had last seen him. It was impossible noticing anyone except Sheila and Keith at the ceremony, but she managed to scan the room every fifteen minutes or so looking for him. She wondered if he'd decided not to come to the wedding after all.

"Deidre darling, it's time for your toast," Ms. Betsy whispered in her ear with a glass of champagne already in hand.

Deidre bent down to get the toast she had written on paper the night before out of her purse until she realized that the hostess had not brought her things to the head table. She looked toward the back in an attempt to try and signal someone, and then stopped when she made eye contact with him. It startled her to see the older version of her son staring at her. Bold features and thick coal black eyebrows and goatee complemented his chestnut brown complexion. He was sitting in the last table in the corner with some other people she recognized from high school. Andre acknowledged her with a nod, and Deidre broke the glance as she rose to her feet at the introduction of her name. Her mind became a blank page as she tried to remember what she had written.

"Sheila and Keith, thank you for allowing me to be a part of your special day. I can say I was there from the beginning of your relationship back in high school. What took you all so long?" she said with nervous laughter to the crowd who had probably thought the same thing at sometime throughout their on-again off-again courtship. "Seriously, you guys . . . Sheila is my best friend in the whole wide world. We've been through everything together in and out of school; some things we vowed to take to our graves. I've seen her blossom into a beautiful woman of God. She deserves all the best, so Keith, I hope you're up to the task. May God bless your lives together with passion and purpose."

Deidre fought back tears as she hugged her friend, and then Keith. She sat down quickly, conscientious of her makeup that she was sure would come running down her face if she kept reminiscing. She had told herself to avoid that uncontrollable cry of hers that sprung from a well of emotion and usually ended in an unflattering snort. Her ex-boyfriend was in the crowd, for heaven sakes. And even though they weren't together, she wanted him to look at her and wish they still were.

Deidre watched as the bride and groom danced together for the first time as man and wife. She and Keith's brother, Kevin, joined them for the bridal party dance that followed. Guests who had stood back in quiet reverence during the first dance now crowded the floor. "The

Electric Slide" was playing as the floor covered over with people crossing over, dipping, and turning to the music. Deidre joined the people on the dance floor because in her mind she didn't think she was committing a cardinal sin by letting her hair down.

She felt someone nudging her way, adding an exaggerated flare to the line dance. She smelled the familiar cologne before spotting him out of the corner of her eye. Dancing had always been Andre's thing. Instead of turning in the direction the rest of the partiers were going, Andre did a quick one-eighty and continued the steps in inverse of the crowd. He danced directly in front of Deidre, almost tempting her as if in some weird kind of dance off. Each time they would dip forward or step left, they barely missed each other. *Was he flirting with her?* She willed herself not to look at him; the fluidness of his torso, the gentle rock of his hips, and the look of passionate intent on his face. She wanted to stop dancing before she appeared to be enjoying herself too much. She could hear Keith say over the music, "Dre always did go against the grain." *That he did*, she remembered.

The deejay took a cue from Sheila's coordinator to cut the music and clear the dance floor much to the crowd's displeasure. The caterers ushered the five-tiered cake to the center of the now-abandoned dance floor. Deidre lost sight of Andre as she took her position just outside of the dance floor and figured no one would miss her if she excused herself to the bathroom before making her exit. She was met with oncoming traffic of people with regular, disposable, and digital cameras, vying for a classic shot of Keith and Sheila feeding one another.

Deidre tried to discreetly look for Andre as she waited patiently behind one of Keith's relatives making her way up the aisle, greeting what seemed like every other person she saw along the way. He wasn't at his table. She spotted him out of the corner of her eye coming back in from the lobby. He carried his over six foot frame with ease. She always thought Dre moved as if he had his own theme music. She debated whether she should stop by his table and talk to him briefly about DeAndre. Before she could cross over to his table she noticed another woman walk up to him. Deidre couldn't tell who she was from behind. She slowed, hoping the woman would keep walking. She found herself analyzing the woman's body language as the woman casually put her hand on Andre's shoulder. *This is crazy*, she thought, *I am the mother of his child. I don't have to wait in line.*

Her eyes locked on his as she approached. "I was wondering if I can speak to you for a minute," Deidre said, towering over the woman who had taken a seat.

"Sure. You remember Lisa Wendall, don't you?" he said.

"Oh yeah; from high school. Hey, I just need to talk to Dre for a second about our son."

Andre led her to the side wall. They were comparable in height, which always made it hard for her to avoid his intense eye contact. Deidre could feel herself blush as his eyes swept over her body appreciatively.

"So what's up?"

"DeAndre is in trouble at school. Got suspended for ten days."

He let out a low whistle. "Ten days? What did he do, hit a teacher or something?"

"No," Deidre said, embarrassed to even admit the truth in public. "They caught him with his hands in some girl's pants. They are calling it sexual harassment."

This time Andre laughed. Deidre stared at him with an expression that said nothing about the situation was funny.

"Are you through?" she asked.

"I'm sorry, but that school doesn't have anything better to do with their time than put out little boys for being little boys."

"The school doesn't tolerate it, and neither will I. This could go on his permanent record. The boy needs to get something else on his mind. He thinks he's as grown as you or I, walking around like some thug."

"It's just a phase."

"A phase?"

"The thug phase is just like the phase boys went through back in our day. Take me for example. I was a break dancing, graffiti artist, and wannabe emcee."

Deidre put her hands on her hips. "Exactly. Tell me something. Did you ever grow out of your phase?"

"See, I'm not even going there with you."

"This is serious. The boy is failing, and all he wants to do is impress his knuckleheaded friends. I've told him that I'm not raising him to be no dummy."

"Guys just want to be down, but then we mature. Maybe not as fast as others would like, but at our own pace. We get our heads straight. DeAndre is smart, but he's a teenager. You know what I mean?"

"DeAndre is such a follower though; he's silly. He doesn't think about his future."

"Where have I heard that before?" Andre said, cocking his head to the side as if contemplating. "Look, Dee, what do you want me to do? You've always let me know that you call the shots. I look forward to seeing him every now and again at the mall when I'm working. I can always call him and talk to him."

"So that's how he's been getting the money from you . . . duh," Deidre said, tapping her forehead with her palm as if to knock some sense into her head. "I knew I didn't see any mail come in from you. I wish you would let me know when you're giving him money, or better yet, just give me the money to give to him."

"There you go. I can't even give my son some money." Andre sounded defeated.

"Do you know what he buys with the money you give him? T-shirts, three to four sizes too big. That's all his wardrobe consists of, white and black T-shirts and jeans."

"Like Ma Mable approved of what you were wearing back in high school. That's why you always changed over Sheila's house. The boy is going to wear what he's going to wear."

Deidre smiled at the mention of his nickname for her mother. Andre never thought her mother liked him, but really she was just as critical of her own daughter as she was of him. Her mom didn't think anyone in their generation had any sense. Maybe she was being just like her mother. The thought sobered her.

"Well, I wonder what I'm supposed to do with your son for ten days. I'm going to have to rearrange my schedule. It's my turn to work the swing shift, from three A.M. to eleven P.M. for the next couple of weeks. I should cart him over to your house."

"Let's do that. I wouldn't mind that at all."

This time Deidre laughed. "Yeah; okay."

"What is that supposed to mean? I've been trying to get you to realize that you and I split up, but I never split on my son," Andre said, getting suddenly serious.

"I've been busting my butt raising *your* son for fourteen years." She raised her voice.

Andre took her arm and led her farther out of earshot of the crowd. "We've had our problems, and other than that time period I returned to New York to deal with the death of my father, I've been there for DeAndre as much as you have let me be. I explained all that to him."

"What did he say?"

"He said that he was sorry to hear about my dad. He didn't get to know his grandfather. I told him I barely knew him myself."

Deidre felt like a heel. "I didn't know about your dad. I'm sorry. I guess I figured you just skipped town. "

"It wasn't like we were speaking then, and now, it's as if you just talk at me. I think there are things DeAndre is going through now that I can relate to better than you can because I'm a man. He can learn from my mistakes instead of making them."

"Maybe," Deidre said.

"Hey, I know neither one of us wanted to get into this heavy conversation at your girl's reception, but call me about this suspension thing, and I'll keep him even if he has to go to work with me."

Deidre nodded her head, not wanting to verbally acknowledge the truce she felt developing between them. She felt ashamed at how she'd let resentment and pride keep her from really holding a conversation with Andre before now. Although she had been petty, she was far from ready to commit to an arrangement.

"Wait a minute; I don't remember your number. Is it still the 450 number?" Deidre asked.

Andre cocked his head to the side and looked at her as if he didn't believe her before grinning. "Yeah okay, why don't you get it from *our* son?"

Deidre began to take offense at his smugness, but had to admit that although she never used it, she knew his number as well as her own social security number.

There was an awkward silence when a videographer approached them.

"Do you all want to say something to the bride and groom?" he said, handing the microphone to Andre. *Andre and a microphone . . . oh boy*, Deidre thought. A red light signaled that the camera was recording.

"What's up, Kevin and Sheila? Oh, oh Sheila. Oh, oh, oh, oh, Sheila," he sang a line from the Ready for the World song. This is Dee and Dre, like old times." Andre unconsciously put his arm around Deidre. "We have been through some times. Remind me to burn your playboy files. Seriously partner, we were there with you guys from the beginning, and now, here's to new beginnings. You wanna say something, Dee?" he said, passing the microphone.

Deidre remembered the conversation she and Sheila had earlier about DeAndre getting closer to his dad. "To new beginnings."

Chapter 5

DeAndre picked up the phone on the third ring, ending the conversation early with his friends.

"What took you so long to get to the phone?" Deidre said.

"I was getting ready to paint," DeAndre stammered. He had strict instructions to stay in the house and finish painting the bathroom in their basement. His mother conveniently decided the stale pinstripe wallpaper had seen its better days right after he got suspended from school. She felt that it was adequate punishment to have him steam, scrape, and strip the walls clean in the afternoons before painting it a vibrant blue. He knew she was trying to teach him responsibility through hard labor.

"Make sure you crack a window down there when you are painting," Deidre said.

"Okay."

"What else have you been up to?"

"Nothing"

"Nothing, huh? Why are you talking so fast?" Deidre asked.

"I'm tired. You got me doing the work of about five men in the basement," he complained. "Can you bring me home a smoked turkey sandwich and some more Smores cereal?"

"Don't tell me all that cereal is gone already. All you must do all day is eat. Gosh, I forgot you were a human garbage disposal," Deidre said. "Let me run over to the deli before it closes and get this sandwich. Everything else will have to wait until Monday. I'm tired too."

"All right," he said.

"Set out some clothes for church, 'cause we're going to Sunday School. I don't feel like fussing with you in the morning. I get off at eleven."

"Okay," DeAndre said, before saying goodbye to his mother and depressing the talk button.

After waiting a few minutes after hanging up with his mother, DeAndre dialed the twins' number.

Robert, the oldest, picked up the phone almost immediately "Dog, why'd you hang up?"

"Yeah," Rajah chimed in, picking up the other extension.

Robert and Roger Dempsey had been DeAndre's best friends since they moved to Kettering when he was four years old. DeAndre clung to them like a triplet, fitting comfortably in the middle of their two personalities. Robert, or Rob, was like the crew leader who could, like his mother often said, "talk a poor man out of his last dime." Anything that the three of them did or didn't do was usually decided by him. Roger, called Rajah, more out of habit from their preschool vernacular rather than an intentional nickname, was a class clown. Deidre and the twins' mother usually asked that the three of them be separated into different classes ever since the three of them ended up receiving a failing grade in conduct in the same first and second grade classes.

"My moms was checking up on me. She already got me on a military lockdown with crazy chores during the day. I know I better answer the phone when she calls," DeAndre said, plopping down on his mother's bed as if he were exhausted just talking about it.

"Well, I hope you ain't too tired to roll with us to this party," Rajah said.

"Dog, you're not hearing me. I'm punished. I don't think another one of your aunt's card parties is worth getting in more trouble for." DeAndre sighed.

"Naw, it's not that," Rajah said.

"D, you're not even going to believe this," Rob screamed into the phone.

"Yo, you sitting down, man?" Rajah asked.

"Yeah, I'm sitting down. What's up?" DeAndre was getting tired of the hype man routine.

"Lonnie Parker has been telling everybody all week that his mother was allowing him to have a party, right."

"Lonnie Parker?" DeAndre wondered why this boy's name suddenly seemed significant to him.

"Yeah, Lonnie Parker is in your last period class. Yo, keep up. So apparently his father said he didn't want the party getting out of hand with the whole school trying to be up in his basement. So he comes to school yesterday with a ticket thingy so you can get in." Rob paused. "Guess what's on it?"

"Take a wild guess," Rajah said.

"What?" DeAndre didn't feel like guessing.

"Afro Yu Gi Oh," Rob shared.

"My sketch? Hold up. Where did he get that?" DeAndre said of his distinctive African American version of the popular Japanese animated character from television.

"Lonnie Parker is doing his thing. Lonnie Parker is turning fifteen." Rob was apparently reading from the front of the invitation.

"I don't know, but he ran off like a hundred copies. I asked him for an extra one for you since you were suspended," Rajah said.

"Oh yeah, Lonnie Parker," DeAndre said, still trying to think about when he recently heard his name. "Lonnie Parker doesn't even hardly come to school but he managed to straight steal my picture of Mini-me. Does it have my signature?"

"Yeah, on the bottom," Rob said.

"Dee something," Rajah added.

"Dee Scribble, that's how I sign my work now. That means he put out one of my newer versions."

"Dee Scribble? That's hot. That's going to be your new nickname. Everybody was talking about the ticket with your drawing on it," Rajah said.

"Yeah?" DeAndre said, happy to hear his work was at least appreciated by his peers.

"I say we pull him up at his own party," Rob suggested.

"Yeah, he can't just steal your art," Rajah added.

"Naw, man. I'll deal with Lonnie later. I'm in enough trouble."

"Look, the party jumps off at eight. You get dressed and meet us at the corner. It's only going to take us fifteen minutes to walk up there. Your mom doesn't leave work until eleven. That gives us plenty of time to bum rush the snacks, get our party on a little bit, then find Lonnie and ask him what his problem is."

"You'll be home in time to fake your mother out, go to sleep, and get up in the morning for church," Rajah said.

"Yeah; all right," DeAndre said, playing along with what he hoped was a joke.

"Dog, anyone who knows you and your drawings knows that Lonnie straight punked you. What if he takes your drawing to that place in Iverson Mall and get it put on a T-shirt like you are always saying you're going to do?" Rob asked.

"Yeah, ain't that like against the law or something?" Rajah said.

"Yeah, copyright law; against copyright law," Rob said.

"He must have just found it somewhere. I doubt dude is stupid enough to use my signature drawing, and then invite me to the party with my work on the ticket."

"I don't know, but he better ask someone," Rajah said.

"You owe it to yourself as an artist, if you want to be taken seriously, to stick up for yourself. We got your back."

"Yeah."

"Naw, dog, I appreciate it though. Like I said, I'm not trying to be serving a life sentence on punishment," De-Andre declined.

"Yo, trust me on this one; you do not want to miss this party." Rob said.

"You got that, dog." DeAndre didn't even consider putting himself at more risk to get in trouble.

"Yo, Rob, I guess we'll have to dance with Kenya," Rajah teased.

"You know Lonnie and Kenya are cousins, right? She definitely is going to be there," Rob said.

Snap, DeAndre thought. That was where he remembered hearing about that kid, Lonnie. Kenya was a girl that DeAndre joined the teen Sunday School class at church to get to know. They eventually exchanged phone numbers in the back of their Sunday School lesson book and became boyfriend and girlfriend over the phone during a late night conversation.

Kenya didn't attend Pemberton Middle like the rest of the kids their age in their area. Instead, her mom put her in an all girls Christian academy. She lived a good twenty minutes in the opposite direction of the twins' house in a town called Largo. The twins thought that Kenya was a figment of DeAndre's imagination and an excuse of his for not taking an interest in any of the girls at their school until they started coming with him to go see her after school. When they got tired of standing there, she had a few of her friends meet with them at the neighborhood playground to even out the boy/girl ratio. Once there, he knew the twins could entertain Kenya's girlfriends still clad in checkered uniform jumpers while DeAndre stole a few minutes alone with her, awkwardly staring and trying to make her laugh. Every once in a while, she would ask about her cousin, Lonnie.

Now he was excited at the prospect of spending time with her at this party, again without the watchful eye of his mother, her mother, or their Sunday School teacher, Sister Neale. He had reconsidered tonight's plan. Kenya was worth getting in trouble for.

"An hour and a half, and then I'm out," DeAndre said.

DeAndre dressed in several layers under his Washington Wizard's basketball jersey and topped it off with a jean jacket. He flipped through his mini sketchbook and noticed the jagged edges of a page recently ripped out of his book. *When did I lose that page?* Another variation of his Afro Anime stared at him from the next page so he stuck the cardboard end of the book into the front of his jeans in order for the picture to hang over his pants like a belt buckle. DeAndre left the phone off the hook as he set out to meet up with the twins. He knew that if his mother called back, she would think he was on the Internet when she heard the busy signal rather than getting the beep from call-waiting.

DeAndre met the twins at the corner of Croft and Tucker Streets where the houses on his street crossed the entrance into a development of townhouses where the twins lived. Rob and Rajah were lanky boys, all legs and arms, but not at all clumsy like some teenage boys getting use to their new height after a growth spurt. Rajah looked to be a blurred version of his brother with softer features that illuminated his carefree spirit. They both wore black down feather coats that made them look twice their actual width. The coats, like all the items they received from their father, were now their most prized possession, which made dressing alike bearable for them, at least for the winter. Although it was below freezing, neither of them wore a hat like DeAndre. Rajah wore a bandana tied to the front and knotted on his forehead, leaving the ends sticking out above his brow like deformed bunny ears.

"What's up?" DeAndre said, extending his palm to Rob for their ritualistic handshake, then doing the same for Rajah before saying, "Boy, you look like a broke-down Tupac."

"I know you're not talking, son." Rajah said. "Your Air Jordans need to go into retirement. You got up here quick as a mug. I can't believe you were going to sell us out until you heard your girl was going to be up there. Dang, you pressed."

"Your mama," DeAndre said as a generic comeback to his friend's insult. The minute he said it he regretted it because he knew Rajah was going to comeback with something good.

"It's yo' mama. Yo mama so fat, she has to use a blanket as a washcloth. Don't start with me, son." Rajah backed up to get some room as if he were about to take DeAndre on in a fight. "Yo mama got one toe and one knee, talkin' 'bout call me Tony. What's up?"

Rob and DeAndre burst into laughter, falling into one another for support. DeAndre put his hand up in surrender to the undisputed "yo mama jokes" king. That was

Rajah's special talent. Rob could talk his way out of any problem, DeAndre had his sketches, and Rajah had the jokes. He had a keen comedic timing that didn't allow his face to crack a smile until the punchline was delivered and his brilliance confirmed with laughter. When he retold a funny story or cracked on someone, he had a command on the language that was not appreciated or assessed in school. There he was deemed learning disabled. DeAndre and Rob knew that making mention of his special classes in school was an insult for which he had no comeback.

The force of the wind stopped their laughter as they moved toward Route 202. DeAndre crossed in front of the twins to the edge of the sidewalk closest to the wooded area just in case, by some slight chance, his mother or any of her informants were watching. He walked backward against the wind's assault. He thought about his mother and how disappointed she had been of him lately and felt a surge of guilt for openly defying her by going to this party. DeAndre watched as they trekked farther and farther from their neighborhood, and he wanted to run back home like a child playing chase getting the okay to, "come out, come out wherever you are." The challenge for him was to get home before being tagged out.

Chapter 6

The party was in full swing when DeAndre and the twins got there shortly after 8:30 P.M. Lonnie's father, a menacing man at six feet two, greeted them at the door. DeAndre didn't know if Rob picked up on it, but he surely wasn't going to start any trouble in this man's house like he and the twins discussed on the phone. He had come to see Kenya, not get tossed out on his butt.

Lonnie's father looked to be having a party of his own upstairs as several couples crowded around a dining room table filled with food and beer.

"Are you keeping count of how many of these kids we got downstairs?" Lonnie's mother asked. "Looks like Lonnie passed out more than forty invitations at school. This was your idea to let the boy have a party."

"Do you have an invitation?" Lonnie's father said, ignoring the woman. Music and chatter floated to the upstairs from the open doorway.

Rajah pulled two invitations with the identical sketch of DeAndre's on it. Rob pulled up his massive jacket to produce his own from his back pocket. Lonnie's father yielded the way to the basement after giving them another threatening stare. Rob bolted down the steps followed by DeAndre and his twin.

The basement was almost entirely filled with boys and girls from their school who were gathered together in groups, acting like strangers. Rob, Rajah, and DeAndre gave the same hearty handshake to some of the fellas that always symbolized kinship between black men; to others not within their grasp, a more contemporary head nod. Lonnie Parker, who was dressed in Allen Iverson wear from head to toe, gave them a backward nod from the deserted dance floor. DeAndre made his way to the remnants of snacks left on the corner table. When he returned, Rob and Rajah had moved in front of a couple of girls who looked to have used the same lipgloss. DeAndre joined them, searching the faces of girls that occupied the only couch for Kenya. He hadn't talked to her since his suspension and hoped the twins were right with their assumption that she would be in attendance.

The DJ struck the right cord with the crowd as he played the latest cut from a Dirty South rapper that had just the right tempo for the dancers to try out the latest dance, the crypt walk. Rob, getting no takers from the girls he was trying to impress, flung his coat on an old pool table where everyone else had placed theirs and bopped to the middle of the floor. DeAndre and Rajah watched as Rob and the other dancers attempted the choreography from the videos seen on *BET* and *MTV*. The music worked as the perfect icebreaker to integrate the dance floor. A few girls, confident enough that their blouses and low rise jeans would not reveal more than they intended, danced in a group.

DeAndre and Rajah decided to relieve themselves of their coats as Kenya came down the steps with a girl, who by appearance, could only be Lonnie's sister. Kenya wore faded jeans and a peasant blouse with the matching jean jacket. Her micro braids were sectioned and bundled in two ponytails. Kenya always looked neat, he thought, always fashionable, always covered. Her glossy brown skin reminded him of the painted on chocolate of a black Barbie doll's. Her eyes seemed to glance over DeAndre and Rajah as if they were invisible, leaving DeAndre feeling foolish for waving at her as she and her cousin walked the perimeter to the opposite side of the room and found a space on the couch. He waited in that same spot in hopes that she would notice him.

The next time DeAndre looked at his watch it was ten o'clock. They had been gone for two hours. Rob and Lonnie seemed to be competition as to who could stay on the dance floor longer. The crowd was chanting, "From the windows to the wall . . ." along with the record which was the teen equivalent to the party chant, "the roof is on fire." Mr. Parker, who was sent by his wife to chaperone the party, walked up behind Rob, who was in heaven, sandwiched between two girls as their arms swayed right and left to the beat. He signaled to the DJ to turn the volume down as he spoke.

"Look here, the grown folks are upstairs. If any of you feel like you're grown," he said for the third time that night, each time more slurred than the other, "come on upstairs so I can show you the door."

The DJ, a man whose age was somewhere between the crowd upstairs and the crowd downstairs, didn't even wait until Mr. Parker was all the way up the stairs before starting the cut over again. Rajah had abandoned DeAndre as some of the boys turned on the Play Station in the corner. DeAndre didn't feel completely comfortable standing alone. As he could recall, the last birthday party that he had been invited to, he brought a gift and sang "Happy Birthday" to the glow of candles on a cake.

He hadn't been to a party with his peers that his mother hadn't confirmed with a phone call and driven him there personally. He had been with the twins to their Aunt Trudy's card party that eventually ended up much like this one with loud music playing in a basement filled with couples, seeing how low they could bend and how long they could last on the dance floor. But they were grown folks, and the only reason DeAndre was allowed to go was because he was spending the weekend with the twins. His mother, like Lonnie's father, always made the distinction between the behavior of children and adults.

The kids in attendance at this party thought they were adults. Apparently there wasn't any middle. They went from playing games and watching a clown to anything they could get away with doing in the shadows of the basement. DeAndre saw Rob dancing so close to Teesha that from DeAndre's vantage point, her hair looked like an extension from his head. And Rajah was about to lose the rest of his allowance betting on the winner of a video game. Curse words were bouncing off the rafters more than the music itself. He knew Kenya's mother didn't know what was going on in this basement.

What's with her, DeAndre thought. By now, he knew Kenya had not only seen him but had rolled her eyes at him a couple of times. She was mad at something, but for the life of him, he couldn't figure out what. He just wished he could fix it so he could see her double dimpled smile return.

DeAndre began walking in Kenya's direction when he saw an empty spot on the couch next to her where her cousin had been sitting. She balanced her elbow on her knees and rested her head on her hands. He could not mistake the look of disgust when she realized he was approaching.

"What do you think Sister Neale would have to say about us being at this party?" DeAndre said, sitting right beside her.

"She'd march our behinds to Sanctuary Hour so we can pray for forgiveness for just hanging out with our friends and liking rap music," Kenya said, temporarily relinquishing her perturbed look to crack a smile, then snapping back into a disgusted grit.

"You couldn't come over and speak? Or were you just going to ignore me?"

"Where's your little girlfriend? I thought maybe she might be here with you."

"Girl, you know you're my girl."

"Do not call me that. As far as I'm concerned, you are nothing to me."

"Wait a minute, what's up?"

"What did they tell me her name was? Lorraine something? I heard you were feeling on her booty in gym class, and your triflin' behind got suspended for it. You didn't even tell me you were suspended, but that's all right. You probably didn't think I'd find out, you dog."

"I can't really get on the phone when my mother is home, but tell whoever has been spreading my business that I wasn't feeling on Lorraine. I don't even like her. I was—"

"Save it." She put the palm of her hand right in his face. "I'm through talking to you. Do me a favor and leave me alone. I don't want to go with you anymore."

"What?"

"You heard me. I thought you were different because you went to my church." She got up. "But I guess I was wrong."

DeAndre watched her walk away. One of his class-mates grabbed her hand, trying to get her to dance with him, but she yanked it away and headed up the stairs to the solace of her family. DeAndre felt as if she had just slapped him in the face. That was the harshest he had ever heard Kenya speak. He looked around to find a couple of girls laughing at him.

"Man, forget her. Forget this wack party." He looked for his partners and walked toward Rajah who was closer. He grabbed him by his neck. "Squad up, son, they are about to feel the power of Afro Yuh Gi Oh up in here. Where's twin?"

"Squad up," Rajah yelled over the music, holding on to a now apprehensive DeAndre who only intended on being brave in front of Lonnie, not a huge audience. The dance floor cleared at Rajah's battle cry as guys tried to figure out their alliances.

Rob linked up with DeAndre and Rajah as they bopped with bravado like Dorothy, Scarecrow, and Tin Man off to see the wizard. Lonnie signaled to the DJ to cut the music, who took it as the perfect opportunity to go upstairs and take a break.

"What's the problem?" Lonnie asked.

"You the problem, son," Rob said, pushing DeAndre forward.

DeAndre felt like a little boy playing a grown man's game. He couldn't believe they were actually busting up Lonnie's party. It felt like he was in a scene from a movie. He thought about what the twins had said to him over the phone about defending his art. He thought about how he was going to make it home in the next 30 minutes before his mother found out. He thought about his dad, who hadn't been there to teach him how to really defend himself. Then he thought about Kenya and how she wouldn't listen to a word he had to say. She was the one who made him believe he was an artist when he would show her his doodles during Sunday School class.

"You see this here," DeAndre said, lifting his jersey and taking his sketch from his waistband and pointing to it. "It's signed Dee Scribble. That's me. I drew that."

"So," Lonnie said, genuinely confused.

"I know you are not going to insult this man by saying 'so' when you ganked his sketch," Rajah said.

"I found it, liked it, and made a copy of it. You got a problem with that?" Lonnie said.

"Yeah, I do," DeAndre said, knowing that if he said very little, the twins would carry the rest. They always stuck up for him, and this time, they seemed really offended that anyone would use his drawing without his permission.

"It is not even that heavy," Lonnie said to the crowd, turning his back on DeAndre and the twins. By now, the jury was weighing in. From their response, the three of them didn't have a strong argument; not enough to stop a party anyway.

"I think you owe my man an apology or compensation or something. He is an artistic genius. His stuff don't come cheap," Rob said.

"Yeah cheap, like yo mama, standing on the corner with a sign around her neck saying, will draw for food," Rajah said, pretending he was an artist studying a model before painting a canvas.

The crowd responded with oohs as if they were an audience at a boxing match and Rajah had delivered a blow.

"Boy, you must be crazy," Lonnie said, looking at the stairwell as if his mother could actually hear the insult, "or should I say retarded." He began pointing. "Why don't you, No- Rhythm, and Dumbo get to steppin' then?"

"Man, who you calling dumb?" Rob said, taking Lonnie's insult of his twin brother personally. Rob and Lonnie were in a standoff in the middle of the dance floor. They were standing soldier straight with their chests poked out, daring each other to make the next move. DeAndre felt the whole scene had gone a little too far and pried his way in between them in an attempt to break them up so they could go.

"I'm calling your brother dumb, locked away in the retard wing all day," Lonnie said, bolder now that there was some room between them.

Rob started swinging and Lonnie swung back. DeAndre found himself in a windmill of arms. His body was keeping them from landing any punches. The crowd stood off so they could accurately report the fight to their peers at school who weren't fortunate enough to get an invitation. DeAndre got shoved from behind, knocking Rob to the floor. He swung around and instinctively landed a blow across Lonnie's jaw. Everyone was stunned, especially DeAndre.

"Where's my piece? This kid is dead," Rajah shouted, throwing coats off the ping pong table until he got to his. He tossed the identical jacket to his twin while DeAndre grabbed his jean jacket before it hit the floor.

It took a minute for it to register. Someone yelled, "He's got a gun."

It was like someone turned on a siren; everyone scattered behind tables, couches and even the DJ booth. Rajah went into a scene from a gangsta film, searching frantically in his pockets for a pretend gun. Only DeAndre and Rob knew that dramatics were Rajah's defense mechanism. Unfortunately, all the kids present had been exposed to a scene like this before, either real or in the media, and for a few minutes, they thought they were in their own gangsta film. Lonnie called out for his father. That was Rob's cue to lead the way upstairs, while De-Andre followed, dragging Rajah, who was still in character. They passed the DJ who was on his way down the stairs now.

Once upstairs, they ran past the dining room where Mr. Parker and friends danced to their own music, oblivious to what was going on in his own basement. Once outside, the boys continued to run a quarter of the way home. DeAndre was in flight until the cold air rushing into his lungs collided with his adrenaline-induced exhaust. DeAndre stopped. He bent at the waist with his hands on his knees. When the twins realized he had stopped, they doubled back to see what was the matter.

"I can't believe we did that, I can't believe it," De Andre said. For a minute he felt as if he were going to hyperventilate. "They thought you had a gun. Did you see how scared they were?"

"Forget Lonnie, man," Rob said, more so to Rajah who was wearing his wounded puppy look. "You showed him who was the dumbo."

"Are you for real? That whole scene could have gotten real ugly," DeAndre said, regaining his breath. "What time is it?"

"Dog, it's 11:20. We got ten minutes, and you are SOL." Rob said.

This time they started running and DeAndre didn't stop until he was at his front door. He had beaten his mother home. The clock read 11:36. He peeled off his clothes immediately and threw the unnecessary layers in his closet. Although he was under a sheet and comforter, he felt a chill that didn't go away.

He thought about Kenya. Where was she when they were putting on a show in the basement? Thoughts of her helped his heart rate return to its regular pace. In his mind, they were at a party again. Kenya flashed him that double dimpled smile from across the room. Before long they were dancing, not that solo, competition, break-a-sweat dancing either, but rather grown folks dancing. In his mind, they were close enough for him to get drunk from her scent of sugared fruit.

DeAndre drifted off to sleep. He didn't hear his mother enter their home at 11:55. He also didn't hear the phone ring slightly after midnight.

Chapter 7

Deidre was speechless on the phone with Mrs. Parker as she listened to her explain what had happened in her house no more than an hour ago. *How could that be?* Each time she started to open her mouth to tell Mrs. Parker that she must be mistaken, that her son was at home painting her basement and waiting on snacks until he fell asleep, she thought about DeAndre and knew it was true. Her son had gone to a party with the twins. As they were leaving the Parkers' to come home, they got in a fight with the woman's son, and one of them said they had a gun which caused frenzy in their house.

Deidre heard a beep and Mrs. Parker clicked over to the other line without saying excuse me. She thought about hanging up, but felt as if she owed her the courtesy of hearing her out.

"That was another parent calling me asking me what in the world was going on at my house tonight," Mrs. Parker said upon her return.

"Let me get this straight. DeAndre and the twins had a gun?"

"Hello?" A male voice said from another line inside the Parker household.

"I'm on the phone with the mother of the boy who acted a fool at Lonnie's party." Mrs. Parker shouted as if the person on the other extension was hard of hearing.

"Hello?" The male voice said again.

Deidre's head was pounding to the rhythm of her heart which felt as if it were going to force itself out of her chest. It was apparent from Mrs. Parker's shouting, as well as the man's slurring on the other end of the line, that the adults at the party were drunk and in no way adequate supervision for a teenage party.

"Mrs. Parker, did anyone see a gun?" Deidre said, joining in on the yelling.

"No, they ran out so fast. I saw this boy with his hands in the inside of his coat. I hit the floor because you know, I'm from Southeast D.C., and I knew what time it was. The kids downstairs were screaming. My son said that as soon as they hit the door, one of boys said, 'Sike-a-boo-boo.' He then pulled out a handful of Fritos and tossed them all over the floor and they all ran."

The man on the other end of the line broke in. "They better be glad I didn't catch 'em. I would have—"

Deidre interrupted, not wanting to think of what she would have done if she were in their shoes or what she would have done if this man put his hands on her son. "I apologize for the way my son has behaved. He's a good kid really. It's just peer pressure that's got him acting so crazy lately."

Deidre's mother always said that stupidity was dangerous. The game DeAndre and his friends played tonight was all of that and more. Mrs. Parker said that minute DeAndre and the twins tore out of her house like some street thugs it was like chaos with the remaining kids practically running all over each other to get out of the house themselves. Mrs. Parker found out from her son what had happened, and her niece gave her their number to call.

Deidre had listened as Lonnie's mother went on and on about what was wrong about the younger generation today. In Mrs. Parker's opinion, it was young boys like DeAndre and his friends who were to blame for everything from drugs, violence, and the overall deterioration of the African American race. Deidre took offense but held her peace.

Deidre hung up the phone with a promise to handle the situation and immediately set out for DeAndre's room. It had been several years since Deidre had to put her hands on her son to discipline him, outside of the occasional whacks upon his head when he slipped up and got smart with her. Usually when he got himself in trouble she would send him to his room so she could contemplate a suitable punishment, like no telephone privileges or forbidding him from hanging out at the mall or the recreation center with the twins. She just figured he was getting too old for her to be, as her mother put it, 'whoppin' up on him.' She had seen other parents slugging on their teenagers as if they were in a boxing ring. In her mind, there was a thin line between sparing the rod like the Bible said and provoking a child to wrath. She treated DeAndre like a young adult. As long as his behavior wasn't flat out defiant or disrespectful, she let him deal with the consequences of his actions, such as getting a failing grade on a missing school assignment or having no money after spending his allowance on junk. This time he had crossed the line.

Deidre swung open the door to DeAndre's bedroom and yanked back his covers.

"Get up!" Deidre shouted. "You can hardly be sleep considering you just got in not too long ago." Deidre waited until he sat up fully in the bed.

His expression alone had "busted" written all over it.

Deidre was like a massive tidal wave taking him unaware, pelting him with her hands as well as her words.

"So you just think you don't have to listen to a word I say in my house. You can do what you want, when you want. Did you honestly think I wouldn't find out that you were out of this house without permission?" she said, punctuating each sentence with a slap across his head or anywhere the blows happened to land.

"Then you don't have sense enough to stay out of trouble when you're out. You all had those poor people thinking that you really had a gun. What if they had called the police, or better yet, what if his father had a real gun upstairs and shot at you for acting a fool in his house? Did you ever think of that?"

Deidre was silent for a second and DeAndre knew better than to say anything. He was probably thinking his worst nightmare had come true. His mother did have 24-hour surveillance on him.

"Number one, you don't know those people." Deidre used her fingers to make her point. "Number two, I don't know those people, but they think they know me. I am the one with the unruly son who gets suspended from school one week and gets in fights at people's birthday parties the next. You don't know how embarrassing it is for me, as a mother, to have to hear from other people about the stupid things my son does. Then I have to sit and explain to them that I'm doing the best I can to raise you.

"What is it, Dre? What has got your mind thinking that rules aren't made for you?" Deidre said. She rarely called him Dre; that's what she used to call his father, but when she did, the conversation had gone to another level.

"I dunno. I mean nothing," DeAndre said. "I'm sorry."

"Your father used to be the same way. He'd shrug his shoulders as if his actions didn't need explaining. I won't have that same nonchalant I-don't-care-about-anyone-but-myself attitude from you also. You need to know that there are limits."

Deidre was pacing now and mumbling to herself. She went over to his desk and dresser, knocking things over as if she were looking for something. She stopped at his chair piled high with his sketch books and drawings on loose leaf paper in a folder. Deidre noticed him eyeing the pile with great concern. "What are you hiding?"

"Nothing." He stood up in horror as his mother flung his books aside and picked up his folder bound together with rubber bands, "Mom . . . no!"

"I'm not worried about these papers. I want some answers. Are you using drugs?" she said, sending his papers soaring across the room. She pushed his chair out of the way in an attempt to get a better look at his desk. "Answer me."

"No," he said. "God!"

Deidre was shocked by his tone. He gathered his sketches into a pile inside the manila folder, placing a few that were torn on top. He held them tight under his arm as he made his way to his desk to tape his pictures back together.

"Oh, God, what am I doing wrong?" Deidre said, sitting on the edge of his bed. "Lord, help me."

Deidre's pleas rolled into sobs. The urge to hide her vulnerability in front of her son caved under the weight of shear helplessness. She had always managed to put on a brave face in front of DeAndre. Even when she and his father had argued and eventually broke up, she had always assured DeAndre that it would be all right, although it wasn't. This time, she didn't have an answer; she didn't know her next move.

DeAndre joined her on the opposite side of the bed. Temporarily engulfed in his own shame, he began mumbling his version of what went on. He was talking a mile a minute. Through the single trail of tears trickling down his cheek, Deidre could see her little boy.

Deidre was through. She didn't want to hear anything he had to say. "All I know is that you will compound trouble on top of trouble. Where does it end? When does common sense and the values I taught you kick in, huh? Forget about using the phone or seeing the light of day for that matter. I'm serious; no phone, no privileges, nothing."

DeAndre inhaled sharply in an attempt to put the remaining tears in reverse. He shrugged off the impression that he cared and shut down. The semblance of her little boy was gone.

Chapter 8

Liberty A.M.E. church held a Sanctuary Hour before the eleven A.M. service so that the members could unload their weekly burdens on the altar before worship began. Those requesting special prayer from the stewards in charge needed only to fill out a prayer request card and leave it in the marked box outside of the main sanctuary. Deidre filled out the card in great detail. It was her prayer that God would give her a discipline plan because, presently, she was clueless as to what to do with DeAndre.

Deidre was surprised that DeAndre was up and preparing for church without any prompting from her. Once they hit the doors of the church, Deidre deposited her prayer request card in the slot outside of the sanctuary doors, and DeAndre took off for Sunday School.

As soon as DeAndre met Deidre in the main sanctuary after class, she yanked him down the aisle with her to the altar. The altar area was packed with people fidgeting nervously, sniffling into fresh handkerchiefs and mumbling their own prayers. Everyone else stood in the aisle or bowed their heads at their seat. The goal was to pray until something happened, or at least, until a person felt better about their current situation. Deidre began to pray silently to herself, keeping a firm hold onto DeAndre's wrist in hopes that he would pray also. The lights were dimmed in the sanctuary, and everyone began praying aloud at the same time. The collective prayers sounded like a swarm of bumble bees until a gradual hush came over the crowd which was the time the congregation listened for an answer from God.

Associate Minister Kenneth Steele approached the podium in the pulpit halfway through Sanctuary Hour as the organist played the hymn, "Sweet Hour of Prayer." Minister Steele, a self-proclaimed prayer technician, was skilled in the art of calling upon the name of the Lord and weaving congregational requests into a corporate prayer while preserving the members' anonymity. He went over the request cards for special prayer in his office a few minutes prior to Sanctuary Hour every Sunday, much like Pastor Tatum reviewed his sermon outline before worship service.

An admitted former cocaine addict, Minister Steele had shared, on numerous occasions, his belief that a person couldn't be truly saved or delivered until they confessed that they were powerless without God Almighty. He seemed to pride himself in bringing people to the point of powerlessness in his prayers so they could stop relying on themselves, and look to the Lord to restore them. He called it killing them softly. Deidre squeezed DeAndre's wrist even tighter when Minister Steele got to her prayer request.

"Lord, bless our children. They are a gift from you. God we've tried to raise our children right, but it seems that in today's time, the devil has dangled every kind of temptation in their view. Our children, dear Lord, are running the streets at night, strung out on drugs, having sex, and having babies. Young children have lost respect for their elders and are throwing their lives away because they have dropped out of school," Minister Steele said in his best TV evangelist voice, wherein the word *Lord* was in its own extraordinarily high octave.

"Oh Lord, I have a mother here who is almost at her wits end with her teenage son. She's all alone, Father, trying to make a difference in this young man's life. Lord, he's getting in trouble in and out of school. Let her know that you hold them both in the palm of your hand.

"Lord, help this mother with her son. Keep her son away from the wrong crowd and wrong influences as he seeks to assert his independence. Let him know that there are rules he must follow starting with the ones his mother has set in her household. Provide a hedge of protection around him when his mother cannot be there. Then, Lord, place a male role model in her son's life that will help shape him into a productive young man."

Minister Steele went on to pray for others who submitted a prayer request. *That was it*, Deidre thought. She'd raised him, taken care of him when he was sick, and made sure he went to church, but it wasn't enough. Now, DeAndre needed a man to teach him to be a man. It was a bitter pill to swallow.

The lights were turned up at the end of the hour, and the praise team was in position to sing during the transition between Sanctuary Hour and worship service. Deidre opened her eyes and rubbed them until they adjusted to the light. Only then did she let go of DeAndre's arm. He took off for the door.

"Don't go far," Deidre said as she looked for Sheila and Keith who should have been home from their honeymoon by now and ready to commune with the rest of the world. Instead, she saw Larry Wilson. He was a Steward of the church that was typecast as Jesus in every Easter play since Deidre had been at Liberty. His slender build made it easy to harness him to the cross for the crucifixion scene. Although Larry was an active member of their church, there was something lewd about the way he stared at her.

Larry was Deidre's 'in case of an emergency' man. Most of the men at Liberty attended a Promise Keepers Rally and conference in the nation's capitol with Pastor Tatum called, Standing in the Gap. The men came back with a determination to serve God through serving others. Pastor Tatum tested their commitment by challenging the brothers to "stand in the gap" for the single sisters of the church. He asked the men to make themselves available when one of the single sisters, who stood that particular Sunday, had an emergency such as needing a ride, needing their lawn mowed or their driveway shoveled in the winter. Deidre thought the whole idea was very chauvinistic and sat down, taking herself off the 'helpless sister' list.

Larry Wilson found her anyway. He extended his phone number and his services for, as he put it, 'emergencies and recreational non-emergencies.' Deidre was sure this was why he was approaching her now.

"Sister Deidre, how about I take you to dinner next week so we can discuss how I can stand in the gap and help you with your son?"

Deidre tried with all her might not to be disgusted. She came in feeling helpless, but not desperate. He was trying to weasel a date with her in exchange for some positive male guidance for her son. It wasn't that she didn't want help. It occurred to her awhile ago that the only people who could bridge the gap in her son's life were the stubborn people who wedged it in the first place; his parents. It was confirmed this morning by Minister Steele's prayer.

"Thank you, Larry, but his father and I will handle it, with the help of the Lord, of course." Deidre said, leaving him standing in the aisle.

Deidre felt empowered to rectify the situation with De-Andre. They wouldn't be staying for service. She was going home early to put her house back in order.

After leaving the church, Deidre knew there were two things she must do with DeAndre. The first was to make amends with the Parkers for DeAndre's antics. She had tried to raise him in a Christian home. That meant they were supposed to admit when they were wrong. She told him that she was taking him to apologize in person one day that week.

"Ahh, Mom, naw," DeAndre said, shaking his head emphatically.

"You are going to apologize to those people for causing a scene in their house when their son was nice enough to invite you to his party. And I want you to stay away from this Lonnie kid in school," Deidre said.

"Oh you don't have to worry about that," he said, rolling his eyes. He shifted his entire body toward the passenger side window as if he were trying to take up as little space as possible.

"And the twins will probably be grounded too, after I talked to their mother this morning. That should give you plenty of time to get yourself together and start acting like you got some sense."

"I can't believe you called their mother. Can you make my life any worse?"

"Who are you speaking to?" Deidre looked around and even glanced through the rear view mirror to see if there was anyone else in the car her son could possibly be talking to in that manner. "I'm doing the best I can with you."

"I couldn't tell," DeAndre said, trying to buffer the impact of his disrespect by talking under his breath.

"Everything that comes out of your mouth is disrespectful, so close it. I'm not playing, DeAndre. Don't open your mouth again," she screamed.

As far as Deidre was concerned, that could just as well be the starting gun for his silent treatment. DeAndre put his head back on the headrest and closed his eyes as if he felt the same way.

When they got home, her head was hurting and her chest was heaving as if he had given her a physical blow.

"Pack your clothes. You're going to your father's for the week," Deidre said, barely getting through the door.

"What?"

"You heard me."

"I don't want to stay over there," DeAndre said.

"It's not about what you want anymore. You have broken my trust, and it will take awhile for it to be mended."

"So you're going to send me to stay with a man you can't even stand."

"I never said I can't stand him. What I did say was that you and he are just alike. So maybe he will have more success dealing with your attitude and disciplining you than I do."

Deidre felt she owed him a better explanation than she had to offer right now. She knew it must have been mighty confusing for DeAndre when she and his father split up. They went from cohabitating to barely seeing one another. Deidre and Andre both agreed, during one of their rare peaceful conversations, that the best explanation she could pacify their then six-year-old son with was that the break up was a problem between Mommy and Daddy. For his sake, they were supposed to try to settle their differences. What Deidre did not want to admit is that she was the one that dropped the company line and shared blame-filled rants about her ex with their son whenever she was angry with either of them. She had repented each time, but she never made it right with DeAndre. Obviously he had internalized a lot of what she had said.

"I don't see why I have to go."

Deidre wanted to say she didn't know why it was necessary either. She didn't know why he wouldn't abide by her rules anymore. Instead she said, "Just get ready to go."

"I mean, I still have to finish the basement," DeAndre said. "I said I'm sorry. I promise I will stay in the house."

"Too late," Deidre said, taking his suitcase out from the closet and walking past him.

"Mom?"

All of this was too much for her to take. Deidre dropped the suitcase in front of his room and left. That was the third time within a twenty-four hour period that she'd let him see her cry.

Chapter 9

Andre Hicks decided to wait twenty minutes after speaking with Deidre to call her back and make sure he was clear on what he had agreed to do. He had just finished recording in his journal the amount of sets and repetitions he had completed for his upper body workout with his free weights when the phone rang. Deidre sounded weary when she explained DeAndre's latest defiance at home. He knew she had to be truly at the end of her rope with their son to have called him for assistance. In the eight years since they had broken up, Deidre had never come to him for help. He had offered, but she never accepted. He knew she was doing the best she could to provide their son with a stable environment when at times he couldn't, so he empathized with her. He even ignored her, "like father like son," comment about DeAndre's self-sabotaging behavior.

That would have been a true classification of Andre when he and Deidre were together, but not now. He was determined to change his life sparked by the premature death of his father and his obsession with the cult phase of body synergy led by former Olympian and Revolutionary gym owner, Bo Donovan. *An awakening*, his best friend, Keith, called it. Andre called it releasing his demons and regaining his peace. He looked at his goals taped to the inside cover of his journal. Building a relationship with his son was at the top, right above laying off the booze and becoming a Bo Donovan Fitness Trainer.

Right after Andre and Deidre broke up for the last and final time, he received a call from a relative in New York. She told him that his father, Harvey Hicks, was in the hospital and that he had been asking to see his only son. Andre was in between jobs, and Deidre wasn't speaking to him, so he decided to make the trip to get away from the stagnation in his own life. He took everything he could carry in his Toyota Celica. He wasn't sure when he would be back to retrieve his old life.

"It's complicated," was the answer given to a thirteen-year-old Andre by his relatives when they intervened and decided that his dad couldn't continue to care for him. After his mother had been hit by a car and died the year previous, Andre's father grieved by keeping busy working as a ticket agent at the Greyhound bus station by day and being a full-time drunk at night. Brooklyn was too open a range for a teenager to roam unsupervised, so his father's siblings picked straws as to who would raise their brother's only son. A week later, Andre went to stay with his uncle's family in Maryland.

Andre remembered thinking how ironic it was to hear the doctor speak of complications that left his father with only an estimated few days to live. Andre didn't expect the floodgate of emotions to engulf him when he saw his dad hooked up to all those machines used to sustain his life. Cancer had ravaged his once bulky frame. Once again, death came to steal away his family. Although Andre was grown and had lived apart from the shell of a man lying on that hospital bed, he never felt more like an orphan then he did at that moment.

Now Andre wanted desperately to put the pieces together for his son. He had a chance to reconnect with DeAndre at an age where a manchild needed his father the most. He promised himself he wouldn't foul this opportunity up even if he had to painstakingly work through the once complicated relationship between him and his son's mother. Andre picked up his cordless phone, sat on the edge of his couch and called Deidre back.

"Hey, Deidre, this is Dre. I was calling you back to get the details of our little arrangement with DeAndre," Andre said. "Have you told him yet that he will be with me for a week?"

"Yeah, not too long ago," Deidre said.

"What did he say?"

"I didn't wait for his reaction. I'm not trying to hear anything else out of that smart mouth of his right now."

The line was silent for a moment. Andre reflected on his own thoughts, but was cautious as to what he voiced aloud. It felt good talking to her civilly again, but he warned himself that a lot of their conversations started out that way.

"I hear you. Just as long as he knows that you're not just shipping him away," Andre said.

"Well, isn't that what I'm doing?"

Andre could hear the exasperation in her voice. "I don't know, but I see this as an opportunity to raise our son jointly. I know you don't want him to feel like you no longer want to be bothered with him so you're giving him to me. You know how I felt when I came here from New York."

Andre figured Deidre was afraid that if they began to raise DeAndre jointly that she would somehow lose the leverage that she always held over Andre's head. She was the responsible one and he was not. He planned on being the epitome of responsibility.

"So what's the lowdown? What is my assignment? I know you have the whole week scripted out for me."

"I just need him to be away from this neighborhood where he keeps getting in trouble, you know. Watch him; he is sneaky."

"Okay, let me get a sense of the rules you had set up so we can be consistent. So he is punished and the whole nine, no visitors, no telephone?"

"I was allowing him to use the telephone to keep track of him, but not now. The first person he'll probably want to call is Kenya."

"Who's Kenya?"

"She's his little girlfriend from church."

"I know you are not letting that knucklehead date."

"Not date, he's much too young to date," Deidre said, borrowing a line from Kenya's mother when Deidre had joked about their children's infatuation. "As far as I know they just talk on the phone and see each other at Sunday School."

"Are you for real? As far as your mother knew that's all we were doing when we met in high school. Kids are more advanced at his age."

Andre had to reflect on the time when they were in high school together. He would be the first to admit that having a girlfriend was more than he was mature enough to handle at that time. It was like being addicted to a drug. He couldn't get enough of her, and despite her squeaky clean upbringing, he coaxed her into meeting him at the mall and once even skipping school with him, all without her mother's knowledge. Although they were not sexually active until after graduation, each encounter alone moved them closer to that reality.

"Talk to him about her. You know, have the talk."

"The talk?" Andre said.

"Yeah, the sex talk," Deidre said, as if she were mad she had to spell it out. "You know like a real father/son conversation."

There was a long pause before he spoke again, "Why do you do that?"

"What?"

"Take every opportunity to rib me about not being present when DeAndre was younger, which we both know wasn't entirely my fault. I hope from now on that we can put our feelings aside for DeAndre's sake."

Andre wasn't sure what Deidre's feelings were toward him. Their relationship was the last serious relationship he had been involved in. He felt the need to tell her how much his life had changed since they were last together. He figured if they continued their parental partnership an opportunity would arise to iron out their past.

"You're the one that sounds a little edgy. I mean, if you have a problem with me telling you what I expect, we can just forget the whole thing," Deidre said.

"C'mon, Dee," Andre said, exhaling deeply into the phone. He began imploring a breathing technique that helped him to remain calm. "Let's start over. Everything before this point is in the past."

"You're right, the past is the past," she agreed, "That's why the hair has got to come off. Wearing those corn-rows has got him walking around here like he's the man. I figure you can take him to your barber. I would have done it myself, but I figure I might nick the boys head on purpose as mad as I am at him right now."

She had left him to do all the dirty work. Andre knew that he couldn't treat DeAndre too nice because he was on punishment, but he couldn't treat him that bad either because he wanted to foster a father/son relationship. He had to find a middle ground.

"Should I pick him up or will you drop him off?"

"You can pick him up," she started then fell silent as if in thought. "No, I'll drop him off and pick up a few things at the market for him to eat."

"Deidre, I have food. Just drop him off at seven this evening, I got the rest covered. Of course you know I live in the Suitland Parkway Apartments off of Pennsylvania Avenue, the first building, apartment 202. "

They got off the phone after an, "all right then." Andre didn't know what he expected. They weren't together anymore. He wasn't even sure they were friends. There was nothing left to be said.

Andre was attempting to cook lasagna with eggplant and tofu from a Bo Donovan cookbook when Deidre and DeAndre arrived. Deidre stood there as if she didn't know whether it was appropriate for her to come in and visit or drop DeAndre off at the doorway. Andre came to the door and grabbed DeAndre by the head and rubbed it as if he were a puppy despite his perturbed expression.

What a family portrait we make standing here as if we're strangers, Andre thought. "What's going on, son?" Andre said.

"Nothing," DeAndre mumbled.

"Well, make sure he completes all his work for school," Deidre said after a lull in the conversation. "He's back to school a week from tomorrow."

"We got it covered. That's one of the many things we have to go over, right son?" Andre said, yielding the way for DeAndre to come into his apartment.

DeAndre just shrugged as if to say, *whatever.* Andre figured DeAndre probably couldn't figure out why they were being so cordial all of a sudden or why they were trying so hard to involve him in their conversation. They surely didn't consult him when making this arrangement.

"If there is anything you need, just call," Deidre told DeAndre.

"We should be cool." Andre spoke with more confidence than he felt.

"Bye, DeAndre," Deidre said, waiting for a response. "Don't make me embarrass you. You better get out here and say goodbye."

DeAndre came to the doorway and Deidre pulled him to her. She didn't give him a chance to resist. She kissed his cheek. Deidre and Andre watched him tear away and walk through the doorway into his father's house. Deidre turned to leave when Andre stopped her.

"Deidre," Andre said, "thanks."

Chapter 10

Andre instructed his son that he would be sleeping in the living room on the sleeper sofa. He turned his 32' television to *ESPN's Sports Center* and waited for DeAndre to roll his suitcase down the hall to the second bedroom which was a mini gym. DeAndre grabbed his sketchbook from his backpack when he returned and started working on a sketch, not really interested in *Sports Center*.

"You're working on your homework, son?" Andre said, going into the open kitchen to check on his lasagna that was baking. "Let me know if you need any help."

DeAndre hadn't said a word since he had been there. Andre rationalized that he probably was trying to feel him out, but he wasn't going to let him get away with not speaking the way he did at home. Andre returned from the kitchen back to that same spot in the reclining chair next to the couch.

"Are you hungry, son?"

"You can stop calling me that now," DeAndre mumbled. "I know you're my father."

"What?"

"You don't have to keep calling me son. I know you're my father."

"Okay, I won't call you son if it makes you uncomfortable. What does your mother call you then?"

"What does she call you?" DeAndre didn't take his eyes off his sketch.

"I'm the one asking questions," his father said, trying to think of a different approach. "What does your girlfriend call you?"

"Girlfriend?" DeAndre said. "I don't know what you are talking about."

"Kenja?"

"Her name is Kenya. . . ya, Ken*ya*, and she calls me Dre."

"I thought you didn't know what I was talking about. I think I'll call you Deuce."

"Deuce?"

"As in Dre number 2. I'm number one around here."

"Yeah, all right," DeAndre said dismissively.

Andre could smell the aroma of his main dish, so he went into the kitchen and cut off the stove. He could see why DeAndre's mother was tired of his mouth. It wasn't so much what he said, but how he said it that made it disrespectful. He debated whether he should say something now, but decided he would wait to say something about DeAndre's mouth later. First he would try to get to know him a little better over dinner. He used a pot holder to pull the dish out of the oven.

"Yo, Deuce, bring your work in here to the table."

Andre heard his son's sigh from the living room before he appeared in the doorway. Andre thought at least he wasn't crazy enough to ignore his request. As soon as he could get it through DeAndre's head that he wasn't on vacation and wasn't going to get any peace, then they could work on his attitude. Andre noticed DeAndre had brought his headphones into the kitchen with him as an added hint that he wanted to be left alone. He joined his father in the kitchen and sat at the opposite end of the table where his father was serving up two plates of lasagna.

"No headphones at the table; it's rude." Andre said. The boom of his voice startled DeAndre who removed the headphones, but made sure his father could tell his displeasure by sighing heavily.

"What's in this?" DeAndre said, wrinkling up his nose.

"Eggplant. It's good. It's a substitute for red meat."

"Naw, that's all right," De Andre said, taking a piece of garlic bread before pushing the plate away.

"You're going to be hungry because this is it for tonight," Andre said, devouring the first piece of lasagna in three bites. "You could stand to eat a little healthier."

"Yeah all right," DeAndre said sarcastically. "How do you know that I don't eat healthy at home with my mom?"

Andre paused. "Look, this isn't a competition between your mother and me. We are trying to do this thing the right way, and raise you together. Besides, I had your mother's cooking; her mother is from the South too, all they know how to do is cook with butter, grease, and salt pork."

"But it's good though," DeAndre said.

"I didn't say it wasn't good, but this lasagna is slammin' if I do say so myself."

Andre pulled out a bag of salad from the refrigerator's crisper and shook up an olive oil mixture he had prepared earlier as dressing before cutting another huge slice of lasagna." So let's get back to this girlfriend."

"Let's not," DeAndre said, with the headphones draped around his neck.

"Excuse me?"

"I'm just saying, maybe I don't want to talk about me and her." DeAndre played with the remainder of the lasagna. It was actually good, but he needed it to be re-heated. "I don't want to talk period."

"Okay, well you can just listen then. If you want a bootcamp relationship this week, then that is what you will get. Let me give you the rundown. First, you're going to lose the attitude. I'm going to get you a towel set and blanket so you can get your rest. Tomorrow morning we're going to the barber shop to get your dome shaped up, so take those cornrows out."

"Man, it's my head," DeAndre said.

"Yeah, well, you couldn't get your act together at home, so just like your mother promised you, the rows have got to go. You're going to complete your homework and go to work with me everyday."

They ate in silence for a while. Andre took the tray of lasagna and put it away with the salad before leaving the kitchen. Getting his son to open up was going to be more difficult than he had assumed. He thought it would be as simple as two guys rapping to one another, but DeAndre had a major chip on his shoulder. He would give the boy his space for tonight and try again tomorrow to chip the ice.

DeAndre stayed in the kitchen to stay out of his father's way. He thought about getting on the telephone, but he felt as if his father would be lurking in the background trying to hear his conversation. He wanted call the twins and tell them that staying with his father was far from the fun and games they expressed when coming back from a rare visit with their dad in Florida. DeAndre crept to the doorway. His father had pulled out the couch, made his bed, and was camped out on the nearby recliner. So he just had to wait him out. Just as he started sketching again, his father came in for a bowl of ice cream.

"I see you're an artist," Andre said. "Wait a minute. Is that supposed to be your mother? That is real good, son."

DeAndre cringed. It was too late for him to conceal his drawing, so he just stopped working as if he were annoyed. In his drawing, his character was sneaking in after being out at a party and had to morph the mind of his mother who was reporting him missing to the police on the phone. He had drawn a lightning bolt going through his mother's ear and extending out the other causing her to drop the phone. DeAndre was adding detail to the background inspired by the wood grain in his father's cabinets.

"Don't let me stop you," his father said, finally getting the carton of ice cream from the freezer, a bowl from the cabinet, and spoon from the drawer. He carved three large scoops before holding up the cartoon as an invitation for his son to get some. DeAndre snatched his sketchbook away as if his father were intentionally trying to drip something on his work. "My bad."

DeAndre took this as an opportunity to leave the kitchen. "I'm going to take a shower," he said. He hated feeling as if he had to report his every action to his father, but his police probing demeanor almost demanded it.

"Yeah, okay. I left you some towels on the coffee table. The bathroom is the first door to your right in the hallway."

DeAndre secured his book bag underneath the sleeper sofa before taking the orange towel set to the bathroom with him. He took his first breath since being at his father's house. The bathroom was small with no apparent color scheme matching the towels with the bathmats or toilet seat cover like at his house. On the sink was the book, *The Power is Within You, A Book of Daily Mantras* by

Bo Donavan. DeAndre couldn't believe his father bought into the hype surrounding the buff older guy who was prone to shouting on television infomercials, although his father's physique resembled a member of his clan.

DeAndre turned on the shower but chose to wash up at the sink instead of actually using the shower. He already felt overexposed, with his father getting the lowdown from his mother and his not really knowing his father's story. *Where had he been all these years?* He looked in the medicine cabinet to find an assortment of multivitamins, over the counter medicines, and one prescription bottle for a medicine called Zantac. He filled his hands up with warm water and immersed his face in it. After washing himself, he turned off the shower and left the bathroom. His father was now in his bedroom with the door left ajar.

"Goodnight, son," he heard his father say as he went down the hall.

DeAndre got his walkman and headphones once again from his book bag and turned the radio on to hear his favorite song. The artist, Lil' Lizard, was rhyming, *there's no place like home.* DeAndre bobbed his head to the beat and thought about his mom and their home. He used the remote to cut off the television before settling in the middle of the bed.

Only after he turned off the light on the end table did he see his father's light go out. The sound of his dad's door shutting sounded oddly like the clank of the lock and key on a jail cell.

Chapter 11

Deidre used the first three days without her son to thoroughly clean her house. She shed the layers of its old inhabitants leaving boxes and bags of her mother's, father's, and even Andre's old stuff in the front to be picked up by Goodwill. She could not get over how quiet it was in the house. Not that DeAndre made a lot of noise except the occasional muffled sounds of the television and radio beyond his closed bedroom door. The decision to allow DeAndre to spend time with his father had silenced her conscience that had plagued her mind with guilt since shutting Andre out of their lives years earlier.

Deidre remembered Andre coming to her out of the blue saying, "I can't do this anymore." That was it. He offered no other explanation before he packed his things and left. But then he kept calling her as if, in hindsight, he was trying to salvage something from a fire he had set. Deidre refused to listen to a word he had to say. She was too busy picking up her own pieces and moving on.

Now Deidre rambled through her house singing the

old church hymn that went, *Blessed quietness, holy quietness, what assurance in my soul . . .*

1252 Fordham Drive was the same house she grew up in as a child. Her mother and father managed to move into the house at the very end of the Civil Rights Movement, which saw an emergence of an African American middle class. Blacks spread from the sections of DC into the nearest Maryland suburbs like peanut butter on bread, her mother, Mabel Collins, told her, often chasing their white counterparts, not quite secure with integration, farther out into neighboring counties.

Her mother and father were strict Christian parents who had their girls in church three times a week: Wednesday Bible Study, Saturday Evangelism meeting and street witnessing, and Sunday Morning Worship at the Independent Bibleway Church. Deidre's mother, who outlived her husband by twenty years, relied on the aide of the church to help raise her girls until her daughters hit their teens and fell under the spell of what she called, Belzeebub's boys. That was the name her mother gave boys who didn't come courting on her girls properly when they reached an appropriate age. Andre Hicks, who didn't drop his super cool act for anyone, definitely fit that category.

Deidre inherited the faded wall paper, squeaky floors, and a basement that flooded every time it rained heavily from her mother who moved back to her birth home of Iverson, South Carolina when she reasoned her daughters no longer appreciated the protection of her prayers or the wisdom of her advice. A mandatory family gathering at Thanksgiving was all either Deidre or her sister could stomach of their mother's testaments of sanctified superiority and constant scrutiny of their lives.

Deidre tried to make herself available for a weekly phone call from her mother. She decided to initiate this week's call to her mother to tell her about DeAndre's temporary living arrangement before she found out from her sister, with whom she had spoken earlier. She pushed the first speed dial button on the cordless phone while she pulled out a tea bag to brew in a kettle of water she was boiling in the kitchen. Her mother picked up on the second ring.

"Hello, Mom. How are you?"

"Blessed and highly favored," Mabel Collins said. "It's about time you called me for a change. I tried to get you the other day but you weren't in, as usual. Your cousin, Melvin, was up there in your part of town."

"Mom, didn't I give you my cell phone number?"

"Cell phones are for people who like to run the streets. I would think you'd come home sometimes, especially with my grandbaby. Put him on the phone anyway. I haven't talked to him in a month of Sundays."

"DeAndre is with his father," Deidre said, bracing herself as she sat at the kitchen table. "Andre has him all week."

"Mmm hmm." Her mother started humming that monotone melody that seemed to roll into a hymn.

"Mom, did you hear what I just said?"

"Yes," her mother said, "and I surely think it's about time."

Deidre was used to her mother saying anything to be contrary with her but she never remembered her being a fan of Andre's to warrant that response. "I'm surprised to hear you say that."

"Why? It's no need to harbor grudges. What's done is done. It's time to make that boy stand up to his responsibilities."

She was one to talk, Deidre thought. "Well, Momma, you've also made it quite plain that you were always against our relationship."

"I just knew the boy was as wild as the day was long, and look what happened."

"Well, you never really gave him a chance."

"Oh, but you gave him one, didn't you? I knew what would happen. What I was against was the two of you fornicating and shacking up like you weren't taught any better; especially since you were brought up saved and in church."

"That's just it, Momma, I wasn't saved then," Deidre said, returning to the stove, wishing like anything that the water was ready so she could take in the calming effects of chamomile.

Deidre could hear her mother gasp, and then the line went silent. It was the familiar silence between them saturated with hurt and disappointment. Deidre always felt as if her mother wanted her to apologize for something, and that wishful apology was the only thing that could condition the air between them. She just didn't know what she'd be apologizing for.

"Well, I guess you just figured you'd send your mother to an early grave with that comment," Mable Collins finally spoke.

"We grew up in a church where everyone over the age of five was considered saved and was instructed like grown ups to 'work out our soul's salvation' like anyone knew what that meant. There was no Christian education, just people shaming other people who were sinners or just flawed so people like you could feel you had exclusive keys to the kingdom," Deidre said.

This time the silence scared Deidre as if she might actually have slain her mother with her words. She felt like a little girl again, ready to apologize and even more ready to be forgiven. "Oh, Mom, I'm sorry. That didn't come out the way I intended."

"Well, excuse me for trying to make sure my daughters wouldn't spend eternity in hell."

Deidre could imagine her mother clutching the tiny

gold plated cross around her neck that her father had given her many Christmases ago.

"I'm sorry if I sound ungrateful. Honestly, I'm thankful to you and Daddy for giving me a religious foundation. I know I disappointed you when I allowed myself to get pregnant out of wedlock." They hadn't spoken about the pregnancy in so long the words almost got caught in her throat. "I needed you, Momma. I always knew that I was the reason you moved back to Iverson."

"You didn't stop to think how it felt for me to have a daughter tell me she was pregnant barley two years after your daddy died? I'm just thankful that your daddy didn't live to see the day that his daughter would live with a man she was not married to."

"I needed you, Momma," Deidre said again. "I was twenty-something, pregnant, and scared."

"You were all set in your own apartment and going to school. Then you get pregnant and go from bad to worse by letting him move in with you."

"Dre was my mainstay. I felt you had discarded me. It wasn't right in God's eyes, and I realized that after awhile."

"You came to your senses only after I told that boy that I would offer you and my grandbaby a stable life in that house on Fordham if he left."

Deidre was stung speechless. Did her mother just confess to somehow orchestrating the break-up between her and her first love?

"I told you when you started seeing that boy and inviting him around the house that it was moving too fast. I just couldn't be around. Do you understand? I just couldn't be around."

"Yes, I told myself that when I was sitting in this house alone with my baby boy. I can't believe you drove Dre away," Deidre said, staring straight ahead. She went into autopilot, the mind numbing state she was accustomed to clicking on when their conversations got too much for her to bear. The whistle from the kettle brought her back to a painful reality.

"I knew it wouldn't last."

"It could have lasted if you would have accepted us. We could have gotten married. It would have been tough, but you and Daddy were married young," Deidre said, sending her tea bag afloat in a mug of hot water.

"The two of you knew nothing about sustaining that type of arrangement. You were fast to believe that he would eventually marry you. How many boys in your generation are done window shopping and ready to make a purchase in their twenties? You all give up too easily or sell your soul, like you were doing. Look at your sister, married one hot minute. I wasn't going to let that happen to you. The difference is people in my generation had sense enough to stick to their original agreements."

Was her parents' marriage just an arrangement? Deidre thought back to her childhood memories growing up. She didn't remember a lot of what she considered to be evidence of love like hugs and kisses shared between her parents. All she remembered was order.

"Are the two of you getting back together?" her mother asked after a long sigh.

"That's the furthest thing from either of our minds. We're just working on an *arrangement* where DeAndre can see the both of us."

Deidre put down her tea cup and clenched her forehead with her palm. The thought about reconciling with Andre had played with her mind on and off since they broke up eight years previous, and being in contact with him had only intensified that feeling. Deidre didn't dare tell her mother that. She felt as if too much had been said already, and at the same time, not enough.

Suddenly Deidre wanted to convince her mother that everything was all right so that they could go back to their forced and superficial relationship and get off the phone. She wanted to assure her mother that she could have the keys to God's kingdom even though her daughter did not live up to her expectations.

"Well, I've found my center now, Mom. It is in Christ. I found a church that is built upon the foundation that you and Daddy established, and it has really nurtured my need to learn about Christ. I've turned my life over to God since then, Momma. I'm trying to shed all of that guilt from the past," Deidre said while shedding a tear.

This time the silence was unbearable. Deidre felt as if she were caught in a maze. She didn't know when she would be free and the pain would end.

"That's all I've been trying to get you to do since you were born," her mother said as she began to hum that monotone melody that rolled into a hymn.

Chapter 12

A ndre felt as if he had finally found a way to connect with DeAndre on a deeper level. DeAndre had a talent he never remembered Deidre mentioning in her smug way of bragging about their son's good qualities as if the genes could have only come from her side. Andre, at one time, had thought of himself as an artist using spray paint and the neighborhood walls as his medium. Compared to the thoughtfulness of his son's sketches, his own were more like rebellious gibberish, but it left some pretty good burners, as they were called, around town. He decided to take his son to one of those faded sites on the way to work and get his opinion on it.

He drove into the parking lot of a 7-Eleven store. The building sat cattycorner to a major intersection, but the bricked side where they parked bore graffiti of school, neighborhood, and even gang allegiances. From the car window, Andre pointed out the stonewashed blues and greens of a globe with buildings of a city scene in the back. His crew's throw-up, which was at the top, read: World Wide Out to Get U Crew. After a few minutes of deciphering the code of graffiti to DeAndre, he drove off. Andre waited for some sort of comment or critique of the work itself, but didn't get any. If anything, his drawing inspired DeAndre, as he began drawing while Andre avoided potholes in the road as he drove to his job.

At a stop light, DeAndre shared an intergalactic scene he just finished. "This is world wide. Our world can't be just the earth. When they sing, 'He's got the whole world in His hands' at church, they're talking about heaven and the earth. God made it all . . . planets, moons, and stars. That's the world."

Andre shook his head in amazement as he entered the mall parking lot. *We all are thinking too small when it comes to his talent.* Municipal Road was flanked between a run-down shopping center and a fashion mall. Both sides were Andre's security beat from 3-10 PM, and since De-Andre had become ward of his father for the week, it had become his beat as well.

They checked in at the information booth in the center of the mall where Andre, his colleague, Ernie, and usu-ally, Norma Jean, the mall staffer, locked their personal belongings in the waist high lockers mounted below the circular counter. Ernie, the veteran security guard who had 17 years of seniority on Andre, usually left it up to Andre to cruise both sides of the mall by foot or take the mall's manual shift mini jeep over to the other side. At eight o'clock, when the five proprietors left on the shop-ping center side and Norma Jean called it a night, he claimed a seat within the circular booth, leaving DeAn-dre to drag a chair from the nearby food court until clos-ing.

"Hey, Andre and Boy Wonder," Ernie said as they en-tered the booth.

"Norma Jean, how are ya, beautiful?" Andre said, re-trieving his security radio from his locker before closing it with his dinner inside. "This old man hasn't been giving you any trouble, has he?" Andre said, referring to Ernie.

"You know I can protect myself. I got a fresh can of pepper spray if he gets out of hand," she replied.

"Anything happening?"

"A lady caused a disturbance over at the accessory store about an item she couldn't return. Knocked over a display of earrings and necklaces on her way out. Manager said a couple of teenagers capitalized on the drama and got away with a stash of merchandise."

"Did anyone pursue?" Andre asked, knowing full well no one did, especially not Ernie.

"By the time they called over here, the lady and the girls were headed toward the door. Apparently they were working as a team. I figure since they were headed that way, I'd let Chris handle them."

Chris was hired independently by JCPenney to do store security, so like Ernie, he was resolved to stay stationary. Andre made a note to head in that direction first to make sure that the trio had, in fact, left the premises and to check in with Chris on the other end.

"I hope you logged it."

"That's all I'm going to do. The manager got into an argument with the woman and can't even give me a description. Then she expects me to spend my time going upstairs running back surveillance tape of the exit," Ernie said, blowing wind through his teeth at the absurdity.

"Ernie keeps telling them they should run the feed from the cameras down here at the desk," Norma Jean added.

"And I asked them to hire some more people. It's not happening," Andre said, adjusting the volume on his own radio before securing it in his belt holster. "I'm going down there. Deuce, stay in this immediate area until I come back, and Ernie, have your ears on."

Andre got a couple of yards before returning to get the keys to the gate and the security jeep from Ernie, who was smoozing with Norma Jean. *Lord forbid if anything major ever actually does go down.* Andre knew he was basically on his own. As far as back-up, he would have to rely on his training and bystanders willing to use their cell phones to call 911.

As Andre had imagined, Chris was unaware of anyone or anything suspicious when Andre talked to him. He proceeded outside to the mall security jeep from its spot near the JCPenney Automotive Department and drove the perimeter of the mall. The only thing that made him feel sillier than guarding the middle-aged man dressed in the Easter Bunny or Santa Claus suit center court in the mall during the holiday season was standing at a stop light next to someone's monster SUV waiting for just the exact moment to cross over the four lanes at ten miles per hour to get over to the shopping center side.

Andre made sure to check in with the store managers and staffers at the stores assigned to him. He waved to the owner of a small pharmacy who looked as if he wished they would just close their side and give him an excuse to retire. Andre once asked the Asian man, who was on an apparent smoke break, why he didn't rent space on the inside of the fashion mall. His reply was, "When people sick, they want to get in and out."

That is how Andre felt entering into the security field. He never figured five years later he would still be working security. The main attraction for keeping his current mall placement was the 5,000 square feet, state of the art, Bo Donavan Body Fitness Center that opened last year.

He immediately got a membership and began working out constantly, or like today, would pass the bulk of his remaining hours in front of the gym with his friends.

On the way back from checking the shopping center side, Andre found DeAndre sitting at a round table in the food court with his walkman on and sketchbook open. Andre rapped his knuckles on the table and signaled with his hand for DeAndre to join him down the other side of the mall. Walking along the store fronts and looking inside was like viewing a film reel to reel where the scenes changed at a timed interval. A pane of wall to wall glass that seemed to have been recently squeaky cleaned from top to bottom displayed polished hardwood floors dotted with people postured on mats.

"Yo, he looks like he's about to burst a blood vessel bending like that," DeAndre said.

"He is engaging his powerhouse."

"What?"

"Your powerhouse in your torso area," Andre said, sticking his hand in DeAndre's stomach, causing him to take a step backward. "The powerhouse is the origin of your breath and blood; therefore, it is the source of all your power."

"Dang, you sound like a commercial. You should be working here."

"Yeah, well, it's not that easy."

"How hard can it be to learn a few exercise routines? Anyone can tell you got it down pat," DeAndre said.

"You have to be trained at Bo Donavan University in all aspects of the program: philosophy, nutrition, and health to be a certified Bo Donavan trainer."

"And?"

"Drop it, Deuce," Andre said, moving on to the opposite side of the door that gave a full view of the cardio room full of cycles, stair climbers, and treadmills. "I've got a lot going on right now. Maybe once we get you focused in school, then maybe I can get you to help me with my studies. I haven't taken subjects like science and math in like twenty years."

Andre thought of Deidre when he used the word, 'we' in relation to helping their son get on the right track. She would have told him to enroll in Bo Donovan University immediately. She never let the grass grow under her feet when it came to her dreams. She knew automatically that she wanted to be a store manager, to supervise people and attend important meetings, so she went to school full time right out of high school, before and eventually after DeAndre was born. She was so desperate for any sign of drive out of him when they lived together to prove to her mother they could make it, but he was content with the occasional construction job here and there. What she really didn't know was Andre was paralyzed in his own insecurities. He was scared that he would soon be a father without a constant paycheck. She began to believe, like her mother, that he was worthless. He had to admit that they put him in a box, and he crawled up in it and stayed there.

As soon as Andre and DeAndre got settled in the information and security booth, it was time to lap the mall again before closing. It amazed Andre at the amount of people that spilled into the mall in the last twenty minutes; some just dropped off with no way to get home. Store clerks stood guard at the gated entrances as cashiers rang up last minute patrons. Closing time was at nine thirty, but Andre couldn't leave until every last person left the premises.

The last ones to leave every night were the women at Hairtopia, a hair salon. Perfect weaves, perms, and braid extensions could not be conformed to the mall's scheduled closing time. Andre constantly reprimanded Annette, the salon owner, about double booking customers so close to closing. To his surprise, at 10:15 P.M., Annette and another stylist were sweeping up hair remnants off the floor and there were no customers to be found.

"Ten minutes, ladies," Andre said, deciding to secure the entrances before walking the ladies to their cars. Andre had gotten to all the entrances except one before noticing a woman coming into the entrance he was about to close.

"Lisa?" Andre said to his old classmate that he had seen recently at his buddy, Keith's wedding. He remembered Lisa and her flirtatious ways being the topic of many arguments between Deidre and him. Although he'd had no interest in Lisa, he liked it when Deidre was jealous.

"Hey, it is nice to see you again," Lisa said, hugging him.

"I was about to lock that door. The mall is closed."

"I know. I just finished getting my hair done, but when I got outside my car battery was dead. I was coming back to call someone."

Andre sighed loudly. He was tired, and he could tell that these late nights were taking a toll on DeAndre after three days of shadowing him. "I'm sorry to hear that. Let's see now, maybe we can call a tow truck or something."

"I'm not worried about the car tonight. I just want to get home. I've been up since five thirty this morning." Lisa said, leaning against Andre's chest with one arm extended while briefly adjusting her shoe.

"Lisa, this is my son, DeAndre." Andre introduced. He turned toward DeAndre who was eyeing Lisa suspiciously. "She went to school with your mother and me," he told his son.

"I know you don't want to see anyone coming at closing time. Since I was just getting my hair done, I threw anything on, grabbed my money, and forgot my wallet and cell phone," Lisa said, brushing her leather coat back to place her hands on her hips.

Andre looked at her fashion forward sweat suit and tennis shoes so white they looked to have come right out of the store. "So you're looking for a ride home?"

"I don't want to hold you two from Deidre."

"Oh he doesn't live with my momma," De Andre added.

Andre noticed Lisa's eyebrow arch up in surprise just before he said, "I guess we can take you home on the way out."

"Great, I'd love that," Lisa said, her smile lingering. "I really appreciate this, Dre."

"You sure you want to leave your car here?"

"No problem. Someone would be doing me a favor if they stole that thing. I'll get someone to come get it in the morning."

"You got everything, Deuce?" Andre said as Annette and her associate rounded the corner. DeAndre nodded, lifting his backpack off his shoulder for his father to see as if it were obvious. Annette stopped to see if there was anything she could do to help her loyal customer. Lisa was emphatic that she was in good hands with Andre.

DeAndre went outside to wait as Andre went back to the security booth and dialed his password into the commercial security network that monitored the facility at night. Lisa waited for him at the door as he pressed the button for the handicap exit.

"You know what? This takes me back. I would have given anything back in high school to have you escort me home," Lisa whispered. The grip she had on Andre's arm told him she still felt the same way.

Chapter 13

Deidre watched as Andre attached the Velcro strap of a sleek sports radio in the valley between his bicep muscles and put his headphones in place outside of his apartment complex. He had not seen her as she pulled up, and she did not signal her arrival. He wore a spandex teal and navy blue long sleeve shirt and navy blue jogging pants, that although were probably insulated, didn't seem to Deidre to be enough clothing to protect him against the early April wind. He jumped up high in the air several times as if being propelled by a trampoline, the sum total of his warm-up, before taking off out the main entrance and to the right down the thoroughfare.

Deidre could no longer view his reflection from her rear view mirror after adjusting it as far to the left as possible. She had to admit she enjoyed the sight. She had always thought him to be beautiful. She didn't term beautiful in a feminine sense, but rather a sculpted work of God, particularly his bold facial features outlined by coarse jet black hair on the canvas of his caramel complexion. Andre had bulked up so much in the eight years since they had broken up. She had to smile at the thought of how scrawny he used to be in high school. It didn't matter then; her only physical requirement was that her boyfriend be taller than her own 5'8" frame. She wondered how else he had changed over the years.

Although she was skeptical at his growth in the responsibility department after this morning's conversation with their son, she had to admit he had finally become financially self sufficient. Deidre viewed the height of his apartment building where she had dropped her son off four days earlier. It was obvious he had moved on.

Deidre thought about the conversation she had with DeAndre earlier that morning. She had tried to get in touch with her son several times the previous night. She told him she had wanted to make sure he was completing his assignments for school, but actually she missed him and just wanted to hear his voice.

"Where were you all last night? I tried calling three times. I know that on Monday I caught you in around 11:00," Deidre had pointed out.

"I had to wait for him to finish work and stuff," DeAndre had told her, as if she were annoying him, although the conversation had just begun.

"Who is him?" Deidre said, knowing full well of whom he was referring. "That's your father. Call him that, okay? Now where were you all?"

"We were at the mall, and then we went over his friend's house."

"After work?" Deidre said.

"Yeah."

"Your dad had to go over a friend's house after work? At 11:00 at night?" Deidre asked.

"Yeess," he said as if she were an imbecile. "I think he

said she went to high school with y'all . . . Lisa something."

DeAndre had asked her something about the twins.
Deidre could not remember her reply or the rest of the
conversation. All she could think about was that Andre
had taken their son over a woman's house after 11:00 P.M.
Before she knew it, she had told DeAndre to be packed
and ready to come home the next day because she would
be by to pick him up. She couldn't believe that Andre
couldn't put his social life on hold for one week while his
son was in his custody. She was enraged that he had their
son hanging out with him like they were friends or something. Lord knows what DeAndre perceived of his father's relationship with his *friend*.

Deidre had to wonder if she would be this upset if he
had been visiting any other friend. She knew exactly who
this *Lisa something* was. She was the same Lisa Wendell
that had been following after Andre's scent since high
school. No wonder she was all up in his face at Sheila's
wedding. *They were an item,* Deidre thought, and it infuriated her that she was the last to know.

Deidre was taken by surprise by the anger she felt; so
much so that she prayed that God would send her a
word to combat the strong emotions. Usually she started
the day with the scripture from her Bible-in-One-Year
listing. This morning, she had a specific need that led her
to the Bible concordance to help define what she was
feeling.

The scripture she had read and meditated over that
morning was from Song of Solomon, which said, love is
strong as death and jealousy is as cruel as the grave. *Love
was strong all right*. Here she thought that Andre must
have loved her so much to sacrifice his home and possibly their relationship by making a deal with her mother.

Up until she talked to her son, Deidre thought Andre may still love her. After her morning devotion, she was convinced that she didn't want to dig her own grave pining over Andre Hicks any longer.

Feelings aside, she had to do what was best for her son. Deidre thought about going upstairs, leaving Andre a note, and taking DeAndre home while he was still on his morning jog, but the God in her wouldn't allow it. She owed Andre more respect than a Dear John letter. He should at least be able to tell his son goodbye. She unbuckled her seat belt and got out of the car. Before going inside, she glanced toward the main entrance to see if, by chance, Andre was on his way back.

Deidre was allowed access to the apartment building by a cable installer going back to his truck. She could hear music blaring from the television or radio playing beyond the door when she reached Andre's apartment. She knocked several times before she heard the music muted.

"Who is it?" DeAndre asked.

"It's your mother."

The door gave way to expose a living room draped in clothing. She immediately noticed DeAndre's hair standing all over his head and almost got mad all over again. He was wearing a plain black, long sleeve shirt and was ironing a gray screen print T-shirt of a duck with a long bill decked out b-boy style with a baseball cap pulled over his eyes, blue jeans sagging off his butt, and a platinum rope chain around his neck. DeAndre's suitcase lay open in front of him and was empty.

"Hey, where's your father?" Deidre asked, interested in his perspective. She walked over to where he was ironing and planted a wet kiss on his forehead before he could protest.

"He went to workout. I told him I didn't want to go, so he said stay here and pack," DeAndre said defensively.

"What's with all these clothes?"

"He had me up in the morning washing clothes downstairs." DeAndre hadn't looked up from the shirt he was ironing. "He said he didn't want me dragging smelly clothes home for you to have to wash."

"Well, I need a place to sit, and you know I'm not about to watch any of these nasty music videos."

Deidre had almost forgotten the smacking sound her son made when she asked him to do something he didn't want to do. It made her realize why he was at his father's in the first place. She would have to let him know in no uncertain terms that nothing had changed; she expected him to follow her rules. *But what if he didn't?* she thought, in a temporary wave of uncertainty. She would just stay on him; wear him down with her unrelenting involvement in his affairs, just like her mother had done.

DeAndre clicked the television off altogether as if to declare that if they couldn't watch his videos, they wouldn't watch anything. He began testing clothes with his hand to see if they had dried thoroughly since the time he laid them out. As if the pressure of his mother watching him had gotten to be too much, he began throwing everything into his suitcase.

Deidre noticed a few uniform shirts embroidered with the name Hicks hanging from the blinds above the heating unit and thought about all the times she avoided Andre after the break-up. Now she was in his apartment. She thought that by avoiding him she could avoid her feelings for him. It had worked for awhile. Now she waited.

"When did your father say he was taking you to get your hair cut?"

"He didn't."

"Oh well, that will be our first stop this afternoon. Good thing I took the afternoon off."

"Man," DeAndre said in disgust. Deidre wondered if he were mad because he had to get his hair cut off, or from the prospect of having to spend an evening with her.

"Get me a drink of water, please."

This time she got a heavy sigh as he took his time bundling his remaining socks and tossing them in the suitcase before going into the kitchen. There was a cutout in the wall between the two rooms that looked like a serving counter. Deidre leaned across it to inspect the cleanliness of the kitchen. DeAndre picked a warm bottle of spring water out of a case on the counter top.

"Ice and a glass, please, sir," Deidre called to him.

Deidre was observing how well DeAndre carried out her orders when she heard keys in the door from behind her. She jumped as if she didn't want to be caught lounging in Andre's apartment when he wasn't there. Deidre thought about how she no longer had the liberty to do many things she took for granted when they were together like lounging around, asking questions about his personal life, or just casually touching his arm or leg as they spoke. That's what made it so weird to her. He was officially her ex, which made speaking to him about as awkward as addressing a complete stranger.

Andre looked slightly winded and flushed at the cheeks, but pleasantly surprised to see her.

"Hey," Deidre said.

"Oh hey. Dag, you're here already?" Andre dropped his keys on the table next to the door. He spread his arms out in a questioning gesture. "What's up? I thought I had him until Sunday. Sunday to Sunday makes a whole week."

"Don't worry about it. He's got school on Monday, and I can't expect you to get him ready."

"What's that suppose to mean?" Andre said as DeAndre came into the room to hand Deidre the glass of water.

"I mean that he has this conference Monday morning at nine to re-admit him back to school; he has to get ready. You haven't even taken him to get a hair cut like we agreed. I don't want to hear why he should continue to sport the cornrows, and I don't want any excuses from him. He needs to get his tail back in school and pass the eighth grade. It seems like I'm the only one who will make sure he'll do that. I guess I shouldn't have expected much from this arrangement." Deidre took a sip of water to ease her throat that felt as if she had swallowed sand.

Andre started to say something but didn't. He was never one to scream and shout; he always appeared cool, which infuriated her more. Deidre could tell he was taking deep breaths from the heaving in his chest. He looked from DeAndre to Deidre before saying, "Can I talk to you in the back for a moment?"

Deidre followed him up the hallway. She was sure that DeAndre was wondering what was going on. Nothing was coming out of her mouth the way she wanted it to. She broke the cardinal rule by starting an argument in front of their son, which made her look petty. Now she had to make him believe that the whole thing wasn't personal. She just wanted to get her son and go home.

He led them to his bedroom in the back of his apartment and left a crack in the door as if he were also concerned about being alone with her. The smell of a strong after shave clung in the air. He removed a stack of clothes folded neatly on the corner of the bed to his dresser as an invitation for her a sit. He finally sat at the head of the bed when he realized she preferred to stand. Out of the corner of her eye, Deidre could spot a framed picture of the two of them on either side of DeAndre's bassinet.

There was a crease through a portion of her face that was folded back.

Deidre could not tell if her image was folded like that to fit into the frame or if it were an attempt to block her out. *At least there isn't a photo of Lisa anywhere.*

Deidre could see the pained expression on his face as he wiped it vigorously with his right hand. "What was all of that about? Just when I think we've come down center street, you make a turn on me."

"Look, no offense, but DeAndre has only a few more days until he's back to his regular routine. I just thought that since I was off I, could make sure he's done his assignments."

"Since you were off you could have waited to pick him up later, at least let me have another day with him. We were in the process of creating our own routine."

"Think about it this way. Now you can have your freedom to hang out with whomever you please, whenever you please," Deidre said. The words were leaping out of her mouth before she had a chance to censor them.

"What?" Andre said, looking genuinely confused.

"I have a problem with you taking our son to some woman's apartment after work." Deidre didn't share that she knew who the woman was, but she was prepared to refresh his memory if he played dumb. "He doesn't need to go gallivanting with you on your little escapades."

"Escapades? Oh boy," Andre said, shaking his head. "Did our son happen to tell you I was taking this *woman* home because the mall was closing and her car battery was dead? Or had you already jumped to your own conclusion? So is this what this whole thing is about."

"No, that's not it at all," Deidre said, feeling her face flush with embarrassment. She cleared her throat. "But for real, according to DeAndre, you all get in pretty late every night; yesterday, a little later than usual. I know it's a chore getting him up in the mornings. Can you really say that you've checked over or even helped him with his school work? Today is the only day I can make sure the entire packet is done. I want to make sure his work is right so he can get full credit."

Her words hung out there for a while as Andre thought about it. "Yeah all right, if you're sure that's all it is." Andre walked toward the closed door. His hand was paused on the door knob. "The other day you called me because you needed me to help you. I don't know what's changed all of a sudden, but now I need you to help me to keep the connection I've established with my son. Don't shut me out, please."

Deidre made an agreement to help him with a head nod. Andre led the way into the living room where De-Andre had the television back on. He had the volume up loud on a sports program. His bags were packed and there was nothing left for them to do except leave. Deidre hesitated in the short hallway that linked Andre's room, the bathroom, and linen closet into the open space of the living room.

"All right, dude. It's been real," Andre said, extending his palm for his son to shake. "Remember, listen to your mother. Both of us don't want any stuff from you when you return to school. Ya hear me?"

"Yeah," DeAndre said, frowning.

Deidre could not tell if he were actually upset to be leaving his father or preparing his attitude for his return home.

"Look, maybe I'll get you next weekend or take you and your boys out for pizza or something."

DeAndre looked as if he didn't know how to respond when he saw Deidre appear into the room. Andre was swinging his arms as Deidre grabbed DeAndre's suitcase by the pull handle and walked past him.

"All right now," Andre said to them both, taking down one freshly laundered uniform shirt.

DeAndre put on his headphones and followed Deidre out the door; a silent change of the guards.

Chapter 14

DeAndre sat in Price's barbershop around the corner from his house. His mother dropped him off after dragging him on errands all morning. He thought for a moment that he would be able to escape his date with the clippers when Deidre walked him inside and saw the line of men waiting to get their hair cut. What she did not know was that Bentley, Chuck, and Big Tom, eternal high schoolers from the neighborhood, weren't actually customers, but rather fixtures at the barbershop when they weren't on the street corner. DeAndre saw the trio in the morning when he walked to the twins' bus stop to go to school and well into the night if he were out late.

DeAndre remembered this one kid that got picked on so badly by Bentley and his crew. Bentley called him over to their side of the street. He started with the boy's glasses that had lenses that were Coke bottle thick. Then he started comparing him to Steve Urkel from the TV show, *Family Matters*. The boy's nose started bleeding. A drop must have gotten too close to Bentley's tennis shoes that he made the poor boy shove a leaf up his nose and hold it there with a stick while he continued ridiculing him. De-Andre thought the boy was going to pass out.

The boy was so traumatized when they were done that he stopped riding the bus altogether and started walking to school because, of course, everyone else joined in, even kids from their own school who are just as vulnerable to that type of humiliation. They almost had to laugh at the poor sap, DeAndre thought at the time, or risk becoming a target themselves.

DeAndre's mother walked up to Earnest Strong, the barber, and told him that she wanted DeAndre's hair cropped close as if she were placing an order at the drive through window. She left DeAndre with her cell phone to call home as soon as he was through. Strong, as he was known, and a few others laughed at his mother's adamant request. DeAndre sat in the quarter of space left in the second chair occupied by Big Tom. He sat to the side resting his elbows on his knees to allow Tom more space.

"What we got, Strong? The third young buck this week whose hair was longer than their momma's?" a patron said.

"I don't know what's up with these young dudes man, growing their hair out like the ladies." Strong said, taking the clippers to the nape of a man in a suit while pointing to the row occupied by guys with various lengths of cornrows and twists. The same row where DeAndre sat.

"What's wrong, Strong? You scared that we gonna put you out of business?" Chuck said.

"Yeah, I am. I'm worried someone will walk past this window right here and get a good look at those naps in the back of your head and run scared," Strong said, using the clippers as a pointer. "Please, don't let me keep you gentleman from your jobs, job search, or whatever it is you do all day."

"I got a job," Chuck said. "I'm on the Work Study Program."

"More like work release," the man in the chair said, giving everyone except DeAndre and Chuck a good laugh.

"Okay . . . ya'll got jokes," Chuck said.

"How do they still let you continue on work study, and you don't even go to school anymore?" Bentley asked.

"I started the job at the beginning of the school year. My boss doesn't even know I got expelled. I work half a day, two times a week. I don't know about the rest of these bustas."

"Why are you not at work now?" Big Tom said.

"Same reason you not," Chuck replied. "I don't feel like it. You need to be worried about yourself."

"Yeah okay, break it up. Y'all gonna have to clear out of here anyway. You know on Thursdays they bring some of the old guys over from the assisted living complex down the street. I need my seats."

"Oh heck naw, I'm not fixing to sit up hear and listen to them old dudes talk about World War I, civil rights, and crap. We out," Bentley said, popping up, leaving Big Tom scrambling to push himself up.

"So Strong, when are you going to hook me up?" Chuck said.

"With what?" Strong asked.

"A hair cut. I got my expulsion hearing coming up Friday."

"Fool, I could have been had you out of the way. How was I supposed to know you were here for an actual hair cut this time? Plus you got those bush ball thingys all over your head. I hope you don't think I'm going to touch them. I cut hair; I don't style it, playa. You don't make no sense at all; you know that? You are going to have to come back later."

Chuck started banging out a beat on the backrest of the

chair, as if he hadn't just been insulted by Strong. The three of them left singing, "Keep it Gangsta."

"We'll be back," Bentley said.

"Be with you shortly, cuz. Do me a favor and take the rest of your cornrows out for me. I got one, two," Strong said to DeAndre, counting the actual patrons from visitors, "two people ahead of you."

DeAndre began working at the seam of one cornrow by yanking at the middle stitch with one finger until the hair started to unravel. He attacked a few more while staring at the neon blue display to his mother's phone as if it were a foreign object to him. How long had it been since he had talked to the twins? It was close to three thirty; their school was getting ready for dismissal, so he figured he'd call the twins to leave a message at least. DeAndre noticed the bar graph that indicated the range on the phone kept diminishing as he punched in the twin's area code.

"I'm going outside to make a call," DeAndre said as if asking permission.

"All right, you'd better get back in here before that van pulls up. They got those old guys on a schedule, you know."

DeAndre sat on the barber shop's stairs enjoying the fresh air. He saw a police officer pull up to the red light directly across from where he was seated and thought about his father. *My dad is at work by now*, DeAndre thought. He wondered why his mother hadn't let him stay a whole week at Andre's place. He sensed the tension between his parents as they emerged from the back bedroom at his dad's apartment and figured that it would be awhile before he saw his dad again.

DeAndre pulled out his mother's cell phone. He felt like a kid with a new toy and the freedom of the whole afternoon to play with it. He dialed the twins' number.

Before he could activate the call, he noticed Bentley and Chuck crossing the street and heading in his direction. For a moment he thought they looked like they were after him as they strode stern-faced in front of several moving cars while swinging their meaty fists. Chuck had taken his knots loose and his hair stood frightfully all over his head. DeAndre's heart began beating a mile a minute as they closed the gap between them. They didn't give him time to move to the side before they were upon him, walking up the stairs on either side. DeAndre could feel one of them stop just past the step he was on.

"Strong hasn't gotten to you yet?" Chuck asked?

DeAndre sat petrified like Chicken Little waiting for the sky to fall. He didn't even realize that one of them was talking to him. He was just waiting for them to go inside.

"Hellooooo!" Chuck shouted.

DeAndre took the phone away from his ear and slowly turned around to find Chuck staring down on him from the next step and Bentley doing the same from the top of the landing.

"Has the van been through?" Bentley asked this time.

"No, no, I haven't seen the van," DeAndre replied, and then slowly brought the phone back to his ear in relief as he heard the door open and shut.

"Little Man, let me hold your phone," DeAndre heard from behind. This time he knew Bentley was talking to him. He didn't have to contemplate should he or shouldn't he. He just prayed he meant in this vicinity and for a short amount of time. He handed over the phone to Bentley like an elderly lady would her purse to a mugger. He watched him dial some digits and disappear around the corner.

Chapter 15

DeAndre crunched through the graveled driveway to the street's edge. He looked both ways as if he were about to cross the street—as if he didn't know in which direction Bentley had walked off with his mother's cell phone. He didn't see a soul on the sidewalk. He stayed there a moment just in case Bentley had ducked in one of the store fronts to complete his call and stood on his tip-toes trying to see into the valley of Manor Ridge, a community park that led foot-bound travelers like Bentley and his crew from the neighborhood into the commercial district. *Bentley couldn't have gotten that far*, DeAndre thought, although he was unsure how long he had sat stunned on the stoop of the barbershop before getting up to look. His toes began to cramp, and he rested back on the heels of his Jordans. From his vantage point, he had two alternatives: get his mom's cell phone back or die.

DeAndre thought about making a call to get some help. He put his hand in his pocket before he realized that his now empty pockets were no longer the safe hiding place for his mother's phone. He smacked his forehead the same way he and the twins did one another when they did or said something stupid. How would he tell the twins he needed help? Then he smacked his forehead again before thinking about how crazy he must appear smacking himself on the side of the street.

Lord, help me, DeAndre thought, before muttering it aloud. He had often heard his mother offer the same plea before she figured out a solution to a problem. If it worked for her, then maybe it could work for him. Besides, God knew his voice. He remembered kneeling bedside and having lengthy conversations with God over similar matters. Things like this were always happening to him; accidents, or situations he would surely have not gotten himself into if he knew the outcome.

"God, help me," he said with his face turned up toward the sky. This time he didn't care who saw him or who may think he was going crazy. Maybe the onlooker would be an answer to his prayer and help him get his mom's cell phone back before she came back to see what was taking him so long. He had to at least tell Strong he was still here. That way he could shave his head the way his mother requested. *Strong might as well cut my head off.*

The door sensor chimed when he entered. Strong barely looked up before saying, "I thought you had left, young buck."

"Can I please use your phone?"

"There is a pay phone in the back," Strong said. "Wait, didn't I see you with a cell phone earlier?"

DeAndre moved swiftly to the back of the shop, not bothering to answer his inquiry. He dunked his fist into his sunken jeans pocket and had to pull his pants up to at least waist level from the force. He found two quarters and was surprised to find that it was the exact amount of a phone call from a pay phone. That meant he had one call, just like the convicts in a prison.

DeAndre stood frozen at the phone. He couldn't believe that he'd forgotten the number of the last person that could possibly help him out of this situation. He looked up at the ceiling as if to say, "God, I'm still waiting on you," before it occurred to him that he could dial information toll free to get the number for the Municipal mall where his father worked. He carried no paper to write down the number the automated operator rattled off, so he had to memorize it. A woman answered the phone politely and assisted him in transferring his call to the Security station. He hoped his father was not on rounds.

DeAndre didn't know if his father could actually help him. All he knew was that if he didn't get his mother's phone back, she would inevitably send him to live with his father permanently, which outside of changing schools and missing his friends, didn't seem like such a terrible thing at this time. Norma Jean picked up the phone and informed him that his father had just started patrolling the south end of the mall. *That's it; I'm through.*

"Wait a minute, let me see if I can't catch him," Norma Jean said with a few heavy sighs as if scouting for DeAndre's dad was the most she had done all day. "I think I see him talking to a few guys from the gym over at the food court. I'll radio him or send Ernie over there to get him for you."

DeAndre took that time to pull out the two remaining cornrows while he waited.

"Are you still there, little Andre?"

"Yeah I'm still here."

"I hope you're all right and this isn't an emergency. Your daddy is on the way"

DeAndre didn't respond. He wasn't quite sure what he would say to his father, let alone nosy Norma Jean. He thought it funny that she'd said, "Your daddy is on the way." He remembered his own mother saying that many times to him when his father had a planned visit just to later inform him that Andre had called to cancel. He tried his best for the past four days to avoid the words *dad* and *daddy*. To him, it gave the man too much credit that he hadn't earned yet.

"Deuce? What's up, man? What's going on? Hello?" his father said.

DeAndre realized he was just holding the phone. He finally answered, "I'm here."

"What's up? Where are you? Is your mother all right?"

"Yeah, everything is fine," DeAndre said, realizing his father was really concerned. For some reason, he felt wrong for calling his father on his job for such a silly thing.

"C'mon, Deuce, you called me at work; you never do that. Something must be on your mind. Where are you?"

"At the barbershop on Addison by Manor Ridge," De-Andre said, wondering why he was having such a hard time getting the problem out. He halfway expected his father to guess exactly what was wrong with him.

"Okay, so you're scared to get your hair cut. You think all your buddies are going to laugh at you?"

"Yeah . . . .I mean, no," DeAndre said, thinking about how the twins would fry him when they saw his skinned dome.

"Well, what's done is done. I can't really do anything about that now."

DeAndre could tell his father was losing patience. After all he was at work. How does one tell their father that they gave away one of their valuables and now was too scared to ask for it back. As buff and muscular as his dad was, he would probably laugh.

Andre broke the silence. "Well, I was planning to call

you later tonight. See if you were watching the Wizards game. So I'll talk to you tonight, all right?"

"Dad," DeAndre relented, saying the only word that might keep him on the phone.

"Yeah, son?"

"I'm kind of in trouble." DeAndre knew once the first sentence was uttered that he would spill his guts. He filled his father in on everything from being dropped off by his mother with instructions to call, up until the point where he was waiting like a gump for Bentley to return.

"Do you want me to come over there and get the phone back?"

"No."

"Deuce, you can't just let this boy have your mother's phone."

"I know, but I don't want him to think I called the authorities on him or something," DeAndre said, thinking of his dad in uniform. "That's not cool."

"The boy has got your phone. He has to expect that you'll ask for it back. So do it. What's the problem? Does this boy go to your school? Wait. Is this the boy from the party?"

"No," DeAndre said. How could he make his dad understand? "He's in high school. He hangs around my neighborhood."

"Ooooh, I see," his father said.

DeAndre didn't know how his father received his revelation, but was relieved. Now he waited for Andre's revelation. Maybe this was his answer from God. Many times in Sunday School they had discussed how God can show up in the most unlikely way, like the eye of the sparrow, just to watch over His children. Hopefully God was putting on a 6'2", 230-plus-pound frame.

"You're still going to have to confront this guy," Andre

told him "But this is not the time to prove how bad you are and get all rude and disrespectful. Tell him straight up, you need your phone. Just like that, real urgent-like. The bottom line is that he'll respect you more if you stand up to him instead of just giving in. Do it outside the shop if you're worried about the crowd. If he still doesn't want to give you the phone, there are adults inside you can tell. Okay?"

"Okay," DeAndre said.

"You sure you don't need me to come over there?"

"No, I can handle it."

"All right?"

"All right," DeAndre said, anxious to get it over with. The problem was that Bentley had not returned yet, and there was no guarantee that he would. DeAndre was too antsy to sit and wait, although he was next. He would go outside and wait for Bentley like his father suggested.

"Hey, Strong, man, I'm going to stand outside," DeAndre informed him.

"Whatever man, I'll be flipping the closed sign before you decide to get your hair cut," Strong said, and before DeAndre could get out the door he heard him say, "I tell you, this is an ignorant generation."

DeAndre walked to the sidewalk's edge and decided to go in the direction he had seen Bentley walk to head him off at the path. He passed an old vacuum cleaner repair store and was almost past the convenience store when he spotted Bentley. He was licking an ice cream cone and his other hand held something in it that he used to scratch his scalp. *Is he using the antenna of the cell phone to scratch his nasty head?* DeAndre fled from sight as he saw Bentley approaching the door and ran back a-ways to simulate a chance meeting. Bentley looked his way and continued in the other direction as if he didn't recognize DeAndre.

"Hey," DeAndre said, then cleared his throat and repeated it again to Bentley who was now headed toward the barbershop. "Hey, I was looking for you."

Bentley stopped abruptly, causing DeAndre to stop on a dime to maintain a safe distance.

"You talking to me?" Bentley said with a half smirk that DeAndre couldn't interpret.

"Yeah, I was at Strong's barbershop," DeAndre said, as if that should ring a bell. He realized the guessing game wasn't going to work with Bentley.

"I don't know you, dude," Bentley said without stopping.

DeAndre looked at his fading image until he realized he was standing still. Bentley would be at the barbershop soon and he wouldn't have resolved anything.

"Wait," DeAndre yelled louder than he had wanted. Bentley stopped in his tracks. This time his eyebrows raised in an incredulous expression that read, *oh no you didn't just yell at me.*

DeAndre jogged to where he was to clear up the misunderstanding. He tried to remember exactly what his dad told him to say.

"What do you want? You're starting to get on my nerves," Bentley inquired.

"Earlier I let you hold my mo . . . I mean, a cell phone of mine at the barbershop."

"I don't know what you are talking about, shorty," Bentley said. His smirk was back. Before he could turn and resume walking. DeAndre stepped in front of him.

"Can I have my cell phone back?"

"I ain't got nothing of yours."

"Can I please have my cell phone back?"

"Dude, I suggest you get outs my face," Bentley said.

DeAndre felt as if he had run into a brick wall. This was not how it was suppose to go. He wondered how

much it would cost him to get his mother another cell
phone. Hundreds . . . probably thousands when adding
up her monthly bills he would surely have to pay. He
looked at Bentley's smirk that slowly turned into a smile
and knew he was running a game on him. DeAndre felt
himself releasing the fear and taking on anger.

Before he could speak, he heard a car pull to the side of
the road partially blocking traffic. DeAndre was too preoccupied to look and see who it was.

"How are you all doing today? Is there a problem?"

DeAndre heard his father's voice concealed behind a
mall security cap and his Buick Lasbre. From his vantage
point, he looked like an officer or at least someone in authority. He had asked him not to come. *Thank God, he hadn't
driven the mini-jeep.*

"No, Officer," Bentley said, surprisingly polite.

"Son?" The question was aimed at DeAndre

"No problem," DeAndre said, wanting to conceal his
own face so that Bentley couldn't see the resemblance.
He waited for his father to pull off and when he didn't
pull off, DeAndre yelled, "I said, we're fine, Officer."

"All right then," DeAndre's dad said before pulling
away slowly.

This should have been over and done with, DeAndre thought.
His anger was returning but so was the plan he and his
father discussed on the phone.

He looked Bentley square in the eyes and held out his
hand." I need my phone."

"You should have said that in the beginning," Bentley
said, looking over his shoulder to see if, in fact, DeAndre's father was gone. He reached into his back pocket
and tossed the compact phone in the air. It was as if
everything was thrown into slow motion. Bentley jogged
the rest of the way to the barbershop steps and DeAndre
caught the phone and physically dropped to the gravel

below him. He felt victorious as he looked up at the sky. He jumped up when he realized his father could still be circling. DeAndre couldn't see him, but held the phone up just in case he was perched somewhere like the sparrow watching.

Chapter 16

Andre had debated with himself whether or not he should attend the Re-admit conference at DeAndre's school because he wasn't invited. He was late, but he was determined not to let that deter him from continuing to show his son that he was there for him.

Andre followed the rhythmic shuffle of the secretary down a corridor that dead ended at a suite of offices and conference rooms. They detoured past a young girl being restrained by a school administrator who was explaining how she was ready to punch someone. Andre remembered the times he was sent to the office, but was also shocked at the girl's defiance. The hallways were where he used to do his dirt, in front of his peers, where it was their word against his. The office was where they passed down judgment. When the principal or the vice principal would call him into the office, Andre would just stare back at them, but not out of defiance. He was hoping someone could tell him why he was there. Why it was even necessary for him to keep coming to a place where everyday he had clear signs that he didn't belong.

The secretary continued past this scene as if belligerent students were commonplace. Andre followed the woman to the end of the hallway. She tapped on the door, opened it, and introduced him to the assembly before shuffling away.

The room was silent. A quick survey around the room showed very few welcoming faces. Deidre, who wore a maroon pantsuit with a coordinating striped shirt, barely looked at him. Then he and DeAndre made brief eye contact before DeAndre locked back on whatever he was staring at in the center of the table. DeAndre looked surprisingly younger than he did just days before. Andre wondered how a mere haircut could make such a drastic difference. He had on a button up plaid shirt with crisp, clean blue jeans and tie up shoes. *A classic court defendant outfit*, Andre thought, complete with his skin's high gloss shine of Vaseline or heavy lotion. Andre wondered how long it took to come to a consensus on that outfit.

"Let's get Mr. Hicks a seat. I'm Mr. Riley, the principal," he said, standing briefly to shake Andre's hand. Another gentleman pulled a padded arm chair, like the others were sitting in, from the corner and waited for Mr. Riley to direct him. "Let's put him next to his umh. . . . Ms. Collins, so that they can take a look at DeAndre's progress reports and permanent record together. She just signed the Re-admittance form, which just outlines the cause of his suspension and the conditions that he is allowed back to school. Would you rather have your own copy?"

"No, that's quite all right," Andre said, taking a seat. He could feel Deidre stiffen a bit, crossing one of her long legs over the other at the knee before sitting up a bit straighter in her chair. She probably felt that he was there to usurp her parental authority.

"With a little more than a quarter and a half left in the school year, I have asked the teachers to prepare a progress report to show where DeAndre stands academically. I'm sure that this dynamic team of teachers and Mr. Talbert, his academic counselor, can answer any questions you may have," Mr. Riley said as if he were leaving.

Andre looked at his son and could only imagine how he was feeling. It was the same way he felt as a child when a bunch of adults discussed his fate with little to no input from him. Deidre was calm and collected as if playing some strange poker game keeping multi-colored folders within reach as some sort of bargaining chips. Each teacher pushed over grade sheets from a computer generated program that broke down each of DeAndre's grades by quarter, assignment titles, and category weights.

"We have his make up work plus a few previously incomplete assignments that I hope you will consider grading . . . if not for full, then at least partial credit. "Deidre slid the folders over as an offering. "Each folder contains DeAndre's personal apology letter.

"I have to be honest, I don't know if this quarter is even salvageable," Mr. Cleveland, his math teacher, said. "I mean, these kids come to class without any materials and their constant squabbles that take up all the instructional time. I think DeAndre has even lost his math book."

Andre cleared his throat loudly. He wanted to ask Mr. Cleveland if he had even bothered to pick up the phone and inform Deidre about the lost book, but he refrained. He took an instant disliking to Mr. Cleveland. He looked over a copy of DeAndre's schedule on the table to see that his son had math with Mr. Cleveland the last period of the day; after gym no less. Even Andre knew that was a hard subject to tackle that late in the day. He was sure that class was off the hook with teenagers whose mindset was on each other and the end of the school day. Although DeAndre currently averaged a D in English and history, the teachers of those subjects were the only two who presented a ray of hope that his grades, and even his overall attitude, could be turned around.

Mr. Riley invited Deidre and Andre to look through their son's personal record. It was arranged in ascending order by grade. Deidre skimmed through toothless pictures of DeAndre at each grade attached to a few picture perfect report cards from his elementary years. The end of his folder seemed to be padded with carbon copies of behavior reports written in the last year. Andre waited until Deidre yielded the folder to take a close look at each one. Of course, Mr. Cleveland, who just told everyone he had no time for instruction, had plenty of time to document DeAndre's every infraction for his permanent file. Andre felt the anger rise within him. He decided to pick his own spot on the conference table and cool out.

"So what we want you to understand is that DeAndre's problem is two-fold: academic and behavioral," Mr. Riley said. "Your son is by no means unintelligent, but he is one of those children whose academics are being adversely impacted by his attitude and behavior. So our recommendation is that DeAndre be moved to another class if you all are in agreement."

"You want him to go to a new class so late in the school year?" Deidre asked.

"Yes. We feel a smaller class setting will allow DeAndre to focus more: less people, less movement, less distraction," Mr. Riley said, as if he were selling them a vacation package.

Andre couldn't remain silent any longer. He was completely shocked at Deidre's silence. Surely she must see what they were trying to do to their son. He had a feeling in the pit of his stomach that putting DeAndre into this class was like stuffing him into a box and forgetting about him. That is what the system did to him. But now he could see how harmful it was to be placed in a class solely on behavior. Yes, DeAndre was a cut-up and a pain in the neck, but what about his potential?

"This doesn't sound right to me," Andre said. He looked at Deidre who looked off into the sky in serious contemplation.

"We have a quarter left of school, Mr. Hicks. Hopefully with intervention this will be DeAndre's last year in middle school."

"He's talking about what will make a difference right now so that DeAndre can have a chance to be promoted and go to high school next year," Deidre said with a look in her eyes that read, *let's not do this now.*

"He's talking about Special Education, Dee," Andre told her.

Andre was completely shocked at Deidre's refusal to see the handwriting on the wall. He knew her bottom line was to do whatever it took to get him to pass on. They were not impressed by his apology letters and a few days of make-work they probably wouldn't grade. They wanted to brand him as stupid and everyone around the table knew it. Andre looked around, reading the expression on the faces of everyone there before saying another word. Mr. Talbert was nervously clicking his ink pen and Mr. Cleveland was wearing a condescending grin.

"Is this considered a Special Education class?" Deidre finally asked.

"Well," Mr. Talbert started until Mr. Riley put up his hand to halt him.

"Our school is divided into academic teams. We set up

these classes to meet the needs for children like DeAndre who need the extra focus. It just so happened to fall on the Special Education team for organizational purposes."

"That means yes," Andre said sarcastically, "and I say no."

"If I may," Mr. Cleveland said. "We took a lot of time considering what would best help DeAndre, even meeting after school."

Andre rolled his eyes at the balding gentleman. *Bull,* Andre thought.

"One of our main concerns was DeAndre's inability to concentrate on a task," the teacher continued.

Bull, bull, bull, Andre thought. He'd seen this kid zone out the entire world to complete the eyelashes on a person he was drawing, and they say he can't concentrate. *Bull.*

"Wait a minute," Deidre said angrily. "Mr. Riley, what you are describing seems like an ideal learning environment for the entire student body where classes are smaller with a low teacher-to-student ratio. No one wants their child to be singled out. I'm just trying to understand if there are any other options. "

"He said himself that DeAndre was not a stupid boy," Andre said. He turned his attention to the teachers who looked as if they all wanted to squirm out of their seats on their bellies. "I'm not trying to be difficult; really, I'm not. I just need you to tell me in your best professional judgment, whether or not my boy can do the work in a normal setting?"

"Andre, the point is, he's not doing the work." Deidre said.

Why was she doing this? Andre thought. *Why was she siding with the enemy?* DeAndre sighed heavily at that point, as if he had been holding his breath.

"Can you show me some IQ or aptitude test that says my boy can't do the work?" Andre's anger had reached a boiling point. He was now scattering the papers inside his son's permanent file.

"Maybe we should let DeAndre's parents have some time to think about it and discuss this privately. DeAndre could follow his original schedule for the rest of this week. That should give them plenty of time to decide and get back to us." Mr. Talbert said.

"I think that's a good idea, "Mr. Riley agreed, looking at his watch. "We are about ten minutes into the second period. These teachers have administrators relieving them. DeAndre can take his re-admit slip to class as a pass. Our recommendation will stay on file until we hear from you."

Mr. Riley stood to shake Andre and Deidre's hands. Mr. Talbert did the same. The other teachers were not as cordial; taking Mr. Riley's closing statements as an excuse to flee the scene. Andre and Deidre walked their son up the hallway without a word. Andre made a ring around his son's head with his arm and kissed the top of his head at the hall's end. He didn't have the words to massage away all the blows he must have taken inside the conference room.

"What do you think about all of this, son? Do you think you need to be placed in a small class to get yourself together?" Andre asked.

DeAndre looked up at Andre, and then Deidre as if they were giants before shrugging.

"Go on to class," Deidre said. "Remember what we talked about at home; it's all up to you."

"Yeah, you know we also had a talk," Andre interjected, "Keep your head up, son."

They watched him head down the hall. Andre watched

as Deidre leaned her frame against the opposite wall from where he was standing. He thought about how many times in high school they had taken that same stance. In their senior year, she was an office aide the period before lunch, and he would wait for her, or vice versa, in the hallway. No one hung out in the hall adjacent to the office, so it became their place. Outside of dodging the occasional teacher who would enter through the side entrance to the main office, that hallway became their kissing post.

Now, some twenty years later, she could barely look at him. He looked at her and wondered what had happened to them.

"I resent what they are trying to do to our son, Deidre. I really do."

"And I resent how you came down here and complicated things."

They both kept to their corners. "Complicated? Can't you see what they are trying to do?"

"I'm not blind, Andre."

"Does that mean that you are perfectly okay with our son being in Special Ed?" Andre said with an incredulous chuckle. "He'll be just like his little buddy—the twin. Let's put every black male whose hormones are out of control in Special Ed."

Andre felt his anger rising again and took a few deep breaths. He knew from the past that flying off the handle made Deidre shut down, and this was a conversation they needed to have. This was a conversation they needed to have had a long time ago.

"Maybe if they didn't act retarded, they wouldn't be in Special Ed."

"You can't believe that," Andre said, this time turning toward the wall and lightly pounding out the syllables on the wall with his fist to diffuse the anger and regain control as Bo Donovan taught. *She cannot believe that.* "This is just a way to label us." He quickly pulled himself together when he heard someone come up the hall. It was Mr. Talbert.

"Nice to meet you, man," Andre said, recovering quickly. "I'd like to thank you for your support in there. You were the only one I felt knew where I was coming from."

"I definitely felt you. Like I suggested, take all the time you need. They won't make the switch without your consent. In the meantime, I'll try to pull DeAndre into my office and talk to him."

"Thank you, Mr. Talbert," Deidre said

"All right, man," Andre said, shaking his hand as if he and Mr. Talbert were old friends. He waited until Mr. Talbert turned the corner before waiting to see what Deidre had to say next.

"See, he knows where I'm coming from."

"Well, I don't believe their recommendation is some big conspiracy. This is about survival and getting to the next level. I know my child, and I don't think time in a smaller class will kill him. In time, when he goes into high school, in a different environment, when he's more mature, he'll be able to prove himself and shake any label they put on him in middle school."

"Well, you already know my opinion. I'd just as soon send him to another school than to have him in Special Ed," Andre said.

"That's not your decision to make." Deidre pulled tightly on the belt of her trench coat before tying it around her middle. I see where you are coming from, but all these decisions have been pretty much up to me since DeAndre was born. I'm drained, and I'm due into work at three. I'll let you know what I decide."

Andre watched her walk away. He stood there in the

hallway dumbfounded for several minutes before deciding he should leave too. He was beginning to feel like the belligerent girl in the office. It was time for him to get to the gym and go a couple of rounds on the speed bag, because he definitely felt like punching something.

Chapter 17

Deidre had taken a liking to Renita, a cashier at Fresh Gardens Market, the store that Deidre managed. Like Deidre, she was a single mother. Renita had to bring her son, Brandon, to the interview with her because of some drama with her child's father. Conrad, the general manager, had had reservations about their newest applicant, but Deidre wanted her hired and put her on rotation when she made the schedule. Now, Renita was her headache.

"I told my son's father that on the days that Brandon is with him, I expect him, not his mother, to watch our son. He is famous for crying about how little he gets to see his son, but as soon as I drop him off, he calls his mother over to help him," Renita said.

"What's the matter with him seeing his grandmother?" Deidre asked, thinking of how little DeAndre visits with her own mother.

"I don't like her, that's why," she said, rolling her eyes as she opened a bag of chips she swiped from her register lane before going on her lunch break. "And it's not my job anymore to make his life easy."

"That's ugly. You know you aren't right. Vengeance is mine, saith the Lord."

"Now you sound just like his mother with that church talk, and you are too young to be sounding like a fifty-eight-year-old woman."

Renita had again joined Deidre in the manager's booth for her break. It had been about three weeks ago when Deidre had entered the customer service area, which nestled the cubicle sized manager's booth, to find Renita on the phone eating a bag of Doritos. When Deidre questioned Renita about how and why she had access to an area designated for management, she said, "I eat up here with Conrad all the time. After they made those bathrooms opened to the public in the back, I told Conrad I needed a quiet place to eat my lunch. I mean, they don't call it a break for nothing. Anybody can go into staff lounge now. They should just call it a lounge."

Deidre remembered wondering why her training couldn't covet her an employee-free lunch hour. Ever since that conversation, and against Deidre's better judgment, Renita Wallace was afforded management status everyday from 4:30 P.M to 5:00 P.M, or as it seemed, whenever Deidre decided to take her break.

Deidre found Renita to be a much better friend than worker. She had a sense of entitlement that bordered on arrogance. She was perpetually peeved and always in the process of telling someone off. Not to mention she took more than her fair share of days off. It wasn't as if Deidre didn't try to mentor her on basic work ethics, but The Fresh Gardens Princess, as she was often called, just didn't get it.

They were talking about their favorite subject—their

babies' daddies—because Deidre and Renita were single parents, and it gave them unlimited conversation.

"Well, Andre left me a very lengthy message on my answering machine telling me, yet again, what he thinks about DeAndre's school situation," Deidre said.

"I have to agree with brother-man on this one. If they had suggested a special class for Brandon, someone at that school would have got cussed out," Renita said, once again rolling her eyes like she was about to let Deidre have it.

Deidre knew what she meant. She even agreed with Andre at this point. As much as she didn't want her child repeating a grade in school, Special Education was not an option. For some reason she was having a hard time admitting it to anyone else. She hadn't called the school to inform them of her decision, and she most definitely hadn't called Andre back to tell him anything. Deidre knew it was her pride with just a taste of resentment. It took conversations like the one she was having with Renita to make Deidre see herself, and she didn't like what she saw. She was sure that she had gotten her stubborn temperament from her mother, but she wasn't being raised like that now at Liberty A.M.E.

"I just don't have time to deal with all of this, especially since I'm picking up Conrad's slack here. It seems as if he's off every other day. I might as well be the General Manager," Deidre said, stirring up a bowl of soup she had taken out of the microwave.

"Well, you better get it together before they bring in another clone copy of Conrad to be the GM when Conrad leaves." Renita opened up the Time Card ledger and rifled through it.

"Wait a minute, is Conrad leaving?" Deidre said. She wondered if Renita even knew what she was looking through. She came to the conclusion that the Fresh Gardens Princess probably knew about every document of a personal and classified nature in this office.

"Do you think I can get off early tonight?"

"No," Deidre said, becoming frustrated, "and you didn't answer my question. How do you know Conrad is leaving?"

"If I answer your question, can I get off early? I might have a date tonight if I can get my mom to agree to watch Brandon overnight."

"No. C'mon, Renita, I need you to finish your entire shift tonight."

"That's all right," Renita said, lifting out of her chair and straining her eyes to see the master schedule on the clipboard fastened to the wall, "'cause I'm taking off this Friday. And before you even start, I'm trying to see if Quanita will cover for me."

She continued with, "Nope, that won't work, 'cause I need her to babysit. Dang, y'all need to give a sister more leave time."

"You would earn more leave if you come to work more," Deidre said, snatching the ledger from her and replacing it on the desk. "You are amazing, you know that? All you think of is yourself and your social calendar. Did you ever consider how hard it's going to be for me to get someone to cover the swing shift on a Friday if you call in?"

"It's a good thing I'm telling you in advance then," Renita said, taking lip gloss from her Fresh Gardens apron and applying it. "And to answer your question from earlier, Conrad has applied for the GM job in Gaithersburg or somewhere. I came in the office one day, and he was on the computer looking at current vacancies, so I asked him about it."

"I can't believe he didn't tell you," Renita continued. "Gosh, does anybody talk to anyone else besides me? I must be the friendliest one around here."

Deidre would have laughed at that comment if she weren't fuming over the fact that the man she had been helping to open the store for three years didn't have the decency to tell her he was moving on. She single-handedly trained his cashiers and kept them from revolting when he tried and failed to cut their break to ten minutes and their lunches to twenty.

Deidre looked at her watch, reminding herself to monitor Renita's time. She already got enough preferential treatment. "Well, I hope they send in someone more flexible than Conrad."

"Well, what is wrong with you?"

"What?"

"Why can't you be the General Manager? You've taken the training, right?"

"Yeah, but . . ." Deidre paused to sip her soup that already felt lukewarm.

"I remember when I first started working here, I thought you were so stuck up. I mean, you wouldn't be talking to me, but I'd hear you going on and on to Conrad about something you had learned at the Management Training Academy. I guess as if to say, that's right, a sister has got the same training as the big boys."

"It wasn't like that at all."

"I know it wasn't. I don't want to hurt your feelings or nothing, but Conrad never looked at you like an equal. Y'all think I am quiet, but I observe things. When things get hectic around here, you are the first manager he puts on the register. You'll open the Customer Service line, but in that instant, you don't realize you've been demoted. You'll never see Renita go to no fancy training academy and have to work a register. I've even seen you clean up a spill."

"It's called pitching in to help where I'm needed. We're a team."

"Yeah okay, but you've never seen Clark on the register or that other dude he replaced. The one who was here for a week was never asked to clean up an aisle or restock a shelf of creamer that was put in the wrong place. Where are they now? They are probably in their own store, and a cleaner one at that, somewhere north of here, outside the beltway. While you and Lori are still here as Shift Managers helping out where you are needed."

Goodness, have I been that blind? Deidre marveled at the lenses used to make things so clear for her. Renita was like the haunting voice of her conscience.

"So what do you think I should do?"

"Instead of trying to be in every place all the time, I would park my butt right here in front of this computer, because when they post the opening for a new GM for this site, don't expect to get the heads up from Conrad or any of those other district people who give him props for the store you run. Let Roz clean up around here; she's a hater."

Deidre put her cup of soup in the microwave again. *Renita is past her thirty minutes,* she thought. Deidre was resolved to send Renita back to her lane in ten minutes for the entire night without her usual nighttime break at 9:30.

"So what are you doing this weekend that is so important that you need Friday off?"

"NBA All Star Weekend is in DC, and this guy got tickets to Allen Iverson's party that should be off the chain," Renita said, bobbing her head as if she were hearing her favorite song.

"I assume this is the same guy you were trying to go out with tonight."

"You assume wrong."

"Gosh, Renita, I couldn't date as many men as you do.

How many is it . . . four or five?" Deidre said after testing her soup's temperature on a spoon with her tongue before deciding to ditch the spoon and sip the soup like coffee.

"I'm not ashamed to say I'm a serial dater. How else are you supposed to get to the choice cut of men if you don't shop around?"

Deidre thought about that, and then she thought of Larry Wilson. He had called to tell her about an upcoming overnight Teen Encampment at church that would conveniently leave her free for the evening if she wanted to go out. Saturday was her day off, and she wanted desperately to do something for herself. She felt as if she had spent the last few weeks revisiting high school and was ready to be over her school girl crush on DeAndre's father.

Deidre decided to go for it. Larry was, as many single women her age considered, a good catch; gainfully employed, responsible with a Christian outlook as an added bonus. She signed DeAndre up for the stay over at church as Larry had advised. She thought it would be good for DeAndre and would keep him out of trouble.

"I may have a date this weekend," Deidre said, feeling herself blush.

"Girl, that is what I'm talking 'bout."

"I'm just nervous though. I don't want to date someone for the sake of dating."

"What is the big deal? It's a meal or a movie."

"I don't know. Every relationship seems so temporary these days, and I don't want that."

"I know what you want, or should I say *who* you want."

"Let's not go there. I've been there, done that, but I still believe in a soul mate." Deidre said, wondering why she was at work baring her soul over a can of vegetable medley soup.

"I don't. You are brainwashed. Most people in church are nowadays, believing that everyone is looking for the same thing. Well, I'm here to tell you they aren't. Everyone is not dating with the intent to marry forever," Renita said, suddenly serious. "I'm not going to follow after some man my entire lifetime just to find out when I get to heaven that I don't have his rib. That Adam and Eve, soul mate, one perfect person for everyone crap, is for the birds."

Deidre often wondered if Renita considered herself a Christian. Many times her long rants were peppered with Biblical references. Deidre figured Renita spent some time in churches throughout her life, but somewhere along the way, she'd lost her faith. It was probably somewhere around the time when she and Carl, her son's father, had broken up.

"I just want to have some sense that I and whomever I date are right for one another," Deidre shared.

"Get a grip. You're never going to know that starting out," Renita said with confidence.

What saddened Deidre was that she already knew Larry was not right for her. There was a pause in the conversation as Deidre tried to put into words her trepidation. She felt embarrassed about what she was about to ask, basically because she was Renita's supervisor, but mainly because Deidre was more than ten years older than she.

"I guess I've been out of the dating scene so long, that I don't know how you know if someone is genuine."

Deidre was surprised at Renita's silence. Renita looked as if she was seriously contemplating her response. Deidre got a chill at the thought that maybe Renita, who had been dead on with her advice all afternoon, may not actually know. She usually spoke off the top of her head, and what she came up with was golden.

"That's hard, I'm not going to lie," Renita said, pausing to reshape her thumb nail with the emery board she pulled out of her apron. "It's like what you taught us last week in training about how to recognize counterfeit money. You said unless it's real, there will be flaws in its integrity. You told us it would be something we could feel or observe. So what you do, right, is hold that brother up to the light and see what you feel."

Deidre just shook her head. She was surprised to know that Renita was actually listening at the training, and even more surprised to see her apply it.

"Let me go, boss," Renita said as if Deidre were holding her up, "'cause I need to run out later on my break."

Chapter 18

DeAndre was embarrassed that he had chosen to wear his black rugby shirt over camouflage pants to the Teen Encampment at church. All the decorum he saw, as he stood in the registration line, seemed like it was bought at the Army surplus store. As it turned out, the theme for this Encampment was "The War Zone," and everything was draped in camouflage from the partitions separating the large multipurpose room into sleeping areas to the registration table itself.

There were groups of kids, mainly from his Sunday School class, clustered about with red rimmed nametags on their shirts. Most of them looked as thrilled as he felt to be at church on a Saturday. DeAndre couldn't believe his mom thought that it would be cool to have a sleepover at church. This was not one of those voluntary activities. Deidre did not ask if he cared to go. She dropped him off promptly at 5:30 P.M., and he reluctantly joined the end of the line.

"You think they have enough camouflage?" DeAndre

heard Kevin Nebo, an older boy in his Sunday School class, say. "Yo, are you on the committee or something?"

"Naw," DeAndre said, amidst the laughter of others standing in line ahead of him.

"I know, he looks like he's in uniform," said Raymond Lamont, Nebo's lanky sidekick from Sunday School class.

DeAndre smirked. *Even church has bullies.* Nebo and Lamont were the oldest boys in the class and would be the last to admit that their parents made them attend Sunday School like the rest of the kids there. The encampment was for those age 12 to17. Nebo and Lamont were the church's equivalent to Bentley's crew from the neighborhood. DeAndre wondered what hoops he would have to jump through to hang out with Nebo and company during the encampment. Hanging with the younger boys would make him appear geeky.

DeAndre thought about his first week back at school and how he had to constantly defend himself against the verbal attacks of Lonnie Parker. He couldn't get away from him, in the hallway, at lunch . . . everywhere DeAndre turned Lonnie was there with a group of his buddies and general instigators threatening what they were going to do to him. As if that weren't bad enough, they both shared the same last class of the day, math with Mr. Cleveland. He wanted to shout through the intercom system that it was all a big accident how he ended up punching Lonnie. It wasn't even his idea to go to his stupid party in the first place.

That one night had gained him a real tough guy reputation though. People talked about a showdown between him and Lonnie like they were anticipating a heavyweight boxing rematch. He didn't know what scared him more, the actual physical threat or the embarrassment when everyone in school found out that he didn't pose one. The twins claimed they had his back, but they couldn't be around at all times.

Kevin Nebo's brassy voice brought him back to reality. "Check out the honeys. That's what I'm talkin' 'bout. Seems like this retreat is going to be worth while after all. Looks like I'm going to be sneaking on the other side tonight," Kevin said.

"You're going to get thrown out, dog," Raymond Lamont said, shaking his head. "Boy, Reverend Tatum going to be preaching about you tomorrow."

DeAndre took his time writing his name in big graffiti letters on his nametag before turning to see the girls Kevin spoke of. There was Kenya with a nest of braids sitting high on her head. She wore a pink sweat suit with a lime green sac draped across her body. She was standing with a few friends DeAndre identified from the youth choir. He watched as Nebo and a few followers approached the girls, integrating the sexes. DeAndre wanted to follow, but didn't know how he would be received. The last time he saw Kenya was the day she broke up with him in front of everyone.

DeAndre watched like a kid excluded from a game. Nebo must have said something offensive to Kenya's friend, Camille, because she punched him in the arm. Then Nebo grabbed the medallion of Kenya's necklace and leaned in to inspect its surface. He waited for Kenya to haul off and whack him like her friend had done. *Can't she tell that he's just trying to chance a look and feel of her chest?* DeAndre thought. Instead, Kenya smiled at Nebo. Then Lamont whispered something close to her ear, causing Nebo to drop her necklace, and they all laughed.

DeAndre looked on helplessly. What was going on? Wasn't it just two weeks ago that he and Kenya were sitting together in the back of Sister Neale's Sunday School class writing in her pink and blue journal to prevent from speaking aloud? They would make comments about the other kids in the class, and his belly would hurt trying to stifle a laugh. She would write that she loved his sketches, and he would blush thinking he might love her. Then he would draw her something simple like a Hello Kitty or Betty Boop character.

DeAndre set off to find the bathroom and change his pants. It was a good thing he had packed two pairs of jeans besides his Sunday clothes required for church the next day. He pulled his loose and double baggy jeans out of his overnight bag. DeAndre usually wore them together to add the appearance of bulk. He delayed putting them on thinking that he wouldn't be able to stomach staying overnight if Kenya was interested in someone else. He could tell Sister Neale that he was sick and ask her to call his mother to pick him up. For a minute, he actually felt ill. There was no way he could compete with a high schooler for a girl's attention.

DeAndre began to test his lie as he re-entered the multipurpose room. He sat his bag with the others on the boy's side. Before he could get to Sister Neale, he could see Nebo still at Kenya's side pointing in his direction. She waved and looked genuinely glad to see him. He walked over slowly while discreetly tugging at his pants that, although were layered, slid down his waist without a belt.

"Your girl was telling us how you went Scarface at her cousin's party," Nebo said.

"Let me tell Sister Neale you need the prayer chapel open now," Lamont said.

DeAndre swallowed hard. He was sure Kenya would still be mad that he had disrespected her family.

"Yeah, it was viscous," she chimed in. "I was like, good. I can't stand Lonnie, even though he's my cousin."

DeAndre was shocked. Kenya smiled. Puppy love had him anticipating reconciliation. Everyone was looking at him as if they expected him to comment. *Think of something cool to say*, DeAndre thought. "You know me and my boys be wildin' out."

DeAndre dared to stick his hand out. He knew if Nebo gave him dap, then he was in. His hand nearly gave way from the force of Nebo's hand on his.

"She also said she had something to give you tonight after everyone goes to sleep," Nebo remarked.

"Shut up, Nebo, and mind your business," Kenya shouted while slugging him in the arm. Her smiled showed she was more embarrassed than offended.

"Young people, stop playing," Sister Neale said.

The three of them stood up a little straighter at the sound of Sister Neale's voice. Everyone knew she had a relationship with their parents. One bad report from her would send a child into instant punishment with their parents. Sister Neale was the main encampment organizer along with two of her college age sons. There were loads of volunteers keeping the child-adult ratio down four to one. DeAndre didn't know what Kenya had said to Nebo, but there would be no sneaking in this church tonight.

"Gary said they got Play Station hooked up on the boys' side. I got you beat on Madden all day, son." Lamont said.

Before DeAndre could drift off with Nebo and Lamont, Kenya hooked his arm in hers and pulled him possessively over to the side nearest the sanctuary entrance. He was close enough to smell the faint scent of soap on her skin. It left him hyper-charged down to the follicles of hair on his arms. He stood a couple inches above her, and although she still had her arm in his, it was hard to look her in the face. He didn't want to appear as if he were gushing over her.

"I didn't even know that was you with all your hair cut off. So why haven't you called me?" Kenya said, hitting him in the arm she just released.

DeAndre realized that hitting was a secret language with girls. He couldn't figure out what was going through her mind though. She was the one that told him never to call again.

"I was at my father's house," he said, inspecting the toe of his Timberland boots. He was nervous. Although he could talk to Kenya all day, he wondered if fraternizing with the opposite sex was allowed. All the adults seemed to be busy with registration, so he relished in the moment. He sat in a nearby row of chairs and Kenya followed suit.

"That's cool," she said.

"At least you live with your dad."

"That's not my real dad," she said emphatically.

"What?"

"I found out he's not my real dad. He's my stepfather that adopted me when he married my mom. I found out that my mom was pregnant and my real father left her. So you know that would ruin her squeaky clean reputation. When she was dating the man I thought was my dad, they came up with this arrangement. I was six months old," Kenya said, staring straight ahead, appearing to scan the crowd. "I sort of wish I never found out."

"Who told you?"

" My Aunt Grace; that's Lonnie's mom. She blabbed it to me one night when she was drunk."

"At least your dad . . . I mean stepdad, has been there for you since you were small, unlike my dad," DeAndre said, trying hard to make her feel better.

"Whatever. It's funny 'cause I don't know who to be mad at; my mom and dad for lying to me, my aunt for blabbing, or Lonnie who keeps bringing it up like it's a joke. That—"

"Shh, girl," DeAndre said, looking around as if they might have to duck and hide if she had gotten her last comment out. He was seeing another side of Kenya.

"Oops," she said, slapping a hand over her mouth. "Well, I don't even care. I'm tired of trying to be perfect. You know what I'm saying, like my mother; then come to find out she wasn't as perfect as she claimed to be."

DeAndre didn't really know what to say. Everyone, including his mom, believed Kenya was this perfectly bred, perfectly behaved, private school girl. They had always been able to speak freely to one another, but something was somehow different.

Sister Neale summoned the assembly into the sanctuary. DeAndre and Kenya yielded the way so the flow of teenagers could get by. They looked at one another before parting ways. "Later," he managed to say. Nebo ran between them through the double doors, chased by another girl, this time, armed with a purse.

"Stop running. You're not here to play. Matter of fact, let's separate right now- remove all the distractions; girls on one side, boys on the other," Sister Neale said.

The encampment participants were obedient to their leader, and the sexes were divided on opposite aisles of the sanctuary. When most of the participants were seated, Sister Neale began with the formalities.

"Welcome to our first Teen Encampment." She paused as if she expected a round of applause. "Pastor Tatum gave me the task of organizing this overnight experience for you, and I tasked my sons with helping me teach you some strategies to help you survive as a young Christian in the world today. You've all heard me talk about my boys in Sunday School. These are my two oldest sons, Gary and Monte."

Sister Neale yielded the front to her sons, who looked to be in their mid-thirties. Gary was the spitting-image of his mom with his shoulder length dreadlocks held back with a rubberband. Monte had his mom's dimpled smile, but was much darker.

Gary spoke first. "Okay, I'm sure when you came in you observed our effort to paint a theme of a war zone. You may wonder who is at war. My brother is going to read you some headlines that might clear that up for you."

"High school football quarterback shot to death after Friday night's game," Monte read solemnly. "Two teen girls abducted at local mall by an ex-Marine. Local girl accuses science teacher of sexual harassment. Teenage boys forced to rob banks in the area by a local gang."

"From just those few examples, who were the victims?" Gary asked. "If you read the articles, you would find many of these crimes were random, which means it could have happened to anyone who fit the particular profile. That's like me taking each headline and substituting your name or your friends' names into it." Gary gestured with each sentence in order to make a bigger impact.

Sister Neale shared that the theme for this Encampment came from the book of Ecclesiastics. She declared that there was a war going on against young people. De-Andre was puzzled when she spoke of another war going on inside each of them.

"The Bible says that from our lustful nature we war in our members. Go on, get your giggles out," Sister Neale said as several attendees cracked up. She knew the minds of teens hung out mainly in the gutter. "When I say lust, I'm talking about anything you hunger after more than you do Christ. So you could be lusting for attention, material things, or members of the opposite sex. We are in a constant internal conflict to do what's right or Christlike. Even when we have a conflict with our brother or another human being, the Bible, our guide book, says we struggle not against flesh and blood. It's a spiritual war, and we want to spend some time this weekend equipping you to fight that war. So consider yourselves enlisted in God's army. "

They spent the next hour in different groups, role playing. The volunteers acted out skits and explained related scriptures that the participants had to write down in camouflage notepads that had been provided at registration.

DeAndre wrote *what profith a man that he should gain the whole world but lose his soul,* and *the weapons of our warfare are not carnal but mighty to the pulling down of strongholds.*

"There hath no temptation . . . ," a volunteer shared, "but with the temptation also make a way of escape, that ye may be able to bear it."

When they watched their last skit, DeAndre frowned, but wrote down the scripture that was written on chart paper in its entirety. DeAndre wondered if it meant that God watched everyone so closely, and knew everyone so well, that when it looked as if they were about to mess up, He provided a way out. It boggled his mind so much that he had to ask if he had interpreted it correctly as others in his group were heading to the dining hall for dinner.

"If you recognize God in your life, He says there is no temptation out of which He won't provide a way of escape. The problem is that we look at the temptation and feel the pressure to conform, but don't look to God." Gary couldn't resist answering after overhearing DeAndre's question.

"So there's your cure for sin right there," DeAndre said, figuring he had cracked a code.

"Not entirely. God gives us free will, and He allows some things to test us. Check this out, no one is going to be perfect. He knows that we will fall, and He knows sometimes we set out to do wrong, but if we earnestly want to get out, look for the get-out-of-jail-free card."

No one in DeAndre's group stuck around to hear their conversation. By the time he reached the church dining hall, kids were chowing down on pizza variety and salad. Kenya was sitting with some girls. They had forty minutes before another session began that separated the sexes into two different locations, which to DeAndre could only be one topic.

The boys' session was a mixture of Bible Study and seventh grade health class. No one was foolish enough to raise questions and risk sounding like they didn't know about sex, or share knowledge that indicated they had experienced it. The Neale brothers concentrated their lecture on the attributes of being respectful young gentleman and the pressure to be sexually active. By eight o'clock, the boys were dismissed with the option of free time games outside the sleeping area, a Christian karaoke and talent show in the sanctuary, or to get a head start by refreshing in the bathrooms before retiring for the night.

Kenya and her friends were outside the sleeping area swaying as if they were practicing a dance. DeAndre, Nebo, and Lamont naturally gravitated in their direction. Nebo sidled up behind one girl with shoulder length hair, tapped her on the shoulder, and then pretended he didn't do it. She responded with a slap on his shoulder. DeAndre wondered which girl Nebo actually liked at this retreat since he flirted with everyone. Most of the girls tried to ignore the three of them because they were more than annoyed with Nebo's antics at this point.

"Are you going to karaoke?" Kenya said, side stepping to get closer to DeAndre. "Me and Camille are singing."

"I hope you aren't planning to be up her butt all night too," Nebo said. "That's all those pretty girls want you to do."

"Yeah, we're about to go dominate these games," Lamont said, following after Nebo.

DeAndre became uncomfortably aware that he was the only male still lingering. He pointed his thumb in the direction of the boys' sleeping area to indicate he would be going with them. Quickly he began wondering why he was missing out on the talent show to sit with a bunch of guys huddled around a twenty-inch television on a cart plugged up by the back wall. Nebo demanded the next round on a popular video game before plopping down on the cot. He used his duffel bag to prop his head up. In no time, he dozed off.

DeAndre left the sleeping area and joined the karaoke session already in progress. He sat in the corner seat of the front pew. Only four sets of children had nerve enough to sing in front of the others. Kenya and Camille were the last to take the stage. They alternated singing verses of "Jesus is Love." Camille's singing was mediocre in comparison to Kenya's strong, pure soprano voice. DeAndre noticed how comfortable Kenya was with a microphone. She added a syrupy flavor to the song. The two of them won by such an overwhelming round of applause, he almost felt sorry for the other groups.

DeAndre dreaded going back to the sleeping area, knowing that in the morning their parents would be there, and he would not have another chance to talk with Kenya. He wondered if she knew he was at her mercy as he pretended to be listening to the music sitting off to the side alone. He stood up to leave at the same time Sister Neale, looking exhausted, came to tell those remaining to prepare themselves for lights out in thirty minutes. De-Andre felt a tug from behind as the group dispersed inside the multipurpose room. Kenya gripped him around the neck and pulled him over sideways to whisper to him.

"Meet me in the sanctuary at midnight," Kenya said.

"What?"

"Sister Neale told us the sanctuary always remained open. In olden times, churches were never closed for people who needed to pray. The doors to the sanctuary don't have locks. Meet me in the sanctuary, okay? Pretend you have to go to the bathroom or something."

DeAndre nodded his head, then looked around to see if anyone was listening. She let him go and must have noticed he was looking bewildered. She repeated, "At midnight."

"Okay," he snapped as if to shush her.

DeAndre knew he wouldn't be able to sleep for looking at his watch. Nebo and Lamont finally got their chance on the video game. DeAndre contemplated telling them about his rendezvous, but didn't trust that they would keep it a secret. Sure enough, the lights were dimmed, and eventually turned off around a quarter to eleven. Nebo and Lamont's talking and faint snores from others who couldn't hang could be heard in the atmosphere. A few boys did get up to go to the bathroom. One time it got so quiet that the boys could hear a round of giggling from the girl's side and admonishment from the female volunteers. Boys were instructed to use the bathrooms in the back by the offices while the girls used the bathrooms up front by the classroom. He calculated how many steps there were from the bathroom to the sanctuary and how many landmines in between.

At midnight, DeAndre, in his sweatpants and long

sleeve FUBU shirt, stood up and yawned. He walked past a row of cots and almost jumped when he felt someone grab his pants leg.

"Where are you going, son?" Lamont asked.

"The bathroom," DeAndre said loudly, not knowing where Gary, Monte, or the other volunteers were stationed. "That pizza is ripping my stomach up." He grabbed his stomach for added effect.

"Go handle that, 'cause no one wants you busting off all night."

DeAndre's heart was in his chest, and he knew if another person stopped him he probably would really go to bathroom on himself. The back hallway curved around and provided an entrance to the sanctuary by the choir loft. He entered on tiptoes. Kenya would more than likely enter from the front. At first DeAndre didn't see Kenya under the faint light. Only a few lights over the altar remained on like they did during the ritual sacrament of communion. He saw the braids on the top of her head bowed in the third pew as if she were actually praying. DeAndre wondered if he should sit in her row or not.

"Kenya?" DeAndre whispered.

"Boy, sit your butt down," she said, scooting over a little to allow him to sit down.

DeAndre bowed his head like she did. He wished she wouldn't sit so close to him so he could breathe. He wished she would just give him a little room so he could think about what he was doing there. They just sat there looking at one another and everything he had planned to say to her slipped his mind. "So what's up with you?"

"I don't know; what's up with you?"

Although he had been looking down, DeAndre could tell Kenya was smiling as if she were enjoying herself.

"I'm trying to figure out if you are serious or is this just a joke," DeAndre said, deciding to put it all out on the line. Now he was looking her right in the face.

"Does this seem like I'm serious?" Kenya leaned in for a kiss. As soon as her lips touched his, the door swung open. DeAndre jumped up with his body pressed up against the wall as if he were on a ledge. Kenya just ducked where she sat.

"Not in there, Gary. I said in the multipurpose room," they heard Monte say.

They waited for the door to close entirely. Kenya laughed, and as soon as DeAndre caught his breath, he laughed too. He knew it was just a matter of time before they came back or someone noticed they were gone from the sleeping area.

"That was close. Look, I'm going to go back," DeAndre said. Maybe she had something to prove or maybe she hadn't been in trouble like he had the past couple of weeks, but he was determined not to get caught kissing in the sanctuary.

"No . . . stay," she whined. "I don't feel like going to bed yet."

This time Kenya was up in his face. DeAndre would have backed up if it were not for the wall. She kissed him. This was far from the pecks they had previously shared in the park by her house. Once their lips set, his mind began to race. *What should I be doing?* His mind recalled hundreds of love scenes from countless television, movies, and video programs he had watched. Just when he thought, *All right, DeAndre, tilt your head;* she tilted hers. Then Kenya inserted her tongue into his mouth and wiggled it around inside before reeling it back in. He felt his body respond.

"Bye, DeAndre," she said, before heading toward the front entrance.

DeAndre didn't wait until she left before bolting toward the same door he had come in. He thought God
would strike him down right there. He didn't think to
look for a way of escape. He went to bed sure that getting
aroused in the sanctuary was so far past a sin that it
would send him directly to hell.

Chapter 19

Andre waved his gym identification as a formality to his friend, Steve, at the entry desk of the Bo Donovan's Body Synergy Fitness Center located in the mall where he worked. Everyone knew him. On the rare occasions that he had misplaced his card, any one of the receptionists, trainers, or managers could vouch for him. Andre had a platinum membership card, which included exclusive hours at all four local Bo Donavan gym locations, product samples, and reduced rates for fitness conferences with the man himself. He knew the entire product line and wore the fitness apparel routinely when he wasn't in his work uniform. He even purchased the host of vitamins, bottled mineral water, and recently, the Synergy Shakes, to add the mass he needed to sculpt more muscle.

After ten minutes in the locker room securing his duffel bag and uniform, Andre hurried toward the main weight room for his lab. He chose to be grouped with other fitness enthusiasts who were, in his opinion, better conditioned than most of the lab groups focused purely on weight reduction.

Most people were already stretching or warming up when Andre entered the gym. Andre had just fastened the Velcro tabs on his fingerless weightlifting gloves when Melvin Johnson, a former wrestling coach and all around loud mouth, came in clapping. He was short, and his bulging arm and leg muscles made him look even stockier.

"Come on, I'm looking to do ten to twelve. You know how I do it," Melvin announced to everyone, referring to the amount of sets he would complete by the time their session was over.

Andre and Melvin didn't get along. Melvin had a negative or snide comment for everything Andre suggested in lab, like the monthly programs they should follow. He was one of the reasons that Andre had missed the last two lab sessions, preferring not to be confrontational and just workout alone. Usually he didn't let people like Melvin bother him, but he had been in a funk for the past week, ever since Deidre and a man in a silver Land Rover had him questioning every decision he had made in the past eight years. He couldn't shake an overwhelming feeling of regret.

Andre had been tired of Deidre ignoring his request to sit down and talk with him about regular visitations with DeAndre. He had come to her house that Saturday in hopes of finding a middle ground. Although it had been eight years since they had lived together, coming through that tree lined neighborhood gave him the feeling that he was coming home. He had almost missed the house because there was a Land Rover parked in what used to be his spot. A man sharply dressed in tan trousers with a brown striped shirt and necktie left the driver's side of the truck and walked to the door. Andre sat in his car awhile and watched him approach Deidre's door.

At first, Andre had thought that the man may be there on business or had accidentally happened upon the wrong porch, but there was no mistaking the man's destination and intentions when he saw Deidre greet him at the door with a broad smile. The man had put up a finger to indicate he had forgotten something before going back to his vehicle.

Andre looked at Deidre poised at the door. She looked good in a black form fitting jersey dress and low sling back heels. When the man Deidre had been waiting for came back, he presented her with a modest bouquet of flowers, which she accepted before allowing him to enter her home. Andre stayed in stakeout position until Deidre and her guest left the house together twenty minutes later. He had driven home that day feeling like he had traded his prized NBA jersey collection just to see his favorite throwback Wes Uncle jersey sported on the back of someone else.

The only way he knew to get the images of it out of his head was to get into his body—occupy himself physically while disengaging mentally. Andre was about to retrieve his program sheet from the file cabinet next to the locker room door and get started when Eugene Miner, the trainer, came in. Eugene scanned the room and looked relieved when he saw him.

Eugene explained to the group, in a raspy voice, that Andre would be supervising the lab temporarily until he got back from the drugstore. He gave Andre an official pat on the back before taking off to find some temporary relief from whatever was ailing him. Andre felt as if he had just been endorsed as the next presidential candidate. He couldn't believe he was getting a shot to do what he always wanted to do—train others.

"I have your program sheets here," Andre said, placing them on the seat of a nearby exercise bicycle. "We should at least be able to knock down six to ten each."

"Like I said before, I'm doing ten to twelve; the bodybuilder's dozen, baby," Melvin said, stepping in front of him dismissively. He snatched up his program sheet which just happened to be on top.

"C'mon dude," Andre said incredulously. He was in too good of a mood at the moment to let Melvin aggravate him. *I'm in control*, he thought before saying, "Remember, more is not necessarily better; train harder instead of hogging the machine counting down twelve sets at fifty pounds."

Andre soon realized he had been training with the wrong group. While the avid lifters were showing off with Melvin, his group was concentrated more on form and getting the most out of the workout. He had to admit working out with the rowdy bunch was motivational, with every man trying to outdo the other, but he could have been using his talent to demonstrate to the newcomers what he had learned from the Synergy conferences about the importance of weight lifting in any fitness program. He had to start thinking like a trainer if he wanted to become one.

Andre fixed his eyes on the sprinkler in the ceiling as he lay on the bench. Like an accordion being stretched slowly, then crunched together, he lifted up the barbells, then pressed them in, stopping shy of bumping them together, before pulling his arms back down. He snapped out of his trance when he had finished his set and sat up on the bench.

Eugene came back with a cup of coffee from the 7-Eleven. Although it probably wasn't what he needed, the temperature more than likely soothed his irritated throat. He gave the thumbs up and raised his brow as if to ask if everything was okay as he approached.

"What are these fools doing?" Eugene asked as Melvin's side of the room abandoned their work out for a shouting match.

"Someone needs to reel your boy, Melvin, in before I do," Andre said, feeling like a teacher whose class had been disrupted by a troublemaker.

"I know your group is driving you crazy also, asking questions and faking like they can't complete a set."

"I'd work with them any day."

"Work on, my man," Eugene croaked. "Yo, make sure they are filling out those sheets. That's how we justify reserving this time for y'all."

"Cool," Andre said.

Andre was determined to make Eugene proud. Carl Mathis, in his group, was complaining that his chest hurt and arms were burning at the top of his set. Andre looked at his sheet as they set seventy-five pounds to his bar per his request.

"Naw, you are at least one hundred," Andre said, referring to the one rep maximum determined on the first day of lab as the most pounds he could safely lift.

"What do you weigh, 180?"

"One eighty-five," he whined.

"You should be moving up to one hundred. C'mon baby, you got to up the ante. You don't want to stay on the same level, do you?"

Carl gave him an apprehensive look. Andre could see it was going to take more motivation to get him out of his comfort zone. He could see from his sheet that Chris had been charting the exact same stats. He thought about the infomercial for the Cardio Press, Bo Donovan's two-in-one gym system. Although the people who needed convincing in his infomercial were probably paid actors, he borrowed a few lines of Bo's reply.

"Look at this muscle," Andre said, flexing. "It didn't

get that way being stagnant or taking up residence on a plateau. Trust the system . . . I mean your program."

Andre took it upon himself to add twenty-five more pounds to Carl's bar. Two spotters in their group lowered the bar down to Carl. He jutted the weights upward like a rollercoaster on its ascent before his arms collapsed to his chest. Andre relaxed the pace of his counting and started coaxing Carl, who sat motionless as if he were willing the bar to move on its own.

"C'mon, don't punk out," Andre yelled. Carl completed the last of his shaky set with an agonizing groan. "C'mon another set. Here we go," Andre demanded.

It never occurred to Andre that he might be pushing Carl too hard until he cried out again in pain. The spotters literally had to lift the bar off Carl as he crumbled beneath the weight of it. He grabbed his right pectoral muscle as soon as the weight was removed. His cries alerted Eugene and the rest of the gym.

"What happened?" Eugene said.

"I don't know. I tried to get him to do another set."

"He added like twenty-five pounds to my max weight," Carl cried, red-faced, clutching his arms around his chest before curling into a ball. "I told him I wasn't comfortable with the increase. Felt like he shredded my muscle."

Andre didn't understand what was happening. It was as if things were happening in slow motion. He grabbed Eugene's arm as he was following after a feeble Carl and pleaded, "You're supposed to make progress with every single workout, right?"

"Man, that was way too much weight for a newbie to handle. Everybody ain't like you. We work out at eighty percent of our max weight, at the most. Sometimes I do a drop set with them dudes, man. I start high, then peel off with each set," Eugene said, gruffly shaking his head. "You messed up, dude, but hey, you didn't know."

Eugene's last comment, that was meant to let Andre off the hook, had stung instead. Andre didn't want to think there was much about the Donovan Way, his love for fitness, and passion for weightlifting that he didn't know. He was a trainer for one morning and he had messed it up, causing injury to a fellow lifter. No one would want to work with him again. Andre parked himself on the bench as the gym began to clear for the next lab. He wished he had left with the others when he saw Melvin approaching with an empty bar.

Melvin had a smug expression, and Andre prepared himself for whatever he had to add to the situation. "More is not better. I guess you forgot about that." Melvin let out a puff of air and shook his head. "A joke."

This time Andre had no snappy response for Melvin. His worst fear had come true; he had been as obnoxious as Melvin was.

When Andre finally left the gym, he drove off with a copy of *Fitness Training the Donovan Way*, a book Eugene had given him when he told him Carl had probably strained a muscle. Although the gym didn't have a doctor on call, the fitness director at every Bo Donovan facility had advanced training in sports related injuries.

Now Andre was back where he started this morning, living inside his head and thinking about regret. He thought about how he struggled through school and eventually stopped trying, barely making it out of high school. He thought about his employment file at the gym and the gripping fear when he thought of the 30 hours of coursework needed in order to attain the fitness trainer certificate.

Andre was dissatisfied with virtually all the choices he had made in his life. One of those choices had been his break up with Deidre. He had made a deal with the devil, and now he continued to pay the price. Mabel Collins had come to him at the height of his self-loathing and talked him out of his good thing. He, Deidre, and DeAndre had been barely making it in a one-bedroom apartment in Landover Hills when her mother informed her she would be moving back to South Carolina and would be leaving Deidre her childhood home. Two months after they had moved in, Mrs. Collins played her trump card. She had stipulations on her property that only Andre could fulfill. One day she conveniently called when she knew Deidre was in her class at the community college.

"You know Deidre's father was a pillar of that community, and the more I think about it, the more it kills me that you all are living there without being married. Now, I'm not telling you to rush into marriage without being established. Lord knows you rushed enough when you brought my grandbaby in the world. As much as I would love to support your new family, I could surely use the money down here from the sale of my husband's property." She paused for emphasis. "Now I would be obligated to take care of my daughter and her baby. It's hard out here trying to support a baby by yourself, if you know what I mean. You think about it and let me know, but make it your decision; you being the man and all. I don't think Deidre needs to be burdened with our arrangements; not with her going to school and raising a baby too. I'd just deny that we'd ever had this conversation anyway."

His moving out without warning was uncouth. It had blindsided Deidre. He told himself it was only temporary until he could provide a way for his family. He wanted to continue dating, but downsizing their relationship was the ultimate abandonment to her. She tried her best to shut him out of her life. Returning to New

York for two years, unfortunately, helped her create more distance.

Deidre was a good woman. He never thought that after all this time he would still be trying to regain her trust. He still had a reasonable amount of reconciling to do.

Chapter 20

The twins made school bearable for DeAndre. They propelled him through school like rocket boosters that helped to fuel a space shuttle's entry into space, but lately, he was running low on octane. Although DeAndre and Rob had different homerooms, they only had one ninety-minute class before seeing one another again at lunch. Rajah was in DeAndre's sixth period gym class where his quick wit often helped to divert DeAndre's attention from the awkwardness he felt having to expose his pencil legs and bird chest to an audience of his peers in the locker room.

He was left to go it alone in last period with Mr. Cleveland and loud mouth Lonnie. It would be a class he would gladly skip if he didn't need it to pass on to the next grade. Mr. Cleveland was more than happy to tell his mother he was on the borderline and that he held DeAndre's academic fate in his hands. He imagined himself disappearing as he neared the door. It was not a complete vanish like Mr. Invisible. It was more like evaporation where only wisps and vapors remained to occupy the page. He thought about how cool it would be to attend all his classes that way.

As soon as he approached his third row seat, DeAndre heard one of Lonnie's buddies say, "Dang, why is his face so shiny?"

Laughter erupted from his classmates who were already in their seats. DeAndre immediately thought about the extra lotion he raked from Rajah's hand when he poured out too much as they got dressed after gym class. He thought about a comeback but was uncertain which one of Lonnie's friends had said it. Lonnie and his friends were famous for tossing out ventriloquist style insults so that neither he nor Mr. Cleveland could point them out.

"DeAndre, don't start. It was completely settled until you got here," Mr. Cleveland said, writing the remaining problems on the overhead for warm up.

"It wasn't me," DeAndre said, flinging his backpack on the ground. He heard an echo of himself coming from the far right. "I guess that was me too."

"All right settle down everyone."

Most of the times when Lonnie and his friends started in on him, DeAndre ended up fuming in his seat or finding an excuse to leave the room. He couldn't let that happen again. He saw on the class agenda that they were in for a pop quiz. DeAndre figured pop quizzes were a way for Mr. Cleveland to sit at his desk and get out of teaching for a day. He needed to do well.

The warm-up was Mr. Cleveland's way of reviewing. He asked the class the steps of multiplying fractions. When no one answered voluntarily, he called on Lonnie. DeAndre was delighted when Lonnie called out the wrong answer.

"Aha, retard," DeAndre couldn't resist saying.

"See me then, DeAndre," Lonnie said, standing.

"Hey, guys, cut it out."

"Why would I want to see you?" DeAndre said, ignoring Mr. Cleveland's request. "I don't go that way. I got a girl."

DeAndre and Lonnie traded insults, each wanting to have the last word. Their classmates tossed out the ohs and ahs, which they collected like currency.

"I hope you are not talking about my cousin, Kenya. Don't think you are the only one she's talking to."

The response Lonnie got from their peers emptied the bank. The noise attracted Ms. Richmond, his English teacher, from next door. DeAndre knew he was going to be taken out of Mr. Cleveland's class again. He pushed aside a few unoccupied chairs to get to Lonnie. He was postering; he was mad that Lonnie would even suggest that Kenya liked someone else, but he had no intentions on getting suspended again. He knew the two adults in the classroom would not allow them to actually fight.

"What you gonna do?" Lonnie asked.

It seemed as if the whole class, even Mr. Cleveland, who was now standing between the two of them, waited for his response. DeAndre heard Ms. Richmond calling his name. This was his chance to get the last word. He thought about cursing, but decided not to chance it, because that alone may get him suspended, plus, the twins had told him a while back that he didn't even sound right cursing. He figured the best way to go was go low.

"Yeah, what you gonna do?" Lonnie repeated.

"Your mother. Tell her I'm coming over later," DeAndre said before walking out, leaving his unfinished quiz on his desk.

Ms. Richmond called out to DeAndre who went stomping down the hallway to an unknown destination.

"If you keep going, you might as well march yourself right to the office," she said.

Her words stopped his trek. He wanted no part of the

office. He just wanted to get as far away from Mr. Cleveland, Lonnie, and his other classmates before he exploded.

Ms. Richmond caught up to him and grabbed him by his forearm." What's gotten into you, Mr. Hicks? You're out of control. I've never seen you like this."

DeAndre shifted his weight from his right foot to the left. He didn't answer. Big angry tears leapt from his eyes. Ms. Richmond, with a firm grip on his wrist and elbow, guided him back to her empty classroom as if he were blind.

She waited until the door was closed before she began again. "What's going on, DeAndre?"

DeAndre spilled his guts, telling her about the feud between him and Lonnie. He even shared what he thought was a mutual dislike between him and Mr. Cleveland.

"I can hear through these walls. Every day at this time of the day there is something going on over there. It makes no sense to go back and forth every day with this other young man without some kind of solution. It's not getting you anywhere. You all behave exactly the way teachers like Mr. Cleveland expect you to behave: wild and out of control, and he'll keep sending you to the office to be tamed. You're smarter than that. Be the bigger man. You don't need the distractions. What about your grades? I invite you . . . no, I *expect* you to do better, and I know your parents do too."

DeAndre was thankful for the silence and the reprieve Ms. Richmond offered as she went about her classroom chores. She allowed him to stay in her class until the end of the day. He did think about what Ms. Richmond had to say. He didn't hate Lonnie. He hated how he made everything public. It was that scrutiny and fear of not being accepted that made DeAndre just want to disappear.

After school, he preceded the twins off the school bus in hopes of catching up with Kenya. He was met with a summons from an un-groomed Bentley in a Lay-Z-Boy recliner. DeAndre had seen the chair earlier and thought it was put out on the curb with the bulk trash, but now saw it was more of a makeshift throne. DeAndre stalled a moment at the curb as if he were waiting to cross. *What does he want?* He was tired of confrontation, and this time, he didn't have his dad to help bail him out.

DeAndre signaled for the twins to go with him. Before either one of them could protest, he shot them an incredulous wide-eyed look that spoke of their unwritten code to be there for one another. Bentley sat in the midst of a crew of other high school kids who got dismissed just twenty minutes before the middle school. DeAndre didn't expect Bentley's thick, ashy knuckles to be extended in a fist for a friendly pound as he approached his seat. He looked across the street briefly to see if his classmates were watching. Bentley and Big Tom were the most popular guys in the neighborhood, and being accepted in their crew gave a person clout that trickled down from the local high school on down.

"Look. Y'all know Myrna . . . tall, light-skinned, just moved around here?" Bentley said to DeAndre and the twins.

DeAndre nodded, still not trusting his voice to give away just how nervous he was. Myrna and her sister, Gazelle, were model fine with long straight black hair and long legs. They'd moved there from Rhode Island right before the school year started. Gazelle was a seventh grader at DeAndre's school. He knew personally that both Johnson girls were the source of many middle school boys' fantasies from the talk around school.

"Which one of them hoes is her sister? Tell her to come over here," Bentley ordered.

Bentley couldn't be serious. A girl like Myrna was definitely out of his league, DeAndre thought. He didn't want to be a part of what Bentley had in mind, but knew just the same that he would chase Gazelle down and wrestle her to the ground if Bentley wanted him to just to stay in his good graces. Luckily, Gazelle was still across the street talking with a few other seventh grade girls. DeAndre walked along the curb a ways and called for her. He could hear the twins doing the same over his shoulder. She shielded her eyes to see who was calling her as her friends pointed DeAndre out. He had never held a conversation with this girl. DeAndre gestured for her; he felt bad, like he was leading her into a den of wolves.

Gazelle strode across the street gracefully with one of her girlfriends; her fingers curled tightly around the handle of her handbag. She wore a simple white prairie shirt and jeans and low heeled mules. Her hair was pulled neatly back into a ponytail, making her look older than thirteen. She walked directly up to DeAndre as if he were the only one on that side of the street. He figured with all the attention she received, she was used to drowning out crowds of howling guys.

"Hey," she said to DeAndre.

"My man—" DeAndre started.

"Yo, where your sister at?" Bentley said before DeAndre could forewarn her. "Tell her to come holler at me."

Gazelle shielded her eyes again, which DeAndre figured out was her way of sizing a person up. She looked at Bentley so hard that even he had to rake his fingers through his 'fro to tidy himself up. Then Gazelle turned her lip up as if she smelled something rancid. *Why did she have to give him that look?*

"My sister is at work. She works. Anyway, she has a boyfriend back home."

"Yo, she sassed you," Big Tom said to muffled laughter.

"I know this hoe didn't just try to carry me. I know she is from another state and everything, but someone needs to tell her who I am," Bentley said, leaning forward to close the extension on the recliner. DeAndre feared he was about to unload an arsenal of undeserved insults on her.

"Let me get her for you, man," Rajah said with sworn allegiance.

Bentley turned to both the twins who were still in place at the base of Bentley's throne like soldiers waiting for their orders. "Yo, take care of my light work."

DeAndre could hardly believe his ears as one of his best friends added a medley of curse words to the others repertoire of wise cracks in an attempt to demean Gazelle. It wasn't that he hadn't heard Rob and Rajah curse before. It was just strange because they had grown to the point that although those words were customary in their household, they weren't necessary when the three of them communicated with one another.

DeAndre stood between the offended Gazelle and the very offensive Dempsey twins. She just rolled her eyes at DeAndre as if the whole incident was his fault. She didn't laugh it off or curse. She and her friend just did an about face as if in drill team precision and started to walk away.

"Yeah, take your lanky self on. Your parents should have just named you giraffe," Rajah said softening the language after DeAndre shot him an incredulous look. "Dang, girl, I have never seen someone with their tail up on their shoulder blade. She got legs shooting out her neck, y'all." The verbal jabs on someone so classy were corny at best, even from the usually hilarious Rajah.

"Yo, I like these young-uns, man," Bentley said, grabbing his sides and landing back in the chair as if he were an audience member at *Def Comedy Jam*. And they all laughed, not because it was funny, but because Bentley felt vindicated and wasn't mad anymore.

DeAndre looked up the street and caught a glimpse of Gazelle. She shook her head as if to pity how sad and ridiculous they all were to be wasting valuable time on the corner talking about people. That was exactly how DeAndre felt—silly and ridiculous and wasting valuable time—as he rejoined the gang and waited to be dismissed.

Chapter 21

Andre woke up disturbed by a telephone conversation he had with DeAndre the night before. Apparently students at DeAndre's school were chosen to design and paint a mural on one of the walls. DeAndre wasn't selected. Although DeAndre didn't let on, Andre knew it was a major disappointment that he couldn't be involved.

Andre left his apartment early to drop by DeAndre's school. He figured he could skip a workout. Once there, he didn't roam the halls to spy on DeAndre or get a visitor's pass to sit in on one of his classes. He found the Guidance Department, which was ironically on the same hallway as the larger than life mural, still in progress, that DeAndre wasn't allowed to work on. Andre remembered talking to Mr. Talbert, the school counselor, the last time he was there. Andre could tell he was a good brother who had his kid's interest at heart. He felt maybe he could shed some light as to why his son was slighted.

Andre took a seat in a small waiting area made up of three uncomfortable chairs and a circular table with various pamphlets laid out for the parents' benefit. He picked up one that read, "Thinking About Your Child's Future." He held onto it to remind himself as to why he was there. He was thinking about his son's future and his role in it.

The meeting adjourned, sending the three counselors to their individual offices. Before Mr. Talbert could reach his door, the receptionist told him that Andre was there to see him. Mr. Talbert, with a soda bottle in hand, signaled for Andre to follow him inside his office. Andre stood inside the cubicle-sized office not sure that he would be able to fold himself into the space provided between Mr. Talbert's desk and the straight back chair. The small space was neatly organized with bookshelves of resources and framed pictures that served as bookends. Andre noticed a family shot of Mr. Talbert and a significantly shorter woman with two younger boys posed at a scenic location. Andre took a seat and pushed back a few inches before extending his hand.

"Thanks for seeing me without an appointment. I'm Andre Hicks, DeAndre's father. I don't know if you remember me."

"Yeah, yeah, I remember you. So how's it going?" Mr. Talbert placed a stack of papers in front of him in his in-box before sitting back and giving Andre his full attention.

"Everything is cool . . . I mean—" Andre said.

"You still have some concerns about DeAndre," Mr. Talbert said, ignoring his ringing telephone.

Andre didn't know why he was clamming up. He was mad all of a sudden, but he didn't know at whom. He realized, now that he had this opportunity—an opportunity to speak on his son's behalf—that he didn't just want to find out why his son, with such obvious talent, wasn't picked to work on the mural, but he struggled to find the words.

"Yesterday I was talking to Deuce . . . uh, DeAndre, and he told me he wasn't one of the students chosen to work on this mural project." Andre pointed his thumb in the general direction of the mural site.

"I know," Mr. Talbert said, sighing heavily as if he knew this was coming. "The Maryland Arts Council chose our school about a month ago among all the middle schools that didn't have an art program. I've seen your son's work. I immediately thought of him, but because the children would have to miss some class time, each child had to get their teacher's recommendation to participate."

Andre placed his head in his hands. He could guess which one of DeAndre's teacher's didn't recommend his boy, and just like that, an opportunity came and went because DeAndre wasn't ready. Andre couldn't count how many things he'd missed out on because he was messing around in school. Now DeAndre was repeating the cycle.

"You know my son has drawn that pirate ship from memory at home. I'm talking exact replica."

"I can believe it, man. He's an artist in the true sense of the word. This wasn't a little boy that you had to coax into drawing a picture. I know what you are saying," Mr. Talbert said between sips from a bottle of Pepsi on his desk.

Andre shook his head. He felt bad for all the years he wasn't there collecting his son's drawings in an album or posting them on a refrigerator.

"I see that picture of your family—your boys. Does either one of them have a hobby, play sports?" Andre asked.

"My oldest one. He's seven." Talbert looked over his shoulder fondly at a picture of his son. "He's short for his age, but wants to play ball. I signed him up for Boys and Girls league. I'm even coaching. "

"Doesn't a part of you want him to be the next Lebron James?"

Mr. Talbert tilted his head and thought about it for a minute. "Yeah, and hook his dad up with courtside seats."

"Well, part of me wants DeAndre to be the next . . . uh, Charles Shultz."

"See, it's up to us, and their mothers too, to lead them there."

Andre knew that to be true. He felt that same confusing emotion from before, but this time he didn't try to decipher it. He just spoke his mind.

"It is a father's job to guide. My father never took the time to teach me those lessons." Andre said, trying to temper his emotions by taking a couple of breaths. "He didn't teach me the difference between the ant and the grasshopper . . . you know, how to work hard and save. The messed up thing about it was that he wasn't the only one blown away when Momma died. He just gave up. Gave it all up. But where did that leave me?"

"It left you right here ready to do all you can for your son. Everybody doesn't have the benefit of having their father in their lives, but we're not going to leave our next generation out there hanging," Mr. Talbert said, extending his hand.

"I'm sorry. I mean I didn't come in here to bend your ear about the past."

"No problem, man. The word *counselor* is still in my job title." He turned to grab a binder labeled COUNTY SCHOOL DIRECTORY off the shelf. "I got a buddy that works at Malcolm Woods High School. It's a creative and performing arts magnet school. He's the one that put me down with the Arts Council. He's always preaching to me about why the arts are an important part of any curriculum. He's made me a believer. Hold up while I make this call."

Andre listened to Mr. Talbert call his friend at the creative arts high school. He felt as if he were going behind Deidre's back. She had a one track mind when it came to school. Whether he liked it or not, DeAndre was college-bound.

Mr. Talbert replaced the telephone receiver on its base. "All right, my buddy said the school I was telling you about has classes in dance, instrumental and vocal music, drama, creative writing, and visual arts. Because this school is a magnet school, it's not zoned by boundaries, so to get in you have to audition, or in DeAndre's case, have an interview and present a portfolio of his work. The guidelines are online. Here. Let me print them for you." Mr. Talbert whipped around to the computer screen behind him.

"That seems like a lot. You know what, that's all right, man."

"What?" Talbert said, whipping back around again. "Weren't you the one who came in here telling me about your son's talent?"

"Yeah," Andre said over the sound of the printer.

"He's got the sketches at home, right? How hard can it be to assemble a portfolio? This school mixes academics and art. It's ideal. Face it, man, these kids need an outlet. I saw your son looking at the mural the other day. I told him how the resident artist who worked with the children said it took a whole quart of paint just for the bough of the pirate ship. You know what he did?"

"What?"

"Without hesitation he said, 'They are going to need a gallon.'"

The look on Talbert's face told Andre he should be impressed. "Yeah . . . I'm sorry. I'm missing it."

"He visualized that the bough was just a quarter of the ship's length. Do you think he would have converted quarts to a gallon that quickly if Mr. Cleveland had it on his next math test? Everyone takes in information differently. He thinks through his art. You know how well he would thrive at a school that has two and a half hours a day devoted to his art studies?" Mr. Talbert said, appearing more excited than Andre. "Oh and the good part is that by recommendation from his middle school counselor—muah—he could enter the Choice camp, which is like a summer institute. My buddy said that kids who excel there almost always get in without the audition because they work with the staff all summer."

Andre thought about that. He was sold. "I know he would be doing a heck of a lot better in all his subjects. This is almost too much to take. I know it would be great for Deuce, but it's going to be a hard sell."

"Are you kidding me? What did we waste the last hour talking about? You better talk to your son and your . . . I mean, his mother."

Andre was silent for awhile. "I got some atoning to do in my situation, if you know what I mean. I'm trying to build a bridge, but I'm not sure whether she's going to meet me halfway or burn that sucka down. Anything I say is met with an instant rebuttal."

"That's all right. You're not afraid of a little debate, are you?" Mr. Talbert said, extending his hand. "A dad's got to do what a dad's got to do."

Chapter 22

"I'm going to tell you the unadulterated truth this morning," Pastor Tatum said in his matter-of-fact manner. "Repeat after me. We are weak witnesses for the Lord."

Deidre turned to an elderly woman who had clung possessively to her aisle seat when she entered her pew after Sunday School. She hesitated before repeating what sounded like an insult issued from their pastor. The woman smiled sweetly and said, "You're a weak witness."

Deidre just stared at the woman. *Is this woman hard of hearing? Didn't the pastor say we?* Deidre turned to her right and repeated the same phrase to her friend, Sheila, emphasizing the word *we*.

"We are weak witnesses," Pastor Tatum continued. "We, meaning right here at Liberty AME. We, meaning the body of Christ. The Bible says we are to be the light of the world and the salt of the earth. "This Little Light of Mine" . . . remember that song? We're supposed to let it shine. Basic stuff, right? That's Christianity 101, but some of us are undercover with our Christianity," Pastor Tatum said, sliding a tri-fold handkerchief across his upper lip which was usually the precursor of a major point and an even more profuse sweat. He was a fair-skinned man with a sprinkle of freckles to match his reddish undertones and hair which had retreated to the back of his head like a carpet that wrapped around from ear to ear.

"How can you be close to someone and they not know you go to church? How do your friends not see the light of the Lord radiating from your life? Everyone you come in contact with everyday sees you as Evil Ed, Snobby Sonya or Gossipy Gloria. We're Christians when it's convenient to us, and it's not right. We think we have a right to be nasty, bitter, or hateful because we've been hurt in the past, then we sit around proclaiming we are these super Christians. Then there are others of us that are so sanctimonious and haughty that we repel the very people we are supposed to help save. Help us, Jesus, we are poor examples."

There was a modest round of applause that Pastor Tatum waited to subside while catching his breath after that introductory rant. "Some of you are sitting here looking just as evil now. Sue me for slander if you think I'm not telling the truth."

Deidre could not sit still in her seat. It was like her Pastor had turned a huge floodlight on her. When some people felt the poignancy of God's Word from the pastor's sermon, they either stood to their feet and said amen, or began to take copious notes like Sheila was doing. When Deidre felt convicted, she squirmed. She shifted her weight several times, crossed and uncrossed her legs or looked around as if to try and catch the neon arrow hovering above her head that told the entire congregation that the pastor had been dead on about her. She couldn't help thinking about her venting lunch sessions with

Renita at the job that recently had to be taken off site since she was being considered for the General Manager position. Deidre never bothered to offer the love of Christ as a peaceable alternative. What's worse was how Deidre used Renita as her own sounding board to complain about her own situation with Andre.

Thinking about Andre just then made her stop and realize that he had not dropped off DeAndre for the beginning of service as she requested. She had agreed on an every other weekend visitation arrangement with him, and he had agreed to drop DeAndre off to church on time. Where was he?

Deidre looked back at the closed sanctuary doors guarded by two female ushers dressed in black skirts and heavily starched white button-up shirts before looking at her watch. This was just like Andre to try and steal more time. She had to remind herself to focus on the day's message to prevent herself from getting upset.

"Turn to your neighbor again and say, 'Our attitudes get in the way of our witness.'"

Deidre watched as others co-signed what the pastor was saying, including Larry Wilson. Larry, who was sitting in the first pew with the other Stewards, briefly looked around before turning to a man in the pew behind him to repeat the phrase. Deidre and Larry had gone out on a date. Surprisingly she had a good time. He was a genuinely good guy, worldly enough to maintain an interesting conversation, conscientious enough to be charming, and saved enough not to make an advance on the first date. She just wasn't certain if she were ready for a second.

Deidre sat forward and didn't bother repeating anything this time, figuring that she didn't need anyone to tell her about her attitude. She took a pen from her purse so that she, too, could take a few notes of her own.

"So who is going to speak boldly for Christ if the Christians are silent, conflicted, or just plain contrary? We've got the radicals and the rappers. Yes, I said rappers. You all have seen the awards shows where these artists are the first to thank God when they win, but you can't find Jesus anywhere in their lyrics, dance moves, or videos. Some of us get real offended by this, but I'm not surprised at all because the Bible says, saints, that every tongue will confess that He is Lord. That means the Murder Squad, MC Pimpin', Thugalicious, and their booty bouncers will know that the Lord is God." The pastor thought for a second, and then continued. "Wait a minute, I've got a rap. This is for my young saints in the back row." Pastor Tatum bopped from side to side in true hip hop fashion. "They degrade and defile then praise Jesus for style. Yeah, boy," he said, posing with his arms crossed.

Deidre had to laugh. Nobody could tell Pastor Tatum that he wasn't "down." To be a man approaching sixty, he had a way that was appealing to his younger members, as well as the old. That was the main reason that she had always insisted that DeAndre be right beside her in service listening to their pastor. Before Andre resurfaced, Pastor Tatum was one of the only men that DeAndre saw consistently. Deidre knew that DeAndre could gain a lot from a man who made it a point to reach out to the youth of his church by having activities like the encampment that she recently sent him to. This was a major difference from the pastor she grew up listening to at Independent Bibleway Church.

"The question is do we want those seen on BET and MTV to usurp the true message of God and what it means to be a Christian. That is the message that we should be carrying throughout the world. Jesus said in Luke that if the disciples kept silent and didn't declare His eternal kingdom as He rode into Jerusalem, the very rocks would cry out. He's been too good to us to keep silent, y'all."

Deidre placed her hand on her right shoulder pretending to brush it clean so she could glance over her shoulder again. She knew the woman directly behind her was tired of her distracting searches of the back entrance into the sanctuary.

"Are you hearing this? Pastor Tatum has never been so on point," Sheila said, following her friend's gaze. "Girl, exhale. He'll be here. He's with his father; it's not like he's with a stranger. I wouldn't be surprised if he hadn't already slipped into the service and is sitting somewhere in the back with the other kids from his Sunday School class."

"Shh," the woman on the aisle seat said.

Deidre and Sheila looked at each other with an incredulous look. "I doubt that," Deidre found herself whispering to Sheila to avoid any further reprimand from their pew mate. They knew there was no need to get mad at this woman. She represented the old school, hat-wearing aristocracy of the church whose job it was to maintain sanctuary decorum, especially in the ever coveted first ten pews of the church. Her job was also to train the I-paid-too-much-money-for-my-hair-to-wear-a-hat Christian debutantes like Sheila and herself in church lady ways before they passed the torch.

"Ask yourself, who has benefited since you have been saved?" Pastor Tatum said, waiting for the immediate response of some, and built-in wait time for the more cautious response of others who felt it may be a trick question. "If your salvation is only benefiting yourself, then you're a spiritual snob. I'm sorry. So we know that's not the way to go. Neither is being so afraid of witnessing and ruffling the feathers of our unbelieving friends and acquaintances that we blend in like Christians in camouflage. You can have faith with a little more finesse than that. Just act like you know. Act like you know Christ, and that you are different because you know Him. Talk about Christ with your friends and family. Pray for people. That's the best way to witness. Other than that, you're a hindrance and a stumbling block. People will see your joy if you live right, and they'll want to know your secret. People who live in hell will eventually ask for a glass of water, y'all," Pastor Tatum said, before taking a drink from a bottle of water sitting on the pulpit podium.

Deidre leaned her head toward Sheila until her mouth was directly by Sheila's ear. "So would you say I am the spiritual snob or a Christian in camouflage?" Deidre smiled, asking in jest until she noticed her friend's silence. Deidre noticed Sheila glance over to their pew mate, but she remained silent.

Sheila's silence was unnerving to Deidre. *Why didn't she just answer the question?* Maybe it was because Mother Theresa, on the end of their row, had a sudden coughing spree. Deidre nudged Sheila to remind her that there was still a question on the floor.

"Well, maybe you're a little of both," Sheila said reluctantly.

"Explain to me how that can be."

"I can only assume you mean between you and Andre. You're a little snobbish. I mean I think you've always been the good girl who could do no wrong when you were in the relationship, and then the innocent victim in the break-up, and he was the villain." Sheila paused a few minutes to take in what their pastor was saying. She sighed heavily before beginning again. "Now that he has resurfaced, neither of you will admit you've both made mistakes."

Deidre unconsciously clutched her floating amethyst

charm on her necklace. She reached for her clutch purse and tossed her pen back in it before bringing it back down on her lap.

"Don't think you're the only one whose feet hurt from Pastor stepping on your toes. I'm just as much a snob. It's so easy to take the position that I'm saved and secure in Jesus and fooey on everyone else."

This time Keith shushed them and Deidre was thankful. It was funny how people can have a very different view of a relationship they were not a part of, but she had asked. She should have known Sheila would be brutally honest.

"Like our text says in 1 Corinthians 9:22, Paul says I have become all things to all men so that I might save some. You can't put up with people's ungodly mess, but you can't throw them away either. Your lives are meshed with other people's for a reason. Who doesn't deserve to be saved? I was watching news the other night and there was this story about a man that went into a burning building. This building was an abandoned facility, a known crack house, but this man darted inside to save this sixteen-year-old boy. The boy's friends stood helplessly on the sidewalk across the street. I imagine these were some of the same boys who may have introduced him to this lifestyle, done drugs with him from time to time, but they couldn't save him. When this man came out with the boy who was dazed out of his mind, more than likely from the drugs, the reporters asked why he would risk his life for this kid. The man said he thought of his own child. This was someone's child with potential to turn his life around. He said he thought this boy deserved to be saved."

Pastor Tatum ordered the congregation to hold hands and ask, "Who do you know that deserves to be saved?" The woman beside Deidre had such a firm grip that it forced Deidre to give the question some honest thought as the woman gave her hand a final squeeze before releasing it. Andre had been on her mind since the beginning of the service. She had always tried to get him to church, but not necessarily bring him to Christ. She was beginning to see that there was a big difference.

"It might be a sixteen-year-old child. It may be an 80-year-old adult with the potential and no eternal direction. As soon as the man that I mentioned earlier got that young boy to the outside of that building, EMS arrived on the scene. They jumped in to start emergency assistance. Christ needs you to lead people to the threshold. See, because we can't theoretically save them; Christ saves them. We call for people to come to Christ each Sunday, but only God knows if they need resuscitation or life support. That's why we have to beat down that snobbish attitude that makes us think we are doing something by simply quoting scriptures that the unsaved won't even understand 'cause the Bible says the dark comprehendeth not.

"You're talking about spiritual warfare, rebuking the devil and speaking in tongues. You all are not speaking the same language. Find the scriptures that tell of God's love and His sacrifice for us. Take them down the Roman Road so they know how to be saved. Bring them to Christ and let the Holy Spirit begin to teach them the meat of the Word so they can live after that. That's my charge to every Sunday School class, ministry, and auxiliary. Teach your members the path to salvation through the Word so we won't sit back, blend in, or hide behind our salvation."

Deidre finished adding her "Amen," then turned to see if DeAndre had snuck in without her knowing. She could tell by his tone that Pastor Tatum was nearing the end of his message. He always started off with correction, giving his commentary on how they had gone astray, and then ended with instruction. He wasn't one of those preachers who seemed to warm up saving their major points to the end of the sermon when they had reached a feverish pitch. Pastor Tatum seemed to stay on an even keel highlighting his points with rhetorical questions and dramatic pauses.

Just as Deidre was about to turn around and face the front again, she saw Andre's face appear in the framed window of the sanctuary's door. The usher must have noticed him too, because she yielded the doorway open. Deidre could see Andre's hand go up to indicate that he was fine with his entryway view. Deidre popped up and placed her right index finger in the air to get clearance into the aisle from the lady on the corner seat. She moved swiftly toward the exit and paused only to allow the usher to open the door for her.

Andre looked relieved to see her as Deidre approached him and their son.

"What's wrong?" Deidre asked

"Nothing. Look, I'm sorry. We would have been here earlier but Deuce packed only one dress shoe in his bag and we knew you'd be horrified of him waltzing up in church with his tennis shoes on. He didn't have his key and couldn't fit my shoes, so we went to the mall. When we found a pair of shoes, a nice pair of brown Stacey Adams, I wasn't prepared to lay down seventy-five bucks.

"You didn't have to go through all that," she said, looking over at DeAndre who was now peeping through the sanctuary doors himself. She looked down to spot the worn toe of DeAndre's black Air Jordans. She probably wouldn't have noticed his shoes the way the cuffs of his tailored dress pants fell at his ankles. Deidre tapped him on the shoulder and shooed him to join his friends inside the sanctuary. He shared a spirited handshake and a half hug with his father before going inside.

"Now that I know his size, I'm just going to buy him a couple of pairs of shoes. First, I'm going to buy him some tennis shoes. Then I think it would be smart to keep a pair of dress shoes at my house for church."

"Don't bother. He's got plenty of dress shoes at home."

"Dee, I'm not asking you for anything. This is something I want to do."

Deidre looked around at the other members in the vestibule who were coming from the bathroom, getting water, or leaving early. She felt Andre's eyes on her and self consciously smoothed the a-line of her eggplant colored jersey dress with her hand before saying, "What?"

"Nothing, you look great," he said.

"You didn't know I could clean up so well, did ya?"

"Naw, I always knew that."

Deidre felt a flush of heat and knew her cheeks must have been rosy. The door of the main sanctuary opened as a member exited, and she could hear Pastor Tatum's plea. Deidre remembered what she had heard during the sermon. "Why don't you come inside?"

"Naw, I'm not dressed appropriately," he said, referring to his jeans and casual laced up shoes.

"Are you sure?" She wanted to explain to him that kind of stuff wasn't important to her anymore.

"Maybe some other time." He smiled before becoming more serious. "Hey, you've been a hard woman to catch up with. I've tried to call you several times."

"You have?" Deidre said before remembering the double shift she pulled leaving at closing on Friday, and then returning early Saturday.

"I guess you made special plans since you knew Deuce would be with me."

"I should tell you; I've applied for the General Manager position at my store. Although I've been the Shift Manager for the past six years, they're not just going to hand a sister the position. It's killing me, but I'm pulling really long hours. This is the time to really prove myself."

"Just let me know if there is anything you need me to do. I'll take Deuce. I mean we don't have to stick to this every other weekend schedule if it's not working for us."

"I appreciate that, because I may have to be at the store late this weekend coming."

"Just let me know," Andre said with a pause. "Wow, General Manager. That's great, Dee. I hope it all works out for you. I know that's all you've ever wanted."

Deidre froze her smile in place before it slipped. That struck her as odd coming from him. Ironically there was something she wanted as much if not more.

"Deuce and I had a serious talk about high school this weekend. I really want to discuss something with you, and I would prefer not to do it over the phone. I was thinking maybe you could come over Monday or Tuesday so we can talk."

"Let's make it Tuesday," Deidre said, figuring she needed a day to think about going to his house and being in his presence again.

Chapter 23

DeAndre sank into his favorite position reclined atop his mother's extra firm mattress with the telephone cradled between his right ear and shoulder blade and his other hand poised on the channel arrow of the remote control. He was confident that he could continue to enjoy his mother's amenities for at least the next three hours until she came home from work. He was surprised he had passed her telephone check-in. She got off the phone without her usual threat of, "Don't make me come home early."

DeAndre had the volume down on his favorite program, BET's *106 & Park* video countdown show, because he was listening intently to his girlfriend, Kenya, reprimand him for not meeting her at Manor Ridge Park after school like they had arranged. This was the same girl, he thought, that had left him waiting at a designated meeting place many times. It was hard to pay attention to what she was saying when the show's "new joint of the week" came on spotlighting one of his favorite rappers.

"So you'd rather hang out with a bunch of dudes than me?" Kenya said.

"Naw," was DeAndre's immediate response as he weighed who he'd rather let down, Kenya or the mob. "The twins weren't ready to go so I stayed with them. So what's up with your girl, Jasmine, anyway? I thought you were going to fix her up with Rob or Rajah. Then we can all hang out at the park like we used to."

"Forget that. I'm not a dating service. Plus Jasmine goes with this guy in high school which is what I'm about to do. Shoot, I'm tired of messing around with these little boys."

DeAndre tried to figure out whether he should be more concerned with being called a little boy or the fact that the last word was plural.

"Hold up," DeAndre said.

"Hey, this is my song. Hey, hey, hey," Kenya sang.

DeAndre could hear Kenya singing along with the video, a pseudo rap song meant only to spark a dance craze. He could tell she was dancing by the inflection of her voice and muffled sounds of her movements. DeAndre enjoyed listening to her party and eased the volume up on his own television to jam along with it from his reclining position.

DeAndre's throat was dry all of a sudden, and he looked in the top drawer of his mom's nightstand for some gum or a peppermint candy. He flipped through a few loose papers that weren't organized into the containers that divided the drawer when he noticed a folded piece of paper that had some kind of image colored in magic markers. He unfolded the paper thinking maybe his mother had kept something he had drawn for her from elementary school when something fell from the fold. He didn't need his father's high school ID that fell into his lap to identify his bold strokes of graffiti art. It took a minute to distinguish the code of the connected bubble letters that read, Dee Dee and Hickory. He folded it back carefully placing the ID card into the center crease only to open it again. Part of him wanted to hold on to it as some sort of proof that he had been a result of something more than one night when his parents "got hot" as the twins had on separate occasions described their conception.

"Yo, Kenya," he yelled to get her attention.

"What?"

"You remember that Betty Boop I drew for you? We were in Sunday School, and you asked me to draw you a Betty Boop like girls wear on their T-shirts. I drew one on a pink sweat suit. Do you still have that?"

DeAndre realized he was holding his breath through the few moments of silence. He remembered making the character look just like her, and that's what made it special, but obviously not special enough that she would remember it. *Just as long as she still had it tucked away somewhere*, he thought.

"Oh yeah, I don't know what happen to that thing," Kenya said.

"You're wrong. I can't believe you lost that drawing, for real," DeAndre said, regretting that he even brought it up in the first place.

"Gosh, what's the big deal? You'll draw me another one," she said confidently. "What are you going to do this summer?"

"I don't know." DeAndre was still pouting. He hadn't even thought that far ahead. He was still trying to make a difference in his grades so that he could pass on to the next grade level.

"That's right, we get out before you all. Three weeks and we're outta there. I can't wait until summer break because I can't stand my school."

"What's not to like? At least your school has less kids than Pemberton. I guess the teachers are mad strict though, because it's a private school."

"It's an all-girl school, Dre. You don't know how jealous and petty girls can be. That's what I have been telling my mom. How does she expect me to be a well-rounded individual when I only see one segment of the population all day."

"Your mama wants you to stay at your school through high school too?"

"Yep, two months off, and then it's back to boring blah-blah academy. At least being ninth graders, we graduate into a whole different building," Kenya said. "God, I need someone to rescue me."

"What's up now?" DeAndre said.

"The man they want me to call my daddy wants me to spend three weeks with his family in Mississippi. I'm like, yeah right. They are not even my real family. Plus it's boring down there. Everyone is so old and country. And my grandma watches over me and my cousins like a hawk. I wish I could apply for a work permit like Jasmine. My mom told me the only way I can get a cell phone is if I can pay for it, but she won't let me work."

"Sorry, sweetheart, I don't know what to tell you," DeAndre said. "Next year my dad wants me to go to some sort of private school for the arts. I really think it is a plan to try and split up me and the twins."

Just then it dawned on DeAndre that he might have an answer to Kenya's woes, and he was proud to offer a solution. She sounded sad, and that meant that angry was not far off.

"Hey, you should look into it. It's called Malcolm Woods Creative Arts Magnet School. It's in Lanham though. They have kids from all over PG County who attend this school who want to be artists, dancers, and singers, and they'll train you. You could be trained in voice lessons. You'll spend two and half hours a day doing what you love," DeAndre said, impressed with his spin on the same pitch his dad had given him.

"That sounds cool," she said, getting excited, "although my voice doesn't need training. My mom says I have perfect pitch. Do guys and girls both go to this school?"

"Uh, yeah," DeAndre said to the tune of "duh." "Your school counselor can get you into the summer camp by writing you a recommendation. Or you can audition in August for a slot in the freshman class. I hear it's really competitive. I don't know if I really want to go there though. Everybody else is going to Carver."

"Boy, you are crazy. Who cares about everyone else?" Kenya said. "Do you know what this means?"

"What?" DeAndre was lost because Kenya had been speaking a mile a minute.

"If I make it into the summer camp, then I don't have to go to Mississippi, and when I get into this school, I can get the heck up outta Hunt Valley. Yea-yah, hey, hey," Kenya said. This time her enthusiasm didn't correspond with the video they were watching which was now a boy band member gone solo trying miserably to crone a love song to a girl way too old to take him seriously.

DeAndre thought about the possibility of going to the same school with Kenya. He knew from watching a lot of television that guys and girls hooked up all the time in high school. It was funny that after he got suspended both his mom and his dad tried to have "the talk" with him. Thank God they spared him the where-babies-come-from part. His dad told him that there were basically two types of girls, loose and conservative, and that he was better off waiting for the girl he loved and respected to get comfortable enough with him to want to share herself with him. Andre warned DeAndre not to ever pressure a girl for sex. Then he added, "Although I know you're not even thinking about that kind of thing now." His mother, who never really bought his Lorraine Dupree-gym shorts story, said any girl who would allow him to feel on her private parts has no respect for herself. Deidre said intimacy of any kind was a sin and should be avoided.

DeAndre couldn't say he exactly felt pressure to have sex from his peers, but like playing a video game, he definitely racked up popularity points if he could attract a girl and could say that he had advanced with her on each round of play. He already had a girlfriend. He thought of how cool would it be to enter high school with a ready-made relationship.

"You should take me to the dance," Kenya said.

"Wait a minute, what dance?"

"Our eighth grade prom is two weeks from Saturday. I know my mom will let you escort me. Each girl in my class will be present. Hunt Valley Christian Academy, in conjunction with the Central Maryland Home-Schoolers, presents the Eighth Grade Promotional Prom," she said, apparently reading from the actual event flyer. "Tickets are thirty dollars each. A portion of the proceeds goes to the Kencaid Family Shelter."

"O-kay," DeAndre said, not sure that even the lure of hanging out with Kenya would make him want to go to a formal dance.

"Students of Hunt Valley may bring a male friend or family member. Parent chaperones are needed. How pathetic," Kenya added. "I was going to go with Jasmine. We bought the same dress. Hers is in turquoise and mine, of course, is in fuchsia, but then she asked Josh, her so called man, who lives down the street. That messed everything up for me because her mom is like way too lenient and mine is way too strict."

"Wait," DeAndre said, trying to find his place in all of this.

Kenya continued. "I'm going to tell my mom that Josh is really Jasmine's brother. He can drive us. Your mom can drop you at my house. Then I'll have my dad take us both to Jasmine's house. I told Jasmine that we should have dinner at her house so we have an excuse to leave from there."

"Where are her parents in all of this? I'm sorry, but my mom is going to want to meet everyone. She's suspicious like that. She'll line everyone up and start firing questions. You'd think she worked for the FBI or something," DeAndre said.

"Gosh, your mom is a trip. Tell her it's just a doggone dance." Kenya sighed. "Maybe I'll have my dad take us. You know he'll do anything these days to win my love since I found out he wasn't my real daddy. That way, your mom and my dad will be satisfied that he brought us there and we are enjoying ourselves. Then he can leave us and pick us back up."

"What about your mom? What if your parents chaperone?"

"Look, do you want to go or not? My parents are not going to chaperone 'cause they know I'd be disgusted. Plus they trust me. Haven't you heard? Kenya Matthews can do no wrong."

DeAndre wasn't down for any elaborate schemes that he had to now run past not only his mom, but his dad also. He didn't want to burst Kenya's bubble, but her plan seemed to be full of holes, especially when his mother got to investigating. He needed this plan to be airtight before he could run it past his mom. He needed it to be airtight so that Kenya wasn't forced to go with someone else. The whole thing didn't feel right, but what could he do? He was in love. Kenya had his heart and had taken it to a faraway place.

"With Josh driving Jasmine, we can leave the dance a little early, then get back before Daddy shows up." She paused. "You know what people do after proms, don't you?"

It didn't register with DeAndre at first. What did he know about proms? He hadn't gone to his first school dance yet.

"We're going to high school. We can't stay babies forever. Do you love me?" Kenya asked impatiently.

DeAndre wondered if he really knew Kenya now. Sure he loved the essence of who she was once her new attitude and bossiness were drained off. He figured he couldn't spare a moment to really think about it. "Yeah."

"I thought so," Kenya said as if she had previously given what she was about to say plenty of thought. "It's okay when you love someone."

"Huh?"

"Dre, I want you to be my first."

DeAndre struck his chest with his free hand as if he had actually found a piece of hard candy in his mother's drawer and was now chocking off of it. He was at a loss for words. Again he could feel Kenya waiting for a reply, and he didn't want her to lose patience with his inexperience. He thought about her fuchsia dress and what she might wear underneath while the corny love song from earlier played in his head. He thought about his mother's hidden mementos that had fallen from his lap when he sat up and what he could say to his mom to convince her to let him go to this dance. He thought about what his dad said about the types of girls and figured that Kenya was mighty doggone comfortable with herself and him to want to go all the way. Then he tried to think of something real smooth and charismatic to say. Something his dad would say in this very instance.

"Bet. We can do that."

Chapter 24

Andre had prepared entirely too much food for a party of three. He wanted something light and filling, but not too intimidating to those who didn't monitor what kinds of foods they ate. He was going to bake a simple chicken dish. Then he felt the mild spring air and heard his tabletop hibachi calling his name. By the time he ran in and out of the corner grocery store, he had added tuna steaks, asparagus and portabella caps that he always used as a meat substitute in his burgers. Even if they were meatless, one couldn't go wrong with a good burger, he figured.

Now Andre was creating a symphony of sound with the sides of his bowls and the handle of a wooden spoon as he listened to George Benson's "Breezin'" on his kitchen radio. He added the chopped mushrooms to hamburger spices, onions, and other adhesive ingredients such as breadcrumbs and egg whites before doing a spin and picking the beat back up, this time with his index fingers drumming on the counter. He formed four patties with his mixture and had to wipe his hands clean with a dish towel. He sealed the asparagus in foil with a pat of butter, splash of lemon, and a shake of Mrs. Dash.

He did a James Brown slide in front of his marinated chicken halves that he began dissecting, legs from thighs and breasts from wings, when a sharp pain hit him in his abdomen. He braced himself with both hands planted firmly on the counter. He lowered his head and closed his eyes to breathe through the discomfort.

Andre contemplated going to the medicine chest where he knew he had a half bottle of Tums and a fairly new prescription bottle of Zantac. If this was an ulcer, he wondered why the pills weren't working. He opened his eyes when the pain subsided and stared down at his severed chicken. The pink juice reminded him of the blood he discovered earlier in his stools. The thought made him queasy. He shook off the feeling that something might be really wrong with him in an attempt to pull himself together. He had been looking forward to this afternoon with his son and Deidre. Right now, he couldn't stand looking at the chicken he had prepped, so he shoved the parts back into the refrigerator. *The show must go on.* He picked up his plate of uncooked burgers, asparagus, the unopened package of tuna steaks with lemon pepper seasoning, and mamboed to the patio door.

It took him only twenty minutes to rotate the majority of his entrees on the tiny halves of his grill. Andre loved the simplicity of the recipes in his *Grilling from the Core*, Bo Donovan cookbook that he had come to depend on for quick summer meals. He left the two mushroom burgers and his asparagus tent on the grill while he went to freshen up.

After a quick shower, he slid on a white top with black strips that ran down the sleeves and sides, which tugged slightly at his torso and the matching black running pants with cross training New Balance tennis shoes. The radio was still on in the kitchen when he heard a knock on the door. He reached over the ledge that separated the front room from the kitchen to turn it down, but not off. He thought it added a nice touch.

Deidre entered followed by DeAndre who came in and slung his backpack immediately at the foot of the couch as if he had an attitude. Deidre stood just inside the door with a jean jacket over her arm awaiting stage directions.

"Hello, hello, hello, welcome to Chateau' Hicks. Thank you for accepting my dinner invitation. You may take a seat while I set the table," Andre said in his best French accent, ushering Deidre to the couch with his hands before closing the door. "Deuce, what's up with you, boy?"

"Nothing," DeAndre said, hiking his pants up in the back as if the belt didn't help to keep his pants in place. He sniffed the air and zeroed in on the patio where the aroma was coming from.

"He hadn't finished his homework by the time I got home, so he brought it with him," Diedre said, taking an exasperated breath.

"That's all right, we'll get to that. First I want him to come see what his pops got for him in that bag right there by the closet while I take this stuff off the grill."

Andre thought that Deidre was stunningly beautiful, standing over DeAndre's shoulder looking at him lacing up his new Nike Air Flight tennis shoes. She wore dark blue relaxed fit jeans and a frilly peach colored top with oversized brown beaded jewelry and brown mules. She had a way of making casual look chic.

Andre felt that old familiar stirring whenever she was near. He had resigned to the thought of Deidre as his past, the one he had let get away, and the gatekeeper to his paternal dreams, but now he was thinking she had to be his future. He had tried other women during their sabbatical that provided cheap thrills that weren't worth the price of admission. He thought about the guy in the Land Rover he saw over Deidre's house. His job was to make her forget about anyone else.

The idea of reconciling with Deidre was always there, but didn't quite crystallize in his mind until he dropped DeAndre off at the church the other day. He thought he had to have a game plan though. Besides introducing her to magnet school options for DeAndre, he now had the long-term goal of selling her on their family and picking up where they had left off.

Andre pulled three plates from the cabinets and three forks from the drawer, and then set the food up buffet style in the center of the table. Deidre took her seat in the middle of his small rectangular table. Andre didn't want to act like a kid in the cafeteria, but he used his plate as a placeholder to claim his seat directly across from her, leaving DeAndre to sit at the head. He heard the static of his radio between frequencies, and when he looked up, DeAndre was attempting to change the station.

"Boy, don't you touch my station. Put it back."

The radio station was playing a Chaka Kahn hit that Andre immediately started bopping to while he brought out a choice of drinks from the refrigerator. Despite his only child's laughter, he added some hips and arms to intensify his groove. Deidre started to laugh too.

"What do you call that dance?" DeAndre asked.

"This here is Dre's groove. See anybody can perfect a dance that everybody is doing because they have studied a video. A true dancer makes his own moves. Ask your mother how good of a dancer I am."

"I thought we came to eat," Deidre said with a healthy

portion of asparagus already on her plate as if it was all she was going to eat. "Get something to go on this burger while you're up."

Andre could see that DeAndre was on his way to the refrigerator, so he headed toward his seat. "Aww, you left me hanging. You didn't even vouch for my moves on the dance floor. What's up with that?" Andre said, adding a pout as he straddled the chair to sit down.

"Your father was a magnificent dancer, by the way," she said unconvincingly.

"What do you mean was?" Andre said, watching her smirk. "Is that all you're going to have? We got tuna steaks if you prefer. The burgers are—"

Deidre put up a hand in protest. "Didn't ask, so don't tell. I'm trying to be open-minded."

"Do you have real mayonnaise this time?" DeAndre asked from the kitchen.

"No mayonnaise, real or otherwise," Andre said.

DeAndre looked at his father, then his mother, before staring blankly into the refrigerator.

"Your dad is the chef for tonight. I was not asked to bring anything." Deidre said, shrugging and unleashing a satisfactory smile.

"Man," DeAndre said with a huff.

"Grab the ketchup if you'd like and close my fridge," Andre ordered. He turned back to Deidre after he was sure that DeAndre had carried out his instruction and was seated with them at the table. "You'll love it. I put a little steak sauce on mine."

"When in Rome do like the Romans do," Deidre said, lifting her bun to allow Andre to douse her burger with steak sauce before taking a mice-size nibble of her mystery burger.

"Come again?" Andre questioned.

"It's an expression, but it's funny, because this all reminds me of a part of my pastor's message from last Sunday."

"Oh yeah?" Andre said before taking a huge bite of his burger. "Tell me about it."

Andre gave her his full attention. He wanted to do anything to keep her talking. Deidre sighed and wiped the corner of her mouth with her napkin. She could start speaking in Japanese for all he cared. He was lost in her eyes. She had to have the biggest, most beautiful eyes of anyone he had ever seen.

"Well, the whole sermon was about the way some Christians go about evangelizing or bringing people into the faith the wrong way. So in the Bible times, when the early converts into Christianity sat down with another sect, they sometimes clashed over silly things like what was appropriate to eat, whether it was sacrificed and if it was right to share from the Lord's table."

"Yeah, Pastor Tatum is a trip," DeAndre said, joining in. "He said it's like people who decide to eat healthy, and then want to change Thanksgiving dinner for everyone. He said can you imagine you are in Mississippi, you know like the deep south, with a rack of your cousins thinking that you are going to steam the greens and bake the chittlings."

"Sounds sort of like me," Andre said.

"Yup," DeAndre said. "You'll be the one he talked about circling the table with a picket sign protesting pork." That sent DeAndre into a frenzy of laughter.

"I think he was making the point that sometimes we get preachy about the wrong things," Deidre intervened. "Pastor Tatum had us look at Romans chapter 14. It talks about when you're invited into someone's house. There will always be differences in what people say is right and wrong, and we shouldn't stand in judgment. The Kingdom of God and being a Christian is so much more than

the petty differences we dwell on. You shouldn't immediately condemn them for their values, and they shouldn't
condemn you knowing that refraining from controversy
sometimes helps everyone to remain . . ."

"Nice," Andre said.

"Agreeable," she said almost simultaneously, then
smiled.

"Interesting," he said. *So is it safe to assume that she
wants to remain agreeable now?* He was definitely down for
that. Andre saw her bring an asparagus stalk to her
mouth twice before biting into it. "What?" he said, taking
a bite of tuna before putting his fork down. "I feel like
you want to say something. Go ahead and say it."

"DeAndre tells me all the time that you're into this Bo
Donovan Fitness thing. I never would have pegged you
for a fitness fanatic. Is there a certain philosophy behind
it all?"

"The Donovan Way teaches that the body is a fortress
for mind, body, and soul. That's the synergy part, or the
overlap of mind body and soul," Andre said, noticing his
son slowly roll his eyes as if he had heard it all before. He
decided to give the concise version. "It's kind of complicated. He has a whole school devoted to his core princi-
ples. I guess you can say the body plays a key role in
your total wellbeing."

"Oh okay," she said.

"You sound skeptical." Andre tried not to sound offended, but he needed her to know how important Bo's
system was to him. "I get that a lot when people find out
I follow Bo's program. I don't know if it's me or Bo and
his infomercials."

"He is kind of loud and obnoxious, and you're . . . uh . . .
not."

Andre laughed. He knew exactly what she meant. It
took a while to get past Bo and his overzealous Olympian

sidekicks, shouting while demonstrating the core princi-
ples of his system. His infomercials were everywhere, and
Andre found he couldn't really escape them. One day he
caught the tail end of a synergy segment on Saturday
morning television.

"What do you believe in your core? Is it reflected in
your habits?" The sincerity of Bo's question was cap-
tured with a close-up. Andre thought about that seriously as he looked at the beer he had been nursing since
waking up that morning. It was the same brand that
lulled him to sleep the night before. He remembered Bo
saying, "I don't want to just sell you a system. I want to
sell you a lifestyle. The system may cost, but change is
free. Are you where you need to be physically, mentally,
and emotionally? Are you someone you can love down
to the core?" It had been a wake up call.

"Learn to love that burn. Down to the core," Andre
said in Bo's raspy kind of rant. "Seriously though, it is a
revolutionary system."

"I think it has definitely done you some good," Deidre
said.

Andre watched as her eyes swept across his upper
body admiringly. It was subtle, but he had caught her,
and he wanted her to know she was busted. They shared
a moment as their eyes locked and a charge was sent between them. She was the first to look away. *It's mutual.
She's feeling me.* He smirked at the thought. DeAndre was
oblivious as he downed an entire glass of ginger ale.

She cleared her throat in an attempt to recover. "What
I meant is that it is obvious that you are passionate about
it. Why aren't you doing that full time?"

"Now that is a good question." Andre popped up to
get a relish mixture, his garnish of choice anytime he had
tuna steaks, in an attempt to avoid answering the ques-

tion. He had asked himself the same question many times, but never could come up with a satisfactory answer.

"I mean there is a Bo Donovan Fitness Center in the Municipal Mall," Deidre said.

"Is there? I hadn't noticed," Andre said in mock stupidity. He couldn't admit his insecurities. Not in front of his son. Not when he was asking DeAndre to go after his own dream by developing his artistic talent.

"Very funny. I think you'd be an excellent body building-trainer person," she said, sounding genuinely concerned. "I hope your spirit doesn't get neglected in the process with all this work on your physique though."

Oh here we go, Andre thought. He'd long since fought off feeling inferior in the sight of her mother because he didn't belong to a church. At that time, Deidre attended another church right outside of the District of Columbia in Cheverly. He had even visited their small uptight church with Deidre and under the direct supervision of her mother. To be honest, Bo Donovan and his synergy system had done far more to clear his mind and transform his life than that church ever could.

"Do you want another burger?" he asked sarcastically although he could see that she hadn't completely finished the first one.

"No thanks," she said.

"Well, I guess there will be no converting here tonight," Andre said, hoping the innuendo was clear.

DeAndre abruptly left the table to throw away his half eaten burger. The tuna steaks had been a hit; the burgers a miss.

"You'd better get started on your homework," Deidre told her son.

DeAndre plopped back in his chair staring up at the ceiling as if he hadn't heard a word Deidre had just said.

Andre could tell it was angering Deidre that DeAndre could be so blatantly disobedient. DeAndre didn't play that with him.

"Did you hear your mother? Get your homework," Andre ordered.

They both watched DeAndre slink to the couch and bring his backpack down on his lap. He pulled out a book to support the creased worksheet. A few more minutes, and he produced a blue ink pen to begin his work.

"Over here at the table," Andre said, putting a little bass in his voice. That was just like a teenager to dull the mood so quickly with his insolence.

"Can I go into your room?" DeAndre asked.

"No," Andre said firmly.

"You all are talking and stuff. Plus you got that sad music playing," DeAndre said, referring to the format change to slow songs on the show the station called, The Original Quiet Storm.

"We're about to talk about your future and what high school you'll be attending next year. It's important that you be here to share your opinion. Let me see what you have to do," Deidre said, trying to sound equally as firm. They watched their son begin marking his paper so quickly that Andre also wondered if he had read and actually understood the directions, or if he were just randomly underlining words to say he had completed it. Andre knew that game too well.

"Let me see," Deidre asked again.

Andre watched her eyes instantly get weary. He could see deep lines etched in her forehead as she frowned and sighed. Andre slammed his hand down on DeAndre's paper and slid it to the middle of the table causing DeAndre's pen to slip leaving a skid mark trail down the paper's edge. DeAndre sat stunned staring at Andre as if he were crazy, and like anyone in a stand-off with a crazy person, he was uncertain how he should respond.

Andre read aloud the directions. He gave Deidre a look to show that he had her back. She blew out a puff of air before knitting her hands and resting her chin on top of them. Apparently she needed him to step in, Andre thought, and he was more than happy to take his rightful place. Once again, her eyes communicated everything she didn't want to say aloud. Andre could tell that she was relieved, if not grateful.

"You need to drop this attitude and listen to those who are trying to help you, especially your mother. I lost my mother when I was about your age. Your mother has taken care of you all these years. I expect you to respect and take care of her in return. I'm serious. I better not ever see you disrespect your mother again. Do I make myself clear?"

"Yeah," DeAndre said sullenly.

"I suggest you check over your work," Deidre said, raking her bangs out of her face. She turned back toward Andre and said, "And he's supposed to be ready for high school."

That was Andre's cue to begin his spiel. He began telling her about the program at Malcolm Woods Creative Arts Magnet High School. Deidre just nodded her head, reserving her judgment to the end. "Sounds good."

"He's got to be accepted into the program though, but he's as good as in if he is recommended for the summer camp." Andre smiled at the thought that he had an inside track.

"It's a far cry from Carver High. You've obviously done your homework." Deidre said downing the last of her green tea soda.

That was easier than he thought it would be. Andre

shot her a satisfied grin, and she returned it. "I have to admit, I paid a visit to DeAndre's school, and Mr. Talbert said he'd be more than happy to recommend Deuce for the camp."

"I know all about the school. I asked DeAndre about your conversation and checked into it myself," she let on.

Andre couldn't believe she stole his thunder. So much for impressing her. She couldn't just let him have this one thing. He started to get angry when he felt a poke in his shin under the table. He sat back just enough to peer at the flyaway heel of Deidre's shoe dangling off her foot. It was the little things like that he remembered about her in those quiet thoughtful times around his apartment.

He immediately started thinking about the delicate arch of her foot and the muted shades of nail polish she wore on her toes in the summertime. He thought about her soft but solid frame and pouty mouth. He also loved the way her hair fell into her eyes. She always had one of those perfect bob haircuts that made every hair seem to fall into place even when she raked her hand through it like she was doing now. Yeah, she was a control freak, but she drove him crazy in ways he knew that no other woman would.

"I really want him to be recognized for his talents. It can really take him somewhere. I initially went up to the school because I was so mad he had been passed over as one of the students creating a mural in his school."

"Mural, what mural? Now that I didn't know," Deidre said, looking from father to son. "What else have you been hiding?"

Andre and Deidre watched as DeAndre seem to search his mental Rolodex. "Kenya asked me to go with her to their eighth grade prom."

Andre laughed and Deidre just shook her head. He couldn't believe his son was getting play from girls already. He hoped Deidre was ready for the attention De-Andre was apt to receive from other females when he got to that new school and started showing off his true talent.

"So are you asking me can you go?" Deidre asked.

"Us," Andre said. "I haven't even heard of an eighth grade prom, and second, I haven't even met this girl."

Deidre jumped in. "Oh, Kenya is a sweetheart. They are in the same Sunday School class at church."

"Her dad is going to take us or you can just drop me off," DeAndre stammered.

"Remind me to talk to Marilynn about the details in church."

"It's in two weeks. They get out for the summer early."

"My boy got a little private school girl sweating him," Andre said. "Well, I guess the boy is finally off punishment."

"No. I'm willing to make a concession for Kenya's sake, but know this: Mr. Hicks is still on restriction until he brings me a report card stamped promotion."

"Yeah, I heard that," Andre said, pushing himself up from the table after a leisurely stretch. "Help me clear the table and wash the dishes."

It was getting late, and as much as Andre wanted to pull out the covers for them all to camp out in the front room, he knew Deidre would be making her exit soon. DeAndre excused himself to the bathroom. Andre looked back at Deidre through the ledge opening. She appeared to be in no rush to leave. He didn't want to be cocky, but he thought she was really feeling him. Like a chapter he read in *The Donovan Way* last night, maybe the vibe he put out in the air tonight was returning to him. If Deidre was feeling for him half as much as he was feeling her, it had returned ten fold.

Andre turned up the volume on the radio. He wanted

to call the radio station and thank the deejay for selecting just the right songs. They were playing "My First Love" by Renee and Angela, and he wondered if Deidre was thinking about them as she sat there. In his fascination, he accidentally ran the crease of his hand across a knife in the bottom of the sink. The sudsy dish water became tinted as he brought his hand to the surface. The air on his open cut made his hand throb at the site.

"Shoot," he said, making a conscious effort to refrain from cursing. He groaned again; this time from a pain in his abdomen. He began shallow breaths until the pain subsided.

Deidre came into the kitchen wide-eyed. Apparently thinking the cut was the major source of his discomfort. She took a dish towel, and immediately wrapped it around his hand and held it there.

"Do you have a bandage or something?" she asked, still holding his hand to yield the flow of blood that saturated a small area of the dishtowel.

Andre tried to think where he last had his first aid kit. He yelled his son's name.

"Yeah," DeAndre answered from behind the closed door of the bathroom.

"Bring my first aid kit. I believe it's in the cabinet under the sink or in the linen closet."

"Hurry," Deidre cried out.

"I'm fine," Andre said. "It's no rush."

They could hear the commode being flushed, then the faint sounds of movement as DeAndre attended to his next task.

Andre watched Deidre lovingly nurture his wound. She checked to see if the pressure she had applied had helped to stop the flow of blood. He couldn't help thinking they were closer than they had been in years. He loved that he was taller but didn't tower over her. Her lavender scent with a hint of baby powder invaded his nostrils and took over his thoughts. He wondered what she would do if he kissed her. Before he could contemplate the answer, he had lifted her chin with his good hand and his mouth was on hers. He sensed that she was about to pull away when he intensified the kiss. Their kiss had become a sales pitch for all that he had hoped their relationship could be. Finally, she used the same hand that tended to his wound to push him away seconds before their son entered the room with the first aid kit.

Andre was not sure what DeAndre had seen, but he greeted him at the entrance to the kitchen. In one swift movement, he took the first aid kit from DeAndre with his good hand and reached across the counter for his keys. He held up his injured hand to block Deidre's way as if in some kind of hostage situation. He didn't have to look at her to know she was ready to flee.

"Deuce, I need you to go get my mail from the mailboxes downstairs," Andre said, almost flinging the keys at his son. "It's the little keys. The one with sixty-five on it belongs to Ms. Mulligan, the older lady on the sixth floor. Get hers also and take it to her."

DeAndre looked from his father to his mother in confusion before he aimed a nasty scowl at Andre.

"Go, now," Andre said sternly, but DeAndre didn't leave the apartment. He must have taken what he had said earlier to heart, because he looked like he was ready to stand up in his mother's defense. He was like a little solider waiting for his battle orders from Deidre. Andre could only imagine how all this must look to DeAndre.

"Go ahead. Quickly, I'm ready to go," Deidre said.

Andre blew a sigh of relief when DeAndre took off for the door. He turned to face his son's mother and saw that her disposition had changed. Her eyes were downcast and her arms guarded across her chest. Had he been wrong about the vibe he had been receiving from her all night?

"What was that all about?" she stammered. "God, Dre, do you even know what you are doing? Do *we* know what we're doing?"

"We were kissing. I figured we were getting along so well. I think it proved that we haven't missed a beat. Everything seemed so natural . . . like home, you know."

"You abandoned our home, remember? And as far as missing a beat, try eight years."

Andre stood there frozen by her words as Deidre passed by him into the living room. He watched her collect her things, not believing they were back to square one. He regretted not being able to keep his emotions in check.

"I'm sorry for—" Andre said.

"You know what, Dre? I'm sorry. I shouldn't have brought up the past. What's done is done. I've prayed about this; I have, and I've forgiven you," Deidre said, interrupting him, her voice brimming with emotion. "I'm tired and just a little confused right now, and if there is anything that I've learned from my momma it's that God ain't in confusion. So I'd better go."

Andre didn't know what was she confused about. He couldn't think of anything to say to rectify the situation, so he kept quiet. The last thing he wanted to do was make matters worse.

"Tell DeAndre, I'll be waiting in the car."

"Hey, Dee, don't go like this," Andre attempted, but Deidre just shook her head as she made her way to the door. Her mind was made up. He watched her do what she did best. Retreat.

Andre thought about the evening's events long after DeAndre had returned with the mail and his keys before leaving with his mother. He knew deep down in his heart she was still in love with him. It was in her intensity, her conflict, her fight. What was holding them back?

Andre's apartment felt foreign to him. It took him awhile to get his bearings and bandage his own hand. He then popped a pill and prepared to retire, but the radio station was playing Marvin Gaye. He couldn't cut off Marvin. Andre couldn't help thinking about Deidre as he sang along. "C'mon c'mon c'mon c'mon, c'mon baby, stop beating 'round the bush."

Chapter 25

DeAndre wondered how he had become so lucky. How else could he explain an unexpected sleepover with his boys at his dad's crib, even if it was for one night? His mom was picking them up on Saturday night from the mall, so that they would be ready bright and early Sunday morning for Youth Day Services at church.

DeAndre noticed that both his mom and his dad were acting weird after the other night. He assumed his dad had done something really offensive and his mom had to check him on it. Somehow his dad's hand had ended up sliced like a Thanksgiving turkey, and his mom wasn't taking any of his calls for the rest of the week.

DeAndre remembered hearing the brief telephone message Andre left Deidre on the answering machine.

"Yeah, Dee, it's me. (Sigh) Deuce informed me that I was picking him up from the twins' house today since I would have the three of them. (Heavy sigh) You and I both know we're going to have to talk eventually. Just let me know what's up . . . what you're thinking. All right, that's all I'm going to say. Call me."

Yeah. His dad must have done something really bad, DeAndre thought. He didn't spend much time contemplating his parents' drama. This was the perfect time to talk to the twins. He was going out of his mind trying to figure out what he was going to do about Kenya and her request to fool around after the prom. He knew his mother would make it a point to speak with Kenya's mom at church on Sunday, and if she approved of the details, it was on and poppin'.

DeAndre was so anxious just thinking about the requirements of being Kenya's date that he had an ongoing wave of nausea. He figured he must not be normal. Every other boy he knew would kill to be in his predicament, or at least that was the talk. Bentley talked about girls who walked by in the neighborhood and their individual private parts as if they were in a variety bucket of fried chicken of which he had dibs on the breasts and thighs. Maybe DeAndre just wasn't as curious as most, but as strange as it may sound, he was content with his and Kenya's relationship they way it was.

On the other hand, she was sold on the idea of having sex. Kenya told him it was just something she had to experience before starting high school. And since he was the chosen one, DeAndre figured he shouldn't question her timeline. She was fast to point out that refraining from premarital sex hadn't been a hard and fast rule with either of their parents. He was hoping that his buddies could help him this weekend with the more technical aspects of sex, or at least enough to fudge his way through it. Any way he sliced it, he and Kenya were about to commit premeditated sin. All he knew was that if God should question him, he planned on playing dumb and ratting Kenya out like Adam did Eve.

The problem was that DeAndre's dad hadn't left him and the twins alone for more than ten minutes since he'd picked them up. They got to Andre's house a little after seven, and before DeAndre knew it, his father was sitting between them on the floor with one plain cheese pizza and one veggie pizza with a six pack of organic ginger ale, debating with Rob and Rajah about which Spiderman movie was best. DeAndre wanted to ask, *Don't you have to go call my mom or something? Keep trying, she should be home.*

An idea formulated in DeAndre's mind as they rode to the mall in his dad's Buick Lasabre the next morning. He tried to give the twins a warning look to play along as he requested that his dad drop them at the library about one mile from the mall. Andre, who had recently been a major proponent for his education, was even skeptical.

"I have to do some research for this project. It's really important," DeAndre pleaded.

"What kind of project, Deuce?" Andre sounded annoyed. "And why are you just telling me about it? Your mom didn't even mention it to me."

"It's on the Colonial South." DeAndre borrowed the title of his last chapter of his social studies book. "I just got to get a few facts about government, agriculture, and stuff . . . maps, you know."

"I don't like the way you put stuff off until the last minute. You can't do things that way at your new school. I bet it's due on Monday too."

DeAndre watched his father look in his rear view mirror at the twins in the backseat. Rob was engrossed in a song he was listening to through his headphones. Rajah must have felt so guilty about the obvious lie that he added, "I don't have that project, but I'm going to help my man out."

DeAndre's father just shook his head at the absurdity of it all. "I've got to get to work, and you're telling me you've got to go to the library."

"You can just drop us off, and we'll walk back to the mall."

DeAndre couldn't tell if his father had digested his lie. DeAndre felt that he was turning into a habitual liar. He had to keep his ends tied up tight before it all began unraveling on him.

"You get in there and get the information you need," his dad said, rolling past the mall on the left hand side to enter the residential area that nestled the library. "I'm giving you two hours to get back to the mall before I come looking for you. I know one thing, your butts better be where you say you're going to be. Hear what I say?"

"Yes, sir," DeAndre said as he and the twins got out the car in front of the library.

DeAndre led the way into the facility since he was the only one who actually knew what they were doing there.

"Remind me to never sleep at your house again. I'm trying to get to the Game Stop and this kid got me at the library," Rob said once he was out of the car. "That is why we never let you decide anything."

"Look, I've been trying to tell y'all about Kenya since yesterday," DeAndre said, as if briefing them before going in the library.

"Nobody is trying to hear about your girl all the time," Rob said under his breath.

"She told me that she wants to go all the way. And soon; like two weeks from now."

"All the way, all the way?" Rajah asked.

DeAndre nodded his head and widened his eyes, sensing that they could feel how monumental the situation was.

"Word? So what are we doing here? Is she supposed to meet you here or something? Hey yo, what about her girl, Jasmine? I thought you were supposed to hook me up with her," Rob said, taking a sudden interest.

They were blocking the entrance to the library, and had to move each time someone wanted to enter or exit, but they knew they couldn't continue their discussion inside.

"I'm going to look up a book to give me some ideas . . . *know what I mean?*" DeAndre said. "Unless you are trying to school a brother, since you're the one with the experience. What about you and that girl, Neicy, your cousin's friend?"

"Experience?" Rajah asked surprised. "She flashed her *breastesis* to him in the back of my cousin's van."

Rob jutted his lips forward and shook his head emphatically. "Twin doesn't know what went down between me and her. Plus I don't want to mess with her."

DeAndre should have known that Rob was lying about going all the way with that girl when he told him not to mention anything to Rajah. How do you keep something like that from your twin? Why would he lie about something like that?

DeAndre made his way inside with the twins following closely on his heels. He gave his library card to a woman behind the information desk in exchange for an available computer. She pointed the way to station number six along the wall. He hurriedly took the only available seat, leaving the twins hovering over him.

"Watch out, dog," Rob said, pushing DeAndre out of the way. He typed the word *sex* into the browser and pressed enter. The screen immediately began flashing a message that read, YOU HAVE ATTEMPTED TO ENTER A RESTRICTED SITE.

DeAndre slapped Rob on the back of his neck and knocked him out of the way. He pushed the back arrow halting the visual alert. He was used to getting similar warnings on his mother's computer, which locked him out of certain sites on the Internet at home. "I'm trying to get a book. Use the library catalog, not the Internet. You're going to get us tossed up out of here."

"Excuse me, gentleman. May I remind you that this is a library," the librarian warned.

"Shhh," Rajah reiterated, placing his index finger on his lips.

"Just stand there and block the screen," DeAndre said, taking a seat. His fingers exploded across the keyboard as if he were trying to hack into the CIA's mainframe. The screen filled with what seemed like hundreds of titles with the same general call number. DeAndre didn't take the time to write anything down. Committing the numbers to memory, he logged off, retrieved his library card from the librarian and signaled for the twins to follow him to the nonfiction section.

The twins got in covert operations mode, standing on lookout at the end of a row of books. DeAndre scanned the shelves, partially pulling a few books from their place to examine them further. He came across two thick volumes with the words *Illustrated Guide* in the title, and knew he had struck gold.

"Psst," DeAndre said, "I found a couple of books."

DeAndre flashed the books' cover to the twins after getting their attention. The twins huddled around him and the books as they thumbed through each so they all could view the contents. In one book, DeAndre noticed each spread had an artist rendition of a nude, slightly pudgy, middle-aged couple in various positions. The other book showed a cutaway diagram merging the female and male genitalia in different positions. DeAndre found the sketches in one too abstract and the diagrams in the other as impersonal and mechanical as a brochure illustrating how to fit the nozzle of a gas pump into a car's gas tank.

The books weren't what DeAndre expected. He was disappointed that the books didn't show what he really needed to know like how people get to that point. The book with the nude couples that was supposed to be the sex encyclopedia for the new millennium according to a blurb on the back cover didn't even show how two people got that close. DeAndre figured there had to be a guide that showed that.

DeAndre passed the first book to Rob who became transfixed with the pages and slapped Rajah on his neck as he giggled his way through each page. DeAndre tossed the diagram book aside and began taking other books from the shelf. He was looking for definitive answers to his own personal questions. He needed to know how many telephone conversations he and Kenya had to have to get that close. How many sketches did he have to draw for her and how many kisses did they have to pass in the park. Even if they printed that kind of information, DeAndre knew that he and Kenya had not met their quota.

"Why are you pulling down all those other books? Dog, this is the one right here," Rob assured.

"Yeah, but how am I going to check it out? They're not just going to let some kid walk out with a sex book."

"Let me handle this. All you need to do is get another book just as thick to go on top of this. They are not studying the titles that closely when they scan them," Rob said

DeAndre knew exactly what book to get. Once again he led the way across the library to the section of art books labeled in the 700's. He skipped the shelves of books about classic artists like VanGogh and Picasso and went to the cartoonist section where they had books devoted to the father of modern comic books, Stan Lee, and other comic book artists. DeAndre felt like he could spend the day in this row.

"Yo, just pick something," Rajah said.

DeAndre picked *The Golden Age of DC Comics*. Rob impatiently grabbed the book from him and added, "Give me your library card." DeAndre and Rajah watched nervously as he approached the circulation desk. Rob purposely plopped the books down with the spine forward. After giving the librarian, an elderly gentleman with glasses and a curvature in the spine, his card, he engaged him in a conversation about a popular science fiction series among teens. He made sure to sandwich the books between his two hands to assist the man in scanning the barcode.

"Well, they certainly are popular, aren't they? The new one just came out, so it won't appear on our shelves for, goodness, another six weeks; maybe not 'til the end of the summer. You may want to check with someone in the juvenile section, because I believe there is a waiting list already, but we got plenty of books one through six."

"Naw, that's all right. I'll wait for the movie," Rob said with a satisfied look on his face when the man had done his scanning.

"Well, all right. These books are due back in two weeks."

In two weeks I'll be with Kenya, DeAndre thought. Only God knew in what capacity. He began to try and absorb the information from the sex manual as they walked back toward the mall. He became overwhelmed with the images so he closed the book.

Once inside the mall, DeAndre placed both books from the library inside his backpack along with two sketchbooks. He struggled to get the zipper halfway around with the additional bulk. His father was on rounds when they checked in at the security desk, so they left a message for him and continued to the Game Stop on the far end. After a half an hour of watching the mall regulars play Tony Hawk's Underground and NBA Live on the newest gaming system with no hopes of getting a turn, they left. The three of them decided to get a bite to eat at the food court where they ate junk and spent a good portion of the afternoon people watching and making fun of each other.

The mall had more than enough colorful characters to talk about. They could hear a group of people screaming and running and had chalked it up to be a prank until it became eerily silent afterward. DeAndre began to notice the crowd around them had thinned significantly in the recessed food court. *It's rather empty for a Saturday,* he thought, as they began to make their way back to the security station. There were even some stores bringing down their gates. Just then, his father came up behind him and gripped his shoulders tightly with his hands.

"When I say check in with me, I mean find me, wherever I am, and check in with *me,*" Andre said, slapping his own chest. "Do you understand?"

"Yes," DeAndre said. His father began leading him briskly through the maze of seating in the food court by the shoulders while beckoning for the twins to pick up the pace and follow.

DeAndre wondered why, all of a sudden, he was being treated like a child who had wandered away from his parent and gotten lost. He did this every Saturday when he was with his dad.

"The mall exits have been locked for your safety. Everyone needs to follow me," his father announced generally. Then he got on his radio. "I got them Ernie, and I'm bringing them back."

"What's going on?" Rajah asked.

"The mall is on lockdown. Didn't you hear the announcement?" DeAndre's father said.

DeAndre thought he heard something on the muffled intercom, but figured it was Ernie announcing another item brought into the lost and found by a Good Samaritan. They turned into a side hallway that led to the public restrooms, as well as the administrative offices at the very end. DeAndre had a bad feeling as he wondered what could have happened to shut a whole mall down. It had to be a terrorist attack or a natural disaster going on outside.

As if reading his mind, his father shared, "Shots were fired around the beauty shop. We think there might be a few people injured. So we are waiting for the police to arrive."

A collective cry of concern came from the few mall patrons who followed through the spacious office suites divided by cubicles. A few chairs were brought out by the office staff as the others took to the floor, including the twins, to await directions. Ernie and a mall administrator approached as DeAndre was about to tell his dad something.

"Did you secure the south end?" the mall administrator asked.

"That's the police's job. I got my son and his friends. I followed procedure, by alerting the police and calling for a lockdown. Your rickety intercom system is no good, by the way. I had to personally go down the directory to call store managers. That's it. I'm not playing hero today."

"But dad," DeAndre said, looking at his watch that read 6:15 P.M. He bent slightly at the waist to take off his backpack that began wearing on his shoulder, dropping a book in the process.

Time slowed to what seemed like a halt as DeAndre watched his dad stoop before him and come up with what DeAndre hoped was anything but the sex guide. Peaking at the cover confirmed that that was wishful thinking. He figured this must be God's way of exposing his plans to his dad. DeAndre temporarily closed his eyes and braced himself for the start of a heated lecture, until he remembered what he was going to say.

"Dad," DeAndre shouted this time. "Mom. She told me she'd be coming early to shop before actually picking us up. She might be out there."

DeAndre's father bolted for the door. The weighty book hitting the floor simulated the sound of a handgun and gave everyone a chilly reminder of why they were on lockdown in the mall office suite on a Saturday afternoon.

Chapter 26

Andre didn't know where he was going; he just ran. Thoughts of Deidre being in harm's way propelled him on. He took the side hallway back to the expanse of the now deserted mall. His heart pounded in his chest the same way it did when he ran the five miles up Pennsylvania Avenue and back each morning. He didn't have an ID on the perpetrator, or a detailed report on the incident: he just had to get to the mother of his child.

Andre switched off his radio, not wanting to draw attention to himself just in case the "perp" was still on the loose. In a lockdown, mall workers were instructed to get as many patrons out of the halls and into their store before closing their gates until being further instructed. Most people panicked when the initial shots were fired, and many absentmindedly risked getting shot themselves by storming the nearest exit doors. A surge of people ran past the security station screaming their own versions of what had happened, which sparked Andre to alert the police and call for the lockdown.

Andre had no idea where Deidre could be. The mall had over 120,000 square feet of commercial and retail space to cover. He remembered DeAndre saying she came early to do some shopping. The north end housed a few specialty shops, but mostly urban outfitters for a younger crowd. Deidre was a namebrand girl. The south end had the department stores and the more high-end boutiques where he was certain she would prefer to shop. The south end is also where the beauty parlor and the shootings occurred.

Andre stopped at the security station and got Ernie's revolver out of the metal safe. His colleague didn't like wearing his holster when he was sitting down, which was all of the time. Andre recalled the mall manager expecting him to pay for his own weapons training course, practice range time, licensure fee, and revolver when he started this job at the beginning of the year because as he put it, "A mall this size only needs one armed officer, and Ernie is, after all, a combat veteran." Andre knew his supervisor was just being stingy with his operating budget and didn't want his security guys using the mall's guns and training for their after hours moonlighting gigs at clubs and nursing homes.

Andre was dragging his heels completing the required training module. He was becoming dissatisfied more and more with his job. He was tired of walking blindly into other people's disputes and problems like a sitting duck before the hunting range. He was the one with the least experience, but always expected to complete the rounds and investigate every complaint.

Once again when everybody else moved away from a problem, he was forced into the trenches. He had to find out what was going on. He moved laterally along the wall with the revolver at his side. He came upon the scene of the crime and was relieved to see the boys in blue busily putting down police tape to mark of the area of investigation. The crime scene covered a large area from the beauty parlor all the way to the door of the promenade. Andre couldn't ignore the article of clothing and splatters of blood as he approached a stocky officer chewing gum.

"I'm the security guard on duty that placed the call. I need to know how to proceed so that we can get these people home with as much order as possible," Andre said, thumbing in the direction of the gated stores.

"It's going to be awhile before we evacuate this place. I've got three witnesses from the beauty shop that need to be interviewed and the guys from the bureau got to get in here before we let people traipse all over my crime scene," the officer said in a thick northern accent. "You need to talk to the chief about the evacuation plan because it's murder out there on the parking lot. The press got wind of it, and now we got vigilantes about to tear down this building to make sure their loved ones are all right."

Andre swallowed a huge lump in his throat when he asked, "What exactly happened?"

"Domestic," The officer said as if he dealt with that sort of thing all the time. "The worst kind."

"Was there anyone injured . . . you know, fatally?"

His questions were waved off as another uniformed cop approached him with a roll of excess barrier tape.

Andre was careful to walk around the tape to get a peek outdoors. The parking lot was packed, and several police cars, with their revolving lights still flashing, were parked in the tow-away zone. He looked back at the three women, two of which Andre identified as employees of the beauty parlor. They were all huddled together on a mall bench;

faces drained of make up and stained with tears. He knew they could answer his questions, but that would be out of order to launch his own personal inquiries.

Andre pushed through the disengaged automatic doors. He approached the man he assumed was the chief with the gray suit and credentialed lapel.

"Andre Hicks, mall security," Andre said with a hand extended.

"Right," the chief said, ignoring his hand. "You're not the one I just talked to in the office?"

"No, sir, I've been . . . uh, monitoring the lockdown."

"Well, excuse me for saying this, but your people don't know their pie holes from their butt holes. I asked Moe a question, and he's got to ask Larry. Tell me you aren't Curly."

"No, sir," Andre said, although he knew he was only as smart as his leadership.

"I was hoping they sent you out here with the evacuation plan that I asked for to downgrade this nightmare to a bad dream."

"Evacuation plan, right. I'll get on that," Andre said.

"I'm glad someone knows where it is. Tell the mall manager it's required for a public facility."

"What happened?"

"Well, a girl decides to get from under her boyfriend's thumb, insert her independence with the backing of her beauty shop girlfriends. He leaves, waits for her to come out and shoots her at point blank range in the middle of the mall. Then thinks it's the OK Corral and starts firing into the crowd."

Andre felt his blood run cold. *This cannot be happening.*

"Luckily, you got a real maze out there in the parking lot. He didn't get real far. Tried to take a shot at the first responders. My boys had to take him out. Got another scene about fifty yards from here. So we may have to re-route everybody coming from this end," the chief said matter-of-factly, then switched up and got real stern. "Now, go get me that plan."

Andre snapped out of his trance, "But chief, who was injured?"

"Are you kidding me? I didn't memorize the names. There are three in all though. They're on their way to PG Hospital with the girlfriend and the perp in body bags."

Andre didn't need anymore prompting. He practically slammed into the glass door in his haste to get inside again. He had unfinished business, and it wasn't drafting an evacuation plan. He had to find Deidre. It was the only way to prove she wasn't on the way to the hospital.

With no impending danger to himself, Andre began to go store by store looking for Deidre. He kept thinking there was no way he could go back to the office to face his son without any information about his mother. Although some stores had the extra assurance of a heavy tarp, most only had a metal gate that divided the people on lockdown from the outside mall. Andre could see the petrified eyes of people who tried their best to be silent and remain hidden as he called through the gate, "Mall security . . . bear with us . . . we'll be starting evacuation shortly. I'm looking for a Deidre Collins. Deidre Collins . . . is there a Deidre Collins in there?"

There were only two remaining stores on either side of the anchoring department store at the end: a bookstore and a jewelry store. Andre knew finding her in a department store would be like finding that needle in a haystack. He yelled out Deidre's name in desperation and heard a response come from the jewelers.

Andre hurried over to The Diamond Galleria. It took some persuading before the Ethiopian proprietors raised his gate midway to allow Andre to enter. He saw Deidre crouched in the middle of the U shaped showcases. She was the sole customer in the store. Even with the lights dimmed, he could see overwhelming relief wash through her initial excitement to see him. She began to cry as he approached her. She stood, as if expecting some kind of consolation, then sat on a stool sensing he was unable to give what she needed. He wanted to hug her, kiss her; he wanted to weep, but he could not do any of these things.

"Oh my God, Andre," Deidre cried. "The boys. Where are the boys?"

"The boys are fine."

"Oh, thank you, God," Deidre said.

Andre put a hand up to halt any further questions. He had forgotten that he had his radio turned off the entire time and felt the need to check in now that he had some news to share.

"Hicks, you're crazier than I thought you were. Why in the world didn't you have your ears turned on? What's going on out there?" Ernie's voice yelled through the radio speakers.

Andre could tell that Deidre and the proprietors huddled on the other side of the glass cases wanted to know those answers as well. He kept that in mind as he thought about his response. There was really no way to gloss over an otherwise horrendous event.

"We got two fatalities and three injured on their way to the hospital. The shooter was one of them taken out on the south lot by the cops. We need to get the chief the evacuation plan, pronto."

"Well, you need to get back here. You know nobody knows what they are talking about."

"For heaven sake, tell Roland to get the floor plan of the mall out and go from there," Andre said, losing patience for a moment. "One more thing, tell my son his mom is all right."

Andre clicked his radio off once more.

"He shot her?" Deidre asked with her head hanging in disbelief. "Oh God, I was right there. I thought about getting my hair done, you know, like get a walk-in appointment. Then I thought maybe DeAndre could use that money for whatever he may need for Kenya's dance. I saw him come in and grab her arm. I left, you know, like I don't need that kind of scene. Oh God, I never thought anything like this would happen."

Andre ignored the signs that warned against leaning on the glass showcase. He propped on his arms and looked down upon the diamond solitaires and platinum bands. It didn't help to hear that she was anymore closer to the fire than he had originally thought.

Andre remained silent as he thought about what he wanted to say to her in the aftermath of such senselessness. It took a moment, but when he finally spoke his voice was surprisingly calm and sure.

"When I left you, all those years back, I always thought you'd come back to me. I mean, that was the hope. You know, like the old saying, when you love someone, you can let them go and eventually they'll come back. I believed that," Andre said.

Andre placed his finger on Deidre's lips to silence her before she could comment. He looked in her wide fawn-like eyes for the first time since entering the store and slid his hand down her cheek to caress it. He didn't care that the Ethiopian couple brazenly watched them as if they were characters in their own soap opera.

"I know you've been avoiding me, and believe it or not, I'm not trying to bring anymore stress in your life. The other night when I kissed you, I just thought . . . I thought you had come back to me; that's all," Andre said, standing and taking one last look at her before walking to the entrance and bending to clear the gate. "The boys are in the mall office. You can come and get them when the lockdown is over."

Chapter 27

"People come into our lives for a lifetime or just a season, but definitely for a reason," Emmanuel Brown, the adult Sunday School teacher, said. "How are you impacting the people in your life? What do you think is the reason God places people in our lives?"

"To show God's love," said one person.

"To help you learn about yourself," said another.

Deidre sat in confusion on the third row of the church's classroom. This discussion didn't correspond with the lesson she had marked in her Standard Lesson Commentary they usually used for class. She was amazed that she had even made it to class that morning. The events of the day before had taken a toll on her and left her with a fitful night's rest. LaKeisha, the twins' mother, having heard about the mall shooting incident on the television news, met Deidre at her house at 10:45 last night to collect her sons. It was doubtful that she or DeAndre would have the stamina to stay for the Youth Day services, but she at least wanted to be in the house of the Lord to show her gratitude for sparing them from being the victims of a violent crime.

"Those were all good answers. Well, that's going to be our focus for this class. If you've been in church the past couple of Sundays, you know that Pastor Tatum charged us all with bringing at least one of our loved ones and acquaintances unto the knowledge of our Lord and Savior Jesus Christ. Our goal is one soul. He's serious about this, folks. He met with his teaching staff this past week. He told us to think about it like this; most people will recommend their favorite restaurant to someone before they offer Christ to even their closest relatives. What do you think about that?" her teacher said from the front of the classroom, peeking often at a sheet of paper that, no doubt, was his script for today's discourse.

There was a period of silence. Deidre felt it spoke volumes about how viable Christians had become in the world.

"What if you've been down that road?" a lady named Marilynn Mathews shared. "It's a waste of time and breath speaking to some of my relatives in regard to religion."

"What if God felt that way about you?" said a flat voice from the far right who Deidre immediately identified as her best friend, Sheila. A few *amens* followed from others in the class.

The teacher nodded and said, "That's a good point; God didn't feel that way about us when He repeatedly offered us salvation. Don't get me wrong, there are some people who don't want to know Christ and aren't going to change no matter what you tell them."

Marilynn turned in her seat to face her critics behind her. "I think you all are misunderstanding me. The only commonality I have with certain people in my family, even my own siblings, is the same surname and a slight resemblance."

"Let's not forget we've got to pray for people. Sometimes that's all we can do," the teacher's soft spoken wife said.

"That's a good point." The instructor took a turn to speak again. "Pastor was clear that he's not talking about some radical evangelism here, but rather equipping everyone so that we are comfortable and willing to explain our faith with those who come to us. You're not handing out flyers on the corner about that restaurant you love either, but at least you're open and prepared to talk about it should the opportunity arise."

"I was at that teacher training with Pastor also," Brother Carl Stephens echoed. "Don't just think of this as Pastor Tatum's assignment for us, but God's. 'Cause I'll tell you one thing, the devil is not going to miss his chance to tempt and devour those we miss."

"Well, it makes a lot of sense to me. It's my desire that my entire family be saved," Sheila said.

"Your entire family? Good luck," Marilynn's husband scoffed. "I'll believe that when it happens."

"Remember this isn't some scorecard of people we can parade down the aisle at Sunday service. Salvation is about acknowledging and forging a relationship with Jesus. It doesn't even have to happen in church," Brother Brown said.

Deidre was surprised by that comment. She thought the pastor standing at the altar doing his best Bob Barker, "Come on down" routine was a precursor to salvation.

"So what are we supposed to do? Give everyone a Bible and hope they find Christ?" Marilynn said.

"That's a start. That's why we are here today. Where in

the Bible can you direct someone to find God's gift of salvation?" the teacher said, once again relying on his script.

"John 3:16," Deidre found herself saying under her
breath until she was encouraged by the lady beside her
to repeat it louder.

"Sure, that's what Pastor calls a nutshell verse. It has
the major components of God's love, His sacrifice of
His only son for us which buys our salvation. Romans
10:9 is another nutshell verse. Hopefully you have your
Bibles and something to take notes with. Pastor would
like everyone to learn the Roman Road."

Brother Brown explained that certain scriptures
through the Book of Romans, known as the Roman Road,
provide scriptural evidence as to the relationship God
desires to have with all of mankind through His Son,
Jesus Christ. He used the stubby remnant of chalk to
write Romans 3:23, Romans 5:8 and 12, 6:23, and 10:9-13,
which most wrote down to reference later. Deidre tried to
imagine flipping the pages of the Bible with Renita at
work, or even Andre, and sort of felt like Marilynn when
she started to doubt the probability of that happening. In
the interest of time, Brother Brown summarized the path
to salvation from those scriptures and a sample prayer
that professes newfound faith. He encouraged each of
them to journey down the road themselves during their
personal Bible study time.

After Sunday School and a brief conversation with
Sheila, promising her the full details of the mall incident,
Deidre caught up with Marilynn as she was about to
leave.

"I think a lot of people felt the way you did in class
and just didn't say anything," Deidre said by way of a
greeting.

"I know. My family will surely crowd around my

honey-baked ham at Easter, but let's see how many fill
my row during service. They're hopeless."

"They might surprise you one year," Deidre said. "De-
Andre tells me that Kenya wants him to take her to her
eighth grade promotional dance."

Marilynn scoffed. "Kenya also wants to be Beyoncé,
but we both know that's not going to happen. Kenya will
be going to the dance with her best friend, Jasmine. Jasmine's brother has already agreed to take them. Really,
Deidre, you might be anxious for your son to grow up,
but if you don't mind, I'm trying to keep my daughter as
innocent as I can, for as long as I can. Stop encouraging
this little infatuation your son has for my daughter. I
mean, really."

Oh no she didn't. "You know what, Marilynn, I'm sorry
you mistook my intentions. I can assure you, though,
the infatuation is mutual. The way I see it, we could encourage our children to have healthy *friend*ships or dis-
courage them, and let them hide their relationships
behind our backs. I'm sure you'll have your daughter
do the right thing and un-invite my son." *No wonder no
one in her family can relate to her*, Deidre thought, stomping away.

Marilynn sounded eerily like Deidre's mother, who
proved that she would do anything to keep her and
Andre apart. Maybe she wouldn't have rebelled so much
if her mother was willing to at least get to know Andre.

Deidre thought about her own relationship with
Andre now as she walked out to her car. As much as the
mall events were on her mind for much of the night, the
brief conversation she had with Andre in the jewelry
store had weighed upon her heart. It felt oddly like an invitation and a resignation at the same time. Deidre felt
herself resenting the mixed emotions he conjured up. She

and Andre had had their season, but just like he pointed out, now he was back. Could she trust him with her heart again? Her heart wanted to believe, but that was a question for him, and she couldn't wait any longer for his answer.

Chapter 28

Deidre stared at a fly trapped on the inside of Andre's car. He started a diagonal pilgrimage up the passenger side window before trailing back down. This was the third such trek Deidre had witnessed before Andre rolled the windows up to set the air conditioning. She agonized knowing that the fly could not free himself because he could not figure out what direction to go in. She swatted at the fly, but he barely moved. Deidre figured he had been trapped so long that his natural instincts had begun to slow, leaving him defenseless.

"Can we cut the air off and open the windows?" Deidre asked.

"Yeah sure," Andre said, eyeing her suspiciously while manipulating the control panel of his dashboard with one hand. "It is rather chilly in here. Although I'm not sure it is from the air conditioning."

Deidre hadn't said much of anything to Andre since he picked her up from her house. She called him when they got in from church and told him that they needed to talk. He agreed. She told DeAndre, who was only interested in sleeping for the rest of the afternoon, that she would be back in less than two hours.

Deidre met Andre at the door when he arrived. She didn't know exactly what she would say to him; she just knew she didn't want to be cooped up indoors when she said it. He suggested the neighborhood parks of Manor Ridge and Watkins, but she turned down those recommendations. Those parks were filled with children and childhood memories of being young and in love and having to hide it from her mother. He was taking her to Allen Pond in Bowie to put some distance between the past and where they were now.

"How did you sleep last night?" Deidre asked him.

"Amazingly well after a hundred or so push-ups and a hot shower," Andre said, stealing glances of her as he drove.

"Only you would do push-ups after a night like that."

"It was all I could do not to make a beer run, and I haven't touched alcohol of any kind in two years."

"I know what you mean. Yesterday was crazy. I mean, at one time during the lockdown, I thought I was actually dreaming the whole thing that is . . . until I saw you," Deidre said, thinking about how she heard his voice piercing through her prayers as she sat in the jewelry store. He took his eyes off the road temporarily and she shared a nervous smile with him.

"Now it's all over the news. I don't know what's worse, being there or reliving it over and over again every half an hour on television. I can't watch the coverage. Tomorrow, I'm back to work. I was hoping we could just close down the mall for a few days to regroup. You never know how unprepared you are until something like this happens. I mean, we didn't even have an evacuation plan mandated by state law."

"Experience is your best teacher. I know I'll be praying

for the salon owner and the other girls that got hurt. I think they said the owner's name is Annette."

"No doubt," Andre said, shaking his head in agreement.

"Do you pray, Andre?"

He sucked in a lungful of air before answering. "I was praying yesterday."

Deidre nodded her head. She was praying now. It was one of those prayers where she didn't pick a desired end, but just left the outcome to the wisdom of God. She felt a certain ease and security with Andre, which left her vulnerable to be hurt again.

At that moment, Deidre realized that she had lost track of the fly. She thought maybe he had found freedom from the slight crack in her window until she spotted him at the base of it. It was as if he had given up. Deidre decided to help him with his release by rolling her window all the way down this time. The breeze caught his wings and reminded him that at one time he could fly.

Deidre felt Andre staring at her after pulling alongside the curb to park. They departed the car and drifted toward the pond's edge. The park was a refreshing change of scenery from the commercial congestion in and around Prince George's County. The manmade lake was deceiving from its view from the street. Only those who actually walked the trail knew how far back the lake sat in the forest of trees.

"Do you want to walk the trail?" Andre asked.

"No," Deidre said, claiming a nearby bench under the shade of a tree. She could barely keep her thoughts straight. She didn't think she could handle walking and talking at the same time.

Deidre was not the outdoorsy type; she suddenly felt something crawling up her arm. She brushed at her arms, exposed from the elbow on down beneath a short sleeve cotton blouse. Andre deciding to stand, twisted at the waist as if he were warming up for the walk anyway. She remembered that he had always found it hard to sit still. That was just one of the differences between them. She took that opportunity to really look at him, but noticed she was not the only one. Just off his shoulder, Deidre caught sight of an attractive woman enthralled by the same subject. She was perky with short, reddish twists design in her hair that was pushed back with a headband. She looked to be preparing to run, incorporating some stretches of her own.

Deidre couldn't blame the woman for her gaping stare. She had already thanked God for the unseasonably warm spring day and the sight of Andre in his grey muscle shirt. Besides his biceps, there was a newfound confidence that was alluring to her. He was so much different, and she had to ask herself if he were the same guy she had fallen in love with. Deidre really didn't want to be swayed by his magnetism. She wanted to test to see if they still had a connection on a much deeper level. She watched the woman head toward the path in a light jog, and decided she'd also do what she came there for.

"Dre," she said, motioning him over and tapping the bench for him to sit next to her. When he took a seat she began. "Let me start off by saying that I think you are doing a great job stepping in with DeAndre, really. It hasn't been at all awkward like I thought it would be."

"But," he said, unmoved by her compliment. He looked at her and turned up the intensity in his eyes, questioning her. "I feel a big fat 'but' coming at the end of that statement. C'mon with it. I've been waiting for you to define this chasm between us."

Deidre didn't know if he spoke out of arrogance or ignorance. In eight years, how could he possibly not know what had been eating away at her? "I know about the little deal you and my mother made when you left."

Deidre noticed he was not so quick to respond this time, and she was glad so she could continue to get out what had been bottled up inside her since finding out the truth.

"I have never been hurt like that in my life," Deidre said, experiencing the return of the pain with the flow of her words, "and by the two people I cared about most in the world."

Andre prepared to defend himself. "You know your mother had it in for me from the beginning. She—"

"Please, Dre. Stop, all right?" Deidre said.

"So what, I can't tell my side?"

"She's my mother, okay. That's a relationship I'm try-ing to salvage. I know how she can be, I really do, but I can't let you bash her any more than I will allow her to bash you," Deidre said, thumbing over her shoulder as if her mother were standing there.

Deidre wiped a few tears from her eyes, and Andre bent at the waist to rest his forearms on his knees. This was going to be more difficult than she thought.

"The worst part was that both of you made a decision about my life without consulting me. My mom went on to South Carolina and you went about your merry way. I guess you all were like, 'Oh, Deidre is strong. She will be okay on her own with a young toddler.'"

"You know that's not how it went down," Andre said, facing her again rather than the pond.

"Oh really? The way I saw it, neither you nor my mother could handle the situation *we* got ourselves in, so you both bowed out, but Deidre was supposed to sur-vive. Let me tell you . . . I was petrified everyday going to work, going to school, and holding down the house-hold," Deidre said.

"That was not the way it was supposed to happen. I couldn't make you understand that I still wanted to be there for you guys and to support you," Andre said. "You put up a wall that was impenetrable. What was I supposed to do?"

"Knock it down," Deidre snapped back, not knowing where that came from.

"I don't believe this." Andre shook his head. "All that time I was begging for you to hear me out and let me in. Now you're telling me that I should have played the caveman role, grabbed you by the hair and shook you till you came to your senses."

Deidre brought one knee into her body and clasped it with her hands as she sat on the bench. The woman from earlier came into view. Could she have made it around the entire lake that quickly? Deidre watched her come and go ahead of another pack of park-goers taking advantage of the trail. Deidre didn't even know why she was so worried about this woman. Maybe it was that this cute and apparently, athletic woman appeared to be a good match for Andre. He must have many women chasing after him, yet he was here with her, trying to figure out where they went wrong. His voice brought her focus back to their conversation.

"I agree that your mother and I left you in a terrible position. I have beat myself up for eight years knowing I wasn't the man you needed me to be."

"I had no one to depend on, but . . . but God," Deidre said, looking skyward; the revelation hitting her like a ton of bricks. *Everything happens for a reason. Accept what God allows. Forgive him,* her quiet inner voice was telling her. She felt an avalanche of pain and disappointment begin to dislodge.

"I must admit now, in hindsight, that your mom wanted the best for you. We weren't ready for that kind of relationship," Andre said, as if he had received the same revelation as she had.

"She was right on many levels," Deidre agreed. "We shouldn't have been shacking up, sharing a bed every night like we were man and wife. We shouldn't have been doing a lot of things."

Deidre didn't know whether to take his long silence as an agreement, so she remained silent also, taking in the scenery and listening again for the voice of God. She knew now that she had given herself to Andre in an attempt to fill the void left by her mother's emotional and eventual physical abandonment.

"Believe it or not, I did put some thought into my exit," Andre said. "What I didn't expect was my father's illness to take me to New York and keep me there for nearly two years. You have to admit though that even before then our relationship was on very shaky ground. I believe you even threatened to throw me out a couple of times. You were angry, and always dissatisfied. Admit it. Your boots were strapped to kick me to the curb."

"Was I supposed to stick around for your slow process of growth? I mean, since I was such a tyrant, what made you stay around as long as you did?" Deidre asked.

Deidre watched Andre rise from the bench to face her. She wrapped her arms around her chest as if to protect her heart.

"C'mon, Dee, do I have to spell it out?" he yelled. "I was foolish enough to think that loving you was enough. Maybe I should ask you the same question. If you were smarter, more mature, and had it all together, what were you doing with a slackard like me?"

"We were in love, sure, but love didn't pay the bills when you kept switching jobs every other day," Deidre said quietly, hoping he would bring his volume down also.

"Forgive me that I hadn't nailed down my life's path in kindergarten like you. That just proves to me that you began to lose respect for me. So yeah, when your mother reinforced that I wasn't good enough for you, I left. I figured I'd speed up the process and have you hate me for leaving rather than stay with you and let what we had turn into loathing."

The truth was hard to hear. Deidre never hated him; she didn't think it were possible. *Lord, what are we doing here?* It felt like they were going backward into resentment. She wondered if rehashing the past was a moot point. She knew now that their separation back then was inevitable, a way for God to get her undivided attention. Back then she wasn't seeing or hearing from God when she was focused on Andre.

Andre sat on the very end of the bench with his back toward Deidre now as if he were done with the whole conversation. She could see the jogging woman bend the corner in the distance. The woman unleashed a broad smile at Andre who was staring straight ahead. The woman's smile seemed to shorten to a smirk as she passed him and made eye contact with Deidre. Good ole' woman's intuition was telling her that this woman could sense the tension between them and was more than willing to help Andre pick up the pieces if things between them didn't work out. The scene urged Deidre on.

"Why didn't you try?" Deidre asked.

"I told you, your mother convinced me that leaving was the only way she'd help you," he said through clenched teeth barely looking over his shoulder when he spoke.

"Not that, I meant when we were together. Why didn't you try to get on your feet? To help me." Her thoughts took over where her voice left off. *To marry me.*

He turned himself on the bench slowly dragging his

long legs over with him. He flung his head back as if to give the question some thought before rubbing his eyes with the palm of his right hand. "I don't know, Dee. Back then, all I was hearing was static, you know, feeling like a cast-off, insecure, the whole nine. I couldn't man up and be there for you replaying that track over and over again. As much as you went through with your mom, at least yours was alive. I wasn't with my parents. I felt sorry for myself." He blew air through his lips and swatted the air with his hands. "That was the past though. I'm tired of blaming. I've found it only weakens you."

"And now?" Deidre said breathlessly, realizing she had a lot riding on his response.

"Now, so much has changed. I'm sure of who I am and what I have to offer. Like I said in the mall, I knew it was only a matter of time before I got back at you."

"What does that mean?" Deidre asked. He was a man of big gestures like the kiss the other night and his hunt for her in the mall the day of the shootings, but she needed the reassurance of his words . . . a vow.

"That means I want another chance to be with you and our son."

Deidre closed her eyes temporarily, allowing herself to drink in the possibility before her internal alarm warned her she had been there, done that. "I just don't know if it's healthy to go backward."

"We're not going back. We are just seeing if we can pick up where we left off. As far as I'm concerned, we've got unfinished business."

"How can we just pick up where we left off? We promised we'd never let go last time, and we both let go."

Andre shook his head in disbelief and laughed. "We were young. Wait a minute, I know Ms. Got-it-all-together-micro-manager is not scared to try."

"Don't you think I have reason to be just a little apprehensive?"

I haven't given you a spirit of fear, Deidre felt in her spirit.

"This has got to work, Dee." Andre stooped to her eye level. "We've got everything it takes to make it work. I'm telling you that you don't have to be scared. I've got you."

Deidre smiled. Everything Andre was saying was being confirmed in her spirit. "How are you so certain?"

"Because it's what I want," he said. "Anything I want, I will invest all my energy into. That's just how it is now; the way it's supposed to be."

"Let me guess, a Bo Donovan principle, right?"

"Yes," Andre said. That unleashed a rumble of laughter from both of them that ended in an anticipatory haze. He extended his hands to help her up. "So what do you say? Let me be nice to you, and you be nice in return. We can pretend that there is no difference between forgiving and forgetting. Isn't it worth a try?"

Deidre nodded, not trusting her voice. She felt a chilling breeze race up her spine. She had found her wings. By the time Ms. Bouncin' Beauty came around for the fourth time, Deidre was walking toward the car arm in arm with her man.

Chapter 29

Deidre adjusted her earpiece and flipped open her cell phone to silence the chorus of Kirk Franklin's, "Looking For You," that she had chosen for a ringtone. She was hoping it was Andre, and although she was preparing to go over to his apartment, she never tired of talking to him. Instead she heard Sheila's voice.

"Hey, Sheila, girl," Deidre sang.

"I'm glad I wasn't really waiting on you to tell me how you and my godson are doing after the mall incident."

"Girl, I'm sorry," Deidre said. Sheila's sarcasm was doing little to squelch her obvious cheerfulness. "We're fine. I believe it has scared DeAndre a little, although it's hard to know what's the deal with a teenager. He's with my sister this weekend. Give him a change of scenery, you know."

"So what's up?"

Deidre felt as if her good friend was fishing for something; she decided to play coy. "Nothing, what's up with you?"

"Come on, Dee, you're holding out on me. Keith called Andre when I couldn't catch up with you. He told him you all were back together."

"It's been less than a week. You know I was going to tell you."

It wasn't as if they had sent out announcements about their reconciliation. They hadn't even told their son, although Deidre knew he had to suspect something when his dad was a guest at their dinner table one night that week. He was also a regular caller on their phone line speaking briefly with DeAndre if he happened to answer before asking to speak to her. Deidre would steal away or whisper replies to his inquiries of, "What are you doing?" She felt like she was thirteen again, love struck and finding great interest in conversations about nothing in particular.

"No, I think this is definitely redemption. I'm happy for you. So what are you up to?" Sheila asked.

"Like I said, DeAndre is out of town, so Dre and I are going to hang out and watch a couple of videos at his house."

Deidre told Sheila she had reached the video store, which meant she had to get off the phone. She was not one to hold a conversation with someone while she walked the aisles of a store, so they said their goodbyes. Sheila hung up with a sing-songy, "Okay," that was a tad judgmental, almost as if to say, *if you say so*. Deidre didn't know what her problem was, but couldn't concern herself with that right now. She had movies to retrieve.

It had taken more than thirty minutes in the video store, not because she didn't know what she wanted, but because the store was so crowded. Deidre didn't know so many people rented DVD's on the weekends. She settled on two of Tyler Perry's latest movies until she lucked up and got a copy of an action flick that she knew Andre would enjoy.

As Deidre drove to Andre's apartment under the cover of nightfall, she felt a part of a special sorority. It had been a while since she felt like one of the selected rather than the rejected. She pushed number 96.3, the adult mix, from her automatic radio settings that had a ballad of undying love playing that she sang along with until she reached her destination.

To her surprise, Andre had company when Deidre got to his apartment. Andre took the movies out of her stunned hands and planted a kiss to the side of her gaping mouth as she stared at a smiling Sheila and Keith sitting on Andre's couch. Not only were they crashing her date, but had done a whodunit move and beat her there.

"What's going on?" Deidre said, thinking she must surely be on a hidden camera show.

"We're going bowling," Andre said, tidying up something in the kitchen.

"Bowling?" Deidre didn't spend a good deal of her afternoon agonizing over what she was wearing to sling a twelve-pound ball around. She finally chose a belted khaki shirt dress over black skinny jeans that silhouetted her shapely legs. Someone was going to tell her something. She turned to Sheila. "Didn't I just talk to you?"

"Yeah, it didn't sound like your plans were sketched in stone, so Keith and I thought it'd be fun to go out like old times." Sheila avoided Deidre's gaze.

"But I'm not dressed for bowling."

"Unless you're on a league, there isn't a dress code for bowling." Sheila said.

"I don't have any socks," Deidre said through her teeth. She looked at everyone's casual footwear, and then to her own Cole Hahn wedged heels.

"You can borrow a pair of mine. It's fresh from the pack, so it hasn't been stretched yet. C'mon," Andre said. She followed him up the hall, but not before sending Sheila a look that read, *you're in big trouble.*

When they got to Andre's bedroom, he began to substitute a gray T-shirt for a striped polo. She sat on the edge of his bed and watched as his undershirt rose up, exposing his chiseled chest in the exchange. Deidre felt suddenly conscious of her primal desire as if she were front row at a strip tease show. She rose from the edge of his bed, not wanting to be eye-level with his waist in the event he wanted to change his pants as well.

"Where are you going?"

"Nowhere," Deidre said, occupying herself with the knick-knacks on his dresser to avert her eyes. "Just wanted to see what kind of cologne you were wearing these days."

"You see I've graduated from Brut and Old Spice. I've stepped it up just a bit," Andre said, checking his completed look in the mirror.

She really wanted to get his take on their date crashers, so she sat back down when it was evident that he was done changing and said, "Did you know Sheila and Keith were coming over?"

"Keith called me about a half an hour ago. They told me they had talked to you on your cell phone. He started talking all this trash about my bowling skills. You know I can't turn down a challenge." Andre took her hand before pulling her up and into him. She allowed him to kiss her. "Plus he made a good point. This is our first time out the gate in awhile. I want to take you out and have some fun. We got reservations at ten, so we got to get going if we are going to grab something to eat on the way."

"Reservations for bowling?" Deidre asked.

"This is a popular spot. After league bowling is over, parties can make reservations and bowl until two A.M."

Deidre twisted her lips to the side and resigned herself to a night of bowling. Plans had obviously been made and confirmed around her.

"What's wrong?" Andre asked, going to his wardrobe and tossing her a new pair of his crew socks.

"Nothing, baby. Let's go."

Deidre paired with Andre as they entered into friendly competition with their friends. The four of them bowled five games before calling it quits. Deidre had not heard so much trash talking and macho bravado in a non contact sport. Andre entertained everyone with his own victory dance, more along the lines of a Temptations side scoop and spin, every time either he or Deidre scored a strike or spare. A misstep during one of his celebrations sent him tumbling into the lane. Deidre couldn't help but laugh from the score table.

"Oh that's funny, huh? Do I amuse you?" Andre asked, approaching her as if he were angry.

Deidre covered her wide grin, but nodded her head in the affirmative. He smothered her with his strong arms until she fell backward. He kept her dangling over the chair like a villain would his victim over the edge of a cliff. He gave her an innocent smack on the center of her mouth, then came back for more passionate seconds. Deidre pulled away before it got out of hand at the same time that Keith swatted at them prompting them to, "Cut it out."

Deidre was enjoying herself so much that she almost forgot about being upset at Sheila until Sheila got up to go to the bathroom. Deidre excused herself too.

The modest bathroom was deplorable in its condition.

It reminded Deidre of a high school bathroom with its one-ply toilet tissue and stalls painted a slate blue and covered with graffiti. Deidre grabbed some tissue just to have handy after deeming that the available stall was not up to her minimum standard of cleanliness. She waited for Sheila by the sinks.

"Gosh, I haven't had fun like that in a long time. Keith and I need to get out more often," Sheila said, approaching the sinks after using the facilities.

"So because you and Keith have fallen into a comfortable rut, that gives you cause to tag along on my date?" Deidre said, looking into the long rectangular mirror above the bank of sinks to check her friend's reaction before checking her own reflection. "C'mon, one minute you're on the phone asking what I'm up to, the next minute you show up and change my plans. What's the deal?"

"I figured you didn't have a dating plan in place, so I came to help you out," Sheila said, washing her hands vigorously with a dried up shard of generic soap. "I knew if I told you that you would blow me off."

Deidre winced at the sight of the overused soap as she tried to remember where she had heard that term before. She knew the term, dating plan, must have been coined at church, but she couldn't remember the context.

"What?" Deidre said, failing the memory test.

"You remember First Lady taught that purity class for the sisters. I know you remember she told us that nowadays you got to have a plan when you're dating to keep yourself sexually pure. She suggested that we date in groups to keep from putting ourselves in compromising positions. Friends help friends keep their clothes on and their integrity intact, remember?"

"Yeah, right. But that was for singles," Deidre said, waving her off.

Deidre felt Sheila lift her left hand and turn it back and forward as if to examine it for an engagement ring or wedding band. Deidre yanked her hand from her friend who was now laughing at her. Deidre's cheeks became flushed with embarrassment as she pulled lip gloss from her cosmetic bag and applied it a little too heavily.

"What I meant was that this is not new to Andre and me. He's not someone I just met who might still be in that groping stage. We have a history." Deidre puckered her lips.

"Yeah, and the two of you have conceived a child out of wedlock within that history," Sheila reminded her. "Girl, I know how it can be. After Keith and I got back together a year ago, it was hard for us to refrain from sex. We'd call ourselves spending a quiet evening at his house. All of a sudden, a lone hand on the back of the sofa turns into a whisper, which turns into a neck rub. Then before you know it—"

"Okay, I get the point."

"The point is I had to want Christ more spiritually than I wanted Keith physically or otherwise."

Deidre digested that last statement. Sure, she needed God more, but Andre ran a close second when it came to her desire. "Honestly, I wasn't even thinking along those lines; a few kisses, maybe a little snuggling. We were just trying to get some time in before DeAndre comes home," Deidre said fluffing a section of her hair.

"You might not have thought about sex, but I can assure you that homeboy has, the way he's been looking at you all night like you're something good to eat."

Deidre had to smile because that was the effect she was going for. She immediately felt convicted. What would she have done if they had stayed at his apartment and the urge hit them to be intimate? Would she have been able to bow out gracefully? Would she have wanted to? She closed her eyes and shook her head as the image of his chest flashed through her mind.

"Have the two of you ever been able to stop after a few kisses and snuggling, or was that just foreplay?" Sheila asked.

Deidre didn't have to say a thing; they both knew the answer. She reminded herself that that was before her rededication to God.

"Look, I know my relationship with Dre can't be a sprint to the bedroom if I want to march down the aisle," Deidre said, temporarily making eye contact with herself in the mirror. "Regardless of how much we both may want to have sex, we can't share the prize *this time* until we cross the finish line."

"You've got to communicate that to him. I think it is both healthy and reassuring if he wants to have sex with you, but he'll respect and appreciate you more if you stick to your beliefs."

Deidre was thankful for her friend. Sheila was right; she had to have a plan. Even when she was unsaved she had a plan even if it weren't any more than a can of mace and enough money to cover her end of the meal and a cab ride home. She truly believed that Andre was the one she was suppose to be with, but there was a lot they needed to discuss before they proceeded.

"Let's get out of this nasty bathroom," Deidre said with toilet tissue poised to shield her hand when opening the door.

"Yeah, my work here is done."

The foursome was quiet on the ride back home. It truly must have been a long time since her friends had an outing, because Sheila had dozed off in the short time they had been driving. Deidre was keenly aware of Andre's thigh pressed against her own in an attempt to get more space for his long legs in the cramped backseat of Keith's car. She felt a heat radiate within her. She turned her entire body to the side to look out the window. Their first date in more than eight years was coming to an end.

Keith dropped Deidre and Andre off in the parking lot of Andre's apartment building a little after one thirty in the morning. They both exited the driver's side in a failed attempt to leave without disturbing Sheila. Deidre didn't hear them pull off immediately and felt as if they were her parents watching to see how passionate their farewell would get.

"Bye, girl. Call me," Deidre heard Sheila say before they took off.

Andre must have felt Deidre start to drift toward her own car, because he grabbed her by the forearm and playfully pulled her along as he proceeded toward his building. She pulled against his arm slightly in feeble protest. This time he got behind her and guided her by the hips, tickling her in the process until they reached the outer door.

Darn that Sheila for talking up this dilemma, Deidre thought. She and Andre had to discuss the parameters of their relationship soon. She'd much rather it not happen in the lobby of his building.

"Dre, I think I'm calling it a night."

"Stop playing," Andre said, holding open the door to the glass enclosure after unlocking it. "What about the movies?"

Drat. The movies. "That's right, I'll just come up and get the movies so I can return them," Deidre said, walking past him and stopping before the second door.

Andre stared at her to see if she were serious, and Deidre put her poker face on to show that she wasn't bluffing. It was oddly like a standoff.

"C'mon, Dee, why are you being a party-pooper? We spent all of our quality time with Keith and Sheila."

"Exactly," Deidre said, thinking about her conversation with Sheila.

"Wait a minute. Deuce is sleeping over your sister's right?" He approached her and stood too close for her liking.

"Yes, you know he is."

"Okay then. Why can't we have a sleepover of our own? I can make it nice and cozy for us." He threw open his arms and shrugged his shoulders as if the choice was evident. "What's up?"

I'll be doggone, Deidre thought. He had thought this through. She took in his entire body from head to toe. Temptation was a fine, wellbuilt, caramel-colored man. It would have been so much easier to walk away from him if she didn't remember his scent, his touch, and his rhythm. It had been a long time. She wanted more than anything to stay with him that night. She wanted to stay forever.

"We need to talk. Don't you think we're moving too fast?" Deidre said, wondering if he could sense the war going on inside of her.

Andre chuckled. "Since when is eight years too fast? C'mon."

He encircled Deidre's waist with his arms and sealed the invitation with a kiss. It was a breathy open-mouth kiss she felt was entirely too intimate for a public place. It didn't speak to the love they shared all this time, nor was it an ode to their shared parenting. He took liberties kissing her on the corners of her mouth, then her chin on down to her neck, letting anyone who happened to be watching know that they had at one time been lovers. She felt naked. Her desires exposed for the world to see.

Deidre now knew the meaning of *discombobulated* as she stood there in total conflict. Andre released her, walked through the second door and held it open for her with one hand, confident now that her inner lioness would instinctively follow him to his den. Deidre prayed right then and there for strength, knowing there was nothing else within her own power to combat what this man was putting down. Where was Sheila now? She said nothing about taking these last few steps alone. Forget the movies, there was no way she could go any further without going all the way.

"Look, I'm gonna go." Deidre's voice was barely audible.

Andre came back through the door and stared as if she were a ghost. She tried to hide the strife in her eyes that pleaded with him to surrender her. He gave up on words and came to her once more. This time he got desperately close, clasping hands with hers, and they danced toward the door, or at least she thought she felt her body sway . . . or swoon. She felt the extent of his desire. He dropped his face into her neck and breathed in as if trying to inhale her scent, and she breathed in also, trying to strengthen her resolve.

"I want you," Andre whispered.

Something in her mind clicked at that moment. She could remember a time when she wanted nothing more than to be totally possessed by this man, and would have given over her mind, body, and soul at his mere request, but his comment brought something else to mind. *A virtuous woman knows who she is and whose she is.* It was the theme of this year's Woman's Season at church. Andre Hicks may want her, but he had yet to put a ring on her finger. She owed God her purity because He gave her a second chance to get love right. She couldn't let them mess up again.

"Don't make me beg, Dee. I want you," Andre said in a vulnerable whimper that transferred all of his power over to her.

Deidre pulled away from him to put some space between them. She looked into his eyes and said, "I know, and you're making it hard for me to say no. I want us to wait. So I've got to go before we do something we might regret. I got church tomorrow and I'd love it if you'd go with me. Call me."

Deidre didn't wait around this time. She pecked his cheek as a salve offering before pushing through the glass doors.

"You know you're wrong, right?" Deidre heard him shout from behind the doors as they came to a close.

So wrong, that I'm right, she thought.

Chapter 30

"You can wait in here, Mr. Hicks. I'll be back in a minute with your orders," a young woman in brightly colored scrubs said, yielding the way to the small lounge in the inner office directly across from the receptionist area.

Andre nodded to an elderly gentleman that was already seated there. He figured that the people asked to sit in this lounge, as opposed to the outer waiting area, had already received their verdict and awaited the details of their sentencing. He resisted the urge to ask the gentleman across from him what he was in for.

Andre rubbed his hands alongside his restless thigh muscles as if trying to warm them. He hadn't noticed the television was on until he heard Bo Donovan's gruff voice. Bo was a guest on one of those national morning shows demonstrating exercises from his new fitness program. Andre almost laughed aloud. This was the last thing he wanted to watch now.

"Do you mind if I switch the channel?" Andre asked, looking for the remote with urgency.

The man just shrugged, indicating with his finger that the remote was more than likely kept by the receptionist who had a side view of the television. Andre couldn't wait for approval; he walked to the TV and clicked it off manually.

He decided he needed something to drink and helped himself to the office vending area as well. He pulled out two crumpled dollars and considered himself lucky when the machine graciously accepted the worst for wear. As luck would have it, three of his selections for juices and water were empty. He decided on a diet soda and cursed when a regular cola barreled down the chute.

Andre didn't have the energy to go back to where he was previously seated, so he crashed down in the nearest seat, opened the can and gulped a mouthful of the soda. He felt the immediate burn as it traveled down his throat and took another big gulp of the unsavory beverage, welcoming the searing effect. He ignored his ringing cell phone, pressing the volume down until the vibrate feature was activated. The phone signaled for a second time and Andre checked the display to see who was calling before answering.

"What's up?" Andre said, deciding to stand and turn toward the window to avoid the disapproving glance of the man across the room. He saw the sign outlawing cell phone use in the office. He just didn't care. "Yeah."

"Hey, babe, where are you?" Deidre asked him.

"Where are you?"

"At home. It's my late day, remember? I thought we might start walking like we talked about."

"I can't," Andre said.

"Oh." Deidre was surprised at his curtness. "Okay, so when am I going to see you again?"

"I don't know."

There was a long torturous pause. Andre stared out the fifth floor window and planned his escape.

"All right, what gives? What's wrong with you?" Deidre asked.

Andre didn't know. After today, he didn't know anything anymore. "I guess I'm not used to my friends being so concerned about my schedule."

"Friends?"

Andre baited her. He could tell she was taken aback. He checked over his shoulder to find a practitioner in a lab coat explaining something to the old man, and took that cue to jump head first into a verbal sparing match. "Yeah, friends."

"That sounds like a bad word coming from a man who was saying otherwise in the park the other day."

"I've been wondering why in the world we even went through all that in the park. You made it evident Saturday night that you're not ready for our relationship to progress. So, no, the word friend is neither good nor bad. It is what it is."

"I told you on the phone—" Deidre started.

"I know you told me that leaving me hanging that night had nothing to do with your relationship with me, but everything to do with your relationship with God," Andre recalled. "That sounds good and all, but what I really think is that you're just not feeling me the same way I'm feeling you."

"I can't believe this. You were perfectly fine with my explanation the other day."

"Well, I got to thinking. We both decided to pick up where we left off. I just didn't think we had to go all the way back to high school to do it. I wasn't asking you to do anything we haven't done before."

"You are the one acting like you're in high school. We

are not the same hormone driven teenagers. So I know I'm not asking too much of you to wait," Deidre said. He could hear the hurt in her voice.

Andre's pride hurt more than anything after Deidre left him standing in the alcove of his apartment building. Like now, he wanted nothing more than to wrap himself up in her womanhood and let their pleasure make him forget about any and everything. His logical mind was telling him that it didn't have to be all or nothing. His logical mind was also the first one to hit the door when he received the news he received that morning.

"I want to honor God and myself in the process, by abstaining from sex until marriage. I want our relationship to be right in the eyesight of God."

"Is that some kind of policy they teach you in church to insure you get married and live happily ever after? If that's all you got to do to be happy, sign me up. Get the license. Let's do the marriage thing ASAP."

"I hope you are joking. Forgive me if I don't jump at that half-hearted, lame excuse of a proposal or whatever that was." Deidre sighed so hard it sounded like static. "You know·what; you didn't strike me as a man who would usher a shot-in-the-dark proposal because you were lusting and wanted some. And I definitely am not the one to accept for fear of losing a man I barely had to begin with."

It's better that you hurt her now than later. "Look, forget I said that, okay? It's really not a good time. I've got a lot on my mind right now."

Andre had often toyed with the idea of proposing to Deidre. He had sense enough to know that a ring would not remedy what was wrong with their relationship.

"Ugh," she moaned out of complete frustration. "What about DeAndre?"

Andre thought about all the time it took to get back

into his son's life. He hadn't really had a chance to talk to him since the mall incident, not the man-to-man kind of talk that current circumstances warranted.

"Nothing has changed. Nothing has changed at all." He tried to sound convincing even to himself. "I just need some time."

Deidre's irritation was a third party on the line. "I guess DeAndre will be in his twenties before we hear from you again."

"No. I'm not going anywhere. I just need time. Please, let me figure some things out, and I'll get back to you."

"Whatever. Give your son a call when you're feeling better," Deidre said sarcastically, like there was no way in the world she was going to waste her time waiting for him to come around. The dial tone told him that she was finished with the call, as well as the relationship.

Andre didn't know when he would feel better. He had been at the doctor's office the majority of morning trying to find out when he'd get better. What started out as a routine visit with a minor complaint of abdominal pain, ended up being an interrogation into his past followed by what seemed like a body cavity search.

The details of his medical history got sketchy when he had to go back a generation. His father had died of cancer, but what kind? Apparently that little tidbit was important because that put him into a risk category for the disease. After a surprisingly painless, yet mentally mortifying, rectal exam, Dr. Jefferies detected something in his body that concerned him.

A polyp. The term seemed so harmless. Dr. Jefferies explained to him that some cancers begin in growths known as polyps in the wall of the colon. A single polyp is not enough to be alarmed, but rather the size and amount of polyps they find indicate to doctors that the polyps might be a concern. The doctor performed a fecal blood test on the spot, sending Andre's specimen to the adjoining lab with his physician's assistant to gather further evidence.

The same nurse that escorted him to the waiting area now approached with what seemed like a portfolio full of papers.

"Here you go, Mr. Hicks. Sorry to keep you waiting. Dr. Jefferies would like you to make an appointment at County General Hospital as soon as possible for a colonoscopy," the nurse said, helping herself to the chair next to him.

Andre turned sideways in his chair to face her. He couldn't have heard correctly although her voice chimed like a bell. He wanted to shush her. What happened to confidentiality and why wasn't Dr. Jefferies explaining this to him? That's what he hated about the HMO approach to health care. It felt like they were being herded like cattle instead of treated like people.

"I thought the doctor said that we would wait for the blood test to come back before we do any further tests."

"Oh we test those with litmus paper in our own lab. Takes seconds. Let's see," the nurse said looking at a file that was underneath the other papers. "Says here, your fecal occult test was positive, so Dr. Jefferies thinks that a colonoscopy is our next course of action to be sure."

What else needed to be done? He had the family history, blood in his stools, and cramping in his abdomen. It was apparent. He was a goner.

"Certain things you eat can render a false positive blood test, and the rectal exam might miss upper colon polyps," she said, as if reading his mind. "With a colonoscopy, the doctor can remove polyps during the exam and test them later for cancer. The only way to rule out colorectal cancer is to have the colonoscopy."

Andre gripped his head in his hands as he half-listened to her explain the procedure with the tri-fold brochure. She pointed to the hospital's surgical appointment line number listed on the orders.

"Dr. Jefferies is going on vacation for two weeks, so it's best you get this done at the hospital by the time he gets back. We can make the appointment for you and fax over the orders if you'd like. That's the easiest way, but we always like to give our patients the option of picking a convenient day."

Andre nodded his head, and the nurse excused herself again. Nothing about this was convenient. In fact, the timing couldn't be worse; just when he thought he could have it all with Deidre and DeAndre. He thought about the last time he'd seen his father's disease ravaged body lying in that sterile hospital bed in New York. It wasn't fair to his family to force his way back into their lives just to subject them to the agony of watching him waste away. He didn't think he could do that to them.

Andre felt betrayed. Something like this wasn't supposed to happen to him. Colorectal cancer usually occurred in much older men. He was forty and in the best shape of his life, or so he thought. He didn't eat red meat and drank more that the recommended eight glasses of water a day. He worked out twice a day to increase his cardiovascular capacity, strengthen his body, and to ward off the effects of aging. How could Bo Donovan lie to him, convincing him that he was strong when he really wasn't?

The nurse returned. She was a little too professional for Andre. His nurse acted as if she were doing a commercial for the National Cancer Society. She made it seem like Andre should be relieved that they caught something like that during an office visit. Apparently colon cancer was the second leading cause of death, because those pesky polyps were often too small and remained undetected until it was too late. Early detection didn't feel like a blessing to him. It felt like a death sentence.

"Okay, we got you all squared away," she said, handing Andre a copy of his orders for his procedure that would occur in a little less than two weeks.

If it were that easy to square away, they could just give him a pill and send him home to sleep it off.

Chapter 31

Deidre unlaced her tennis shoes after getting off the telephone with Andre. She used the opposite foot to pry her heel loose before flinging them as far as she could across the room. They felt as if they were two sizes too small. She didn't customarily wear tennis shoes, so she was sure that the last time she had worn them was also the last time she attempted to workout. She was hoping that working out with Andre would put a little more consistency to her hit-or-miss exercise regiment, among other things.

Just seven days ago, Deidre had packed her heart and emotions, prepared to give their relationship another try. She couldn't believe they would not be taking that trip to forgiveness and lasting happiness together. She felt God was urging her to forgive him and try again. *But for what, God? To have my heart broken again?* How could she have read this wrong?

Ambivalence was a place she didn't desire to be. Deidre was seething, but could not completely rid her mind of thoughts of being intimate with Andre once more.

Glimpses of his toned chest kept flashing through her mind again and again. Perhaps she should have given in. She was almost positive it would be all that she expected and more. Just as quickly as the thought popped in her mind she reminded herself that the kind of pleasure wrought by physical intimacy was fleeting. Sex had not secured their future in the past.

The internal conflict brought her into the kitchen. Dejection had a sweet tooth, and she opened her freezer prepared to feed it. Deidre pulled out a half gallon of ice cream before thinking about the time. It was barley eleven A.M. The thought stopped her in her tracks. There was no amount of Chunky Monkey ice cream that could soothe her heartache.

Deidre needed to hear from the Lord. She prayed all of the time, and she had prayed about her and Andre more times than she could count. What would make this time any different? Right then and there she decided that she wouldn't eat anything, but rather add fasting to her prayers. Deidre understood fasting only as the abstinence from food, but called Sheila, as always, for all things scriptural. Sheila picked up the phone on the third ring.

"Hey, girl, I don't mean to bother you on your job, but I need to pray about some things," Deidre said after their customary greeting.

"Wait a minute. I'm at my desk. You sound awfully upset. I'll be glad to pray with you; just let me call you on my cell phone from the bathroom."

"No, Sheila, that's all right, girl. This is something I've carried to the Lord before, and I'm not certain about His answer. I think I'm going to take the morning to fast and lay it before the Lord once and for all," Deidre said. "I called because I remembered that you had participated in the corporate fast at church. I guess I'm wondering what makes a fast different from any of your other prayers and meditation."

"Well, Pastor Tatum told us that many people in the Bible fasted to bring God's attention to a special issue in their lives. He anointed our heads with oil and prayed with us. He also charged us to not just refrain from food, but from all distractions. You may have to stay away from Mr. Hicks today so you can get your breakthrough."

"Oh, that won't be a problem," Deidre said, not wanting to give too much away.

"The goal is to hear from God, so fasting and praying is like an exchange with God—like a conversation. Stay close to Him in thought and in prayer, then expect to hear from Him through His Word or the impression of the Holy Spirit."

"Thanks, Sheila. You're the best."

"I just wish I had known you were fasting before I ate that Krispy Kreme doughnut in the conference room. I would have fasted with you, but I can always pray in agreement with you. I know everything will work out."

They talked for a little while longer until Deidre felt a rumble in her stomach that indicated hunger. Either she was going to do this thing or not. "I'll talk to you later," Deidre said, deciding not to delay.

Deidre did as Sheila instructed, asking God's blessing over a bottle of extra virgin olive oil before anointing herself for her time of fasting and prayer. Her initial prayer felt more like a laundry list, petitioning God about her promotion, the maturation and overall well being for her child, and finally, some clarity or closure with Andre. She figured while she had God's ear, she might as well put all her concerns out there. Now she had to listen.

It was hard for Deidre to still herself. Mentally she was always going: guessing, planning, and evaluating. She usually counterbalanced the noisiness inside her head with the mindlessness of the television when she got home. Deidre took her study Bible from her nightstand and was embarrassed to find she hadn't even read through the Book of Genesis in her quest to complete the Bible in one year. She only had to scan back to the previous chapter to remind herself of what she had read, which was about Joseph.

Joseph, the son of Jacob, was known as the dreamer among his brothers. Because his father favored him, his jealous brothers plotted to kill him, settling later to sell him into slavery instead. She read from that point on to find out that just by interpreting Pharaoh's dream, Joseph was made ruler over Egypt.

Deidre didn't know what she was supposed to glean from the life of Joseph. She didn't know what she was doing. Like most Christians, she relied on her Pastor to walk her through the interpretation of the Word. Deidre made it a point to review the text of each message over the course of the week in her office at work, making sure to follow closely any advice, or as her pastor called it, spiritual practices. Deidre heard Pastor Tatum say many times that it would make his job easier if his members would go directly to God for themselves. That was Deidre's intention.

Deidre put the Bible down and turned on the radio while she piddled around the house. Remembering she was on a fast, she tuned the stereo from the Rhythm and Blues station to one of the many gospel stations in the DC Metropolitan area. Deidre recognized the unmistakable voice of Daryl Coley coming from the speaker, and she took a seat to take in not just the musicality of the arrangement, but his words.

Sovereign, sovereign, the Lord, my God is sovereign . . .

Unexplained tears flowed freely from Deidre's eyes.

The song took away her anxiety about not receiving an immediate response from the Lord. It reminded her that God didn't work on her timetable.

When it neared one o'clock, she decided to call her job and take the rest of the day off. She expected to speak with Carol, a demure white woman from Rockville, sent to babysit their little store in the hood in the interim. Instead, she was forwarded to Mitchell Graham, her fellow managerial candidate who was starting his own probationary period at the helm of her store. He was fast to tell her that absences led to a breakdown in the service provided to their customers and should be avoided except in extreme cases of emergency.

He spoke hypothetically about the consequences of abusing leave that left her furious until she began to reflect on her impeccable record at Fresh Gardens that spoke for itself. She felt she didn't need to justify to him why she needed to be off. He was a candidate just like her. *No matter what others thought about Joseph, God promoted him because he provided an invaluable service to Pharaoh,* she thought. God was sovereign. Instantly, she felt that the situation at work would ultimately work out for her good.

Deidre turned off the radio and prayed, feeling the Lord working on her behalf. She turned back to the story of Joseph, realizing that there could be a message planted in the text by God just for her. Just like that, the text opened up to her, and she was able to draw parallels to her own experience. She read from chapter forty-two to chapter fifty, which was the end of the Book of Genesis. Without the aid of his family, Joseph was able to develop a plan that helped all of Egypt to survive seven years of famine.

Deidre thought about the eight years that she and DeAndre endured alone without Andre or her mother. God developed her confidence and character by bringing her to Liberty AME Church. In the end of the text, Joseph crossed paths again with his brothers who came to Egypt out of desperation to get rations that Joseph stored away for this barren time. He ultimately forgave his brothers and sent for his entire family to come live off the wealth he'd been blessed with.

Deidre marveled at the fact that Joseph was not bitter at what his brothers had done to him. In spite of what they had done, he was willing to share with them all that he had gained. He was able to forgive the people involved and see the sovereignty of God's plan. She was trying her hardest to be that wise.

Deidre's name wasn't Joseph nor did she live in Biblical times. She wanted to wipe her hands of Andre Hicks for good, but they had DeAndre, and he needed his father. She kept replaying the conversation she had with Andre earlier that morning in her head. This time she tried to separate his words from the hurt that they caused her. He told her he needed time and that he had a lot on his mind right now. Pride was telling her that she had spent enough time on him. But what was God saying?

Deidre thought about the acronym P.U.S.H., which stood for pray until something happens. She dropped to her knees at the foot of the couch.

"Father God, forgive me for my sinful, self-centered, and self-righteous nature. I'm tired of trying to figure everything out. I want to be like Joseph and accept my struggles, knowing that they will only make me stronger. You know my heart. You also know that Andre has occupied a big part of my heart. I'm trying to do as you have instructed and forgive him. I feel like I can't do this again, Lord. Help us to sort things out, to truly forgive and be healed for DeAndre's sake because right now, we're not even speaking the same language. We need an interpreter, a third party mediator or something . . ."

I'm your third party. It won't work without me.

She felt His impression. God's spirit was speaking to her right there in the midst of her prayer. It was nothing spoken aloud like the voice of the Lord coming to Moses from the burning bush, but rather an imprint on her soul that wasn't there before and could undeniably only be put there by God.

God was speaking. It was her job to listen. Was He saying there was hope for her and Andre, even though they both didn't have the strength to hold on?

Once again, she felt a mark on her soul. *Let me complete your love. Make the introductions.*

Chapter 32

DeAndre was obsessed with a sketch he was drawing. It was unlike the comic sketches he had done before. It was more like a painting or mural on a legal size sheet of paper from his sketchbook. A muse so strong that it brought him away from the television and to his desk every chance he got, to shade and to add countless layers to the thicket already in this drawing. In his gut he felt he was bringing about perfection of some kind. It tormented him with each detail. It was grander than his present thinking, grander than his present skill set, and he wished he was already at Malcolm Woods Creative Arts Magnet School so that he could learn more techniques to actually pull off a piece like this. Unknowingly, he was bringing to light the confusing mix of emotions he had been experiencing for the past two weeks.

The sketch was of a modern day Garden of Eden. Except instead of having just one couple, Adam and Eve, his garden had three. A nude and fleshy Adam and Eve looking much like the couple in the book he checked out from the library, crouched on the perimeter of the page looking inward toward the next couple while almost submerged in coiled ivy and grapevines.

Over the course of the week, DeAndre had dreamed about this slender younger couple, fighting with each other, fighting for control, fighting to come alive. He wrestled to portray that struggle. He settled on the girl emerging from the ivy, racing forward toward the center of the drawing. The boy, with only his face and hands exposed, reached out for his partner, trying to catch her before she fell into the recessed area of the forest floor.

At the heart of the drawing was a man and a woman lying juxtaposed on the forest floor like the twins slept the night of their sleepover. There was fear on everyone's faces. Eve covered her mouth with her hand to shield a scream, and Adam's eyes were wide with fright. The young girl looked over her shoulder with panic while the young boy's expression showed the desperation of trying to save her. The third female's eyes were slits, her mouth twisted in anguish while the man beside her bore the same sick and demented smile DeAndre imagined the armed man wore the day of the mall shootings.

Desperate for color, DeAndre had bought assorted color chalks from the Dollar Store on his way home from school. He was a sketch artist and cartoonist who, until this drawing, never thought color necessary enough to use his allowance for the right tools. Now he was using his fingers to mix brown and green onto the shrubs and painstakingly wiping the excess with tissue. He added character to the leaves and branches by outlining with his dark granite pencil.

It was at this point that DeAndre took in how good his drawing was and thought that he may actually want to show this to somebody one day. He knew it was complete. Flipping his head back, he looked up and imagined his finished product drawn on the ceiling like Michael

Angelo's Sestine Chapel. He turned over his masterpiece and signed his real name in his neatest penmanship rather than his alias, *Dee Scribble*. DeAndre struggled to come up with an adequate name for his drawing. When an apt title didn't come to him, he looked at the clock which read twenty minutes past six, then tried to find what he had done with the cordless phone.

Calls between him and Kenya were few and far between after she had called him, rather remorseless, and relieved him of his escort duties. It was around the same time that DeAndre realized he would not be able to honor her request to be her first anyway. He was relieved, yet scared. She stated that her mother preferred she not be in the company of boys, so she and Jasmine would go to the dance together. That meant nothing to DeAndre who figured her mother must have been standing near. Kenya found a way to do whatever she wanted, and as he was finding out, she not only preferred to be in the company of boys, but lived for the opportunity.

DeAndre wanted to at least be offered a Plan B, and when he wasn't, an argument ensued on a different conversation. He told her she wasn't ready for sex for which she replied, "If you're scared, say you're scared, but don't try to put your fear on me." He laughed it off, but knew she couldn't have been more right.

Tonight would have been their big night. This was the night that DeAndre had planned to wear his new suit that now hung in the closet with the rest of the church garments his mom had bought for him. He waited to call Kenya on this day, right before she was in the throes of getting ready. He wanted her to tell him she wasn't going. He wanted her to say that staying home would not make her half as miserable as being at the dance without him. DeAndre found his mom's cordless phone on his bed, so he took a seat and dialed Kenya's number. She picked up on the second ring.

"Hey," Kenya said, shouting over the loud background noise.

"You getting ready?"

"Yeah, my aunt's got me sitting under the dryer with big doo-doo rollers in my hair."

"Don't forget to take a picture for your boy, all right?" DeAndre said, lying back on his bed.

"Yeah, okay," Kenya said.

There was a long pause that neither DeAndre nor Kenya were eager to fill. They were both waiting on select words that did not come.

"Yo, have fun. . .not that much fun. . .you know, since I can't go with you."

"All right now," Kenya said, sounding ready to get off the phone.

"I'm going to keep my momma's phone in my room to call you tonight when I think you're back. . . make sure you got in safely."

"Boy, don't ring my phone tonight," Kenya laughed, but they both knew she was serious.

"So what I got to do; bring your mother a dozen roses to church for Mother's Day so she can let me take you to the next dance, or what?" DeAndre said.

"Boy, shut up. You are crazy."

"Well, I'm going to let you go. I just finished drawing this insane picture. I got to show it to you."

"Oh yeah, that reminds me, did you get your letter?"

"What letter?"

"From Malcolm Woods. I got my letter today. I'm going to the Choice Arts camp, baby," she sang. "We are going to have so much fun this summer."

"Oh snap, I didn't even get the mail on the way in."

DeAndre hiked his pants up one good time from the back before starting down the hallway toward the door.

"Well, check it and tell me on Sunday."

"Bet," DeAndre said before hanging up the phone. *Sunday will always be our standing date,* he thought, taking comfort.

DeAndre practically skipped to the mailbox. He emptied the contents from the mailbox attached to the front siding. He dropped the mail on the sofa and riffled through the letters, looking for the green uppercase letters he had come to know as the school's letterhead. He found the letter toward the bottom of the pile and ripped it on the side before realizing he had also torn another letter at the same time in his haste. He tossed the other letter aside and extracted the letter from Malcolm Woods.

The letter was made out to him. He only had to read the top two lines before realizing this wasn't the good news he was expecting.

Dear DeAndre Hicks,

Thank you for your interest in Malcolm T. Woods Creative Arts Choice Summer Camp. Unfortunately, this opportunity can only be afforded to those upcoming ninth graders recommended for placement in our program. Feel free to apply again next year when you meet our qualifications.
Sincerely,
Patrick Ramsey
Principal, Malcolm T. Woods Creative Magnet High School

DeAndre could not understand. In an instant, his hopes were dashed and angry tears flooded his eyes. Maybe Mr. Talbert had omitted something from his packet. Maybe he just wasn't good enough.

DeAndre knew his parents would be terribly disappointed. Just when they seemed to be getting along so well, he goes and fouls up. It probably would cause them to get into a huge argument about what they were going to do with him now. DeAndre quickly stuck that letter and the one he accidentally opened in between the cushions of the couch and the armrest. His plan was to show his mother next week after Mother's Day. He gathered all the other mail in a neat pile and took off for his room.

At least he would be going to Carver High with everybody else in the neighborhood, including the twins, DeAndre thought as he wiped his eyes for the final time. His communication with the twins had also been limited since all they wanted to do was hang out on Bentley's corner these days. He tried his hardest to fit in, but everyone else was acting weird toward him. Apparently busting up someone's party awarded its share of cool points, but as the story goes, having a father who single-handedly took out a gunman in the mall parking lot was not. DeAndre didn't care enough to correct his misinformed schoolmates. He wasn't pressed about losing cool points with Bentley and his crew, but losing his best friends was another story. He didn't fret it now; he had four years at the neighborhood high school to get back in their good graces.

DeAndre was lying across his bed when he remembered his drawing. If only that review board at Malcom Woods could have seen it, he would be a shoo-in. He picked up his masterpiece and studied it. Then he grabbed his Bic rolling writer and wrote, *We're in Trouble Now*, as a title.

Chapter 33

Although Deidre was all dolled up in a dusty rose colored suit with a red corsage for Mother's Day, she didn't feel like celebrating motherhood. A visiting minister had preached the typical Mother's Day message, highlighting the various traits of the mother of all mothers, Mary, from her immaculate conception to her front row seat at her son's crucifixion. Deidre could only think about her own story of how she managed to isolate her son from his father, then reconcile with him, just to run him off again. Not to mention her relationship with her own mother that was far from ideal.

Deidre declined the usual invitation for her and DeAndre to tag along with Sheila and her mom, Ms. Betsey. She felt bad because they usually dined at some upscale restaurant in D.C. Today, Deidre didn't mind buying two value meals from a fast food place as long as she could eat it in the privacy of her own home.

Deidre and DeAndre were so hungry that they ate at the dining room table before changing out of their church clothes. Theirs was truly fast food, prepared hurriedly and getting less edible with each passing minute. Between bites of a double charbroiled burger and washes of heavy carbonated soda, she initiated conversation with her son about his post-suspension life. He categorically denied any after effects from the mall incident and his recent debacle with Kenya. She needed, more than anything, for him to open up to her. She needed to understand the only person she truly had left in this world.

"Everything will be all right in time. You'll see. When I get this promotion and you get over to that new school, we'll forget all about what's been happening lately," Deidre said.

Deidre waited for a response. DeAndre just looked at her blankly as if he didn't know how to respond. *Come on kid, throw me a line.* He must have read her mind, because he gave her a half-hug around her neck before throwing his burger wrapper in the trash.

"Happy Mother's Day, Mom," he called to her.

"Thank you, baby."

"I'm going to take a nap now."

Deidre waved him on with her hand as she began to clear her own place. She didn't want him to see the tear roll down her face and feel obligated to stay and cheer her up. She couldn't explain why she felt tired after a good night's rest and achy without the pain. She took a seat on the couch, resisting the urge to retire herself. She knew sooner or later her mother would be getting in from church, and would be expecting a call from her baby girl.

Deidre reared back in her seat and braced herself before dialing her mother's number.

"Hello, Mother. Happy Mother's Day."

"Well, well, ain't this a surprise."

"What? You know I couldn't forget my momma on Mother's Day," Deidre said, refusing to get pulled into negative banter. "I know you were decked out in all your white today."

"I tried my best. What about you? I hope you gave the Lord His due today."

"Yes, DeAndre and I went to church. I had on my nice new suit and my red corsage," Deidre said proudly of the tradition. Her mother taught her to wear a red lapel corsage on Mother's Day to represent that her mother was still living.

"I would have thought you'd wear a white one seeing how infrequently you see or call your mother. Maybe you thought I done dropped dead here in Iverson. I was telling your sister earlier that it never occurs to you girls to surprise your mother and visit on a day other than Thanksgiving."

Deidre shifted in her seat as she would have done as a child being reprimanded. The force of her hips surfaced two letters that appeared to be stuck down in the cushions. Both letters were ripped open—one addressed to DeAndre and the other to her.

"Maybe we'll plan for that next year," Deidre said, pulling out the latter. She began reading.

"I decided not to wait on you all to decide to visit. Plan to bring my grandbaby down right after school lets out for the summer. I think Donna said the kids get out in the next couple of weeks. I'm going to throw a big barbecue, 'cause Lord knows when I'll see my kin folk again."

"Oh no," Deidre said in response to the letter she had been reading instead of listening to her mother rant. It was from DeAndre's school.

"What's wrong with you? You'd a thought I said something horrible by wanting my family nearby."

"Wait a minute, Momma. I just found a letter that obviously DeAndre was trying to hide from me. It says that he hasn't met the minimum requirements of eighth grade, therefore he's not being promoted to the next grade unless he takes a course in summer school."

Deidre heard on the news that the county was cracking down on social promotion or advancement to the next grade based solely on age. Deidre agreed with the crack down after watching the broadcast; she never thought it would hit home. DeAndre had failed math, a core subject. How could this be happening to her child?

"Where were you? You and that father of his are to blame. What were the two of you doing when this baby was struggling in school?" her mother said.

That was a good question. Had they been as vigilant as they could have been after DeAndre returned to school from his suspension? Deidre knew his grades wouldn't be great, but she surely didn't think he would fail altogether. She was mad. They had two good weeks left of school. Deidre wondered if there was anything that he could do to make a difference.

"Momma, I've got to go. I'll call you next week, okay?" Deidre said, hanging up before her mother could share her final thoughts about her neglect.

Deidre shouted DeAndre's name so loud she scared herself. "Get out here, boy."

It took a minute before her son appeared, groggy from an unexpected awakening like he did the night he thought he had gotten away with sneaking out of the house to attend that party at Lonnie's. She wondered how long he thought those letters would stay stuffed between the couch cushions.

"How dare you hide mail addressed to me?"

DeAndre threw his head back and grabbed his face with his hands. His eyes darted back and forth as if he were trying to think of something to say to rectify the situation.

"Huh, what do you have to say for yourself?"

"I wanted to see if I made it into that Creative Arts camp. The other letter I ripped on accident."

"Well, this one here says you're going back to Pemberton Middle School in the fall unless you make up a math class this summer."

"I failed?" DeAndre said. His eyes widened and his chest began to heave. He was obviously devastated by the news. Deidre almost felt sorry for him.

"Yup, tell me what good was hiding the letters going to do?"

"I knew you'd be mad and I wanted you to have a nice Mother's Day. I was going to show you on Monday, honest."

"So you did this for me? How about studying? Why couldn't you do that for me . . . do it for yourself?"

Deidre wanted to heap shame on him. She wanted to take out the eight years of pain and frustration from dealing with his father, the guilt and shame she carried from her mother, plus the fourteen hours she spent in active labor, all on him. She wanted him to know how disappointed she was in him right at this moment. "Like father, like son. He failed tenth grade, now you're failing eighth grade."

Deidre felt terrible as she watched her son's eyes widen then glass over at this confession. He couldn't even look at her. She covered her eyes with her hands and began to rub circles with her fingertips. She didn't know what her aim was, but she was so far off the mark with that cheap shot.

"I'm sorry about what I said. It was way out of line. This is not about your dad. It's about you. I'm just so disappointed about this situation. I'm disappointed about a lot of things right now. This can be rectified though. This is your life. You need to start acting like it. Ask yourself do you want to return to middle school next year when all your buddies are off to high school?"

"No."

"Summer school costs, DeAndre. I'm not going to waste my money unless you're going to take it seriously and apply yourself. In fact, you can kiss your entire summer goodbye, because after this session is over, I'm going to find little odd jobs for you to help pay for this class."

Deidre thought back to her morning in church for some sort of comfort. What would Mary do in this situation? *Mary had the perfect son.* Then Deidre thought about the Book of Genesis that she was still studying in the mornings before work. There was something about Benjamin, the youngest and only full blood brother of Joseph that she had missed before. He played a key role in saving the family. Both Joseph and his father, Jacob, protected Benjamin. Joseph wanted to see him before he revealed himself to his other brothers, and Jacob didn't want to let him out of his sight. The success of the family was tied into making sure that Benjamin was well and hadn't been mistreated by the same brothers who sold Joseph into slavery. The focus was on the child.

Deidre decided right then and there to take a new approach. DeAndre would be her focus and that meant acting in her son's best interest, even if that meant keeping the lines of communication between her and Andre open. It wasn't going to help matters to berate her son or his father like she had done in the past.

Deidre said, "Go call your father and tell him."

Deidre watched DeAndre take off down the hallway. She lowered her head from the weight of her own shame before lifting it once more. *This is a setback, but we'll get through it.* She didn't know how, but she had to have faith that it would all work out.

Deidre smoothed the wrinkles in the front of her new suit as she stood. Although she vowed the focus would be on DeAndre, it was still Mother's Day and she was going to lounge for the rest of the day.

"Someone owes me a Mother's Day card," Deidre said, passing DeAndre's door as she made her way back to her own room. She could hear DeAndre on the cordless phone with his father, and she hoped they could hear her. "Make that eight."

Chapter 34

Deidre started her work week like she always did: with the corporate spec sheet on a clipboard walking the aisles to make sure new sales items were marked with arrows and old ones were taken down. Their store had lost hundreds of dollars honoring reduced prices on items incorrectly marked. The store was a mess since Mitchell took over. Carts full of returned or otherwise ditched items remained in the front of the store because he neglected to assign an associate after each shift to re-shelve the items. Deidre could only estimate the amount of perishables that would have to be trashed in all that mess. The majority of the other items would have to be reduced for fast sale.

Deidre had not seen or heard from her competition all morning. Usually Mitchell made his presence known by revamping some policy and disrupting the order it took her and her predecessor, Conrad, five years to achieve. Deidre wanted to satisfy her own curiosity and check the company's intra-web for other stores seeking General Mangers, but didn't have sole access to the manager's booth nowadays. She remained on the floor working along with her staff to return the store to some semblance of order before it drove her crazy. She was watching Renita count the money in her drawer before clocking her in for the shift at the Customer Service booth.

Ironically, Renita helped her out tremendously at the Customer Service line. One night, Deidre was trying her best to man the area. Ever since their store constructed the special aisles and started selling beers and wines, including some "top shelf" items kept behind the counter at the Customer Service register, Deidre lost her people skills. Deidre resented the fact that her store, and just three other urban locations in the local Fresh Gardens chain, was forced to sell "spirits," cigarettes, and process money orders and wire transfers on top of settling other customer disputes at the Customer Service line. Apparently her customers were so untrustworthy that even baby formula was kept under lock and key.

The usual end-of-the-work-week line was forming when Renita came off break. Deidre, who never had been a drinker, tried desperately to find the brand of cognac and cigarettes for a man in line when a lady in the back of the line with a case of beer in each hand called out for her to hurry up. Renita asked what the man needed and quickly helped Deidre retrieve them. When the heckler called out again, Renita asked her, "Where you got to go?" like she was a close friend privy to that information.

The woman, eager to share, said a couple of her co-workers were getting together as she put her cases of beer down and slid them forward with her foot. To which Renita asked, "Can I come?" Deidre noticed she said this all the while taking over ringing up and tendering cash to the current customer. Her comments seemed to entertain the crowd. "I'm serious. I get off at nine," Renita added. By the time the lady with the beer got up to the counter, Renita had an invitation to a party and Deidre had a Customer Service Associate.

Carole called out for Deidre just then to join her in the office. She and Renita shared puzzled glances wondering what was so urgent that would preempt the change over of shifts. She carried the two remaining money bags marked for the evening cashiers into the booth with her.

"Close the door, will ya? Besides the fact that this thing has no ceiling, the walls also have ears," Carol said from her seated position. Deidre knew she was referring to Renita, the conductor of the grocery store grapevine that was stationed right outside.

Carol was well into her sixties with a round face and homespun bun of blond hair. She had been with the company a long time. When corporate gave managers a choice to wear business casual like Deidre always sported, or in corporate logo, Carol chose the latter, wearing her blue and green embroidered blazers and blouses with pride. Deidre liked her immediately because she was fair in giving both she and Mitchell their due time to prove themselves and treating them with equal respect.

"How would you rate yourself as a managerial candidate? How do you think you've done?"

Deidre froze for a moment thinking that this was a trick question. "I think I handled the store responsibly responding to the needs of both the staff and the customers. I'm constantly making sure that our quality, safety, and customer service are up to the standards. There are some areas that still need some work. Our bakery goods have consistently undersold for the past six months. Each time the Ottenburg truck pulls up, we're discounting and discarding half our inventory from the week before. I believe that's due in part to our outdated floor plan. Those beer and wine aisles have blocked the view of the bakery from the entrance and check-out lanes. I'd love to put in a bid for a corporate 'floor-lift' the next renovations cycle."

"Deidre, Deidre," Carol said, finally getting a word in. "I think you are great. I think you've done a wonderful job."

"Well, thank you," Deidre said with a sigh of relief.

"That's why, you've got the job," Carole said with a pat on her hand.

"I've what? Where's Mitchell? I mean, is his time over? I can't believe this," Deidre said, bringing praying hands over her mouth and nose.

"We both know we had to let Mitchell have a chance to appease the big boys, but I wasn't about to let buddy boy bring the store down. We told him yesterday that there was no need to come in. He'll be reassigned as a shift manager. I've been around awhile, and they trust me when I tell them we've got our man, and in this case, woman. Congratulations."

"Oh my gracious, thank you, Carole. This is incredible news, and it couldn't have come at a better time."

"Well you deserve it. If you don't mind, I'm leaving early. I've been on the phone all morning with my son-in law. My daughter went into labor around two o'clock this morning. I'm going to be a grandmother."

"Wow, well congratulations are in order for you as well. By all means, go and be with your family."

"I know the store is in capable hands."

"I'm ready," Deidre said, walking her to the door of the tiny office.

"You sure are."

Deidre smiled broadly in Renita's direction. Renita signaled for her to come over and Deidre put up her index finger to indicate that she would be a minute. She waited until Carole had exited the building before seeing what Renita wanted.

"Where's Carole going?" Renita asked.

"She left for the day. Her daughter is in the hospital about to have a baby, and guess what?"

"What? Why are you cheesing all over the place?"

"I got the job. This is my store." Deidre did a Broadway musical spin in the middle of the store." I'm the new General Manager."

"Oh yeah," Renita said, waving her hand above her head as if she were the one receiving a promotion. "Does that mean that Mitchell is gone for good?"

Deidre nodded her head. "He's been reassigned."

"That's what I'm talking about. Carole knew she better reassign him before I did," Renita said with her fist clenched like she was about to fight.

"Girl, is that all you wanted? I've got to go clock Cydney and Rachal in," Deidre said, holding up the money bags she had in her hands the whole time she talked to Carol.

"Your man came by when you were in there meeting with Carol."

"What man?"

"Your ex," Renita said with pursed lips as if to suggest Deidre knew exactly who she was talking about.

"How did you know it was my ex? You've never seen him."

"Toffee brown, security guard, stuck on fine," Renita described.

Deidre looked over her shoulders to her cashiers at registers five and six who both had a line of two or more people. Their relief cashiers hadn't made it up front from the lockers in the employee break room yet, so she figured she had time to get the scoop from Renita.

"What did he say?"

"He asked for you. Said he had some movies of yours he needed to return, but he didn't want to leave them with me."

"So where did he go?" Deidre asked, with a hint of desperation in her voice.

"I didn't ask him all that, but if I didn't know he was your ex, I would have tried to holla at him. This is the guy you're holding out on?"

Deidre shushed Renita. She regretted telling her about the other night she and Andre had gone out and how hard it was for her to resist his charms. Deidre made her way from behind the customer service area to give the other cashiers the appearance that she was on her way.

"We'll talk about it later," Deidre told her.

"At lunch?" Renita questioned.

"Yes, but it will be the last lunch of the day," Deidre said, before walking away.

Deidre quickly dispersed the cash allotment for each cashier's drawer and bagged the money from those cashiers clocking out for the day. She returned to the office to prepare the bank documents for the night's drop. She tried to reach both Sheila and her sister to tell them the good news, but was unsuccessful. Back out on the floor, Deidre instructed her stock room clerks to create a display of ten pound bags of dog food prescribed in a corporate email that inadvertently got left off the sales circular when she heard Renita's voice over the store's PA system.

"We need a GM at the customer service station. We need our new GM at the customer service station."

Deidre walked through the produce aisle to access the front as quickly as possible. She was going to kill Renita. Obviously she was abusing her duties to pull a prank of some kind. Applause erupted from her staff as she reached the front. They were clapping for her. She swelled with pride and brimmed with emotions as many of her colleagues that she worked alongside for years left their posts and registers to congratulate her on the news that Renita readily broadcasted. She turned toward the culprit and saw Andre standing in front of Renita's register.

The notion that she could deny any romantic interest in Andre flew out the window at the sight of him. He was distinguished in his uniform and could still make her heart leap. She walked over to him as her ovation died down and everyone had gone back to their regular duties. She signaled for him to follow her outside to avoid public scrutiny.

"I did it," she said, as if he weren't just in the store and heard the announcement himself. She was dying to tell someone and thought it ironic that he was the first one to know. "I'm the new General Manager."

He opened his arms to give her a congratulatory hug and she gladly walked into his embrace, forgetting her vow to be done with him. "That's great. I'm happy for you," he replied. He held on longer than she expected, and when he finally released her, she noticed his eyes had such a profound sadness in them that it temporarily put a damper on her otherwise perfect day. "I brought back those movies. I know you need to get them back to the video store."

"Yeah thanks," Deidre said, taking the videos still in the bag from him.

Their eyes carried on their own conversation. His eyes, red rimmed and weary, were downcast avoiding the direct questioning of her piercing eyes.

"I want to come over and talk to Deuce, if that's all right with you."

"That'll be good," Deidre said. "What are we going to do with him?"

"I don't know. I figure I'll have a better idea when I speak with him. He just failed a class. It's not the end of the world."

"Well, I'm following your lead. He's not telling me anything. He keeps everything bottled inside. I don't want to get in the way if you can get him to open up," Deidre said.

Deidre really didn't want her feelings for Andre to get in the way of God's assignment either. She was trying to forgive him.

"All right then, I'll let you get back to your store. I'll see you later."

Deidre watched him walk across the parking lot. It didn't get any easier watching him walk away.

Chapter 35

Andre knew that Deidre probably had given up on him coming over and talking with DeAndre as he had promised earlier in the week. He finally knocked on her door at 8:45P.M. Thursday night. It had taken him four days to get himself together. He had his pre-operation work-up at the lab where Dr. Jefferies wanted to be doubly sure of his contributing factors that he ordered a more extensive stool test kit for him to complete at home. He didn't know if he were being psychosomatic during all this, but he just couldn't come around Deidre and his son for fear that he would reek of a deadly disease.

Andre hadn't made up his mind what, if anything, he would tell Deidre and DeAndre about his diagnosis. Bottom line is that he didn't want Deidre to feel obligated to have to care for him like another dependent. He had come to the conclusion that his diagnosis should not have a bearing on what kind of father he could be presently.

Deidre greeted Andre at the door in a plum v-neck top with scalloped lace around the edges and grey trousers. Her plush ballerina-style slippers and mug of hot tea indicated that she had been home long enough to unwind. He remembered those slippers from the time when they were together. He also remembered the calming effect hot tea had on her in the evenings no matter what the season. He was truly homesick.

Deidre barely spoke as she yielded the way for him to enter.

"Sleepy time?" Andre said.

"Earl Grey. I'm not quite ready to retire. I'm working on a report on the computer. Come on in."

"They got you bringing work home now, huh?"

She moved from the doorway toward the living room, and he followed. "That among other things, but I enjoy it."

Andre ignored her wide-eyed stare that queried him as she turned to face him, perhaps about his absenteeism or maybe because of his haggard appearance. "Is Deuce still up?"

"He should be. He got out of the shower not too long ago. I made him sit here after dinner and watch game shows with me like we used to do," Deidre said through vapors rising off her mug. "You can go on back."

Andre felt her on his heels and thought maybe she'd be joining in on the dialogue when she stopped in front of the bedroom across the hall that had always been her home office. DeAndre's door was closed and the canned laughter from a television sitcom could be heard through it.

Andre knocked and waited for permission to enter. By the time DeAndre had given Andre the verbal okay, he was lying across his bed. His night clothes consisted of a short sleeve T-shirt and extra long shorts.

DeAndre looked like Andre felt. He looked frail without the weight loss. His eyes were dull and his lips were pouted, letting Andre know he wasn't up for a conversa-

tion. Andre signaled for him to scoot over on his bed to
allow him to sit. He thought long and hard about what
he'd say to his son in lieu of all that had gone on the past
couple of weeks and decided to say what he wished his
father had said to him on many occasions growing up.

"How's it going?"

"Fine," DeAndre said, never taking his eyes off the
television screen.

"You're fine, huh? That's not what your mom told me.
You're sleeping all the time and not talking on the phone
with your friends."

"I'm tired. Can't I take a nap when I get home from
school?"

"Hold up," Andre said, searching for the television remote. "We're just worried about you. Let's turn this television off so we can rap awhile."

DeAndre breathed in deeply, but thought twice before
sighing too loudly. He pushed himself off the bed to grab
the remote on his nightstand. After turning the television
off, he plopped back on the bed and rolled to his back
with his arms under his head. He stared into the ceiling
as if there was something written there.

"Look, I came all the way over here to—"

"You came just to repeat everything that Mom has told
me over and over for the past few days?" DeAndre said
under his breathe. "I know I'm punished. I know you all
want me to work hard this summer to make sure I get to
Carver and not return to Pemberton Middle School next
year."

"Hey, what about Malcolm Woods?"

"I didn't get in," DeAndre said as if his father were an
imbecile.

"You didn't get into the camp, but there is still a way to
apply to get into the school in the fall. What's up? Don't
you want to go to this school and learn more about art?"

Andre stared down at his son. DeAndre just shrugged. Could he show up after being a 'Johnny Come Lately' father and make his son go to this school against his will? Andre didn't know why, but right now DeAndre was behaving as if his will had been broken. He had to make him see that this was an opportunity that he couldn't miss.

"It's not too late. Where are those papers I gave you when I first told you about the school? Find them." Andre slapped the bed with his request. "C'mon, Deuce man, you were hyped about this two weeks ago. We both were."

What a difference a couple of weeks can make, Andre thought as he watched his son poke around his desk in slow motion. He would feel a lot better about going into the hospital knowing that DeAndre had a plan of action which included getting into this school. Andre felt sure it would be all downhill from there. It always seemed that he came out of the doctors feeling worse than when he went in. He was sure once he was in that hospital gown and invaded by that scope on that operating table that treatment would become a way of life and the hospital would become his new home.

"I want to tell you . . ."Andre started, resigned to share the tragic news.

"I got it," DeAndre interrupted. The same manila folder he had given his son was in his hand. He handed the folder to Andre and took a seat next to him.

"Yeah, let's see." Andre scanned the contents. "Okay, the Magnet school auditions are August 1st."

"I have to audition?"

"Visual Arts applicants must present a portfolio, you know like a collection of work samples."

"Dang," DeAndre said, reclining on his side, and resting his head in his hand. "I got to put together a portfolio and go to summer school at the same time. All I got to do is show up at Carver. Plus all I have are sketches. They want something fancy."

"I know that it seems like a lot, but you can handle it. Carver is a second-rate school for someone with your talent. You've got to try. This is your future," Andre said. "There is nothing worse than seeing other people succeed knowing you could have done it also if you had just tried."

"Like you and the Bo Donovan thing?"

"What?" Andre said, patting his chest.

"Anyone can see you spend fifty percent of your time at work visiting the gym. That's probably why you even work at that mall."

He's a clever kid to swing the interrogation light off himself and onto me, Andre thought. DeAndre wasn't saying anything about his career options that he hadn't contemplated seriously himself, especially after the shootings. Bo Donovan University had two intensive summer trainings, but just like everything else, pursuing this plan was placed on the shelf after visiting Dr. Jefferies.

"You're right. At one time I did want to be a fitness coach, but growing up, school was not my favorite place. I struggled."

"Mom said you were kept back a year in high school."

"It's true. So you see, returning to school after so much time has been something I've been avoiding. The Body Synergy program is not easy either, let me tell you. I would be studying science, math and health all over again."

There was silence. Andre felt compelled to bring closure to this issue even though he had not firmed it up in his mind yet. He was there to offer sound advice to DeAndre; now it was time that he started leading by example.

"How about we both try? You pass your summer school class and we wow these people with your sketches at the audition," Andre said, looking into his son's eyes that he noticed were as wide and as beautiful as his mother's, "and I'll enroll in Bo Donovan University. I have something coming up that might prevent me from being in the first session, but I'll definitely hit the second. How about it?"

Andre smiled faintly as his son nodded, sealing their deal. The whole deal was predicated on too many outside variables. DeAndre had to pass his summer school class. When that happened, Andre wasn't sure his teacher would turn around a grade in time to meet the minimum grade point average requirement. Not to mention the outcome of his colonoscopy and subsequent treatments. They were in the need of several small miracles.

Andre and DeAndre talked about the portfolio. The school required the student's interpretation of styles such as abstract, charcoal sketch, and a still-life to be included in the portfolio. Two student choices rounded out the collection.

It was 9:55 P.M. when they packed up his sketchbooks and placed other sketches into the protective covers of folders and report covers. Andre felt privileged to finally be trusted to view his son's work and only hoped he would be around to see his work recognized by others. It was getting late, and he had one more order of business.

"So now that that's out the way, where are the books you checked out at the library?"

"The . . . books?" DeAndre said, stammering.

"Yeah the books you had to have for your project. There was one book in particular I'm sure contained all the information you needed."

Andre noticed DeAndre had not moved, but found it hard to keep his eyes fixed in the same spot.

He continued. "I'm trying to figure out, though, how

did you use *The Ultimate Illustrated Sex Guide* to explain colonization?" Andre pretended to ponder for a minute. "Now get the books. Unless you'd rather your mother take them back to the library for you."

DeAndre didn't say anything. He didn't have to; *busted* was written all over his face. For the third time he got up, but this time, he slinked to the closet. He bent over and went digging as if he were excavating a fossil. He pulled two huge books from the depths and placed them in front of his father.

"There wasn't any project, was there?"

With his eyes downcast, DeAndre shook his head, but that was all he was offering.

"What's this all about? Why'd you tell me you were going to the library for one thing, but come out with another?"

"The twins and I saw it, and I was curious about the pictures."

"Okay, now you think I'm a chump. I know guys your age get curious, but to make an urgent pit stop to the library lets me know something else is up with this. I thought we already had this talk. Didn't we talk about sex, babies, and protection?"

Andre didn't know why, but he felt personally offended. Then it dawned on him that sex was another thing that his own father never talked to him about. He had to discover on his own, but DeAndre had a father willing to help him figure stuff out.

"Come on, don't clam up on me. I'm not here to bust you out. I'm your dad. We're supposed to talk about this stuff. I even came prepared," Andre said, unfolding a large drawstring bag from the sports store that DeAndre's new tennis shoes came in. "This makes the difference between me walking out of here with your books out in the open or concealed in this bag."

DeAndre thought about it. "I guess I was trying to get some ideas."

"Whoa, tell me you're not seriously thinking you're ready for sex, and who . . ." Andre said, standing and hitting himself upside the head. "This all happens to coincide with your little date with the private school girl. Deuce, man, I'm telling you, you're biting off way more than you can possibly chew. What's the rush? You're just fourteen. I told you never to pressure a girl for sex. It's not cool."

"I didn't. She just felt it would be the perfect time to, you know, do it, before going to high school."

"Thank God her mother made her dump your butt," Andre said, chuckling before he could censor himself. DeAndre had a pained expression and rubbed his left forearm as if he'd just been pinched hard. Andre covered his mouth and shook his head. He couldn't believe this. "My bad. Let me get this straight though. This was her idea? This is the same girl your mother has been bragging about being so sweet."

"She is nice," DeAndre said, rising up in her defense.

"Son, nice girls don't offer themselves up that easily, especially not at fourteen years of age. Have you even kissed this girl?"

"Many times," DeAndre said proudly.

"I'll put it like this, your little girlfriend will be real popular in high school, but it won't be because of her personality." Andre looked at his son's sheepish expression and knew his last comment had gone over his head.

"She's not my girlfriend anymore anyway. I called her after the dance and she told me she just wanted to be friends."

Ouch. Andre could tell from his son how much that phrase can sting someone who wasn't expecting it, *like Deidre.*

"You're all right, right?" Andre said, swinging at him as if he were in a boxing ring to encourage him to brush it off, or at least, dodge the blow. "I mean you're cool, right?"

"Yeah, except she got accepted into the camp instead of me, so she'll be going to my same school if I get in."

"The school is huge with lots of other girls."

"I know," DeAndre said, lying on his side again with his head propped on his hand. "My Sunday School teacher said good relationships start from friendships. Good friends last a lifetime, right?"

Andre didn't have many friends. He thought about his old crew and his buddy, Keith, the man who he would more than likely ask to drive him to and from the hospital next week.

"Can I ask you something?" DeAndre asked, bringing Andre back to the present. "What happened between you and mom? I mean why aren't you still together?"

Andre thought about an edited version. The look in DeAndre's eyes was telling Andre that he was asking him to be transparent so he could learn something.

"You don't have any tape recorders going, do you?" Andre said, smiling. "I don't know if I ever told you, but I think it's important for you to know that you were conceived in love. Your mom wasn't somebody I wanted to just sleep with. We were in love, and honestly, I still care for her deeply. I just think that back then we were immature, and when you're immature, you ask for more than you need and take even more."

Andre didn't know if his son understood what he was trying to say. He lay down beside his son and mirrored his position before he continued, "Your mom gave a lot. I think she turned her back on a big part of who she was— her spiritual side—just to stay with me. She wasn't ever going to be happy that way. You're never going to grow in a relationship until you know who you are, what you want . . . and you don't compromise that for anyone."

"I always wanted . . . I mean, when I was little, I used to pray that you all would at least start speaking again, and you know."

His son's childhood wish choked up Andre, and he took a moment before beginning again. "You might have guessed, but recently your mother and I have been—"

"In negotiations," DeAndre finished.

"Yeah, we're in negotiations," Andre chuckled. "Since being back in you all's lives, getting to know you over again, and loving you as my son, makes me love her even more as your momma and vice versa. " Andre lifted himself off the bed. "As a matter of fact, I better go talk to your mother now before she goes to bed and I fall asleep right here."

"You're not going to tell her about what we talked about, are you?" DeAndre asked.

"Naw, I don't think that will be necessary. Keep your head up these last few days in school. Hear me? Remember our deal."

"A'ight, Dad," DeAndre said, extending his hand in a mannish manner.

Andre pounded his son's fist. "It's been real. You can always ask me anything. I mean anything. Just give me a chance to figure it out first before you expect an answer."

Chapter 36

Andre darkened the doorway to Deidre's office to find her pajama-clad, but not bound for bed. She was still staring at her computer screen. He felt tired but knew he wasn't ready to face the sleeplessness that awaited him when he got to his apartment. He was starting to realize, in the short time since his diagnosis, that he didn't have many people he could call on to keep him company.

"Hey. Waiting for me to leave?" he called out.

"I almost forgot you were there. I'm still playing around with this software. Know anything about system requirements and installing software?" Deidre asked with her eyes still squinted at the screen.

"Sorry, can't help you there," Andre answered. "Can I steal you away for a minute?"

"Yeah, I've been on this thing too long anyway, but this application is supposed to make some of the store's files and databases accessible to me at home if I can get it to load completely. I keep installing and uninstalling. Let me get this other document ready to print and I'll be right out."

Andre made his way into the living room and collapsed onto the couch, another fixture from the time when they were together. It was a tan faux-suede that had a sweet spot in the corner where the armrest was a little loose, but still firm enough for him to relax on while watching television or gazing out the window. He rooted around until he found that spot in the corner, and he rested his head back on the oversized cushion. He didn't hear Deidre enter the room.

"Did DeAndre do any talking?" Deidre said, startling him. "Or did he just sit there waiting for you to get tired of talking?"

"No. We had an exchange going, a very interesting and enlightening exchange." Andre planted his arm on the armrest to prop his head.

"Good, then I'm sure you learned more than I've managed to." Deidre sat in the arm chair across from him with her legs crossed at the knee. "I've really tried to be sensitive and let the fact that he has to go to summer school be his punishment. Other than that, I think he's still weirded out by the mall and maybe a little mad at Kenya, you know, about the dance. "

"He told me they're friends." Andre put both his hands up. "He's okay with it, so let's leave it at that."

Andre did not want to go into everything he was able to get DeAndre to share with him. His son was depending on him to keep his confidence about his teenage curiosity and not blab it to his mother.

"I guess history is repeating itself," Deidre said matter-of-factly.

Andre sat all the way up this time and clasped his hands together as he rested them on his knees. "I know, one minute we are on play, and the next we're on pause."

"Let's stay on pause," Deidre interjected. "Let's just be blessed that we're here and we're at least speaking, and go from there. This stuff with DeAndre failing in school has proven that he should really be our focus right now."

"Right." His voice was unable to hide the same regret he saw in her eyes. "So why don't I feel blessed when I got a son with about as many worries as his old man and a relationship I haven't managed to get right in eight years?"

"We just took me out the equation, remember? And for the record, we both can't get it right. We're missing a key ingredient," Deidre said, studying the hem of her satin pajama top. After picking at a few strings, she allowed it to fall flat and stared at Andre with new resolve. "As far as the blessings go, faith puts me in the right frame of mind to deal with everything that's going on."

"Yeah well, I haven't been in my right mind for days . . . weeks. You might even say years. Do I look like I'm in my right mind?"

Andre made a crazy face that made Deidre chuckle. *If she only knew the truth,* he thought.

"I guess you know what you need then. You need Jesus."

Andre couldn't tell if she was being serious or patronizing, but decided to change the subject. "Remember when you first started going back to school at night, and I was home with Deuce?"

Deidre smiled and shook her head at the memories. "Yeah, and every week I'd come home, and you all had made a trip to the emergency room for something."

"It wasn't every week, but I didn't expect the child's poop to take on that shade of green." Andre scrunched up his face.

"That's 'cause you never changed any Pampers," Deidre said, with her hand on her hips. "But what about the time you let him shove peas in his nose."

For some reason the memory of his son's nose packed and pouring with pea soup was now hysterical to Andre. He laughed until he dropped to his knees on the floor. When he was exhausted, he either got really irritable or really silly. The latter was apparent now, and he continued to take Deidre down memory lane to a time when they both were together and everything between them appeared fine. He needed to laugh and hearing her laugh soothed him.

After forty-five minutes had passed, Deidre was also sitting on the floor with her back against the armchair, holding her stomach and panting as if she couldn't take any more. "It's getting late, and you got me cracking up on the floor like a fool. I know you didn't wait around to talk about old times. What do you want, Dre?"

You, he thought. "I know, I know, I ain't got to go home, but I got to get the heck up outta here, right?"

"Kinda. Do you know what time it is?" She paused as if waiting for him to make a move, but he didn't. "For real Dre, what do you want?"

"I want what you have," Andre said, unable to put his feelings into words. " I came over today thinking you would be so angry at Deuce, that he'd be taking up residence in the shed out back, and so furious with me, for, well, you know. But there is something about you that's always so strong. I want that peace."

"God will give you peace," Deidre replied, her face taking on such an ethereal quality in the glow of the lamp directly overhead that Andre thought he was dreaming.

"Okay, I see a recurring theme here," Andre said, now searching out the wall clock that read close to midnight.

Conversations about God and religion in the past always ended up with a measuring stick and him coming up short.

Andre thought about his own ideology. What did he believe in? He thought about how much credence he had put into his body strength and his workouts. It all seemed to amount to nothing in the face of real trials.

"You said it yourself, you've got a lot of worries. Well, I have the privilege of taking those worries to the Lord. That's why I can have mercy on that son of ours and can even reason with you," Deidre said, kneeling before him, then standing.

Deidre put up a finger to indicate for him to wait. "Let me show you something. It'll take one minute."

Andre watched her take off down the hall. He could hear her bang on DeAndre's door, telling him to cut off the television. He couldn't hear DeAndre's reply, but could tell they were having a conversation. Andre found his spot again on the couch and closed his eyes for what he thought was only a moment. He awoke to find his shoes off and Deidre tugging at his legs in an attempt to straighten him out on the couch.

"Dag, I dozed off," Andre said, attempting to right himself.

"You're fine. I was just trying to make you more comfortable," Deidre said.

"Good, 'cause I don't think I can drive home. Feels like I haven't slept in days," he murmured.

Andre fought to keep his eyes open. He watched Deidre lay what looked like a Bible on the end table next to his head before cutting off the lamp. He could see her shadow pulling a plaid blanket off her easy chair, which she unfolded and draped over him.

"I'm going to bed," Deidre announced.

He watched her form start to disappear down the hall. He had to tell her one last thing. "Hey, you know what I learned from our son?"

"What's that?"

"The word friend is a good word; and in our case, it's a very good word."

Chapter 37

Deidre felt like a brooding hen protecting one of her young all night as Andre slumbered on her couch. She peeped in on him when she got up in the middle of the night to use the restroom. She watched the deep swell of his chest as he breathed in. She listened as the air expelled in a loud snore. She urged DeAndre to go about his morning routine quietly so not to awaken his father, and then hastened him off to school. Having showered and dressed herself, she debated about how long she should allow him to sleep.

Deidre noticed that Andre stayed in the same position all night, lying on his right side facing the back of the couch. She approached him and gently touched his arm to wake him. When he didn't stir, she left her hand on him, closed her eyes, and began to pray over him. She prayed for his soul. Reminiscing with him the night before was bittersweet. He seemed to be enjoying himself so much. With every bout of laughter came sadness though. She wanted so desperately to fix it, fix him, fix their relationship. Deidre realized now that she never

had a problem sharing God with Andre. She had a problem sharing Andre with God. She wanted him all to herself. Fortunately, she knew better than to play tug-of-war
with God.

Deidre felt she missed the perfect opportunity to travel
down Romans Road with Andre. Her mind kept telling
her: *It's as simple as recommending a restaurant; make the introductions.*

When she opened her eyes at the end of the prayer, he
was looking up at her.

"Hey," she said, startled. She backed up, giving him
room to kick his legs over and sit up.

"Serving me my last rites?" he asked, wiping his face
with his hand and rotating his neck until it cracked before sitting up. "Am I that bad off?"

"I don't know, are you?"

"Very funny." Andre let out a loud moan while standing erect and stretching another few inches above his
6'2" frame. "Excuse me while I go to the bathroom and
get myself together."

Deidre made her way to the kitchen. She usually preferred to grab something quick to nibble on before rushing off to work. She wondered if Andre would be
hungry.

"What time is it?" he asked, after using the facilities.
He joined her in the kitchen and sat at the table opposite
the stove.

"Almost nine thirty." Deidre noticed he was still in no
hurry to get home. Soon she would be setting off to work
herself. "Are you hungry?"

"Starving."

Deidre went on the hunt for something in her refrigerator. She spotted the white butcher paper from Fresh
Gardens' seafood counter. "I bought this halibut on Mon-

day, thinking you were coming over then to talk to De-Andre."

Deidre noticed his flattered expression before continuing, "I guess I expected too much. That is, I expected too much of my culinary skills. I didn't even know how to prepare it. Do you fry or bake halibut?"

"You can bake or pan fry it. I got a great recipe for soft tacos with halibut in one of my Bo Donovan cookbooks that you can have. It's so good. Deuce would love them with a little sour cream."

"You can just make me a copy," Deidre said, settling on bagels and the last quarter of cream cheese spread. She placed the clear bag containing the bagels, cream cheese and two knives on the table with two paper towels. She joined him at the table. Although he signaled for her to fill her bagel first, she made sure to leave some spread for him.

Deidre thought about what it would be like cooking for him again. Her mind naturally gravitated to the possibility of them being together and caring for him as a companion.

Are you being fed the same thing?

Deidre closed her eyes to welcome the guidance of the Holy Spirit. Andre's voice brought her back to reality.

"I see you're already dressed for work." He was swirling the cream cheese on one half of the bagel with a knife.

"Yeah, I'll be leaving soon. I'm strictly eleven to seven now. No more working to close for awhile. I begin hiring a new shift manager for the night shift today."

"Sweet."

"What about you? What time are you going in?"

"I'm not," Andre said with a mouth full.

"Oh, you have the day off? No wonder you were burning the midnight oil. Let me tell you, DeAndre was so surprised, almost happy to see you sleeping on the couch this morning. I wouldn't let him wake you though."

Deidre returned to the refrigerator, this time for something to drink. She chose orange juice and carried the carton and two small glasses to the table.

"I think I'm getting to him," Andre said. "I convinced him to pull together a collection of work to audition for a placement in Malcolm Woods after all. I'm taking him to get some supplies this weekend."

That was great news to Deidre who overheard DeAndre telling the twins about summer school and attending Carver next year like it was part of the status quo. "Did he tell you he didn't want to go back to the mall for awhile? I was worried we were going to have to work something else out for the weekends he is with you."

"Yeah, he doesn't want to admit that what happened in the mall really scared him. Don't worry about it though. I'm not working this weekend."

Deidre almost missed her glass with the spout of orange juice carton as she poured it. "When do you work?"

"I'm taking some time off."

"Obviously," she remarked, "but for how long?"

"I don't know, Dee. I'm just taking some time off, all right?" Andre helped himself to the juice.

"Is there any reason why?" Deidre searched his face for the answer.

"It's nothing," Andre said as he gobbled the last bite of bagel before licking the excess cream cheese off his thumb and forefinger.

"Why are you being so evasive?"

"'Cause it's not your burden, Dee," Andre said, exasperated.

It amazed Deidre how fast they could go from pleasant to uneasiness. Why was he here? Obviously he didn't trust her with the truth.

"You come up here obviously exhausted, looking like the walking dead, conk out on my couch, and now you're taking an indefinite amount of time off from your job. A red flag goes up."

His smirk told Deidre that he expected she'd say as much. "After all these years, aren't you tired of trying to figure me out, trying to help me with my issues? This is not like the times when I was short with my half of the rent, and I needed you to cover for me."

"Oh I see. This is about pride and your male ego. When I had trouble with DeAndre, I had to come to you for help even after what happened with us in the past. That's why we are not alone on earth, Dre. We all need help sometimes."

"Well, you can't save me this time. "Andre swished his orange juice around in his glass.

Deidre felt his words rang with so much truth that it must have been the reason the phone sounded. Deidre grabbed the wall extension and told Sheila she'd call her back without letting her get a word in. This was her opportunity. "You're right. I can't save you, Andre, but I can help you get to the one who can."

Andre drained his glass. He balled up his paper towel and kept it clenched in his fist. He stood. "For what, so I can sit up in church and be judged? You and your mother have tried to convert me before, remember?"

"I want to show you the difference between believing there is a God and having Him operating in your life. I want to pray the prayer of salvation with you and show you some scriptures that explain the kind of relationship God wants with you."

"I'm okay, all right?" His voice was barely above a whisper. "Look, thanks for letting me crash here. I've got to go."

Deidre watched him leave the kitchen. There was

something about seeing him walk away from her yet again that made her heart race. How many times had she watched him walk away? Had they walked away from each other?

"You know what I think? I think you're a control freak." Deidre followed him into the living room where he had slept. He gave her an absurd expression as if she didn't know what she was talking about.

Now that she had his attention, she continued. "You can't control whatever it is you're going through, and that's driving you crazy. It's not me trying to control everything, it's you. And it's not me retreating this time, it's you. Just like when we broke up, you're shutting me out with no explanation. As much as I've wanted to shut you out of my life. As much as I've wanted to stop feeling what I'm feeling, I can't."

Deidre felt as if she'd hyperventilate if she didn't take a breath. She grasped the back of the armchair for support.

"I can't either," Andre said softly.

"I just feel that if you really cared for me, you wouldn't keep shutting me out like that. Not again," Deidre said.

Andre dropped onto the couch with a loud thud and an even louder sigh. There was a long pause. His jaw clenched. His temple tightened with thought. "My doctor thinks I may have colorectal cancer."

"What?" Deidre clutched her chest, unable to hide her horror.

"Yeah, deal with that, because I sure can't."

"Wait, I don't understand. Where? I mean, when did you find out?" Deidre stammered.

"A week ago during a visit with my doctor."

Did he say cancer? She plopped just as hard onto the chair. Pieces of the puzzle from the last couple of weeks began falling into place in her mind, but now her heart was breaking.

"And, they already know you have cancer?"

"It's kind of consistent with the way my life is going right now. I've been having symptoms, and I have a family history. To top it off, Dr. Jefferies felt something in my colon. They want to do a procedure next week to be sure."

"So there's hope, right?" Deidre said, her hands in a praying stance. She looked to him to assure her, but his expression didn't register optimism. "You might not even have it."

"I'm not getting my hopes up. My father withered up and died of this very thing." Andre's voice was unexpectedly hoarse.

She waited on her own words of comfort that she could share. *God. Why him? Why now? What do I say?*

Tell of my love.

She was up and at his side. "You can't give up. God will bring you through this."

"I'm not in that frame of mind right now. Don't you get it? I'm angry, let down. My body betrayed me," Andre said, flexing his bicep. "What have I been working for all this time, changing my lifestyle and working out all the time so I can have muscles on top of cancerous cells?"

His despair pierced her heart. "The Bo Donovan regiment has been great for you, but it's just that, a health regiment. Faith in God is a way of life. I believe He wants you to turn to Him."

"Is that what God wants from me? Some sort of deathbed plea bargain? He knocks one foot in the grave so I can see the light?"

She grabbed his hands and squeezed them within

hers. "He wants to reveal Himself to you. Pray to Him like that time in the mall. Let Him know you want a relationship with Him. He promises He'll be there with you even in your time of need."

They sat there quietly holding hands. Andre rested back into the cushions of the couch as if he were contemplating what she said.

"I don't know, Dee. It's hard to process this whole thing," Andre said.

"Just think about it. It's not about what I want you to do. It's not about the church. It's about making a connection with God."

Andre nodded at the wall clock as he rose from his place on the couch. He bent to kiss her forehead. "I know you have faith enough for the both us. I appreciate your concern. At least I know you'll be praying for me."

Deidre sighed loudly as she escorted him to the door. "You know I'll be praying all the way to the hospital."

He raised his brow in confusion. "No, Deidre. This is why I didn't want to tell you. I can't expect you to take off work just to take me for an in and out procedure. You've got your hands full with the new promotion. Deuce is out of school next week. And aren't you going out of town to your mother's?"

"I'll handle my mother. I'm going to tell her that I need to be with my friend next weekend. As far as my job goes, I'm the manager, remember? You're not the only one who can take off work," Deidre said with a hand on her hip.

Andre opened the front door to the outside and sunshine poured into the doorway. Streams of sunlight bathed and warmed their faces. He turned to face her.

"I can't talk you out of going with me, can I?" he said with a weak smile.

Deidre just shook her head. She noticed his hesitancy

as he looked up and down her street on his way to his car. She wondered what he was going to do with himself during his time off besides wait for a premature death. She called out to him.

"If DeAndre and I come over with the halibut later, will you make those tacos for us?"

Andre smiled and gave her the thumbs up.

Chapter 38

Either Deidre was making Andre nervous, or he was already scared to death. He was unusually quiet. They arrived at the hospital thirty minutes before his scheduled procedure and took a seat with the other patients and loved ones buying time with general interest magazines and handheld devices. She took it upon herself to assist Andre with his registration forms since he seemed preoccupied. It gave her something to do. She was like a settlement officer giving a synopsis of the form and pointing out where he should sign. She found another ink pen in her purse and settled in to complete the general information on the next page.

"Andre Maurice Hicks," Deidre sang, writing his full name as she would in her notebooks back in high school. He smiled at her weakly before dropping his head back to the paper in his lap.

The next line was asking for emergency authorization in the event that he couldn't make decisions on his own. Technically, she wasn't even his girlfriend. *DeAndre, who was now with her sister and his cousins in Iverson, South*

Carolina for a week, was his next of kin. She started to put down her information for emergency contact purposes, but decided to ask him first.

"Dre, where it says—" Deidre started.

Andre grabbed the clipboard from her. "You don't have to fill out all of that. All they need to know is who is paying." He leaned over sideways toward her to extract his wallet from his back pocket. He pulled out a blue and white insurance card and began filling in the blanks before signing and dating it.

"But—" Deidre started again.

"Trust me, Dee. They have all they need to know in their computer. This is basically just a duplicate of forms to waste your time when their operating room gets backed up." Andre took the clipboard back to the receptionist.

Deidre looked around the waiting room where she would spend the next three or four hours. A maze of vinyl cushioned seats faced either the small mounted television or the tinted glass window overlooking the parking lot and ambulatory entrance. She heard Andre's stomach rumble when he returned to his seat. He had been instructed not to eat anything past midnight. Deidre held off from eating the cereal bar she had in her purse. They heard a nurse call Andre's name from the side door and walked toward her.

"Hello, my name is Megan. I'm the pre-op nurse, and I am going to get you prepared for your procedure."

"Oh," Deidre said, realizing that this was where they would part ways. "So I'll just wait out here then."

"All right," Andre said, handing over his watch and wallet to Deidre.

"Your guest can come back in a few minutes to speak to the doctor," the nurse said, referring to Deidre. "I'll come and get you after I get Mr. Hicks situated and get his vitals."

"No, I'll just see you later," Andre said, as if he were just going to the corner store. "Go get yourself something to eat or something."

"The lady said I can come back," Deidre said practically through her teeth. *I hope he doesn't think he's getting rid of me that easily* "You must have forgotten who you were talking to."

"Megan, meet Miss Persistent," Andre said.

Deidre watched as the nurse waited for Andre to walk through the door. Back in her seat, Deidre pulled out her daily devotional and her mini Bible. The day's lesson was from the Parable of the sower. It told of a man sprinkling seed for an impending harvest that Jesus used as a symbol of His Word and His way. The success of the harvest depended on where it was planted. Some seeds were plucked away immediately. Some fell on stony ground; some among thorns, and a few grew and thrived in fertile soil. Her seed just walked through the door to await his operation, Deidre thought. It remained to be seen how fruitful her efforts at reaching him had been.

When the pre-op nurse came to get her, she was led down a corridor to an open room with several beds separated by a wrap around curtain. Andre was in the next to the last compartment. She realized why he didn't want her to come back. There was nothing more vulnerable than a man in a flimsy blue hospital gown and cap hooked to an IV. He tried to paint on a brave face when she approached. She stood near the head of the bed on the right hand side as the nurse closed the curtain to afford them some privacy.

"You couldn't resist the urge to see a brother in his skimpies," Andre said. When Deidre didn't reply he countered with, "I'm all right."

"I know," Deidre said. "They do thousands of procedures like this every day. It's in and out for goodness sakes."

"So you can leave and come back later."

"Why are you in such a rush to get rid of me? Am I making you nervous by being here?"

"Not at all," Andre said, adjusting himself in the bed. "I know this is not your scene. You've done enough waiting around for me to fill two lifetimes."

"This is an entirely different thing."

"I know. You've got important things to do in your career, a life to live. I just don't want you taking up the habit of waiting on me, because I may not get better."

Deidre waved off the melodrama. She didn't want to go there with him. As if there was any place she'd rather be. She had to believe that the Lord had a bigger plan for Andre, which included restoring him to good health. She thought about what she had just read about the seed of Christ she attempted to plant in his heart. "Let's put an end to all this talk about not getting better. I've learned that if you pray, it eliminates the need to worry. Can I pray for you?"

Deidre was pleasantly surprised when he nodded his head. She closed her eyes to trap a tear that was about to fall. After a moment, she grabbed his left hand and began. She prayed for the outcome they both hoped for, speaking those things as if they already were. She prayed that the seed of God's love would take root in his heart. Then she petitioned God to bless every doctor, nurse, and attendant that he came in contact with during his time in the hospital.

As if on cue, the very doctors Deidre just prayed for entered. They introduced themselves as the surgeon and anesthesiologist. Andre introduced Deidre by name only with no title of possession as in, his friend or his girlfriend. They smiled at her politely as they explained each phase of the procedure briefly to him. Deidre faded into the background, listening. The surgeon explained that after Andre was put under anesthesia, he would use a scope driven by knobs to search for and extract polyps. A complete analysis of those polyps would be done within a week after the surgery. The entire procedure from start to finish would take two and a half to three hours at the maximum.

Deidre decided she would leave with the doctors to give Andre time alone to mentally prepare. She encouraged him to say his own prayer. Both of them had successfully tried to stay within the boundaries of the friend zone the week leading up to his surgery. Signs of affection were limited to a kiss on the cheek or forehead, and a bear hug. This time when she leaned down to kiss his forehead he arched his neck to met her lips with his own. She left the room praying to God that his kiss could be hers to enjoy for a long time to come.

Nearly five hours later, Deidre was moving too fast for the automatic doors and had to slow herself down before she went crashing into it. She had gone to the nearby mall after leaving Andre and got caught up in a two-day sale and traffic from an accident on her way back to the hospital. A fifteen-minute drive had taken forty-five as they awaited authorities to clear the scene. She was one of the fortunate ones to scoot by in the left hand lane after the ambulance loaded up the injured and took off. Deidre appeared to be in a race with the emergency vehicle as she raced toward the same hospital. She had to get back to Andre.

She noticed the lobby had cleared out significantly as she hurried toward the family waiting area. There was no way to know if Andre's surgery was over or had run long. She was clueless. She approached the door to the surgical area despite the signs that read, AUTHORIZED PERSONNEL ONLY. She noticed the panel on the wall that allowed those authorized access by some sort of ID pass. Then she remembered that this area wrapped around from the pre-op entrance in the main lobby that she was led through that morning and decided to try that route.

Back at the receptionist counter, the woman stationed there wasn't giving Deidre eye contact, much less trying to understand what she was trying to say. Deidre was beginning to get angry when the door opened and a familiar voice summoned another family back to Pre-op. Deidre left her fruitless efforts with the receptionist for more promising ones.

Deidre hoped Andre's pre-op nurse, Megan, remembered her from earlier. Her face didn't register recognition, and the woman and her daughter she was escorting back were similarly confused.

"Miss Persistent?" Deidre said it as if Andre's pun from earlier would ring a bell. "I came in earlier with a man who was having a colonoscopy at 8:30. It's close to one now. I left out and was late getting back. I'm not sure if he's in recovery or just how the procedure went. Can you find out for me?"

Megan's face softened at her plea. "I'll check for you after I get these people situated. What's the patient's name again?"

"Andre Hicks."

"You can go in the family waiting area," Megan said, using a chart to point the way. "I'll see if I can get his doctor to come out and speak to you."

"Thank you," Deidre said, taking off in the same direction in which she had come.

It took twenty minutes for Deidre to realize no one was coming. Was there a lost and found for patients? She figured Andre had to be looking for her as well unless something happened to him during the surgery. Her mind flashed back to the forms she filled out for him that morning. *Next of kin.* The thought prompted her out of her seat. She approached the secured entrance to the surgical area with the intention of going in.

Deidre waited until someone came out to gain entrance on their pass. She went unnoticed among the hospital officials in basic blue or green colored scrubs that went about the business of managing the care of their current patient. A curtain whipped open and a team escorted a patient, bed-and-all, to what Deidre could only assume was an awaiting operating room. She caught a nurse tailing behind.

Deidre alarmed the woman by grabbing her arm. The nurse, an average sized woman, gave Deidre a fierce backward glance that showed she didn't appreciate being handled.

"Yes?" the woman said.

"Sorry, but I'm looking for my friend who came back for surgery."

"You shouldn't even be back here. The waiting room is through those doors. Someone will be with you shortly."

"No," Deidre said, reaching out for her, but thought better of putting her hands on the woman again. "I've been waiting. He came in at eight thirty. They said it would take three hours. It's going on five. Please. I've asked at the desk. I've asked at pre-op. Isn't there anyway you can track a patient from back here?"

The alarm in Deidre's voice must have alerted other workers because several appeared out of nowhere poised to intervene. Then Deidre saw Megan. They both headed toward one another. Megan was the first to speak.

"I had Dr. Scafedi paged and was waiting for him to

respond. He's probably making rounds on the other side. Apparently your companion has been taken to the hospital side. If a complication occurred in surgery, more than likely they've transported him to ICU, but I don't see him logged in as a patient on the computer. I was waiting for them to update his status."

Without another word Megan took off to her left and bent the corner. She looked over her shoulder to indicate that Deidre should trail behind her. She stopped at a small counter with a few charts and a mounted computer, in front of a white board. Her back was toward Deidre as she began using the computer which operated by touch-screen technology.

Megan began scrolling with her thumb and punching with her forefinger. Her brows furrowed as if she were digesting the information presented on the screen. She told Deidre that Andre was being admitted to a room on the third floor. That brought Deidre's heart rate down a notch, but she was still alarmed. A colonoscopy was an in-and-out procedure. What could have gone wrong? She had to keep moving until she found out. She thanked Megan and found her way out.

Deidre moved at a pace that matched her heart rate. This time she didn't stop. Dodging oncoming traffic through the automatic doors that were already open, she raced through the breezeway toward the emergency entrance. Uniformed security guards were stationed just inside the doors to log in the traffic and direct visitors. A seated guard insisted Deidre show her photo ID before directing her toward a bank of elevators.

More red tape awaited her on the third floor. Deidre practically threw herself on the counter of the nurse's station and spewed out the same explanation and inquiry she used in pre-op and surgery. The head nurse bore a look that read that Deidre's personal problem and subsequent state of emergency wasn't going to become one of hers.

"And you are?" the stoic woman said with the compassion of a bill collector.

Deidre thought about what she was asking. Somehow she knew her name would not suffice. The woman wanted to know her relationship to Andre before issuing out his information. If the nurse only knew how often she had asked herself that same question recently. What was the real obstacle? It wasn't as if she were there to kidnap him. She just wanted to see him. Make sure he was all right.

"Look, I was told he was admitted to this floor. Can you please tell me what room he is in?"

"Ma'am, Mr. Hicks just arrived on the floor. His attending doctor, much less the nurse on this floor, has barely been in to see him. Until that happens, he cannot receive any visitors. Now there is a lounge around the corner and a cafeteria on the second floor you can use until he is cleared."

"I'll be right here," Deidre said, pointing back toward the small bench outside the elevators. "In the meantime, I'd like to speak to either his doctor or nurse."

"Ms.?" The nurse inquired with mounting frustration.

"Collins," Deidre said.

"Ms. Collins, he was admitted to our care. The doctor hasn't ordered us to call or tell his family anything. From the looks of his records, neither Dr. Scafedi nor any other employee of this hospital is obligated to share his medical information with you. Now if you'd like to wait in the designated areas, then you may have an opportunity to see him when he's been evaluated by our staff and elevated to visitor status."

"But I've been waiting all morning. Just ask him. I'm

sure he's anxious to see me. I brought him here for good-ness sake."

"Are you his wife or an immediate blood relative?" she said, shutting Deidre's explanation down.

Deidre started to lie, but felt the pause told it all. "No." She felt more like a glorified cab driver. She started back toward the elevators and the bench seat beside the window. She couldn't fathom sitting for an indefinite amount of time waiting and wondering. She turned toward the desk and called out to the nurse again. She didn't care who saw or heard her.

"Lord forbid if something should happen to him be-fore I get a chance to talk to him or see him." Deidre de-livered with an exasperated gasp. Tears started.

Deidre didn't realize she was backing up until she bumped into something. Two doctors in scrubs and lab coats stood still as if Deidre had flattened their tires and they were unable to move. She was apologetic. She rec-ognized one as Andre's surgeon, Dr. Scafedi.

"Oh God," Deidre called out, "Dr. Scafedi, Andre Hicks, how is he? Remember I was with him right before his colon-oscopy. Now he's over on this side and no one will tell me anything."

"He had an accelerated heart rate after the procedure that concerned us. We want to run some tests. Do me a favor. Get something to eat or check out the botanical gar-den terrace on the ground level. Come back in an hour."

Deidre shook her head in tearful defiance. She didn't want to leave him again. She wouldn't.

Dr. Scafedi passed his clipboard to his colleague and grabbed Deidre's hand. "This is the Cardiac wing. They have rules. You won't be able to see him until I meet with his attending doctor, Dr. Bloom here, and complete my post-op evaluation with him on my rounds. I'll then have something more concrete to tell you. Let us do our jobs

so we can then suggest how you can help Mr. Hicks recover."

Although Deidre knew the doctor was just pacifying
her, she allowed herself to breathe. A flood of fresh tears
accompanied each breath. She turned and departed quickly,
embarrassed now that she laid bare her emotions in front
of the whole ward. She made up in her mind that she'd
give them an hour, but no more.

Chapter 39

Andre thought he had a heart attack. He thought he had two. One minute he was out cold, the next thing he knew, he was awake in recovery with his heart ticking like a time bomb in his chest. Each time the beats would intensify, he could feel his heart rocking in his chest cavity and felt his pulse in his throat. He remembered bracing himself against the bed. Was this the end? Would he ever see DeAndre and Deidre again? Was he ready to meet his Maker?

Then he remembered his prayer from earlier.

God, I never thought an orphaned boy from Brooklyn should pray. I never thought I was significant enough to be heard. I don't want to be scared anymore. I don't want to be weak. I realize now that I've been scared all my life, and it has hindered me in every aspect of my life. I know you're real. I want you to know me the same way that you know Deidre and Deuce and care for them. I need you to pull my pieces together. Help me through this, please.

The next time his heart rocked in his chest, he repeated his plea from earlier: *Help me through this.* He reached out for a nearby nurse who alerted an emergency team. Somehow amidst the pandemonium surrounding his distress, his fear was gone. That episode landed him in a room on the cardiac ward. He felt his heart stabilize, but by then, he was hooked up to probes so he could be monitored overnight.

Andre used the bedside remote to turn on the television mounted high on the wall to drown out the bells and whistles on his monitoring device and that of his roommate. He immediately identified the television personality although it wasn't his typical format. Andre had never heard of the *Miracle Club* much less viewed it. He wondered what Bo Donavan was peddling now, because he was certainly on television a lot these days. He was poised to turn the channel, but was interested in his curious attire. Bo, who was usually in a muscle shirt and shorts was now in a suit and tie sitting on a couch opposite the show's host, a friendly looking couple. Andre couldn't resist turning the volume up so he could hear better.

"With fame comes a lot of the traps that success can bring," the male host said. "Bo, you've already shared how you grew up with the foundation of our Lord and Savior Jesus Christ. Tell us about your journey to superstardom and how you felt you compromised your faith."

"I'd love to, Grace. I'll be the first to admit that I was cocky starting out, believing in my own strength. God showed my butt quick who was boss. I got humble real quick after not placing in my first Olympics. I prayed to God to help me keep my focus. Return me to that little boy in Texas who desperately wanted to train so that I could make the school's wrestling team. That's when I began chanting prayers like you see in my videos. I started counting breaths, visualization, and other techniques that I use in my program. It all came together when I began to blend the mind, body and soul. I couldn't have won those three gold medals the next time around without God."

"Hallelujah," the male co-host chimed in.

Andre couldn't believe what he was hearing. As long as he had been following the Bo Donovan Way, he never knew Bo had such a strong belief in God. Bo's usual gruff voice took on a smoother quality as he continued.

"As you know, I became very popular after the Olympics in Seoul, Korea. If you remember, I was like the unofficial captain of team USA. My photographs were on all the posters and paraphernalia, basically because I shared the goodwill I felt in my heart for all God's people.

"I think it was your genuine nature that attracted so many of us to our televisions that summer to root for you—some of us that have never watched a weight lifting competition before," Grace said, reaching on the prop table in between the two couches to show a magazine from 1988 with Bo on the cover.

"You bore the fruit of God's spirit. You weren't afraid to be both strong and vulnerable like when you did that tribute to your father from the medal podium," Jim, the male co-host, said.

"I couldn't have paid for that type of publicity that I received after that competition. Like you said, God was ready to elevate me. The war began when I developed my first product line, though, and started approaching companies for distribution. Companies didn't know how to market what one company executive called freak fitness to mainstream America."

"He didn't call it that to your face did he, Bo? I'd be afraid to insult a guy who just won a medal for lifting the weight of a small car," Jim scoffed. They all laughed. "I guess what they were really saying was that they didn't want to market your faith-based fitness programs."

"Exactly, my brand of Body Synergy is really a mixture

of mind, body, and Spirit. Spirit was clearly defined as a oneness with God that allows the transfer of His power in your life. I personally believe that you can't develop and grow without all three. Acknowledging Christ in my core text and in my workout videos became my biggest issue. That alone was threatening to the powers that be; not just at one company, but to every company I went to. Meanwhile the people, the consumers, my fans around the world were waiting for my fitness program. I was struggling with the men in suits about what I believed, what I knew to be true. My true weakness came when I allowed my products, the content of my core theory, to be altered so that the entire package could be marketed and manufactured."

"Unbelievable," Grace said with praying hands and a slow shake of the head.

"So Bo, your Body Synergy line that millions now have in their homes is not what you originally created?"

"The fitness part is the same. We went back and forth about where the power to acquire strength and endurance comes from. We went from God as the source, to calling Him a higher power so not to offend people, to taking the source out altogether."

"The power comes from within," Jim said, repeating the mantra throughout Bo's program.

"That was a key phrase in my system, and I believe that, but who puts it within you? Puts it in all of us?" Bo asked, getting emotional. "What happens when we as humans fail and can't depend on our own might? That is what was being ignored."

"Aww," Grace said, getting the revelation.

"So when they asked you to basically take God out of your program, what did they want you to replace it with?"

"New Age philosophies. There were teams pitching

ideas to me. We compromised on some of the laws of attraction that were close to my original intent. So when I originally talked about, 'with God all things are possible,' the team replaced it with the law to attract the kind of life we want. One of the laws talks about the power of your thoughts to manifest itself in real life. We know, as believers, that God gave us the power to speak those things as though they were. We made it close to Biblical doctrine, but it still was deceptive because it had you believing solely in your own power."

"Now you say your greatest shame will become your greatest triumph for the Lord. When we come back from break, why don't you tell us about the new book, *Core Beliefs*."

"I'd love to," Bo said, a grin now replacing his solemn expression.

The screen filled with the cover of Bo's new book, and Andre made a mental note to get the book to add to his collection. Andre no longer believed in coincidence. He was supposed to be lying there seeing this. For the first time in his life things were becoming clear, and he wanted to thank God for lifting the haze.

The program returned from a commercial break. Bo was explaining the timeliness of his latest venture when Andre's doctors came to visit him. Andre muted the television.

"How are you doing, Mr. Hicks?" Dr. Bloom asked.

"Fine, I think."

"Good, good. Dr. Scafedi and I would like to go over some things with you," the attending doctor said before flipping in a chart.

"But first, we have a young lady who has been waiting to see you. Lovely lady, but I'm sure she is ready to write everyone on the floor a one-way ticket to you-know-where if we don't let her in to see you soon. I have a feeling she'll want to hear your results as much as you do. If you don't mind, I'll get her."

Andre's wide smile gave Dr. Scafedi the permission he needed. He stepped out and returned with Deidre. His heart melted at the sight of her red eyes and less than perfect appearance. His new vision removed all those imperfections. She scurried to his side and he reached out for her hand.

"Hey," he said to her, attempting to catch a tear from her eye with the hand restricted by the IV cord. She grabbed his other hand and turned to give the doctors her full attention so they could proceed.

"Again, I'm Doctor Bloom. Your heart rate had everyone concerned. We thought it might have been a reaction to the anesthesia, but we didn't have a problem during surgery. You were already coming to in recovery. What we do know is that people react differently to stress and trauma. Although you had a minimum evasive procedure, all procedures have risks. The good news is that your heart rate has come down significantly without the aide of drugs. That's what we like to see. You were very dehydrated, so we're running an IV. Has there been a change in your regular routine or eating habits?"

Andre had to recall his reckless abandonment of his eating and exercise routine since finding out he had to have this procedure. "Yeah, I've really slacked off from exercising and taking care of myself."

"We've found, with athletes in particular, it is important to keep that balance. Exercise balances your emotional and mental state and generally relaxes the everyday stresses of life. It could be that the adrenaline of all those emotions just reached a peak. It appears you'll be fine. I'll order a few tests to be sure and probably get you home in the morning. We'll tell Dr. Jefferies to put you to the test on the treadmill to test your endurance on your next doctor's visit. Are you up to the challenge?"

"I can run a mile on incline in just under fifteen minutes," Andre bragged.

"Oh well, no contest. You'll be fine. Dr. Scafedi," Dr Bloom said, deferring to his colleague.

"Well, the colonoscopy was a success. We found and extracted five tiny polyps. One was sizable, maybe the size of a grape." Dr Scafedi paused to show the approximate size with his fingers. "We'll test all of them and get the report to Dr. Jefferies to share with you."

"Is that it?" Deidre asked, dropping Andre's hand in an attempt to get a better understanding.

"Yeah, what about the cancer?" Andre wanted to know this more than anything.

"We worry about the possibility of cancer if the polyps we extracted turn up to be malignant. But you're cured," he said with a sly smile that indicated to Andre a joke had gone over his head.

"Huh?"

"Ninety-five percent of colon cancer is cured by finding and extracting the polyps. Polyps form in the intestines all the time. Some polyps that will become cancerous in some people lay dormant or benign for five to fifteen years. By extracting them in a procedure like you had, in essence, cures the patient of that risk."

"What do we do now?" Deidre asked.

Andre noticed her use of the word 'we.' Maybe she felt like he did, that Dr. Scafedi's answer was critical to how they could proceed as a couple.

"I suggest genetic counseling for Mr. Hicks since he has a family history. It's just good to know your risks," Dr. Scafedi said.

"But what if it comes back?" Andre asked.

"Normally we recommend a colonoscopy every ten years for someone over the age of fifty. With you, we want you to come back every three years."

Andre wanted to be cleared so that he could start life anew. "But—"

"You just make sure you come back at the designated time. Matter of fact, have that young lady remind you. I know she will make sure you're back in here. She's a feisty one. Unless you plan on getting rid of her, you'll be fine."

Andre breathed easy. His new vision was picking up a glimpse of the future. "You're right. She's got me covered."

Andre remembered Bo Donovan talking about a woman at his publishing company who encouraged him to live authentically and tell the truth in his new book, *Core Beliefs*, even if he lost some of his market share. He called her his angel. Deidre Collins also went by that name.

"Well, all right then. We'll be leaving. Good luck now," Dr. Scafedi said, following Dr. Bloom out the door.

Andre didn't quite know what happened to him that day, but he knew it was more than luck. Just like his hero, Bo Donovan, he was coming to know that God was a sure thing. God could have taken him out, in more ways than one, but He didn't.

Andre winked at Deidre. She patted his chest before bending down and hugging him around the neck. He heard her sniffle, and he pulled away so that he could see her face.

"What's up? You act as if you were worried about me. What happened to, 'If you pray, don't worry,'"

"Listen at you," Deidre said, looking at him as if she were trying to figure out what was different about him. "I didn't know where you were or how you were doing.

Everyone was treating me like, 'who are you?'and 'what's your relationship to Mr. Hicks?'"

"I should have made my relationship to you abundantly clear to everybody, a long time ago." *Especially to you*, Andre thought.

"I want to go and let you rest, but I'm afraid if I come back you might be back in surgery somewhere," Deidre said, flashing him her 100-watt smile.

"Oh no, you're not going anywhere."

Andre raised the head of his hospital bed with the keypad on the side of the bed. He reached over to lift the latch that allowed the side safety barrier of the hospital bed to collapse. He motioned for her to join him on the side of the bed. She sat cautiously to the side until he moved over to give her more room. As she lay back next to him, she rested her head on his shoulder. They both closed their eyes in an attempt to rest before the next round of tests.

Andre appreciated Deidre more than ever now. He struggled to find the right words to say to her at that moment. He grabbed her hand and whispered, "You know I love you, right? All this time I have loved you, from high school until now."

Deidre squeezed his hand, but remained silent. Her hand was resting on his chest now, trying to feel its regular rhythm, or maybe trying to read its sincerity. "This isn't just some kind of sickbed confession, 'cause I'm a little hesitant to tell you that the feeling is mutual," Deidre said finally in her wry sense of humor that he loved.

"I've been a jerk. I don't want you to think I only want to please you physically. Forgive me please."

"I know, and I do."

I'm willing to wait on you this time, to win your love, to move at your pace." Andre nuzzled up to her until she covered his mouth with her hand. When she removed it, he continued, "I'll—"

"Go to church with me and DeAndre?"

"I'll even go to church," Andre said, surprising himself at how easily he acquiesced. "Third time is the charm. Give me a chance to show you."

"A chance, huh?" Deidre was laughing at him now. "Like in high school when you told Keith, to tell Shelia, to ask me could you have a chance?"

"Well, sort of, but not exactly," he said, thinking about his awkward attempt to catapult their friendship into a courtship.

"We'll see what God has in store for us. Now, let me take a nap. I'm tired. At least you got to sleep in surgery."

Chapter 40

Parents of students auditioning for the remaining 55 slots of the Malcolm Woods Creative Arts Magnet School's freshman class were encouraged to wait for their children in the alcove and lobby area of the school. DeAndre's parents were not only among the few that ignored that recommendation, but also insisted upon rehearsing what he would do and say when he was called.

"Be yourself. Show your outgoing side, like the way you are with your boys," Andre said.

"But with no slang. Show them you know proper English," Deidre said.

"The only one who can sell your talent is you."

It was unnerving to an already anxious DeAndre the way his father was standing while everyone else sat. Other students looked on as if his dad was the coach shelling out the last minute game plan. His mother must have felt the same way, because she grabbed Andre's arm and pulled him down into the seat next to her. He leaned over in the chair and continued his coaching.

"If they ask about your middle school transcripts, remember you have that letter," Andre said, referring to the letter he obtained from DeAndre's summer school teacher. Although Mr. Watson, his teacher, wouldn't commit to a grade for a class he'd just completed two days previous, he certified DeAndre's attendance in a letter. Malcom Woods started their classes in three weeks. DeAndre's parents were concerned that his lingering grade status would deny him consideration.

"I think he should start off with the letter. Get it out there before they even have to ask a question," Deidre said.

DeAndre just listened. They were both talking over one another and completing each other's sentences the same way they did the day they sat him down to explain to him how their relationship had changed. *Y'all were fooling no one but yourselves all this time*, DeAndre thought. He knew.

One day DeAndre asked his dad why he just didn't move back in with them. His dad was thoughtful and replied, "We've learned we can't rush this thing. Your mother and I living together before we are married goes against what we both believe now to be true. That is the reason your mom and I got into a lot of things we weren't ready for before." His father got a horrified look on his face as if he said something wrong and grabbed DeAndre's shoulders real tight. "I was talking in the context of timing. You were not a mistake. We love you." DeAndre's mother had told him that many times. He was glad to finally hear his dad say it.

His parents were so caught up in talking to each other, that he was forgotten. Names were being called from two different sides of the multipurpose room. There appeared to be triple the amount of kids than slots. When the overweight boy next to him was called, DeAndre was able to slide down two seats to the end, leaving the spaces next to his parents open for the red-haired girl that was approaching carrying a garment bag.

DeAndre first noticed several instruments in black plastic cases on the floor between his seat and the row of chairs next to him. He looked up to find the sweeping mane and side profile of one of his classmates, Gazelle Johnson. Like in school, her beauty and grace rendered him speechless. He stole glances of her out of the corner of his eye while she talked on her cell phone. He remembered the last time he held a conversation with her and wondered had she forgiven him for introducing her to a jerk like Bentley. He was about to find out, because he couldn't justify being so close and pretending like he didn't know her.

"Hey," De Andre said, immediately embarrassed that he hadn't waited for her to get off the phone.

She tilted her head and stared at him, making him feel like a leper until she clicked her phone off and smiled. "DeAndre? What are you doing here?"

She remembered his name. There was something familiar in her greeting that made her seem like an old friend. "I have an audition," he said, stating the obvious without his usual, "duh."

"Me too. For what department?" she asked.

"Visual Arts," he said before explaining further, "I draw." *Very well*, he thought.

"Performance Arts . . . instrumental," she said. He would have guessed choral the way she sang every time she spoke. It was quite magical to him.

"How many instruments do you play?" He looked down at the cases as if he could identify the instrument each case held.

"All the woodwind instruments except the bassoon, and that's only because they didn't have one in my hometown, but I'm sure I could figure it out though. I decided to play the same selection on each instrument. You know, show off a little bit."

"That's hot."

"Oh my God," Gazelle said giddily. She held up a finger, flipped open her phone and turned her body to the side slightly to garner a little privacy for her now urgent phone call.

DeAndre played nervously with the straps on his portfolio. He looked at his parents to see if they had been watching him. His dad was still talking to his mom who was shaping her fingernail with a nail file. He looked up when he heard Gazelle say, "And guess who is here?" He was surprised to hear her say his name as if he were a mystery guest on a teen talk show and her subsequent giggles. *Are they laughing at me?*

"My friend, Tiah, said hi." Gazelle said to DeAndre.

"Tell her I said, what's up," DeAndre said confused. He didn't really know Tiah or the other girls she hung with. More giggling ensued before she hung up the phone for a second time. Somehow he didn't feel self conscious. If he had a phone, he would have called the twins just as excitedly to tell them that he was talking to her.

DeAndre thought about what he knew about Gazelle besides her beauty.

"Hey, I thought you were in seventh grade," he said.

"I was. I actually was skipped a grade before I transferred here, but they told my mom they didn't double promote in this county. I started out in seventh, but my mom kept fighting. In January, I took a placement test with Mr. Talbert and was moved to the eighth. I was in Ms. Marshall's homeroom."

"So you're like super smart," DeAndre said.

"My mom and my sister call me Lisa Simpson," she said, shyly showing a manila folder full of sheet music with a pencil drawing of the popular character from *The*

Simpsons. DeAndre could see the correlation, but couldn't relate the goonish character with someone so lovely.

"Let me see your work," Gazelle said, reaching for the handle of DeAndre's portfolio.

Instinctively he held the strap tighter. "Stop playing, girl. I charge admission for each viewing."

"C'mon . . . please," she begged.

DeAndre felt an unexpected tingle. He would have gladly shown her some of his pieces, but he knew his mother would have a conniption if he started displaying his stuff out in the open.

"Let me show you just how well I can draw by hooking up your folder," DeAndre said, reaching over the divide between their chairs. He used his portfolio as a desk. Pulling a pencil from behind his ear he started on the Lisa Simpson character from the blue dress down to the saxophone. Instead of the yellow spikes that served as her hair, he made the tresses long and flowing with a flip on the end. He handed Gazelle the folder back. He watched as she stared at it in amazement then hugged it close to her body as if it were her most treasured possession.

"DeAndre," his mother called, startling him. "Are you listening for your name?"

"Yes," he replied, hoping to circumvent a major conversation with his mom while Gazelle was sitting there.

"Well, it seems like they've forgotten about you. We've been here close to fifty minutes."

"Go check where you're at on the list, son," his dad ordered.

As DeAndre got up to check the status of his own audition, Gazelle's name was called. She yelled out, "Right here, I'm coming." He watched her look back and forth in a quandary as if she hadn't thought out how she would get her collection of instruments back to the audition room. DeAndre knew his parents were watching and waiting for their command to be carried out. As he stood side by side with the school beauty he knew he had to help her.

DeAndre bent to pick up two of Gazelle's biggest instruments and waited to follow her. She picked up the rest, and they both followed a man to a band room in the back of the main auditorium. The man gave them a quizzical look as they reached their destination. She explained that DeAndre was her friend and that she, in fact, would be playing all of those instruments.

DeAndre placed her instruments to the side of a music stand. He whispered, "Good luck," and then, "I'll talk to ya," as he returned to the multipurpose room to await his turn. Hopefully he'd be seeing Gazelle again in the fall.

His father was gesturing for him when he returned. His mother was standing by his side with disapproval written on her face. DeAndre decided to check in with them before finding the teacher he had checked in with earlier.

"They called your name while you were back there playing Romeo," Deidre said.

"Cut him some slack, Dee. The boy was just being a gentleman," Andre said, nudging DeAndre with his elbow. A sly grin showed his approval.

"Uh-huh," Deidre said, reaching for her purse. She slipped the strap on her shoulder. "We'd better get in there."

"Hold up," Andre said. "We're not going. He is. This is his time to shine. We can't hold his hand through this." He turned to DeAndre. "You've got this. You have a unique point of view. I've seen it. We're your parents and we love you. This is not about us, your boys, or even that girl you just met. This is not a time to let other people's feelings, judgments, or opinions overshadow what you know is right and what's best for you."

DeAndre had a feeling that this school was right for him. He guessed his father had the last say because his mom rested her purse back on her chair and gave his arm a reassuring squeeze. They huddled around him like a family sending a loved one off to battle. He pulled away to join the awaiting faculty escort stationed at the door.

Presenting his portfolio of work to the three members of the visual arts faculty was like an out-of -body experience. He hoped his sketches were strong enough to make an impact, fearing he bombed the interview session. He never figured how comfortable he would feel discussing his work as the panel thumbed through each drawing before replacing it back in his portfolio. These people didn't view his work as mere scribbles or doodles. He noticed the Garden of Eden drawing remained on the tabletop in front of them. They were interested in the method, meaning, and motivation behind each piece; especially that one.

At the end, they asked him what it felt like to draw and how he felt when he created. DeAndre didn't know what kind of answer they expected. He didn't have anything deep to tell them. He decided not to fake an answer and just be real. He told them, "It feels natural, like a pad is a part of my left hand and a pencil is a part of the other."

It was like DeAndre was in a daze when he returned to the multipurpose room where his parents were waiting. It was dawning on him how much he truly wanted to be accepted in that school. He was trying to process what just took place, trying to evaluate what he did and said. His parents, of course, hit him with a barrage of their own questions as they headed for the parking lot.

"Did they comment about each sketch?" his dad asked. *Nod.* "You're so in."

"Did you speak up?" his mom asked. *Nod.* "Good."

"DeAndre, did you give them the letter?" his dad said.

"And explain your situation?" his mom said.

DeAndre sat in the backseat of his dad's car with his parents in the front facing toward him. He waited to the very end to tell the panel that he was still considered an eighth grader until his summer school grade became official. He barely was able to nod an answer before the next question was fired off.

"Wait a minute, Dee, let's let him talk. At the end what did they say?"

DeAndre was an amplifier for the tape that was still playing in his head. "They said exceptions are made for students with exceptional talent."

Chapter 41

"Hey, sweetheart, what are you up to?" Andre asked. He listened as Deidre made cooking dinner and doing the laundry sound good. "I thought I'd drop by if you have the time."

Andre waited for her approval before disconnecting the call. He breathed a sigh of relief that everything was working according to plan. Andre had one more stop before reaching Deidre's house. He passed the security parking area to park in a regular space at the Municipal Mall. He had turned in his resignation shortly after his colonoscopy, but returned to the mall daily to work out at the Bo Donovan Fitness Center. He'd taken the night shift as security guard at a nursing home facility to make good on his promise to DeAndre. He took the first of the many Body Synergy courses at Bo Donovan University's satellite campus forty-five minutes away. He loved the flexible schedule so he could study. The night job also gave him something else to do and somewhere else to be besides at Deidre's, fantasizing about taking her to bed.

It seemed as if his desire for her was made stronger now that they vowed to remain celibate until marriage.

Andre moved faster now. He had come to make a very important purchase. He headed for the bookend of stores on the south end to secure the last gifts for his surprise for Deidre. Once in the car, he transferred his purchases to the gift bags he'd previously bought. He checked the labels he had affixed to each bag before taking off for his final destination.

Andre caught his reflection on the side of his car door when he got out in front of Deidre's house. He adjusted the collar of his blue striped Kenneth Cole dress shirt and kicked out the cuffs on his gray slacks. He looked good. It took a moment for him to gather his packages and ring her doorbell.

The look on Deidre's face was priceless as she answered the door with the telephone meshed to her ear. A peck on the lips was their greeting. She backed up and allowed him space to navigate in and relieve his arm of packages. She was thrilled at the prospect of gifts. He barely heard her tell the person on the other end goodbye as he arranged the bags on her coffee table, moving her centerpiece and magazines to the floor.

DeAndre skipped up the steps from the basement and was the first to speak. "I thought you were coming to help out in the basement. Why are you so dressed up? You going to a funeral?" DeAndre said, playfully popping Andre's collar.

"Naw, partner, no funeral. I came to celebrate." Andre remained stationary waiting for Deidre to replace the phone and join them.

"What's this we're celebrating?" Deidre said, returning. Andre could tell she spruced up a bit while she was in the back. Her headband was gone and her lips were freshly glossed. "You look nice. You smell nice too."

"BMC," Andre announced.

"BMC?" Deidre said, tilting her head as if trying to figure out his acronym.

"Y'all buggin'," DeAndre said, not even trying to figure it out.

"BMC, woman. Haven't you heard?" Andre grabbed Deidre's hand and led her to the chair in front of his display. "Here is eight years of birthday, Mother's Day and Christmas gifts for you. One for each year, 'cause a brother is on a budget. Just my way of saying my heart was here even if I weren't physically here with the gifts."

"Oh, Andre," Deidre squealed. She covered her face with her hands to get over the shock of it all. She popped up and hugged him as if she had opened her gifts already.

"I'm out," DeAndre said, retreating to his room like he always did at the possibility of them getting mushy.

"Wait, get back here. We celebrated with you when you got into school, and took you out to dinner after your first week. Sit your ungrateful tail down," Andre said in jest. He wanted DeAndre to be a part of this. If his plan continued to work out, they'd all be on a plane by next Saturday. "You sit also, Dee."

Although it was barely fall, Andre felt like Santa orchestrating which gifts for her to open first. He had a specific order and each gift was labeled with a number. He held gifts seven and eight close to him to prevent Deidre from tearing into them prematurely. He decided to let her go for it, taking the best view on the couch next to DeAndre.

The first few gifts were functional. Deidre kicked off the house shoes she had from yesteryear to don the fuzzy new pair Andre had bought. She would put to use the Nike running shoes and matching gray and lilac fitness wear on the track now that they often met at the park to workout. He combined two books from the Bo Donovan collection into one gift. Deidre smiled as she flipped through the recipes in the *Core Cuisine*. Andre felt partly responsible in making her a more health conscious cook. He also thought it would be cool for them to read the *Core Beliefs*, Bo's latest book, together.

Andre was on the edge of his seat enjoying the pleasure of making her happy. He watched as she plunged her hand in the next bag blindly and was met with the solid frame of a shadow box. She pulled it out slowly and covered her mouth at her astonishment. He had gathered mementos of their relationship together to make a collage. Some items, like a love note he had written but never gave her in high school and a caricature drawing of the two of them at a carnival, were over twenty years old. Deidre stared at each thing as if she were swept back in time.

Deidre came over to sit between her two guys. She handed the shadow box to DeAndre who was more interested in the sketch than the sentiment. He asked permission to take the gift to his room, no doubt, to sketch his own version. When DeAndre left, Deidre gave Andre five butterfly kisses for the five gifts she had already received. She waited for him to hand her the next surprise.

As Andre prepared to explain the gift in bag six, he felt a fresh dollop of love drop into his spirit. It was the same feeling that made him replace a DVD movie set to add this gift before coming there. It was more for him than Deidre.

As Deidre pulled out the thick leather bound Bible from the bag he began, "I know that this seems like a strange gift because I know you have plenty of Bibles. Actually, I picked this one out for me. I don't know how to explain it, but over the past few months I've changed so much."

He hesitated to go any further. On a day that Andre was fully prepared to make his intentions official and take their relationship to the next level, he now felt compelled to slightly alter that plan. It was time to declare a new love interest. He knew in his heart he'd be offering her a better man after taking this next step.

Andre knelt before her, taking the Bible off her lap. "Dee, God has opened my heart. Even before I started going to church with you and Deuce, ever since I was in the hospital, I've felt like He's been with me. This might sound crazy, but I want to know how ... why, even? I want God to know me like He knows you."

"He does. He knew you before you knew yourself and He's been waiting for you to get to this point," Deidre said.

"A couple of months ago, you wanted to show me some verses in the Bible that you said would help explain salvation. I want you to show me them now so that I can accept the Lord."

Andre watched as Deidre's initial shock turned into the purest expression of joy.

"Right now?" Deidre asked.

"There is no time like the present."

She glanced at the two remaining gifts, then back at him. "Speaking of presentsssssssss."

They both smiled. He wondered had she figured out what the last gift bag held. "Your gifts aren't going anywhere. Neither am I."

"You want me to take you down the Roman Road, huh?" Deidre said, taking the Bible.

"Yes, ma'am," he said, thinking, *you've never led me down the wrong road.*

Andre took a seat beside Deidre again as she flipped the pages of life's manual to the book of Romans.

Epilogue

Six months later

"Like Sam Cooke sang, *It's been a long, long time coming*. But if you really know the two of them, like I do, you know their souls have been married from the start. Their relationship has been like a prayer—a seemingly long, drawn out, yet sincere expose. Like a prayer, it was filled with its share of petitions. There were times when they had to say, 'Forgive us, Father,' 'Help us, God,' and 'Have mercy, Lord.' Now God has given them permission to go ahead with His original plan. We're all witnesses to their love supreme. Thank God that He's still making love stories. Thank God, He's still using people to help each other grow, if they only love and believe on Him. Join me in helping them close this prayer with victory, for there are many more prayers left to be uttered and answered in their lifetime together. Let all God's people say, hallelujah, thank you, Jesus, and amen," Sheila said to the crowd.

Deidre wore a sleeveless gown with pearls and iridescent crystals on the bodice that gave way to flowing satin. Her three-inch heels made her the perfect height for their ceremonial kiss. Her hair was swept away from her face on both sides, then exploded into a pyramid of curls underneath the headband and veil. Andre wore a classic black tuxedo with a fitted shirt highlighted by a black bow tie and vest. They were barely introduced inside the lavish hotel reception site before her best friend, matron of honor, and wedding coordinator began with that rousing toast.

Deidre could feel the modest crowd of fifty gathering in close around the wood paneled dance floor as the DJ cued up their music for the first dance. They each chose a song that would be revealed as a complete surprise for the other. When the first beat of the melody was played, and she felt Andre's arms circle her waist, everyone else drifted away. With her arms resting atop her husband's shoulders, Deidre began to whisper the words in Andre's ear as the record played, 'We both deserve each other's love.'

They drifted side to side effortlessly, as if they'd already boarded their honeymoon cruise ship headed for CoCo Cay, Bahamas and other exotic ports of call. She let him lead as their bodies became the interpretation of the lyrics.

They barely wanted to part at the end of the song as the DJ changed gears and announced Andre's selection for his bride. Andre's feet were already in motion as Deidre recognized the upbeat tempo of Cheryl Lynn's "Encore." It was like an old school dance off. She tried her best to keep up with him before he encouraged everyone standing around to join them on the dance floor. They took turns dancing with members of their bridal party. Deidre spent a minute dancing with Keith and Eugene before pulling her son, who had served as their best man, onto the dance floor. Andre danced in the center of

Sheila, Renita, and Deidre's older sister, Donna, in their blush champagne gowns before going into the crowd to find Deidre's mother seated at the reserved table.

After praying the prayer of salvation with Andre on the night he proposed, Deidre was surprised to find that he had secured three airline tickets to CHS airport in Charleston, South Carolina where once and for all, he could appeal to her mother and make his intentions to marry her daughter known to her in person.

Although Deidre had already accepted his proposal and wore her half-karat diamond engagement ring, Andre respectfully asked for her hand in marriage from Mabel Collins. True to form, Ma Mabel was skeptical about his sincerity. Deidre and Andre had decided on the flight in to cut the ties to the past which meant starting anew by purchasing their own home. Before Deidre could intercede, Andre said to her mother, "I wish things would have been different. I wish we had a chance to truly get to know one another before I proposed to your daughter. I have always loved Deidre, and I feel like Jacob in the Bible who worked for Rachel's hand in marriage for seven years. I have worked to get myself to the place where I am now ready and deserving of a place in Deidre and DeAndre's life. I certainly hope I don't have to work another seven to prove that to you."

By the end of the weekend, even Ms. Collins couldn't resist Andre's genuine charm and was acting as if she had been a longtime supporter of their relationship.

Deidre looked on as her mother and new husband did a two step on the dance floor to the record's end. There were members of her church present. Almost everyone from her Sunday School class had accepted their invitation except Marilynn Matthews who was on a self-imposed exile from church after rumors of her daughter, Kenya, being in a family way at fourteen ran through their Sunday School class. Deidre tried to refrain from judgment and just thanked God for His intervention. She'd take DeAndre's heartbreak over a grandchild any day.

Deidre caught Andre's eye and gave him a knowing look. He tilted his head toward the door. It was time to make their exit. They both went in search of DeAndre who was joking around with the twins by the punch fountain. She warned him to be good for her mother the week they would be away on their honeymoon. Andre slipped him some money for incidentals, but mainly to bribe him so he wouldn't tip their guests off as they snuck out to start their own personal celebration.

No sooner had Deidre and Andre gotten cozy in the back of their limousine than there was a rap on the tinted one-way window. They could see a frustrated Sheila standing with her right hand on her hip. Deidre placed a finger up to her lip to shush Andre as if to trick Sheila into believing they weren't there. Guilt set in. They couldn't just pull off. Deidre thought about how much time and energy Sheila had invested in making their wedding possible in a short amount of time. Deidre used a button on the panel to bring the window down on her side.

"No no no. You all can't leave now," Sheila whined.

"Why not?" Andre jumped in. He gave Deidre who was perched on his lap, a look that read under no uncertain terms were they returning to the ballroom.

"They haven't even served dinner yet."

"That's why we paid for an extensive appetizer bar to keep people satisfied while we took all those pictures. We're good. We'll catch a bite at the hotel."

"C'mon, y'all. This is so tacky. Your guests are here to see you. What about the cake? Dee, you haven't even thrown the bouquet."

Deidre leaned over and handed her friend the champagne colored tiger lilies freckled with brown splotches that was discarded on the floor of the limo. "Do the honors?"

"And the garter?" Sheila questioned.

Deidre wriggled the band down from around her thigh. Andre gladly assisted his wife. Deidre covered her face to conceal the laughter at their brazenness as Andre tossed the delicate elastic and white lace band to a visibly disgusted Sheila.

"Check in on Deuce this week. Make sure he's not pulling a number on my mother-in-law. We love you, but now, be gone." Andre held Deidre firmly around the waist while reaching over to the control panel to officially bring the conversation to a close.

"Wait," Sheila yelled, making Andre halt the pressure he applied to the up button on the window. "What do you want me to tell everyone then?"

Silence lingered for a moment. "Wifey?" Andre said, deferring the response to Deidre.

"Tell them we had to take care of some unfinished business," Deidre said, before giving their driver his cue to pull off.

Reader's Group Guide

1. Deidre's mother disapproved of Deidre and Andre's relationship from the start. Deidre also was overzealous about DeAndre's relationship with Kenya? What level of involvement should a parent have in their child's friendships and courtships?

2. What was meant when Deidre said her mother felt she had exclusive keys to God's Kingdom?

3. How did Andre's past prevent him from developing a relationship with the Lord sooner?

4. In what ways had Deidre been a spiritual snob? In which ways had she been a Christian in camouflage? Are these categories accurate for some of today's Christians?

5. Give examples of how the characters in *The Manual* misrepresented their faith and blocked others from seeing Christ?

6. Sheila reminded Deidre about how easy it is to fall into sexual immorality when dating today. Discuss the necessity of group dating and developing a dating plan.

7. In what ways did DeAndre's experiences and relationships mirror that of his mom and dad's? Deidre learned to rely on God to raise DeAndre alone for eight years. In what ways was his spiritual upbringing apparent in the decisions he had to make?

8. Discuss your feelings about the "recommend the restaurant" approach to evangelism?

9. Andre's hero, Bo Donovan, disclosed how he had to conceal his religious beliefs to reach commercial success. Do you believe that superstars are put in a position to have to choose between their faith and success?

10. What do you believe is the significance of the book's title? What other manuals did the characters consult to enhance their lives?

About the Author

Sherryle Kiser Jackson is a graduate of Salisbury State University, a middle school English teacher, and Educational Consultant. She is a fresh voice in Christian fiction. Her style reflects an honest commentary on her life with Christ. Her first novel, *Soon and Very Soon*, was published in 2007. Jackson describes her novels as too real to be preachy, Biblically based, and out-the-Christian-box. Sherryle lives in Charles County, Maryland with her husband and two children.

Urban Christian His Glory Book Club!

Established January 2007, *UC His Glory Book Club* is another way by which to introduce **Urban Christian** and its authors. We are an online book club supporting Urban Christian authors by purchasing, reading and providing written reviews of the authors' books. *UC His Glory Book Club* welcomes both men and women of the literary world who have a passion for reading Christian-based fiction.

UC His Glory Book Club is the brainchild of Joylynn Jossel, author and Executive Editor of Urban Christian and Kendra Norman-Bellamy, author and copy editor for Urban Christian. The book club will provide support, positive feedback, encouragement, and a forum whereby members can openly discuss and review the literary works of Urban Christian authors. In the future, we anticipate broadening our spectrum of services to include: online author chats, author spotlights, interviews with your favorite Urban Christian author(s), special online groups for *UC His Glory Book Club* members, ability to post reviews on the website and amazon.com, membership ID cards, *UC His Glory* Yahoo Group and much more.

Even though there will be no membership fees attached to becoming a member of *UC His Glory Book Club*, we do expect our members to be active, committed, and to follow the guidelines of the book club.

UC His Glory Book Club members pledge to:

- Follow the guidelines of *UC His Glory Book Club*.
- Provide input, opinions, and reviews that build up, rather than tear down.
- Commit to purchasing, reading, and discussing featured book(s) of the month.
- Agree not to miss more than three consecutive online monthly meetings.
- Respect the Christian beliefs of *UC His Glory Book Club*.
- Believe that Jesus is the Christ, Son of the Living God

We look forward to the online fellowship.

Many Blessings to You!

Shelia E Lipsey
President
UC His Glory Book Club

**Visit the official Urban Christian Book Club website at *www.uchisglorybookclub.net*